Bernice Curler

The
Visionaries

AmErica House
Baltimore

Cover design: Patricia Wershiner

ISBN: 1-58851-154-5
PUBLISHED BY AMERICA HOUSE BOOK PUBLISHERS
www.publishamerica.com
Baltimore

Printed in the United States of America

Lovingly dedicated to my two children, Danny and Dawna, and to my two granddaughters, Teresa and Kim. And in memory of Al, a very special person in my life.

PROLOGUE
Virginia, June, 1828

As morning sun streamed through the windows, it gilded the books that lined the library's walls and sent sparkles of sunshine from the inkwell on her father's desk. It was a room Medora Gaylord usually loved to be in, but as she entered this morning she felt a difference--a tension. Her father's back was turned toward her. "You wanted to see me, Papa?" she asked.

He turned slowly. Lines etched his face, and she felt a grip of fear. "Papa, what's wrong?"

His Adam's apple bobbed as he swallowed and shadows darkened his eyes. "Best to say it straight out," he said. "There's been a duel. Early this morning. Chatfield challenged your Frenchman."

Medora felt the color drain from her face as her eyes went huge and round. "Oh no," she muttered.

"I'm sorry, my dear. It's very bad news." He paused as though he found it too difficult to go on. Then: "Chatfield is dead."

She backed away as though to distance herself from what her father was saying. "Chatfield dead?" Her betrothed. Her very best friend. She clutched her chest to quiet the erratic beating of her heart. Her voice thin and squeaky she asked, "What about Jacques?"

Her father's face hardened as words spilled out in a rush of fury. "Gone. The rascal fled. Chatfield never even had a chance to fire. The dastard escaped to risk being charged with murder."

"Oh, no. No--no--noooo!" Medora covered her face with her hands. "Oh dear God in heaven, no." Her body trembled. Her limbs went limp and she crumpled to the floor.

She was lying on her own bed when she opened her eyes. Tessy, her black servant, was placing a wet cloth on her forehead and mumbling, "I told you, honey. Ober and ober, I told you no good would eber come of that Frenchman hanging around."

Memory returned in a rush of horror--her father carrying her upstairs. Chatfield dead! Jacques gone! Her skin chilled to freezing. She pushed Tessy's hand aside. She had to sort through her terrible thoughts. "Go," she ordered. "I need to be alone."

"Yessum," the black woman said, but lingered. Again Medora ordered her to leave. Tessy still hesitated, then shook her head sadly and shuffled from the room, closing the door behind her.

Alone with the sickness in her soul, Medora's thoughts were in turmoil. Chatfield dead. Next spring they were to marry. It had long been planned by both their families, the Youngstons of the great banking family, and the Gaylords who owned Richmond's most acclaimed emporium. Her hand pressed her stomach and a clammy fear swept through her. *Jacques gone!* What if she were right about the strange changes taking place in her body...

Her throat filled with a choking heartbeat. Her beloved family--paramount in the community--respected by all. What would that do to them? Emotions tangled and snarled like a dropped ball of yarn. *Never able to hold up their heads again--ever!*

Engulfed in the hopelessness, her thoughts went back to the night it began: the night of her sixteenth birthday celebration held at her grandfather's plantation. If only by some miracle she could change it all. If she hadn't stepped out onto the veranda that night for a needed breath of cool evening air. If only Chatfield, always eager to grant her every wish, hadn't returned to the ballroom to get her some punch. If only she hadn't been alone on the veranda when that handsome brougham rolled to a stop.

A young man, handsomely dressed in a black swallow-tailed coat with a white satin cravat, alighted from the carriage and started up the stairs. When he noticed the young lady on the veranda, he stopped short. "Ah, mademoiselle," he said.

She glimpsed snapping dark eyes and a bold teasing smile. He was the most handsome creature she'd ever seen.

He swept off his hat in a gallant bow. "Or do my eyes deceive? As lovely as you are, you must be a vision."

Medora felt herself blush. Her heart did a turn, leaving her speechless. He nodded again and disappeared inside. If only she had left it at that. Instead, she went back into the ballroom to learn who the stranger was. She saw him talking to her grandfather. If she'd casually saunter over...

"Ah, here is my granddaughter now," her grandfather said and introduced her to Monsieur Jacques Rouleau. "A house guest of our neighbors, the Neglers," her grandfather explained. "They met Monsieur Rouleau when traveling in Paris last year and invited him to come to America and experience life on a southern

6

plantation.

"Which I am finding most pleasing," Jacques said looking at her with penetrating eyes. She felt herself quiver and knew she was falling in love.

For the next few weeks Medora remained at her grandfather's plantation, a welcome holiday from the heat of the city and the demands of Madame Tessier Finishing School for young ladies. She loved the grand old plantation and the green rolling hills and could spend lazy days on the veranda with her books and her sketch pad. In the mornings she rode the wooded bridle path that followed the River.

One morning Jacques trotted up beside her. After that there were many rides together in spite of grandfather's disapproval. "An adventurer and a rogue," was her grandfather's assessment. But Grandpapa could not know of Jacques' captivating charms.

During those heavenly weeks her thoughts seldom strayed from the visiting Frenchman and his teasing smile--his soft rich voice: *Ma chere, my princess,* he'd say as he caressed her with those mysterious dark eyes. Her grandfather reminded her she was promised to Chatfield. Jacques Rouleau had no place in her life now or ever.

They met in secret; stolen moments in a garden or in hidden nooks off the bridle path. Stolen kisses--and fervent promises. She was filled with the rapture of being in love, so different from the warm affection she felt for Chatfield. Eventually Grandpapa would relent, and her parents too. They'd never denied her anything she really desired. And she did desire Jacques--with a passion she hardly understood.

Just kisses at fist, so tender, so gentle. They'd clasp each other eagerly, hidden by the thick growth off the path.

"*Ma chere*, I love you. I'll cherish you always," he whispered as his lips, ever so softly, caressed her eyelids, her forehead, and moved down to touch the straight bridge of her slender nose. Her heart pounded. His hand rested on her breast and she liked the feeling.

Then one day he placed her down on the bed of new grass, its sweet fresh scent blending with the heady perfume of summer flowers. His slender fingers stroked and followed the curve of her chin. "If I were an artist, I'd sculpt this beautiful face." His words were echoed by the trill of a bird in the branches above them. The whole world was singing their love song.

Again the kisses. His velvet, moist tongue tasting the sweetness--first her ear, then pecks down her neck to lodge at the pulse beat of her throat. Lips together, semi-teasing. Then eager, more demanding. Her lips opened with an insatiable wanting. His hand brushed her chin with the lightness of butterfly wings. She melted into his gaze--oh, heavenly, heavenly. A shaky sigh escaped. His hands cupped her breast, and she felt a tremor--and a fear--something deeply ingrained. Was this the forbidden fruit she'd been warned of by her mother? By her black servant, Tessy?

He unbuttoned her bodice, a button at a time, and freed her breasts. She was powerless to stop him. His fingers first tickled a teasing pattern and then his forefinger pressed down, ever so gently, on her firm protruding nipple.

"Oh, oh," she moaned. Tantalizing prickles sparked her whole being. His finger touched a special, eager place, and she'd strained for more, wanting what? How could she know? Her heart thudded. Her breath came in little short moans.

"Ah, *ma chere*. You do want me too."

But when he released the bulge held captive in his breeches, she gasped with alarm and was drenched with panic. "No, we mustn't. It's wrong!" She was smothered with guilt. It was her Tessy's voice she was hearing, seeing her black eyes rolling so the whites showed like signals. *Nebber let any gent'lman touch you. If he does, he ain't no gent'lman, and you ain't no lady!*

At first she struggled against his iron grasp. His mouth came down hard on hers, smothering her, his curved tongue probing--and below--the other prober.

When it was over, the tears flowed, but he cradled her with tenderness. "I didn't mean to hurt you, *ma chere*. I really do love you. We will marry. You will be my wife."

She lay in his arms, but full of self-condemnation. Anguished thoughts recoiled at the unforgivable weakness of her own body. She had betrayed Chatfield, her betrothed. She had betrayed her beloved family and all they stood for. *She had betrayed the very principles she'd been taught.*

There were no more rides on the bridle path or secret meetings. What they had done was unforgivably wrong, and no longer dared she trust her own weakness. She returned to Richmond, but Jacques followed her there still insisting they should marry. Medora was torn. She loved Jacques, but there was her family to consider. Chatfield as well. She needed time. Eventually her parents would understand and give in, but she needed time to prepare them. Then came the shattering realization of what was happening in her body. But now, even before she could tell him, Jacques was gone--*never to know she carried his child!*

In the silence of her room, Medora stared with unseeing eyes at the ceiling, racked with guilt for the senseless tragedy she had caused. She thought of her father's grief over Chatfield's death, and her mind churned with questions as she searched for answers. She could go away. Her beloved family need never know her shameful secret. She could leave a note saying she'd heard from Jacques and was joining him to be married. Later she'd write and tell them about the child. They would be heartbroken, but wouldn't that be better...

As Medora tossed her head from side to side, tears dampened the pillow. She loved her home in Richmond, and summer days spent at her grandfather's great plantation. She loved the life she had always had. But most of all, she loved her dear family. She could not add this burden of shame. Her chest tightened into a hard ball of fear. If she did go away, whatever would become of her and the baby? Yet, in her mind the decision had been made. Her lips set in a firm straight line. There was no other way.

CHAPTER 1
Illinois--April 15, 1846

Spring was in the air, but the patches of snow banked around the trees still held a reminder of winter. The villagers with coat collars high to ward off the early morning chill clustered around the travelers to bid them good-by. Medora Dudley, still lovely at thirty-four years of age with her light flaxen hair and eyes blue as sapphire jewels felt she had said all the farewells she could without tears spilling over. She had to get away from the well-wishers. The lump in her throat was too tight, too choking. She needed the shelter of her home--just one more time.

Someone had built a warming fire. A great coffee pot suspended over the coals spread a tantalizing aroma. Medora stepped as close to the fire as she dared without her long skirt touching coals. But the warmth did not reach the chill within her. The chill remained. And the fear. Pioneering again! Once in a lifetime should have been enough for anyone. But that other time, that terrible time, the choice had been hers, *hers alone.* This time it was William's.

A large buxom woman with a shawl pulled around her shoulders, handed Medora a steaming cup of coffee. "Warm yourself with this, Miz Dudley."

"Oh, thank you, Mrs. Stephenson. I do appreciate your thoughtfulness."

Others gathered around. It was overwhelming that so many had come; mothers with babies in arms and little ones tugging at their coats. Young swains too with inconsolable eyes, their gazes following her oldest daughter, Lavinia. And William's associates--his customers, his friends. He had so many. Her friends too; members of the literary society, the church choir, the school board. Everyone was here to wish them well and a safe journey to that far off land they knew so little of, the Mexican province called California!

"We'll sorely miss the Dudleys," was said over and over.

"And we'll miss you," Medora replied. "My yes, how we will miss you." She said it from her heart. Whitherville had become *her* town, and the citizens *her* people. Here she was looked up to--a leader, with no one, except for Will, ever knowing her most shameful secret.

The lump in her throat still corked the tears. She didn't want to leave a memory of a blubbering woman with red swollen eyes. She touched her flaxen hair. The strands were still in place. A wonder after the exuberant embraces. She smoothed her dark woolen skirt chosen for the months of travel ahead instead of the rustling taffeta she liked to wear.

Medora glanced toward the roadway where four white-topped wagons clustered. Three of the wagons were hitched to oxen, the Dudleys' two and the other belonging to their good friend, Anton Zwiegmann. The fourth wagon was the Morgans' mule-pulled outfit. She hardly knew the Morgans.

William was puttering around the wagons, showing them off. *Of course, showing them off.* A couple of neighbors from outlying farms were talking to him. They looked inside the family wagon, stepped back and nodded approval. She could see Will's broad grin glowing with pride.

Medora felt her anger rise as it had so often of late. He could be enthused. Well, she couldn't! That box, twelve feet long and four feet wide with walls of wood and waterproof canvas, would be their home for the next five or six months. For six people! Hardly room for six fleas! Of course they'd not all sleep inside; William and Billy would use a tent. And Torrey? Who knew about that girl?

Plump arms went around Medora's shoulders giving her a hug. "I dread seeing you go." It was Judith, the judge's wife and Medora's good friend. "Our town won't be the same without you."

"Judith, dear, that's sweet of you to say."

"It's true. You've done so much for our little town. Our Literary Society will flounder without you."

Medora squeezed Judith's plump hand. "Everything will continue just the same with you at the helm."

But the fact was that within the entire community Medora was the only woman who had attended a female academy of culture, who could read and write in French, Spanish, and Latin; who spoke a "high-brow" English, as some said, and who had shelves of literary books and subscribed to *Godey's Lady Book*. Whitherville would never be a great city like Springfield, but the women folk liked having some culture and socials at the church, all of which Medora helped organize. This was what she was leaving--to follow *his* dream!

A tide of misery washed over her, drenched her, filled every crevice. Yes, they would miss her. *But how she would miss them and all that Whitherville stood for.*

She had to get away. The tears were too close. She set the cup on a stump, mumbled to Judith that she'd left something up at the house, then turned and ran up the path toward home.

The four wagons were not yet in line although the teams of oxen and mules were hooked and ready to go. Eleven persons were going, the six Dudleys, two Morgans, Anton Zwiegmann, and the two hired hands. At Independence they'd join the larger wagon parties going west.

One of the men who'd been looking over his rig, slapped William's lead ox on his big rounded rump. "Mighty fine animal," he said. William puffed with pride even when the neighbor started joshing him about his new clothing. The wool plaid shirt and heavy twill trouser tucked into knee-high boots were quite a contrast to William's usual attire of starched shirt, white silk vest, dark pantaloons, and well-cut frock coat. "Now ye look like the rest of us honest folks," the fellow said, poking William in the ribs.

William laughed. "What did you expect? I should wear weather duds when I was inside minding the store?"

"Right ye be. Reckon if yer a dandy, ye got to dress like one."

The joshing was good natured, no reason to take offense. For the last eight years William had run the mercantile and the gristmill for Judge Witherspoon who had started the settlement and still owned most of the town. Naturally, he dressed as a man of the trades. Whitherville was a town showing rapid advancement, and most agreed, many of its improvements could be credited to Mr. Dudley and his progressive ideas.

William did have ideas--and the enthusiasm to go with them. He had a positive belief in success, which was the natural progression of events when you had the Lord right beside you. But he also believed that the Lord favored those who did for themselves by putting their best foot forward. In his early forties, William still kept himself trim and hard around the middle. He combed his heavy dark hair, highlighted with red, back loosely to display his high forehead--a sure sign of intelligence some would say. He liked following fashionable trends and sported the new side-whiskers of the day and a smartly clipped mustache. It helped project the look of success. Even now, dressed in the rugged clothing designed for the elements, he still had a look of distinction.

"We've just been funnin' ye, Mr. Dudley. But the truth be, we are all powerful sad to see ye go. Whitherville will not be the same without the Dudleys. Ye and yer missus have brought mighty fine improvements to our town."

William's own emotions were mixed. He was leaving good friends; the townspeople and the farmers who were his customers. He'd miss them all. But he'd especially miss the judge, a man he liked and admired--a man he thought of as his mentor. The judge had paid him well for his services these past eight years. But the fact was, he still had no land of his own, a promise he'd made to his mother years ago. Land here in Illinois was now out of his reach.

But in California the land was free!

He wished Medora wasn't taking the leaving so hard. He knew she was remembering the hard times in Missouri where they'd pioneered at the start of their

12

marriage. But as head of the family, he had to think of the family's future. He had a son to consider, and three daughters. He must have something to pass on to his children, not always just work for another. So now here they were, ready to go.

William glanced toward his friend, Anton, a short-legged German with a flexible face that molded to his moods. Anton was turning a brush in the tar bucket that hung from the rear axle. He sloshed the wheels with a final dab of lubricant. William smiled. Typical of Anton, always so thorough in whatever he did.

"Everything in good order?"

Anton nodded, then frowned. "Except for Morgan. Stubborn as the mules pulling his wagon. But we settled the question who would lead out. If he wants to join our party, we set the rules."

William nodded. He hoped Morgan wasn't going to prove a burr under the saddle in the days ahead. Then he shrugged. He was not one to let problems bother him for long. The Lord would help out with Morgan. William began to whistle. With everything travel-secure, it was time to get going.

Fourteen year old Victoria Dudley, better known as Torrey, looked for her friend Effie among all the ones who came to bid them farewell. Such a hubbub of talking, made it as gay as a summer-day picnic. Children, playing hide-and-seek, scampered and screamed, her four year-old sister Jenny, and eight year-old brother Billy among them. Dusty Dog barked at their heels.

For weeks Torrey had been bubbling with excitement--the planning. And the dreams--night and daytime as well. Mama would say, "There's no time for moonraking now. There's packing to do." But Torrey couldn't help thinking on it. If she closed her eyes tight enough she knew how the wind would feel when it touched her face and tousled her hair. She herself would be at the head of the wagon line on the horse Papa had promised her when they got to Independence. *"Halt. Indians ahead!" She'd hold up her arm. Behind her the creaking wagons would roll to a stop!*

But now was the hurting part--the saying good-by. She and Effie had already shed their tears. It was such a monstrous thought when you considered you might never see your dearest, your very best friend ever again.

And the time was now. Most of these people she'd known since she was a kid. A big lump worked up tight in her throat making it hard to swallow. But where was Effie? Maybe she wasn't coming. Saying good-by was somewhat like dying.

Torrey glanced over toward her seventeen-year old sister, considered the pretty one of the family, looking so much like their mother with the same blond hair, the same sapphire blue eyes. She reckoned Lavinia was feeling the sadness too the way she was looking up at that gawky milksop Otto Meyer who looked as stricken as a hog going to the killing, and Lavinia eating it up. Makes you want to puke. Right now, though, Torrey could almost understand--not about anyone as stupid as that fellow Otto, however. But she knew what it was to be hurting with sadness.

Torrey spotted Effie's mother. Mrs. Stephenson should know where her daughter was.

"Morning, girl," Mrs. Stephenson said as Torrey ran up. "All set to go?"

"Yes ma'am, I reckon so. But where is Effie?"

"'Spect still to home. She was rummaging when I left. 'Spect she's still rummaging."

"Isn't she coming to say good-by?"

"Cain't rightly say about that girl. She's such a lolligager. 'Spect she'll be comin' sooner or later."

Torrey felt uneasy. If Effie didn't get here right soon...

By rights, the Stephensons' wagon should have been in that line too. It was Effie's pa who had first started the talk about going to California. Torrey remembered how excited they'd both been, she and Effie. They'd be traveling together, seeing new country--mountains and prairies, a possible encounter with an Indian or two. Pioneering was a mighty powerful adventure.

But then, Effie's pa changed his mind. "Too risky," he'd said. He had a wife and six children to think of. "And now with all that war talk with Mexico, and California a Mexican province. What happens if war is declared?"

Torrey was glad her father had pooh-poohed the idea. "If there is a war, the United states would certainly win, and so much the better," he'd said. Thanks to goodness, Papa didn't discourage easily.

Then she saw her friend. Effie was running across the field. Her long dark braids bounced out like oxen whips from beneath her knitted cap, and her breath came out in a steamy vapor. Torrey closed her eyes tight to capture the picture. This was a moment she must savor, store in her secret memory box to have for a future time when she needed to relish this ecstasy of pain. *Oh, Effie, if you were only going with us.* She ran to meet her friend.

"I-I-I-I was afraid I'd miss you." Effie's words spilled out in choppy breathlessness. "But I was looking for something." Her right hand was behind her back.

"What've you got?"

"You'll see. First, promise you'll write and tell me everything."

"I'll write every day. Papa says we can post letters when we get to Independence, and then again when we reach Fort Laramie. Oh, if only you were going too."

"I know." Their pain was a bond they both shared.

"I'd just as lief it'd been others who backed out instead of your pa. I'd just as lief certain ones weren't going."

"I know," Effie said again. She and Torrey were of a like mind.

Torrey's brow furrowed. "Like that Mr. Morgan. I saw him take a whip to his mules. But I like Mrs. Morgan all right."

"Sort of peculiar though."

Torrey agreed. But Elspeth Morgan, a skinny, bony woman with eyes that popped out like a toad's, intrigued Torrey with her strange ideas. "Papa says she's full of old backwoods superstitions and that I shouldn't pay attention to her tales. But she should be mighty interesting to have along."

Effie glanced over toward the meadow where Jake and Anton's teamster, Mike Sullivan, were tending the loose cattle and frowned. "The one I'm plumb worried about for your sake is that cheeky Jake Stringer."

Torrey followed Effie's gaze. Jake looked the smart-aleck he was with his soft felt hat tipped to a rakish angle and sporting a fancy leather vest garnished with Indian beads. He had drifted into town a couple of months before and Torrey's father had put him to work at the gristmill. Then, because Jake wanted to get to California, her father figured he'd do fine pushing the cattle.

"You couldn't talk your pa out of taking him--after what happened the other night at the farewell party?"

Torrey's eyebrows squinched together. "Papa doesn't know. You're the only one I told."

"But others must have saw," said Effie, still pursuing the subject.

Others had seen. Torrey had heard a startled gasp when they were out on the dance floor and her hand had suddenly swung up to leave a red mark across Jake's face.

Up until then, she had been having a tolerably good time, even when dancing with Jake until he joshed about the new twin rounds he'd suddenly noticed blossoming on her bosom. All her mother's fault, sewing ruffles inside her bodice to give fullness to what was hardly there. With that smart aleck grin he'd said it must be a sign she was ready for sparking and he was there to oblige.

She had rushed from the room, her face flaming with anger, but he caught her in the darkened hallway. His hand groped and squeezed the slight rounding of flesh where the ruffles were. Her knee came up and he doubled in pain and she got away. That part she hadn't even told Effie not wanting anyone to know. She hated Jake ever since.

"He's still casting glances your way," Effie said.

Torrey's scowl deepened. "Pooh. He casts glances at all the girls."

"But he's really got his eyes set on you, and he'll always be around. I'm frettin' for you, Torrey."

"Geeminy-gee, Effie, I can keep out of his way. I won't let him be mashing." She didn't want to talk more about Jake. She'd as lief forget him altogether. Just then she noticed her father motioning. "I think Papa means it's time we got started."

Effie brought her hand from behind her back and handed Torrey a small hard-bound booklet with gold edged pages and "Journal" printed in gold on the cover.

"I want you to have this to remember me by. I got it for Christmas one year, but nothing happens around here so I never wrote in it 'cept for that first day I got it."

Torrey took it, opened it carefully. Her fingers traced the crisp blank pages. Her eyes misted. "Effie..." The words choked her throat. "I'll never forget you--ever. I'll think of you every time I write in it." The two girls wrapped their arms around each other and a wailing waterfall flowed.

Effie's mother stepped up behind them. "Quit your blubbering and take this to your pa." She handed Torrey a steaming mug of coffee. "He must be nigh frozen working on his wagons, can't take time to warm by the fire."

"Much obliged to Mrs. Stephenson," William said as he shaped his hands around the warm mug. "Ah, this does taste mighty fine."

He smiled at his daughter, feeling a surge of love for this care-free child of his, part woman, part tomboy still. Not a beauty yet, but showing promise. There was no denying she had a special kind of radiance. It sparked in the ruddy brown eyes with the same touch of red that was in her dark auburn hair, and in the vibrant movement of those strong dark inverted V eyebrows like his own that flashed her moods so quickly. It was sinful, he knew, to have a favorite among your children, yet he couldn't deny that Torrey was someone very very special to him.

Now her eyebrows peaked in anticipation. "Are we about ready, Papa?"

"If you can round up the others." He looked toward the fire. Lavinia was there holding on to little Jenny. Billy was down on his knees skimming the other boys out of their marbles. The dog, Dusty, was flopped down beside the boy.

"Where's your mother?"

Torrey shrugged.

William frowned. "I don't see her over with the rest. Go see if you can find her. It's past time we were on our way."

Medora hurried up the path that led through the woods. Her acute awareness of the new spring was a stab of pain; the sweet scent of new clover, the tender greenness of dogwood, redbud, and elder blossom. She would not trod this path ever again. The white frame house appeared through the branches--her home these last eight years. As she approached the steps she saw the lilacs near ready to bloom. And she wouldn't be here--not here to fill the house with its sweet fragrance. *Not to be here.*

The house was cold inside--and bare. An empty house. As empty as she herself felt. Her footsteps echoed on the rugless floor. The less faded spots on the walls were a reminder of where pictures had hung--the portraits of her parents, silhouettes of the children. For a moment Medora stared at the space where her mother's cherry wood breakfront had stood that had held her mother's fine fluted Bristol china and apple-green Spode. *Would she ever have them again?*

They were the last vestiges of her beloved Virginia, the final tie to the great brick family town house in Richmond and to the vast rolling greens of her grandfather's plantation on the James--all she had left of those glorious days. Those few treasures a cousin had sent her after her father's death. Memories. Days gone forever. She never saw any of her family again after she left Virginia to marry William. So long ago. *So long ago.*

Now those family heirlooms were carefully stored in Judge Whitherspoon's attic. He would ship them around The Horn once they were settled. "Unless you'll be back here someday," the judge had added.

They wouldn't be back. That was the terrible certainty she felt. Another chapter of her life to be closed. Like the other one, there would be no turning back.

Medora wandered from one empty room to another. She pulled her cloak tighter about her, shivered from the cold--and shivered from fear. What lay ahead? Miles of travel over plains and mountains, and once again, an unknown country.

She slumped against the wall where her spinet had been. On it, as a child, she'd first learned her scales. Later Chopin, Beethoven. Such memories. Long lost times. She slipped to the floor and buried her head in the skirt covering her knees. She pulled her cloak tighter about her.

Outside the air was crispy still, yet it was as though she could hear the sound of wind. Oh, God--that whistling wind in the Missouri woods. The loneliness of its sound. It seeped through the unchinked spaces of the log cabin. Sorrowful wailing. Would it be like that again?

In the new sparsely settled section of Missouri neighbors had been few and far between. Weeks went by without talking to anyone but Will and the babies, and with Will--there was the insurmountable wall between them. He could have abandoned her after he'd learned she'd lied--telling him she loved him so he'd take her with him. Instead, he had given her protection--and had kept her secret. In return, she accepted the role of a pioneer wife. She had tried to live up to her bargain.

Oh, yes she'd tried, for one who'd previously known only a gay life made up of fashionable people, Madame Tessier's Finishing School for the Refinement of Young Ladies, and cotillion dances in chandelier brightened rooms. Whose big black lovable Tessy did everything for her; buttoned her clothes, brushed her hair, scolded her when need be. And her father and grandfather had pampered her so. Oh God, how life changed in Missouri, living in a dirt-floored log cabin.

She learned what it meant to be a pioneer woman. She learned to cook stews in a great iron pot over fireplace coals, her hands blistering in the process. She learned to make soft soap from leached-out ashes and hog grease; and how to make patch quilts from the remnants of worn out clothing when it no longer could hang on a body. And she learned, frighteningly and painfully, about birthing babies on a corn husk mattress.

But the loneliness had been the hardest to learn.

Will tolerated it better. He had his enthusiasm for the land, and later, when he had his conversion at that Methodist camp meeting, he had his religious faith to carry him through. He'd said about Missouri, "No finer country. God's country it is." He had the same lilt in his voice then that he now used for California. Missouri was "beautiful, fertile, productive. Soil so black, anything will grow." He had staked his claim and built his dreams of great productive fields. *But Will was no farmer. He had never been a farmer.*

And he failed to see the competition he would face with the wealthy slave owners when he didn't believe in slavery because of his own years of indentured servitude.

He also had overlooked the abundance of snakes, rattlesnakes and copperheads. Eventually one had taken the life of one of their babies--her beautiful little golden-haired boy when he was only three years old. Then later, summer complaint took her four-year old Clement, named after her father. *Her little boys left in the ground at the edge of the tobacco field.*

What would it now be in California?

After Missouri's backwoods, Whitherville was Glory Land. Small country town that it was, hardly to be compared with Richmond, but at least here she had neighbors. Life had settled into a pleasant pattern. She was devoted to her children. She was a dutiful wife to the man she'd shamefully wronged. Eventually he'd learned to forgive. Although there had been no love on her part in the beginning, through the years she'd learned to care. She was proud of Will's standing in the community. She was contented living in the neat frame house they rented from the judge. Her family pieces had added a certain elegant charm. And their income was adequate. It even provided some privileges; they'd sent Lavinia to the Female

Academy in Jacksonville for a season. Torrey was to have gone this coming year to learn to be a lady and, Medora hoped, shed some of her sauciness. But now, all that was changed. Everything gone to follow *his* dream.

Torrey pushed the door open. She paused for a moment in the doorway seeing the huddled figure bundled against the wall, the cloak tight about her. "Mama! Mama, are you all right?"

No answer. Only a trembling of the shoulders.

Torrey didn't remember ever having seen her mother cry before. There had been times when she saw a sad wistfulness in her mother's eyes. But tears? Mama was so queenly--so beautiful and perfect--so different from herself. Now, a sob?

Torrey glanced around the cold, bare room. No wonder. She felt sad too with everything gone. Mama loved this house, and she loved her family things because they reminded her of her old home in Virginia. Torrey guessed home could be pretty important when you weren't there anymore. Maybe she'd think that way about Whitherville when they were out in California.

A tear slipped down Torrey's cheek. Sometimes she was shamed when another's crying brought on tears of her own. But this was different. Her choked-up sorry feeling created a closeness to her mother she seldom felt. Mama must really be hurting, leaving all those things she loved. Papa had said only the necessities but then gave in on her blue willow ware. For the first time Torrey really wanted to be able to talk to her mother--say she understood.

"Mama..."

Why was it so hard to find the right words with Mama?

Torrey slid to the floor. If she reached out, she could touch her. Torrey remembered a time, long ago, when she'd lost out on the angel part in the Christmas pageant, a part she wanted so very much. She ran from the church back to this same room. Here, like Mama now, she'd slid into a miserable heap. How desperately she'd wanted arms around her, have loving words wash away the piercing misery that seemed overwhelming. She remembered how Mama had knelt right down beside her and gathered her close in her arms. Yet, she had pulled away. Papa was the one she wanted.

For a moment Torrey's fingers almost touched the huddled figure, then drew back. *What if Mama resisted like she herself had done?*

They sat for a moment, side by side. The silence stretched between them. Torrey groped for what she wanted to say. Some words of comfort. Finally, words tumbled out.

"Mama, Papa says it's time--time for California."

CHAPTER 2

Two weeks out from Illinois and they had sloshed through rain much of the time, the wagons bogged to the hubs in Missouri's red clay. But the last few days had been dry, right pleasant weather in fact.

Eli Morgan led out that morning as he had been doing most of the time. "No reason you should hold back your spirited mules as long as we're traveling through settled country," William had said and Morgan, not having spared the lash on his mules, was soon out of sight. They were following the Mississippi River and the countryside was dotted with farms. Travel was safe enough for a lone traveler during the day, but come nightfall, with the possibility of roaming highwaymen, Eli would always be waiting for them along the roadway.

"Maybe this time Eli's fine mules takes him too far for us to catch up," William said as he urged his mare along side of Anton.

"Ja, but not so likely," Anton replied. "Maybe at Independence he joins another party."

"With all his complaining, you'd think he would," William said and wished it might be so. He didn't look forward to traveling with the contankerous man and his strange little wife over the two thousand miles that lay ahead. He had a feeling Morgan spelt trouble. Then, chiding himself on unchristian thoughts, he added, "Reckon it hasn't been too bad with the Morgans along."

Actually, the odd couple had kept pretty much to themselves. They built their own cookfire and ate their meals alone, retiring to their wagon soon after supper. Just as well, William figured with Morgan given so to cussing. He'd seen Medora shudder when she thought the children might hear. As for Morgan's wife, Elspeth, she was a timid little soul, holding back as though she was afraid to intrude.

Their own evenings around their campfire, after supper was cleared, became right lively. Medora would pour coffee for the older ones and give slices of dried apple treats to the two younger tykes. Jake would play his harmonica as the children sang. He and Anton, and Anton's teamster, Mike, a man of near thirty and not much given to talking, lit up their pipes. Anton, after a couple of deep draws on his Meerschaum, would start on his whittling stick. He had a sure knack for whittling, never letting his hands sit idle, even after a hard day of driving stubborn teams. For himself, William was ready to sit back and just contemplate the days happenings.

Now, riding along side Anton, William felt the trip was going well indeed. He glanced back at their oxen pulled wagons, and felt a glow of pride. He and Anton had their rigs especially built. Hard hickory with wrought-iron reinforcement around the tongue and hounds. The wheels were stout seasoned oak for less shrinkage on the desert. Sound equipment was necessary for the jostling over the two thousand miles ahead. He was concerned for Morgan's old farm rig. Valuable time could be spent if repairs had to be made.

As though thinking along those same lines, Anton said, "Notice how close Morgan is about his old wagon."

William nodded. "He's made that plain. Don't want no one getting too near. Yelled at Billy when the boy crawled under it to get a ball."

"He sold that farm that belonged to his dead brother."

"Think that's it? He's hid his gold in his wagon?"

"Ja, knowing Morgan, banks he wouldn't trust."

The two men fell into silence. The talk on Morgan had run its course. Now the only sounds were the horses walking and the saddles squeaking. Behind them was the roll of the wagons and farther back occasional mooing from protesting cattle as Jake and Mike urged them on. Dusty Dog often darted ahead, sniffing and establishing his dominance of the trail by his liquid signature that he emphasized by vigorous kicks that sent dirt flying. He was a middling sized dog with long floppy ears, a coat mostly black tipped with brown--the reason for his name. A no-account dog to be sure, William figured, but Dusty loved the children so earned his keep. Besides, he came from a bitch that belonged to the judge. The Dudleys owed a lot to the judge.

Eight years before when they arrived in Whitherville they owned nothing but what was heaped in an old spring wagon. A humble beginning to be sure. After losing his farm in Missouri they were on their way to Springfield where William felt he'd have a better chance of employment. But he'd stopped at a farmhouse to ask directions. The farmer, who was Anton, gave them shelter for the night, and William learned from Anton that the judge was looking for someone to run his mercantile store. His past experience as apprentice to a storekeeper in Pennsylvania during his youth and later clerking in Virginia's largest emporium in Richmond, owned by Medora's father, qualified him for the job.

Before long, the judge had recognized William's versatile talents with figures and business. Thus, from the abject poverty the Dudleys had known in Missouri, life in Whitherville became one of moderate comfort. And they lived in the nicest house in the village, the white frame house the judge and his family had originally occupied before building his mansion further out in the country.

It was difficult to leave all that behind. Yet, California had the promise. It was there in the letters printed in various Illinois papers telling about the far-off Mexican province. Glowing letters they were that told of a land of perpetual sunshine, where sweet william and hollyhocks bloomed at Christmas tide and clover stood five feet high. And so rich was the countryside, cattle never had to be fed. The Mexicans were eager for settlers, the letters said. They would give away huge grants of land free if you lived there a year. To William it seemed the Lord had beckoned. California, his *promised land.* He'd made a promise to his mother years ago when he was just a lad. "Strive for thine own land, my son" she had said as she tearfully signed the indenture papers that apprenticed him to a storekeeper. "It's what will make thee thine own man." He gave his promise. Now California's free land meant he could keep that promise. if only Medora wasn't taking the leaving so hard. "I'd say, no-thank-you, much obliged. Whitherville is fine if I can't have Virginia," she'd said when he first told her he was thinking of going. Of course, she was remembering Missouri.

Well, he remembered Missouri too. A time of torn emotions for them both with more to forgive on his part than on hers. But that belonged to the past. Time had healed. California would not be the same as Missouri.

California. It gave him a feeling of humbleness as well as a bursting of pride. New frontiers. Makers of a great new country. Manifest Destiny. The promise of Washington's Western Expansionists was to make this great land of theirs a two-ocean nation, Oregon and California a part of the United states. William felt a trembling of excitement thinking by heading west and settling new land he would be putting his mark on history.

Nooning came and Anton picked a grassy place near a stream. The men unhooked the oxen to graze as Medora and Lavinia started the midday meal. William's gaze followed his wife's graceful movements, enjoying the way her skirt, dark and serviceable as it was, clung to the pleasant roundness of her buttocks. He thought of the crisp, fashionable frocks she'd be wearing if still back home. He felt a burst of gratitude for what she'd given up for him. Never a complainer. Once she'd accepted the fact they were going, she'd said little more. Wasn't easy, he knew, for a woman to tend household chores while traveling. He was glad she had Lavinia to help--and Torrey. William frowned. Where was Torrey now?

At that moment Torrey was at the back of the wagon watching Jake's attempt to herd the loose cattle toward a meadow. One of the young steers had separated from the ranks and was headed for the woods. A look of disgust clouded Torrey's face. You better hurry, you chuckledhead, she thought, before it's lost among those trees. Why her father thought Jake would make a good teamster! Her feeling toward him had not improved during these past two weeks of travel after the incident at the party. Well, she guessed Jake was a hard worker--if only he'd keep his eyes to himself.

Torrey's brows drew together as she saw Jake make a grab for their mule's short mane, something Dulcie objected to. The animal pulled away, tossed her big head and stepped out of Jake's reach.

"That numskull," Torrey muttered.

Even from this distance she could see the set look on the young man's face. Again he made a grab for Dulcie. This time he got a firm grip, tossed his leg up and straddled the mule. His heels dug into her flanks and he flapped her over the head with his soft felt hat. Dulcie was taken by surprise. The mule shook her head with pinned-back ears, switched her tail and took off like a spark dropped into fireworks set for the Fourth of July. She started off with a short pop and a hop, and every now and then a sizzling kick. She stopped abruptly, waved both hind legs high in the air. Jake went even higher. When he came down, Dulcie was gone and Jake was flat on his stomach.

Torrey burst into laughter, but her father started running toward the fallen victim. Torrey followed.

She had not yet suppressed her mirth when they reached Jake. He lay sprawled, then turned slowly and sat up trying to catch his breath. Torrey held her sides as she broke into fresh peals of laughter. Jake had been lucky. Dulcie had picked a soft spot to toss him, one covered by fresh cow turds which cushioned his fall. His face was smeared, his dark curly hair matted, his beaded leather vest streaked brown.

Torrey put her hands across her mouth to hold back the rollicking sound. Jake's eyes shot fire.

"Are you hurt, lad?" William asked.

Jake got to his feet and brushed off the clinging cow dung from his clothing. "I'm all right--but wait 'till I get that dad-blamed mule!"

"You took her by surprise," William said.

Jake made no answer, but Torrey could see he was bristling with anger--not only for the mule. His eyes flashed revenge as he looked her way, and she preened herself with satisfaction.

Unaware of the commotion going on in the meadow, Medora wedged the big black kettle of stew, cooked the night before, into the burning embers. Bending over she stirred the simmering mixture with a long-handled wooden spoon. Straightening, she rubbed her aching back muscles. If she only had a table to set things on. But why complain? What was there to gain? When she closed the door on her home that last time, she had resolved there'd be no more tears. You made the best of the inevitable. She had an example to set for the children.

Medora threw an appreciative glance toward her eldest daughter. What a blessing Lavinia was--always so helpful. Without being asked the girl was already cutting lard into the flour for a pan of biscuits. And Torrey? Medora glanced around. Torrey had disappeared--as usual. Medora sighed. What a difference between the two girls. Even here--Torrey scorning domestic chores, preferring the men's hard labor. Just then she noticed William and Torrey coming from the meadow, a glint of amusement in Torrey's ruddy brown eyes.

"Can you spare me from chores? Jake's got sort of a distraction," Torrey asked. "Reckon Papa needs help unhooking the critters."

Medora shook her head. "Go on. Be gone." Anything to duck women's chores. The girl should have been born for trousers. Torrey's unladylike behavior was a concern. She couldn't help but worry for the girl's future.

Medora turned back to stir the stew but glanced toward the two who had begun to unhook the yoked animals. William threw a rope over to Torrey, but it missed its mark and fell across the head of the lead ox. The startled bovine bellowed and stepped backwards. "Torrey, watch out!" Medora screamed.

"Mama, don't worry so. I can handle these critters."

Jake ran up. "Hey, there girl, what you doing?"

Medora noticed an angry glint in the young man's eyes and wondered about the remains of a stain on his fine beaded vest.

"Helping Papa, that's what," Torrey replied.

"Well, go skedaddle and tend your female chores."

Torrey scrunched up her face. "I can handled these critters good as you, Jake Stringer. You're such a smart-aleck." She stuck out her tongue.

Medora gasped in shock. Such unlady like behavior!

Jake laughed. "Careful now. I might bite it off."

"Never mind, girl," William intervened. "I do appreciate your help, but now that Jake is here..."

Torrey flung down the rope. Her eyes flashed, and her tip-tilted nose went skyward. She swung around and stalked off toward the creek, her long auburn curls bouncing across her shoulders.

That girl, Medora thought. Why does she act so? Why couldn't she learn to use the same finesse Lavinia would use? Jake was a nice enough young man. Not suitor material, of course, Torrey only fourteen. And naturally, Medora's eventual hope was for her daughters to make good matches with educated men of promise when the time was right, which would certainly not include a teamster. Besides, Jake was more or less a drifter, coming from where? Indiana? He'd arrived in town and William needed a hand. Still, no call for Torrey to act so horrid. Would she ever learn?

It was a nagging worry. How could she make Torrey understand, now that she was reaching *that* certain age? How could she make Torrey understand the importance of femininity?--the only leverage we women have. The patterns had long been set. There was no way women could change them.

Medora sighed. *If only we could. But we can't, my daughter. You were born female, the same as I.*

Thinking of Torrey's fractious attitude toward Jake, Medora's thoughts went back to the night of their farewell party and the embarrassment she had known by Torrey's shameful display on the dance floor where everyone could see... Later she had demanded an explanation, but all she got was: "You had to sew those ruffles in my dress. I hate that Jake Stringer," and she'd bounded up the stairs to her room without saying more.

Since then Medora had searched her mind for the answer, even thinking of it now. Had she tried to push womanhood on her child too soon? Well with the several months of travel ahead, she might as well let Torrey be--let her have these next few months of childhood. Let her stay the tomboy she had always been for a little while longer.

The noon meal over, Medora and the girls began clearing, even Torrey pitching in without being told. The two teamsters went off to round up the loose cattle to get them ready to move on. William gave a quick check of his supply wagon to make sure everything was travel secured. It carried the precious food stuff they needed; flour, dried beans, rice, and huge slabs of bacon, enough to last six months, plus a few household items. Only the necessities William had insisted, but gave in when Medora said she wanted her willow ware dishes--to have something besides tin plates for special days like birthdays or the Fourth of July. He buried them in a barrel of flour so they didn't take up extra room. He also gave in on her tin box of books. She needed her favorites; Emerson, Longfellow and Thoreau, and the children needed books for their studies. And of course, he'd need his guide books handy.

Anton's wagon carried mostly his farm equipment plus two large boxes of young grafted trees planted in rich Illinois soil. They would start his orchard when he got to California. A cautious man, he also carried necessary spare parts in case of breakdown while traveling the many miles of treeless prairie. He was a powerful man with enormous energies and liked order, everything neat and in its place. William felt lucky that Anton was his friend, a good man to tie to.

While William checked his wagons, Anton went down to the stream and returned with buckets of water for his young trees.

"You take better care of those trees than most men do their wives," said William with a smile.

"Ja, they produce for me maybe more than a wife."

"While you're petting your trees, I've something else to check out." From his own wagon, William reached for the tin box that contained the books and took out his two guide books. One was the Fremont Report that the government had published with detailed maps for the overland trail. But William's favorite was *The Emigrant's Guide to Oregon and California,* written by a Lansford Hastings who had been to California and knew the lay of the land. It not only told about California, but it showed an easy shortcut to get there--would cut off four hundred miles.

Anton finished watering his trees and came over to where William was sitting with the Hasting's book open.

"Four hundred miles," William said. "That's a fair piece to cut off. Save about a months travel, wouldn't you say?"

Anton shrugged. "Ja, I would say. But I think I like better Fremont's government report. I'm not sure I would trust that Hastings." He looked up, taking a reading from the sun. "Only now, I think it's time we hook up and get on." His eyes twinkled and his mobile face shaped to a grin. "I feel our friend is missing us, hardly able to wait for our company, ja? Unless his mules have already got him to Independence."

Eli Morgan, a big man over six feet with scowl creases between shaggy brows, was waiting--had been waiting impatiently for some time. His wagon had smashed a wheel about an hour ago, probably about the time the Dudleys and Anton stopped for nooning. Eli knew Anton carried a spare.

When the spokes first broke, Morgan jerked on the reins to halt the mules before they pulled the damn wagon to pieces. But the mules were spirited creatures. When he finally got them stopped, Eli jumped from the wagon, his face livid with rage. The wheel was beyond repair. He gave the wagon a lusty kick with his heavy-booted foot. "Goddamned piece of junk."

That bastard German had said as much before they'd left Whitherville which infuriated Morgan at the time, thinking no sonofabitch foreigner had the right to remark on his rig. Foreigners and Mormons--they both stuck in his craw.

Both Zwiegmann and Dudley were so damn proud of their new shiny wagons. Hell, he had good reason for using his old one. It fit his needs when he put in a false floor to cache the money he got from the sale of his brother's farm, and another secret compartment that hid his prized treasure that was going to make him a fortune when he got to Californy.

Now, damit-to-hell, he would need some help to put on another wheel, and he didn't like snoopers around his wagon. Sonofabitch. Damn fool luck. Like usual. He had figured his luck was changing, going to Californy with that treasure.

A scrawny face with bulging eyes poked out from the puckered canvas opening. "What ye goin' do, Eli?"

Eli spun around, his scowl fiercing his face. He was in no mood to be rubbed by her damn fool questions. "What in hell do ye think I'm going to do? I'm a'going to wait here till the others come."

Elspeth pulled her head back into her canvas home. Jest like a damn turtle, Morgan thought. More of his goddamn luck, saddled with the likes of her. He would have left her in Illinois--except for the treasure. Esko, her brother, wouldn't have let him have it if he didn't take her along. Kin. Them kind put so much stock in their kin.

Inside the wagon came the whoop of a cough. Elspeth's head poked out again. "Eli, I need my remedy. My coughs chokin' up."

"Leave it be, damn woman, and get out of that wagon."

Elspeth crawled out of the listing wagon, pulling her shawl tight around her shoulders. She wore a man's heavy shirt, which once had been Eli's, a dark woolen skirt and on her feet a pair of heavy brogans. She started coughing again. Eli glared. More trouble.

"If I had my remedy..."

"Damn you, woman. I'll get you yer remedy. But ye better be quiet about it. If ye let anyone know there's more beside what ye got in yer own little bag--ye'll be wishin' ye never was born."

Morgan hated to get back into the broken wagon, but if it was the only way he could keep the damn woman quiet. More of his goddamn luck.

Seemed bad luck had marked him since the day he was born with his maw dying when she had him, and he learned early in life that he could really count on no one 'ceptin' himself. Not even his paw. He learned that lesson when he was not much more than a tad of thirteen and his paw gave him a patch of ground to plant. His paw had a farm that bordered the Ohio River. The patch was small, but his paw had said he could have it to plant whatever he wanted. So Eli plowed the ground, planted 'taters, ridged the soil up some as the vines grew, ashed them and dug 'em when the vines died down. He got three hundred bushels, figured enough to buy himself a gun.

"I'll peddle 'em fer ye, son," his paw said. Which he did. He sold 'em to a captain taking a flat boat down the river. But then his paw kept all of the money.

Cheated by his very own paw, like that, he decided to run away. He was big for his age, so signed onto a flatboat that was carrying 'taters--probably the very ones he'd growed, he suspected. But his experience on the flatboat proved no better than the one with his paw. After the first run was over, being jest a kid, the pilot cheated him out of his pay. Eli never saw neigh a penny of it.

By that time, he was figurin' that was all ye could expect in life. But now the river was in his blood--a muddy yellow witch that could be mighty peaceful at times, but high-handed when she took a notion. He liked the independent life she offered. He liked the ribald stories the crew told, and the cheap corn whiskey they offered him now and then. He liked the excitement of the free-for-all battles. He learned to use his balled-up fists and to flash a knife if need be. Ye had to, or ye didn't survive.

So he stayed with the river, working the keelboats and the flatboats, up and down the Ohio and the Mississippi. River rats they were called, and he guessed maybe they wuz. He grew bigger, older, wiser, and rougher, but not much richer during the many years he stayed on the river, his damn luck still a bur up his ass. So he went to trapping.

It was in the Tennessee hill country that he came across Elspeth. She had strange smokey eyes and was half-way purdy at that time. She was fourteen and as fresh as a new plucked daisy. He was right taken to her for a spell, until the day she pulled him down to the grass behind a huge boulder where he'd taken her several times before. And she said to him, "Mr. Morgan, I'm afeared ye've got me with child."

"What makes ye think it be me?" he demanded.

"Cause yer t'ony man ever tetched me."

But it took her pappy to do the real convincing. The old man poked the long barrel of his Kentucky rifle in Eli's gut.

"Ye needn't be so hasty," Morgan said to the old man. "I been aimin' all a'time to ask ye if I can marry yer daughter."

"The answer be yes, and ye better make it fast," her pappy replied.

Anyway, about that time, Morgan had been giving some thought to settling down, remembering his more peaceful boyhood days on the farm. If he went to farming, he'd need a woman to do the chores and to supply him with sons who would be able to help with the work. So he took Elspeth to wife, but even there his damn luck turned up like it always had. The first sprout was born dead. The second one lived only two weeks. After that, the others never got far enough to show in her belly.

But when he learned his brother, Lem, had a farm going in Illinois, he figured that's where he should be. Sadly enough, a short time after him and Elpeth arrived,

28

Lem drowned in the river. The sheriff started snooping around.

Eli protested. "I'm mighty grieved right now with the loss of my brother--much too grieved to answer yer questions. Me and Lem was mighty close." So close, in fact, that he'd talked Lem into signing an agreement that if one went before the other, the survivor got all. Of course, Morgan didn't tell that to the sheriff. It was just at that time the migrating talk was strong, and with the sheriff still snooping, Morgan figured it was time he headed west as well. So here they were, Californy bound--with a damn broken wheel.

Well into mid-afternoon he finally heard the commotion of wagons rolling and cattle bellowing and figured that must be the Dudleys comin' at last.

"All right now, woman," he said glaring at Elspeth. "We'll be here a spell puttin' on a wheel, and if ye be jest hangin' around mixin' with them others, ye better be sure yer jaw ain't a'flappin' about that damn remedy of yourn--or what else is in the wagon."

Elspeth nodded. "I swar, I won't say a word. The Lord will plague me if I do."

And as the Dudleys and Anton closed ground between themselves and the Morgans, unaware of Eli's problem, William's spirits still sailed high as his thoughts winged on to that favored land where clover stood five feet high, where with dedication and the help of the Lord he'd realize his dream.
Califoria. The land of promise.

CHAPTER 3
California, Sacramento Valley
May 1, 1846

As the Dudleys were wheeling through Missouri, more than two thousand miles away Steve Magoffison, a tall lanky young man with blond hair bleached almost white from the California sun, was making his way toward Putah Creek in search of James Clyman. He had heard that Mountain Man Clyman was organizing Yankee settlers to resist General Castro's threats and Steve was ready to sign up. He hated to leave his rancho at this time. A young mare was ready to foul--first time around, but the future of his rancho was at stake--the future of all American settlers. Rumors were that the comandante was now inciting the Indians to burn them out to rid the province of the Americans. Recently, the comandante had posted a proclamation at Sutter's Fort that stated that all settlers who were not citizens were to leave the country. If they resisted, they'd be shot. No new emigrants would be allowed to enter the Mexican territory.

Steve wasn't a Mexican citizen, nor was he about to become one. Citizenship required becoming a Catholic and living in California a year. Steve had lived in California two years now, but wasn't about to become a papist. Nor would he be chased from his land. He'd bought a section of an original Mexican land grant fair and square from the original owner who had never put it to use. It was wilderness country on the Feather River fifty miles north of Sutter's Fort. No other sign of civilization, just an Indian rancheria a few miles away, and the Maidu people were peaceful enough. He'd stocked his rancho with cattle and was now into breeding the Palominos. Invited to leave? Hell no. He wasn't about to.

He wasn't a violent man, but there was a time when you had to stand up for your rights. There were enough American settlers here now--and more coming in. *If they only knew*, Steve thought wryly--those emigrants coming with high hopes and dreams of a "promised land." Promised land hell. More like their Waterloo considering what was now happening. Taxes had been raised, and the tariffs on imported goods so high, they'd find they couldn't even afford the necessities once they got here.

But for us who already have our land... If Clyman is organizing the settlers to take a stand, hell, he wanted to be in on it too.

The turn his life had taken in these last couple of years was still hard to

30

believe. He'd been brought up in the political environment of Washington City with his senator father who believed his son would follow his own political career, marry Amanda, his childhood sweetheart, and settle in Washington City. His father's plans. Not his. Ranching had always been his dream--a secret dream to be sure, a dream that became a reality when he crossed the Sierra Nevada Mountains two years before as a member of the United States Topographical Engineering Corps headed by John Charles Fremont. They crossed the mountains in the dead of winter, almost perished in the snow drifts before they got through. Then, he looked down on a valley that gleamed like a jewel; grass so high it scraped the bellies of their horses--wildlife in abundance. Steve knew then he wanted to stay. He took his discharge from the corps along with four others, and wrote a farewell letter to Amanda whom he knew would never want to come here.

Evening found Steve arriving at Clyman's camp on Putah Creek. He reined in Pepieto, his chestnut gelding trail horse.

"Done gone," a trapper who'd been working for Clyman informed him. "He's taking a party of settlers back to where they come from. Reckon they'd had enough of this here Californy and the damn Mexicans and their ass-hole laws."

"I was told he was organizing the settlers to take a stand against Castro."

The trapper shrugged. "He wuz. Ye might find him at Sutter's Fort where he's pickin' up supplies."

"I'll be damned," said Steve. He'd camp for the night and take off for the fort next morning before daylight.

The next day, nearing the fort, Steve slowed Pepieto to a gentle walk. The day had warmed. Spring in California could be like summer. If he were up on his rancho, he'd be out herding his cattle to higher ranges. He'd sure as hell rather be doing that than on this errand of anger. But by God, they couldn't let that tyrant Castro get away with what he threatened to do to the American settlers.

Now cultivated fields spread before Steve. A breeze played across the tender blades of unripened wheat bending them to a shimmering sea of different shades of green. Amazing what Captain Sutter had done here in this primitive country. Seven years before the only inhabitants had been the wild animals and Maidu-Nisenan Indians. Now, on a slight knoll rose the adobe walls of a fort. Bastions atop at the corners emphasized the fort's supremacy of the wilderness. New Helvetia, Sutter called it, after his Swiss homeland. It was becoming a Mecca for the Yankee emigrants who were coming over the mountains in increasing numbers. The reputation of Sutter's hospitality had traveled far.

At the gate stood an Indian sentinel dressed in a green military jacket with red cuffs. Probably one of the uniforms Sutter acquired when he'd purchased the Russian's Fort Ross on the coast a few years back, Steve thought. The Indian

31

recognized Steve and gave him a nod to enter the compound.

Activity bustled inside--the swish of a plane from the carpenter's shop, the clang of metal against metal from the blacksmithy. Sutter was a progressive entrepreneur with many projects going.

Steve tied his horse to a hitching post. He'd look in on Sam Neal first. Sam was Sutter's blacksmith, and had been one of the men who took his discharge from the corps along with Steve when Fremont headed back for the States.

Steve stood in the doorway until his vision adjusted to the dimness inside. The objects came into focus: the rows of hanging hammers and tongs on the wall, the huge bellows leaning against the side of the glowing forge. Acrid smells of burning charcoal mixed with the steam of a horse as manure flew out of a frightened animal being shod. The stink from the paring of the hooves was strong, a sickening smell. Steve watched the man work and felt the warm tug of memories, good times and hardships shared when they'd explored with Fremont.

Sam Neal finished his job, looked up and grinned. He rubbed his blackened hand on his leather apron and reached for Steve. "Howdy, friend. How be ye there?"

He was a long stick of a man in a red flannel shirt and leather breeches. He wasn't old, but he'd lost some teeth so that his cheeks sank in under a long skinny nose giving him a stringy look from head to toe. His eyes shone with a twinkle.

"I'm right fine," Steve responded. "You're looking fit enough to raise hell and then some."

It was always good to be with an old comrade. The last time he'd seen Neal was in January when he'd heard that Fremont had again crossed the mountains and was at the fort. Steve had come down from his rancho then wanting to see his old friends of the corps, especially Brent Kendrick. He and Brent had been boyhood friends, attended Harvard together, and both opted for adventure after graduation and joined Fremont's corps. Steve had seen them once again after that when Fremont and his men camped at his rancho. Fremont had been ordered out of the Mexican territory by Castro and the troop was heading north toward Oregon territory.

Neal pulled a plug from his pocket, offered Steve a chew. Steve declined. He wanted to get to the point of his visit.

"I'm looking for James Clyman. Have you seen him here?"

"Shod his horses just a couple of days ago. Gone now. Up to meet a party at Johnson's and take 'em back to the States."

"Damn. That's what I heard."

"What you need Clyman for?"

"I'd heard he was rounding up the settlers to take a stand against Castro. I wanted to be counted in."

Neal switched the big bulge in his cheek. "Yep, reckon somthin's got to be done about Castro, but Clyman's not the one. Hell, he ain't got no property here to protect. He jest wanted to get in on the fight, thinkin' Fremont was about to lead it. But he got damn disgusted when our old captain took off like a whipped pup when Castro says to git."

"Christ Sam, what's Fremont got to do with our fight with Castro? He's a visitor here, and a representative of our country. He'd be in a hell of a lot of trouble, and our government as well, if he got into a shooting match with the Mexicans when we're not at war--not yet anyway, as far as we know."

"Then why the hell did Fremont build a fort up on Hawks Peak and raise the American flag? Jesus, right above Castro's own headquarters in the Santa Clara Valley!"

A quirk of a smile deepened the groves in Steve's cheek. "It was a rash thing to do, but can't you see? Hell, just the kind of a stunt our old commander would try."

Neal chuckled. "Yeah, like thumbing his noes at the Mexs. But that's what gave Clyman the idea that Fremont was ready to fight. He sent a message to Fremont that him and some of the settlers were ready to pitch in. But when Fremont turned him down, Clyman got damn disgusted and decided to pull out."

"Hell, Sam, Castro is *our* problem, not our government's. It's up to us settlers to make a stand for our rights."

Neal scuffed his chin stubble with his knuckles. "Guess maybe you're right."

"When did Clyman leave?"

"A couple days ago."

"Maybe I can still catch him." Johnson's place was on the Bear River between Sutter's Fort and Steve's own rancho. At least, if Clyman was still there, he could find out who the ones were Clyman had contacted, find out the ones who were ready to get involved.

Just then an Indian stuck his head into the shed. He informed Steve that Captain Sutter had seen him arrive and was inviting him to join him for dinner. The captain set a good table, and Steve was hungry.

"Tell Captain Sutter I'll be pleased to accept his invitation."

"I tell." The Indian said and was gone.

Steve turned back to Neal. "I'll stop in again before I leave."

The main building of the fort, a large adobe structure, was in the center of the compound. An outside staircase led to the second floor and Sutter's main quarters. Several men were already seated at a long plank table, a strange assortment of guests. Some were dressed in buckskins, probably Sutter's trappers who had just

33

come down from the mountains. One fellow wore a navy jersey. No doubt a deserter from a ship in the bay. No questions asked. Sutter always needed workers for his many enterprises. Two men were dressed in business attire. One was John Bidwell, Sutter's head clerk, prim and proper as usual. The other was a stranger to Steve, but he looked like a dandy with his black tie and brocade vest under a dark broadcloth coat.

Captain Sutter, a stocky man, immaculately groomed in a black frock coat and white silk vest, sat at the head of the table. He smiled broadly as Steve entered and motioned for him to join them.

Steve hung his broad-brimmed hat on a peg and ran splayed fingers through his sun-bleached hair, an attempt at grooming. He raised a long slim leg and stepped over the bench, sitting down across from John Bidwell and between the dandy and a leather-clad trapper.

In the center of the table plates heaped with corn bread, eggs, beans, ham, venison, and fresh warm wheat bread were fast dwindling. A surprising fare for the wilderness, and Steve was ready.

He turned and offered his hand to the trapper. "Steve Magoffison."

The stranger swallowed what he was chewing, wiped his greasy hand on his leather-covered leg and reached for Steve. He was tall and spare, as tough looking as a piece of dried jerky, middle years with bloodshot eyes. "H-h-howdy. Ezekiel M-m-m-merritt," the trapper sputtered and then quickly resumed stuffing his mouth.

Steve turned to the man at his other side. "Magoffison," he repeated and again offered his hand.

"Glad to make your acquaintance, Mr. Magoffison. Hastings. Lansford L. Hastings. Lawyer, writer, lecturer--and emigrant guide."

Hell you say, Steve thought. He looked over at Bidwell and exchanged friendly comments. He liked the bright, methodical young man, and often thought what a chore it must be for Bidwell to take care of Captain Sutter's haphazard accounts. The captain had a reputation for generosity, but most of his possessions had been acquired on credit and it was general knowledge how lax Sutter was in taking care of payments.

An Indian poured coffee from a huge black pot. Steve took a gulp and gagged.

"You not like my coffee, Mr. Magoffison?" The captain looked indignant.

Steve raised an eyebrow.

"A little bitter, ja. Ground acorn when coffee runs out."

Steve took another sip so as not to insult his host. He ate the other victuals with relish while listening with a brief nod of acknowledgment now and then to the near soliloquy from Hastings who monopolized the conversation. He boasted how he'd brought a group of young travelers across the mountains this last winter arriving at the fort on Christmas day.

"Mighty risky, chancing the Sierra in the dead of winter like that," Steve squeezed in. He thought of his own crossing with Fremont two years before when the whole corps had almost lost their lives in the heavy snow drifts.

"No problem. We were ten strong men on horseback traveling light. I have an instinct for the wilderness."

Steve's irritation rose. He resented anyone assuming he could second-guess nature. Nature was the dictator in the wilderness, not man. "You were lucky. The Sierra snows can be ferocious." This year, the winter snow had been late in coming. The braggart didn't seem to realize that. Weather could be capricious. There was never a way of knowing when your luck would run out.

Brocade vest continued to look very pleased with himself. His chatter went on. He was now getting ready to head over the mountains again, and the snows hadn't yet cleared. However, he had no question that they'd make it through. He was meeting a party of emigrants at Johnson's, disenchanted settlers who wanted to return to the east. He'd agreed to lead them part way and then mountain man James Clyman would act as guide for the rest of the journey.

Steve looked up in surprise. "Clyman's going with you?"

"I'm not going all the way, only as far as Fort Bridger. Clyman will take over from there on."

Steve wondered what this fellow was up to. "Why only as far as Fort Bridger?"

"Separation point for Oregon and California. There I'll meet the emigrants who are now just starting west. I'll convince the ones headed for Oregon that California is where they should come--with its climate and soil. I'll be there to serve as their guide."

Hastings dribbled honey over corn bread, took a bite, but hardly quit talking. "Seems an awful lot of Americans have an itchy foot to travel these days. I did a lecture tour in the states and I wrote a guide book. Went real well. You'd be surprised how many now are coming."

Steve looked thoughtful. "But what about Castro's new proclamation refusing new emigrants entry? I see it's still tacked out there on one of the posts."

"Oh, Castro. He's more bluff than anything else. With Mexican rule so weak... What we need here are a few more Americans, and we will do like they did in Texas. California's got a great future in store under proper leadership."

Hastings' leadership? Steve was beginning to see the picture. The man saw himself as another Sam Houston! He'd planned it well. The lecture tour. The guide book. Now he'd personally meet the emigrants and lead them to the promised land. King of the wilderness with a built-in following. Steve could see the ambitious gleam in Hastings' eyes.

"Plan to bring them here by way of my shortcut."

"Shortcut?"

"Come south of the Great Salt Lake. I suggested it in my guide book. That way we'll cut off three or four hundred miles of trail instead of going north to Fort Hall."

Steve stared at Hastings with amazement. "Hell, man, that way would be far too risky with wagons. Across those salt flats? And then more desert?"

"Fremont proved it's possible just this last winter."

"Fremont's party was all on horseback, and they'd come up from the south from the Sante Fe with Kit Carson and Alexis Godey breaking trail. You said you put it in your guide book?" Steve couldn't believe what he was hearing.

Hastings looked pleased with himself and nodded.

"Even before Fremont proved it?" What kind of an irresponsible man was this Hastings?

"I had studied the maps. It's an obvious shortcut. And now as I head east, I'll map out the trail."

Hastings pushed aside his empty plate. He wiped his mouth with his handkerchief and looked toward the head of the table. "Mighty fine repast, Captain. Much obliged to you for your hospitality." Rising, his glance included the other members at the table. "If you gentlemen will excuse me, I have a good deal of business to tend to get ready for my trek." Again, addressing the captain. "I'll see you later in your office, Captain Sutter, to settle for my supplies."

He stepped over the bench, offered his hand to Steve. "Nice making your acquaintance, Mr. Magoffison. I enjoyed our talk."

I bet you did, thought Steve, you having done most of the talking. The man was crazy for such a plan. Putting lives in jeopardy? God, those poor emigrants!

But James Clyman would be there, Steve reasoned, and felt somewhat relieved. Clyman, an old time mountaineer had trapped with the Ashley Company years before and knew the country well. Clyman would see the folly. The emigrants would surely put more trust in an old mountaineer than they would in this foolhardy opportunist.

Steve's brows drew together. It still didn't make sense for Clyman to start to organize a resistance then desert the settlers who were already here. There still was a chance he'd catch Clyman, maybe persuaded him to stay and carry on.

Yet Steve couldn't keep his thoughts from straying back to those faceless emigrants who were coming. God, would some actually trust this opportunistic scalawag?

36

CHAPTER 4
The Overland Trail
May 15, 1846

Morning chores completed, Medora climbed up onto the wagon seat wondering what would happen next. A sense of expectancy radiated from the whole camp village. Here, at the start of the prairie, the real adventure was about to begin.

They were a day's journey out from the bustling frontier settlement of Independence. Civilization was now behind them. Fifty or sixty white-topped wagons were assembled along Indian Creek just short of where it emptied into the Kansas River, and more wagons coming. Seemed the whole world must be heading west! The air rang with the excited screams as children darted between the tents and the wagons. Some of the women were still finishing morning tasks while others chatted with neighbors they had not known a day before. Most of the men looked so jovial, cracking jokes as they checked each others equipment. William too, stroking the shoulder of another man's handsome horse, a grin of admiration on his face. Almost everyone was eager to be underway. Except for me, thought Medora. Why did she feel so apprehesive?

Someone yelled, and the men started to gather at the far end of the camp. Medora frowned when she noticed Torrey heading in the same direction. She almost called out. *Torrey, a proper young lady knows when to keep her place. My daughters are going to learn civilized behavior in spite of frontier conditions.* Yet, she didn't call out and sat quietly instead. True, Torrey, was on the brink of womanhood. But the child was still there. It was there in the impatient long-legged way in which she moved, in the way the heavy mass of auburn curls, although restrained by a hank of cord, bounced across her shoulders. Medora felt a catch in her heart. The carefree time of childhood was so short. Why take it away so soon? So Medora sat quietly and just watched as Torrey moved toward the assembly of men.

Some of the other women, as curious as Torrey, were collecting around the outer edge of the cluster of men. Torrey edged closer.

A man jumped to a wagon box and waved his arms to gain attention. "Time's a'wasting!" he shouted. "Some trains have already left. We got to elect us a captain now so's to get started before the good grass is all gone."

There came shouts and noisy agreement.

"I'm putting forth the name of my good friend, Colonel William Henry Russell, 'Owl' Russell to most of us."

More shouts. Some for. Some against.

It reminded Torrey of the politicking that had gone on in Whitherville just before they left when the tall lawyer, Mr. Lincoln, had come riding through their village to gather votes for a seat in Congress. "Stumping," Papa called it. Sure enough seemed they were stumping out here on the prairie. Strange place to be stumping.

She spotted her father in the crowd with Uncle Anton and Mr. Morgan. Both Mama and Papa had hoped to be shed of the Morgans when they reached Independence, although she'd sorely have missed Elspeteh. With all Mr. Morgan's grumbling, seemed likely he'd hook up with another wagon outfit. But here he was, still sticking as close as though they were kin--just because they all started out together.

Torrey pushed toward the three men. Her father put a protective arm around her shoulders. She was glad Papa didn't share Mama's views about "women's place."

The man on the box was still shouting. "This here Colonel Russell served in the Black Hawk War and was also a United States Marshall. We'll be in good hands under his direction."

A tall man in a Panama hat with an oiled-silk cover began shaking hands with the others around him, courteous to all. He gave Torrey a special bow. Then he mounted the box, and his oratory was so grand Torrey decided then and there if only she had a chance to vote she'd sure enough vote for Colonel Owl Russell.

Another voice rose from the crowd. "I've a candidate I aim to propose." A man with a ruddy face garnished with a stump of a bristly red beard took his place on the stand. "I nominate the Honorable Lilburn Boggs, past governor of our state of Missouri."

A roar rose from the onlookers.

"Governor Boggs!" William exclaimed. "Well, we are traveling in fine society." He winked at Torrey. "That should please your mother."

Morgan's face had drained of color. "Hell's fire!" he mumbled. "We're sure in trouble now."

"Why?" asked Torrey. Of course, that was being pert, sticking her nose into men's business.

"Because of the damn Mormons, that's why," Morgan replied. "If they learn Boggs is in our party, hell, they'll be lookin' fer revenge."

William frowned. "Please Eli. Watch your tongue. My daughter is present."

Morgan paid little attention. "Them damn bastards is now headin' west same as us. They could sneak into our camp, slaughter us in our bedrolls!"

Torrey's eyes opened wide. Sneak in! Slaughter!

But her father looked calm enough. "Don't reckon we need worry. If the Mormons are headed west, reckon they're as anxious to get to where they're going as we are. They won't be looking for distractions."

"Ye don't know them fornicators like I do. Can't trust 'em, ye can't. Ain't civilized. Remember, it was Boggs who sicked his militia on 'em!"

Torrey had heard talk like that before as most people were powerful suspicious of the Mormons. Only Papa always said they were still God's children even if he didn't hold to their beliefs.

As it turned out, a majority of the other men must have reckoned along Morgan's lines. They jawed among themselves and speculated on what the fanatical "saints" might do if they learned their old enemy, Governor Boggs, was a member of the caravan. It ended with Colonel Owl Russell being elected as Wagon Master. Even then, some apprehension remained.

However, in spite of the doom-spreaders, the holiday spirit returned and good-fellowship sprouted about the camp thick as the spring flowers on the prairie. Torrey heard some say they'd just be more watchful for the Mormons, same as looking out for Indians and snakes. You had to be cautious of all vermin.

The next morning dawned bright and clear. Everyone was eager to get going. Colonel Russell appointed William to take a count. Later William remarked to Medora, "I'd say, we're a mighty fine cross-section of substantial citizens, mostly prosperous farmers, judging by their equipment."

"Have to be," Medora replied thinking how costly it had been for them. Their savings had been nearly depleted with scarcely little left for starting the new life.

William's voice was buoyant. "We've also a journalist, a couple of lawyers, and a clergyman aboard, but unfortunately, no physician. Came to 119 men, counting teamsters working for their keep, 59 women, 110 children; a total of 288 people, and an estimate of 600 cattle, 150 horses and 63 wagons. I'd say, as fine a troupe of pilgrims that's ever wended its way to the new country."

Later Owl Russell assigned duties and places in line. "We'll have a daily rotation so each family will have a turn at the head of the procession and not always be eating the dust of others."

Only Eli Morgan grumbled. "All them damn orders like he's still running his damn army."

"We're lucky we've got a captain like Owl Russell," said William.

The following day it was scurry time. The men harnessed their teams and the drovers rounded up the loose stock. The clatter of pans and buzz of chatter drifted about the camp as women washed, boxed, and stored their dishes.

Medora, about to empty the smoke blackened coffee pot remembered she hadn't seen a breakfast fire at the Morgon's camp. Elspeth feeling poorly again? It seemed a shame to waste the bit of remaining coffee. She did feel sorry for the strange little woman, but should she continue to encourage the relationship with the Morgans?

They'd hardly known them before leaving Whitherville as the Morgans' farm was several miles from the settlement, and Elspeth had seldom come into town. During the first two weeks of travel the Morgans had kept to themselves until the time Morgan's wagon had lost its wheel.

Then, while the men had worked on the wagon, Elspeth sat alone under a tree, her shawl pulled tightly around her scrawny shoulders as though she were chilled. Medora's heart had gone out to the lonely looking sight and invited Elspeth to join her and the girls with a cup of tea around their campfire.

Elspeth held back at first, then shyly came over. Gradually she warmed to the children and the children to her. After that the Morgans often sat around their fire when supper was over, although it bothered Medora to have her children exposed to Eli's crude language and Elspeth's superstitious tales. Their precious minds were too pliable. In a way, she even regretted she had ever extended that first invitation, the reason she hesitated now. But then...

As Elspeth climbed from her wagon, Medora called out, "Elspeth, would you like a cup of coffee before I pour it out?"

Elspeth paused, then a cautious smile softened her gaunt face. "Mighty kindly of ye, don't likely want to intrude." Her voice was country-soft.

"Of course you're not intruding."

Jenny ran and got her a stool. Elspeth, as usual, sat down spread-knee fashion, the folds of her heavy wool skirt falling around her big man-sized shoes. Medora handed her a steaming cup of coffee.

"Thank, ye, ma'am. Ye be mighty kindly to me."

"Nonsense. What would life be if we can't share with our neighbors." She hoped this time Elspeth would not light up her smelly clay pipe or start another one of her ridiculous yarns. Elspeth's native land had been Tennessee hill country, her "Highland Home," she called it. It had once belonged to the Cherokees, thus, her stories were a blend of Indian and mountain folk lore that so intrigued the children.

Billy plopped down on the grass beside her. "Will you tell us another one of those stories about where you used to live?" His face was bright with expectation.

Elspeth gave a cackling laugh as she reached into her apron pocket and withdrew her old clay pipe. "As I told ye before, my Pappy came from 'Ginny. First white to go up in them thar Smokeys to clear some land. Some of the Injuns is still around, but most got marched away."

Medora's lips tightened when she saw Torrey set down the dish she was drying, her attention riveted to Elspeth. Torrey's imagination was vivid enough. She didn't need Elspeth's wild tales to excite it more.

"I'm sorry, Elspeth, Medora cut in. "There isn't time for a story now. We have to get packed." She handed Torrey a box of washed and toweled tin plates to be put in the wagon.

Elspeth stood up, slipped the pipe back into her pocket and handed the empty cup to Medora. "Thank ye kindly, ma'am. I best get back to my wagon."

Medora hoped she hadn't hurt Elspeth's feelings, but they had to get a move on. She knew both she and William had been wishing the Morgans would drift away after they joined the main caravan. She sighed. It looked as though they would continue to stick as tight as feathers to molasses.

She turned to Billy and told him to smother the coals with dirt then went about finishing her chores. A month of travel was now behind them, but these tiresome tasks would go on for another five or six months; cooking in the open, rain or not, sleeping on the ground if not in the wagon. Day after day the same. She was thankful she was strong and could manage, not sickly like Elspeth. Poor woman. Looking around the camp, she felt real sympathy for the other women who had the telltale swelling under their aprons. How difficult for them. She doubted if there was a single woman in the whole wagon train who had wanted to leave her home for this adventure. It was the men who had the wanderlust notions.

She glanced over toward William. He had finished yoking the oxen and was now rearranging crates in the supply wagon. Arduous work for one who had spent most of his life tending store. *This determination of his to own land!* Business was his forte. Not farming! She thought how handsome he always looked in his neat frock coat and starched white shirt. *To turn his back on what he'd worked so hard for!*

With the last box packed, Medora carried it to the wagon. "Do you still have room?"

"Always make room." William's smile was still buoyant. The month's travel had diminished none of his enthusiasm. If only she could feel the same. William took the box and Medora climbed up onto the wagon and settled herself on the board seat. Resentment was futile, she knew, but there were times...

To uproot his family when he was doing so well handling the judge's affairs. Of course, she knew it tied to his early years and the promise he'd made to his mother. William had told her about his youth--so different from her own--often brought tears to her eyes. He was just a boy when he'd been torn from his widowed mother's care because she was too poor to keep him. He was apprenticed to a shopkeeper and was often mistreated. But he did learn a trade. A blessing, in a way. William had a natural talent for business. He understood figures, and his positive nature gave him an edge for getting along well with people. The judge had recognized William's ability. Now to cast it aside for this obsession to farm land! Medora pressed her hand to her heart as though to stop the hurt. She should have been more adamant, refused to go along with this mad dream of his. But what choice did she have? What choice did any woman have? A man made the decision.

Medora rested her head against the puckered canvas cover and closed her eyes. She must calm her thoughts, take advantage of the few minutes of quiet before the jouncing started. Will was a good husband. She had much to be thankful for. A caring man. A forgiving man. *Better than she'd deserved--considering how she had tricked him into marriage.*

Unwelcome memories. Medora tightened, not wanting to remember the past. But the silent intruder persisted. So long ago. *Jacques.* Her first true love. But she'd let that love betray her--giving in to her own body's urging, forgetting all she'd been taught. The tragic consequences that followed. Memories flooded her with all their horror. Chatfield. She had loved him too, in another way. The duel. Her lover had to flee or risk being charged with murder--and she carrying his child.

Then just at that time she learned the young clerk who worked in her father's emporiium was leaving to pioneer to Missouri. She'd often seen his eyes following her. If she could convince him she loved him too... She would spare her beloved family her shame and her child would have a name.

Medora brushed her hand across her eyes as though to erase those painful thoughts. Better to stay with the present. She fingered the calico sunbonnet that lay in her lap. Still early morning, but she should put it on. With her fair skin, she'd soon be as speckled as a robin's egg. Adjusting the bonnet, Medora tucked a stray end of flaxen hair under the ruffle, then tied the ribbon under her chin.

Idly, she watched the men working with the animals. She should have kept her sketch pad and pencils out to keep her hands and thoughts busy. With her drawings, Medora was keeping a record of their travels.

Ahead and behind the wagons were now jockeying into designated places, some with "California" painted across the back, some with "Oregon." One with "54-40 or Fight," which meant the owners were Oregon bound. Chains clanked, animals snorted and bellowed, and men yelled and swore. The pungent smell of animal droppings wafted stronger than the fresh smell of spring.

Colonel Russell rode up on his fine looking bay. He spoke to William then touched his hat to Medora. "Good morning, Mrs. Dudley. It looks like your wagons are both in fine shape. We'll be pulling out directly."

He rode on, stopping to chat with different ones, probably making suggestions and answering questions. Most of the travelers were novices, just as the Dudleys were. Their emigrating knowledge, like William, had been gleaned from the guide books. William put so much store in that Hastings book.

She looked up at the sky. Only a few gossamer clouds streaked the blue. Thank goodness this day was clear. They'd already had their share of miserable weather since they'd left Illinois. Back home she had always enjoyed the rain, watching it make patterns on the glass windowpanes. *Would she have glass windows in California?* Knowledge of that Mexican outpost was so sketchy.

Now and then, over the animal smells, she caught the sweet scent of bunch and buffalo grass, crushed from stomping hooves. She breathed deeply to capture the fragrance. At home it would be the sweetness of lilacs. They'd be blooming now and she'd fill the house with their sprays.

She squeezed her eyes tight. *Don't think lilacs. Think yellow buttercups instead.* Lavinia had gathered a bouquet this morning for the center of the makeshift breakfast table. How pretty they were. They eased the reality of eating fried pork and gritty camp biscuits from tin plates, and picking a flopping beetle from the pan of milk gravy.

The prattle of high-pitched children's voices broke into Medora's thoughts. A group of children had formed around Billy. Medora warmed to their chatter. Little Jenny hung back, her baby arms around the neck of big shaggy Dusty-Dog for needed security. She was a shy child but now gradually becoming more assertive. No shyness for Billy. Pride and pleasure surged through Medora as she glimpsed her only son. A vigorous child. The center of attention. Probably Showing his treasures. She smiled, knowing what would have come from his pockets: an Indian arrowhead, a hank of string, a rabbit's foot, and his prized cateye marble. It was such a privilege to be born male--and to be the energetic boy he was. She basked in the warm glow of mother-love.

Motherhood.

This she savored, and prayed for guidance to be able to dispense wise counsel in directing her children on the proper course for a satisfactory future. She had little concern for Lavinia who seemed to know instinctively a women's rightful place. She sighed thinking of Torrey. That stubborn intractable behavior of hers. She wanted the best in life for all of her children. But with Torrey? She felt the usual rise of frustration. With Torrey it never seemed easy.

A bugle sounded. Owl had given the signal. However, before the wagons began to roll, a shout came from the tree-lined path that bordered the creek as three horsemen approached followed by a procession of wagons.

"Looks like we've got more coming to join us," shouted William above the noise.

Nine wagons in all. The last one was huge and high-built, looking two-storied.

A stove pipe protruded from the top. Must be a real cook stove inside. Even a side entrance with steps. What a blessing not to climb over a tailgate and worry if your skirts were down. What luxury. A regular house on wheels!

Medora couldn't help the stab of envy. She wondered who on earth the new party could be. Someone of importance?

Torrey was also interested in the new arrivals, her eyes focused on the handsome horses the three men rode, especially on the silver grey. What a beauty! Horses were her love. She'd hoped for one of her own for as long as she could remember.

Papa had said maybe when they got to Independence. Yet when they arrived there: "We have to be cautious. Our funds are limited. We might need to replenish supplies when we reach Fort Laramie. But California. California for sure. I'll get you the finest horse we can find."

California. She wanted her own horse now!

She watched as Captain Russell strode over to talk to the three strangers. They were pleasant looking gentlemen and well dressed, but two were almost old, Torrey figured, if you went by their graying beards. But the man on the beautiful silver-grey was younger, more like her father's age. Torrey puzzled. Something about him seemed vaguely familiar, as though she'd seen him before. Dark curly hair showed bellow his hat brim, and a dark beard well trimmed. But it was the way he held himself that needled her memory--the set of his head on his shoulders like he figured himself a kingpin. Where had she seen him before?

Just then a girl near Torrey's own age rode up and joined the men. Her full skirt fell in graceful folds across the shiny sides of one of the loveliest ponies Torrey had ever seen. A chestnut. Trim of line, proud of stance--a truly gorgeous creature. Oh, to have a horse like that. She felt a rush of envy.

Torrey glanced toward her father to see if he were looking too. He was, but his attention was focused on the black-bearded man, not on the girl and her pony. He also looked puzzled. Then suddenly came a pleased look of recognition.

"Mr. Reed, from Springfield," her father said walking with a sprightly step toward the man on the grey. He stretched out his hand. "Mighty good to see you again."

It came back in a flash to Torrey. The man who owned a furniture factory in Springfield. She had been helping her father in the store at that time, in spite of her mother's objections to her daughter working behind a counter. So Papa had taken her with him on a purchasing trip that proved the most exciting time in all of her life--excepting now, starting across the prairie.

Springfield was an elegant city. After the railroad had been brought through from Quincy on the Mississippi it had become the state capitol. They stayed in the Prairie Inn Hotel. She had a room to herself, not having to share a bed with Lavinia. And while having supper in the hotel's elegant dining room, a real live senator from Washington City, there on railroad business, stopped at their table. Her father had met the senator before when tending the judge's business, so asked Senator Magoffison to join them. Before long they were talking about California. How well she remembered it all.

The senator's son was in California now. He had gone there on an expedition with an explorer named Fremont, and decided to stay. His son now owned a ranch and seemed to be adopting some of the Spaniard's ways. The senator pulled a sketch from his pocket. Torrey was intrigued. It showed a man wearing a fancy embroidered jacket and tight pantaloons slit to the knee. It reminded her of the picture in her mother's geography book of a handsome Spanish caballero astride a gorgeous white horse and dressed the same way.

Papa promised the senator they'd look up his son when they got to California. Stephen Magoffison was his name. Probably now called *Don Stephano*. Her mother was teaching them Spanish so they'd be able to talk with the natives. *Don Stephano*. Not really a native, but surely a real caballero. She could hardly wait to meet him. So it was only natural, when she'd realized the picture in the geography book was ready to fall out with only a bit of a tug, it was now pasted in her journal.

The following morning they'd gone to the furniture factory and had met the man her father was talking to now. Even there the talk got onto California. Mr. Reed was selling his business because he too planned on taking his family west. And here at the start of the prairie, the two men were shaking hands like long lost friends. Strange how things happen.

Torrey moved close enough to hear Mr. Reed introduce her father to his friends. "George and Jacob Donner, brothers of course."

The men shook hands.

"And this is my daughter, Virginia."

Again Torrey looked covetously at the beautiful pony the girl was riding.

Virginia dimpled and said, "It's a pleasure to meet you, Mr. Dudley." She cocked her head to the side just enough to set her long flowing tresses brushing across her shoulders in gentle waves.

Torrey's dark brows pulled together. *I 'low, if she were standing, she'd be making a curtsy!*

Suddenly Torrey felt flooded with unpleasant emotions. It wasn't fair *that* girl should have such a horse. She felt awash with an overwhelming longing for Effie. There were times she so desperately needed her very best friend. Putting up with the likes of Jake Stringer was enough to try a body. But now, she suspected, Virginia Reed would be another cross to bear.

Sometimes life was just too monstrous.

CHAPTER 5

There was dissension from the start over the Springfield party joining their caravan.

"We're already too large. Nine more wagons!"

"Plus all of their stock!"

A lively number, indeed. Among the Donners and the Reeds were thirty-two in all, counting wives, children, hired teamsters, Mrs. Reed's aged mother, and the Reed's hired girl.

"Hell, who ever heard of having a servant girl along when you're pioneering!" complained Morgan.

But the Springfield party was voted in by the majority, and the wagon train started on its way. However, begrudging remarks continued. Not against the Donner brothers, both pleasant fellows and well liked, especially easygoing George. Well to do farmers, they were, judging from their fine wagons and equipment. It was James Reed who was the thorn in the side of many of the other travelers.

Too damn arrogant, some complained. Reed was a Scotch-Irish immigrant, but liked to boast of Polish nobility ancestry, which went against the grain of some. And there were those who were envious of the free time Reed had to explore the prairie while his hired hands did his work. Besides, there was that monstrosity of a wagon his daughter Virginia called their pioneer palace car. A wagon that size was bound to cause delays when they started climbing mountains.

"Sees himself a damn prince," grumbled Eli having heard Reed's claim to Polish nobility. "I see him a damn bastard. Al'ys boasting his horse can outrun any horse in camp."

"Probably can," said William. He was one who felt partial to Reed. "It's a prize winning thoroughbred--a beautiful piece of horseflesh."

Actually, Reed was the kind of man William admired; forthright, vigorous, ambitious--and successful. The same traits William had respected in the judge--traits he himself hoped to emulate. So what if Reed did show some arrogance? Not unusual for a self-made-man. He had come to this country from Ireland as a boy with scarcely a shilling in his pocket, William had learned. He had prospered as a merchant, a railroad contractor, and then with his furniture factory. Reed was a man who got things done, a man it wouldn't hurt to know better. Proper association was always prudent if you yourself had those same ambitions.

But not so for Anton who did not cotton to Reed even though the two had much in common. They had both immigrated to this country as youths with empty pockets and now were both men of means. But no royalty in my background, Anton thought with inward rancor. He'd come from hardworking peasant stock. Peasant born--and peasant destined to be if he'd remained in his homeland with little chance of ever rising above his station in life, the reason he'd come to America. But like Reed, here in this new country he had made his own way and had prospered. Now, often seeing his good friend and Reed in deep conversation around the other's campfire, Anton couldn't deny his rising feeling of annoyance, only a pestering irritant at first, like swarming gnats at milk time. But when the friendship between the two began to get thicker, he couldn't restrain his resentment.

"A blow hard he is, letting others do his work. Ja, for a man to be worth his salt, he should do an honest day's labor, not pay others to do it all for him."

"Why not?" William replied. "If he has the where-with-all to hire it done."

The discussion bothered Anton more than he liked to admit. He and Reed had already ruffed feathers over a spot for parking their wagons. William had remained noncommittal. Uncertainty began to pick at Anton's gut. If it came to a real confrontation between him and Reed, whose side would William take? Anton shrugged his shoulders as though to shed the foreboding. Ach, such foolish thoughts. No reason to doubt William's loyalty. Friends they were. Friends they would remain.

Each day Owl assigned places in line. A daily rotation would eventually give each family a chance to be leader. Starting out, the Whitherville unit was somewhat in the center with the Morgan wagon ahead of the Dudleys and Anton's wagon behind. The contingent from Springfield followed them in line. "Hell, my mules is too spirited," Eli complained. "I can't hold em back behind them damn slow-moving oxen."

"You aim to pull out?" asked William, knowing he wouldn't but wishing he would.

"I don't take to all them damn rules Russell hands out."

"We elected him as captain. But if you think you'd get along better with those redskins--or maybe the Mormons." William nodded toward the vast beyond. "Reckon there's plenty of both out there."

Actually, the earlier apprehension of a Mormon attack had faded, although there were some suspicions that a family of Mormons might be in their own caravan--the large Rhodes family with their many children of all ages which included married ones, their spouses and their children. They had kept to themselves, not mixing with the others. Come Sunday, they even held their own prayer meeting instead of joining the service the Reverend Mr. Cornwall conducted

48

for the others. This added weight to the suspicions.

As for the Indians, they were apparent almost as soon as the wagons had crossed the Kansas. They followed along and begged food and trinkets. Most emigrants had come prepared to hand out glass beads and other gew-gaws. It was known that the Indians were Pawnees, a formidable tribe. The large wagon parties were fairly safe as long as they corralled at night, cloistered the live stock inside the ring and positioned guards to stand watch. However, it would be chancy for anyone traveling alone.

Morgan scowled at William's remark.

"Just a suggestion," William said with a smile.

"I'll thank ye to keep yer damn suggestions to yerself."

William said no more. He tried to ignore the big man's complaints, but often thought how much more pleasant it would be if the Morgans weren't still hanging on to them like leeches.

Now into their second week on the trail, a drenching thunderstorm the day before had forced an early encampment. With only a few scudding clouds remaining, Owl Russell was eager to get underway.

"Chain up, men. Chain up!" he shouted as he made his way around the circle of wagons.

Reluctant oxen bellowed, protesting the yoke and tongue, as cursing bull-whackers "Geeeed!" and "Haweeeeed!", working the animals into position. Dogs barked in excitement and women called for their children to climb aboard. Bawling loose cattle were driven off to one side by the drovers to bring up to the rear of the train. The bugle sounded and the caravan started to roll.

William gave his lead ox, Freddy, a pat on his great broad head, then raised his whip high, cracking it in the air as he yelled "Giddup there!" The huge oxen moved slowly. Wagon wheels creaked in turning. Ahead and behind were the same sounds--the crack of whips, the yowling of animals, the dry screech of axles and the soft gritty digging of metal tires into the ground. The wagons moved out forming a chaotic pattern, a long snake of canvas tops gleaming white in the morning sun, one towering above all the others.

William looked skyward at the scant brushing of clouds, breathed deeply of the sweet clear air and felt a swelling of pleasure for the beautiful day. Thus far, their trek had been without hazards except for Morgan's broken wheel. And now, ahead, behind, and on all sides was the gentle lush green prairie. William, bursting with gratitude, gave thanks to the good Lord for bringing them safely this far. He felt like Abraham going to the "promised land", and knew the Lord would be with them all the way.

He hadn't always had such faith. During his apprenticed years he'd drifted away from his mother's religious teachings. It was later, after he and Medora settled in Missouri, that he had his convincement. It came at a time when he sorely needed the help of the Lord. Pioneering to Missouri had been harder than he'd reckoned with. But worst was learning his bride had deceived him, pretending to love him. *But she carried another man's child.*

He had not learned that shattering truth until after they were married and were already in Missouri. Outraged with fury and hurting with pain, he could have abandoned her then. Almost did. But he'd promised love and protection during their wedding vows. It was much later that he was touched by the Lord and learned the blessings of forgiveness.

It was when word had spread that a well-known revivalist would be coming to a neighboring settlement to gather souls. The parson was a book-peddling itinerant preacher who played a violin. William packed the old spring wagon with blankets and supplies, enough to last a couple of days, and he and Medora took off. It was dark when they arrived where the huge tent had been set up. Medora was swollen with child, it being only a short time before Lavinia was born. In her clumsy state it took some doing for Medora to work past so many others to get to an empty place on one of the log benches--and some doing on his part to check his tumultuous feelings when he looked at her and knew it was not *his* child.

The parson was already playing the violin and working the crowd up to singing and toe-stomping. Then switched to preaching, and at first his words rolled heavy as thunder with the usual revivalists threats of doom. But then he paused. His eyes glistened as his gaze penetrated the audience. Then in place of the sin and doom, he focused on love and faith. "FAITH, my brothers and sisters." It was almost a shout. "Faith--the substance of things hoped for--the evidence of things unseen." His voice was now overflowing with joy. "Put your faith in the Lord, my brothers and sisters, and you'll find all things, yes I mean ALL THINGS! All things are possible if you believe in the Lord!"

William felt a stirring, like the whirring of wings. He shouted, "Amen!" and found himself pushing down to the front. The next thing he knew he was bearing witness.

That evening he did believe. He still believed. There was power in faith. Weren't they now on their blessed way to the land of promise?

On the second day the parson expounded on his preaching of faith adding forgiveness and charity. "Faith has little victory unless you also have charity," he said. "Charity is love. Charity means you can love those who've wronged you. Forgiveness, that's what it is. Hand-in-hand they go, faith and forgiveness."

William pulled back. The faith he could accept. But forgiveness?

The parson's voice was impassioned. "I quote from the Good Book: 'Though

I have faith, so that I could remove mountains, and have not charity, I am nothing.' NOTHING!" he shouted. The veins stood out on his neck. "And there is nothing that so bears the impress of the Son of God so surely as forgiveness."

William felt a swirl of emotions. He wanted to resist, but suddenly he was filled with the spirit. Was it possible he could forgive?

It took time coming. Eventually it did. With the help of the Lord he put the fury aside. He began to accept Medora as the good helpmate she was. In spite of her favored background, she'd courageously accepted the hardships of pioneering with little complaint. Nor did she ever deny him his male needs. As the Lord willed it, he did forgive.

It was harder to forget.

However, he did well in keeping those emotions pigeonholed in the far recesses of his mind, and on a day such as this, they were certainly not thoughts to pull out and examine. Now, here on the prairie, William felt the great swelling of joy as he walked beside his oxen. He raised his head toward the heavens and from his throat--from his soul--full rounded melodious tones poured forth: "Stand up, stand up for Jesus, ye soldiers of the cross."

Others joined in, up and down the line, a chorus of joyous voices. At this point, the travelers were still endowed with the great holiday spirit, their wagons still bright with new paint. Their animals were still spirited and strong. Warm fellowship carried up and down the long line, ringing out in the laughter of the children who peered out from the puckered openings of the canvas covers; in the smiles of sunbonneted women whose nimble fingers were already busy with knitting or patching designs for quilts as they jostled on the wagon seats; and in the good-natured joshing of the men as they cracked their long ox-whips.

"Lift high His royal banner..."

Medora joined in. But only in the first verse. She was sitting on the board seat that was stretched across the front of the wagon, an arm holding little Jenny close. Even though she mouthed the words, her mind was repeating another song--one she'd seen in *Godey's Lady Book* sometime before and had memorized it because she'd thought how appropriate it was. The words went:

> What fly to the Prairie. I could not live there,
> With the Indians and panther, and bison and bear;
> Then cease to torment me, I'll not give my hand.
> To one whose abode's in so savage a land.

Yet, she had given her hand. And she'd gone to a savage land.
Now, for the second time she was going again. Not that she hadn't resisted.

51

There had been bitter words between herself and William.

"You profess to be a Christian. How can you uproot your family? How dare you expose your children to the dangers of Indian country?"

"It's safe enough now," he had replied. "Hundreds have successfully pioneered the way. And believe me, I *am* thinking of my family. I'm thinking of their future."

"There's land here in Illinois."

"It's too expensive. I can't afford it. The land speculators have seen to that."

"Like Judge Whitherspoon?"

Will showed his anger. "The judge is an honorable man."

Medora had felt ashamed. It was a silly outburst and unfounded. She respected the judge.

"Land was cheap when Judge Whitherspoon came. Land is not only cheap, but it's free in California."

In the long run, she had no choice. They would pioneer again. She had fought back the tears--and the fear.

It was part of the bargain she'd made long ago when she took her marriage vows. A wife was compelled to be subservient to her man. It was the law of the land. A wife had no status, no property, not even possession of their children should the husband leave or sue for divorce. One "cleaved unto" one's husband and then obeyed him. Even the Bible said you must.

Medora's thoughts were interrupted by the baying of one of Mr. Morgan's mules. His wagon was in front of theirs. She couldn't see over its white canvas top, but she could hear Mr. Morgan cursing and slapping his reins. She smiled. Mules had a mind of their own, remembering old Betsy, the mule William had used to pull their old wagon when they had traveled from Virginia to Missouri at the start of their marriage. Dear old Betsy. She certainly had a mind of her own. She was apt to stop when Will called "Giddup," and start when he said "Whoa."

But she'd become friends with old Betsy--that terrible time, so long ago. She had to have something alive and warm that she could bury her face in--the rough stubbly neck of a mule--to hide her tears. She hadn't wanted Will to see her crying and start probing with questions--not that soon after their marriage. The loss of Jacques was still such a weight on her heart--and the loss of her dear family. Disturbing memories. Best to let the past lie. She tried to focus on things around her.

William's strides were long as he walked beside the oxen. He switched to another hymn--still joyous. The wagon wheel hit a rut and jostled Medora and Jenny. Medora grabbed the edge of the rough board seat. Pungent warm smells of fresh manure drifted up as the oxen trod through a fresh evacuation from one of Mr. Morgan's mules. Even the smell brought back reminders of old Betsy--how profuse old Betsy had been.

William cracked the whip above Freddy's head, but suddenly the wagon bogged down into a deep mud hole, remnants of yesterday's thunderstorm. William grabbed the ox's yolk. "Come on, fellow, give a good pull."

Freddy bellowed and lowered his massive head. The other five oxen lent their strength. The wagon creaked and groaned. It jiggled and jerked and rolled out of the hole. Different from that other time. That old rickety spring-wagon Betsy had pulled could never have taken this kind of punishment. That old rickety wagon. *Got so she hated that wagon.*

Even after they'd arrived at their destination in Missouri, they still lived in it with only a lean-to shelter added, lived in it until William had cleared some land and started the planting. The awful intimacy of that wagon! *And she a bride!*

Even now, waves of shame flushed through her whenever she'd think of those earlier times. The first time he had touched her she had cringed, knowing what to expect. He had tried to be tender, even apologized for his clumsiness.

"It takes time," he had said. "I won't rush you." He looked at her in wonder. He stroked her hair, tipped her chin to look into her eyes. She'd dropped her gaze, not able to face him.

"The wonder is that you are mine. My pure delicate blossom. I won't crush you in haste."

Pure!

He learned the truth later.

He did take her--in the dark with the wagon creaking. So tense was the moment, it immortalized for her the sense of that time, that place, the sounds of that night. Even now she could relive it, remember the blackness of the forest sky beyond the covering of the wagon, and the single star out there in that blackness. There was the smell of grass, and the chirping of crickets. She could remember the soft feel of the folds of her nightgown protecting her naked legs from the course straw-filled mattress. She could still smell the stale oiliness of the dead-wick of the lantern after he'd snuffed out the light. She turned her back to him, her heart thumping, but still followed his movements by the sound of the drop of his trousers to the floor of the wagon and the tug of his shirt over his head.

He pulled back the rough patch-work blanket and crawled in beside her. His arms reached from the darkness and pulled her against him. She felt his stiffness against her buttocks. His hands groped for her breasts. He rolled her over on her back, unbuttoned the neck of her gown, cupped her naked breasts in his hands and she felt a tingling, like the touching of nettles. He buried his face between her pulsating neck and her soft shoulders, then moved down to the hard points of her breasts. His tongue flecked quickly like a butterfly sampling sweet nectar, then his lips covered the mound, gulped, sucked, kissed, sucked. "Oh, my God," he moaned, and gratefully deposited, around the brown nubs and over the soft pink fullness, his appreciative kisses. She felt a violent trembling, a beautiful yet terrifying sensation. The electrifying tug on her breasts sent shock-waves down to her thighs--a throbbing, an urging in her lower region that somehow felt good.

He drew the bottom of her gown up past her legs, lumping it above her waist. His hands explored the satin of her body. Gently he urged the opening of her thighs. He pressed against her, and the hardness that had prod her buttocks thrust against the mound between her legs. A rough groan escaped him.

Suddenly horror swept her. *History repeated!* Her body tensed, grew rigid with denial.

But he still moved on her--and horror exceeded horror. Afterwards he moaned, "I'm sorry. I'm sorry!" And he kissed her in a fumbling, clumsy sort of way. "My God, I'm sorry. I didn't mean to hurt you."

She lay still, unable to move. Unable to feel.

Later she learned to lie passive to allow him to do what must be done, thankful that it never took him long, and then he'd be peacefully asleep beside her. This was the physical side of marriage that women must accept to accommodate their husbands. The fact that at first she had felt an arousing response filled her with shame. *Strumpet! Trollop! Harlot! Was that what she really was? Like before?*

Even now, at times, when she lay beside William and his hands moved gently across her body, that delicious sensation would ache in her private parts, and she felt raw shame that she should lust for such pleasure. At least she was able to triumph over those carnal desires.

Suddenly a commotion in front snapped her attention back to the present. The Morgan wagon was shaking and she could hear Eli yelling at his mules.

"Dammit! Hold it, ye goddamed critters!"

She couldn't see what was going on beyond the canvas cover, but Morgan's wagon was jostling like a cyclone had struck. William ran forward and she saw her husband spinning, sent sprawling. The wagon lurched and headed toward Will. Medora screamed.

With rattle and clamor, Morgan's vehicle shot on spinning past the wagons ahead, careening like crazy. A woman screamed. Elspeth was inside!

Medora jumped from the board-seat and ran over to Will. He looked a bit dazed but sat up. The wheel of the wagon had just barely missed him.

"Dad blamed mules," he said.

Like the rush of a tornado, Medora caught a flash of a silver-grey horse as James Reed dashed by. He reached Morgan's bolting mules and pulled them to a stop. It was a wonder the old farm wagon hadn't fallen apart.

Morgan jumped down, eyes flashing as he cursed his mules. He raised his whip. Reed jerked it from his hand.

"You damn fool! Want to start them over again?!"

Morgan's fist swung out but Reed was faster. Morgan went sprawling.

By this time, William was on his feet and both he and Medora made a run for the back of the Morgan wagon. Medora tore open the puckered canvas and peered inside. "Elspeth! Elsepth! Are you all right?"

What a shambles! Overturned boxes. A snow scene of mixed cornmeal and flour. A pottery chamber pot with painted blue cornflowers smashed to pieces. Amongst it all, a woman moaned.

William climbed up over the tailgate.

James Reed pushed Medora aside. "Excuse me, Mrs. Dudley. Let me in to help."

The two men lifted Elspeth out. She was bruised and battered and covered with flour. After an examination it was found she had a broken shoulder.

But instead of being grateful that William and James Reed had rescued his wife from the wreckage, Morgan was hostile, eying William and Reed with suspicion, claiming no one had any business in his wagon.

Medora made up her own bed inside their wagon for Elspeth. Later that evening, for the first time since they'd left home, she lay beside her husband in one of the small tents, and they shared a whispered conversation about the day's events.

"Josh, did you ever see such gratitude?" William said. "You'd think we were in there snooping for his precious treasures."

"Treasure?"

"Well, he sold his brother's farm. So his gold is probably stashed away someplace inside."

Then aware of the softness beside him, William's thoughts turned to more demanding needs as his hands groped to find the smooth flesh under Medora's gown. It didn't take long. Soon he was pleasantly and contentedly asleep.

But Medora was still staring into the darkness. An ache still throbbed in her lower parts, and it mixed with a feeling of shame. Again she had desired only what men should find pleasure in--and now--still wanting. Her hand touched her husband. His soft-patterned breathing told her he was not aware, otherwise she would not dare be so brazen. She thought of another time--another place--another man. Of lingering kisses, of gentle unhurried exploring that had aroused her passions until she realized too late the sin she was committing. So terribly wrong. She had tried to stop him, but he wouldn't be stopped. She'd paid dearly for those shameful desires--was still paying.

But this was her husband who lay beside her, as he had these last eighteen years. There had been other times her body had wanted to respond, but with strength she was able to hold back. The dice had long been cast. Only loose women gave into such licentious desires.

For Medora, that night's sleep was long in coming.

CHAPTER 6

To Medora the days seemed endless, each day the same. The wagons lurched in the muddy road, the wheels turned so slowly, and it would go on forever. Often they were pelted by rain while other days the sun burned hot. She was thankful for her sunbonnet, although its wide brim still could not prevent the drying wind-fingers from parching her tender fair skin. The long train made only fifteen to twenty miles a day with the country looking much the same. Still, it had a certain beauty, green and rolling, stretching to infinity.

With the lumbering pace of the oxen, Medora found time for sketching; her solace, lifting her beyond the weariness and the monotony. Feelings and impressions miraculously became substance. She had been told she had talent, and she'd had some training when attending Madam Tessier's School for Young Ladies.

One day, with pad and pencil, Medora wandered a short distance out on the prairie. So intent was she on her drawings, she did not notice someone beside her until a pleasant voice said, "My, that is fine."

Medora turned in surprise seeing Tamsen Donner. She was a tiny bit of a woman in her mid-forties, not quite five feet tall. Although Medora was slender as a willow, her own five-feet-five and a half inches made her feel as though she towered over the petite little woman.

"I can almost hear the cattle bellowing and the wagons creaking in that sketch," Tamsen said.

"Why Mrs. Donner, thank you for such kind words."

"I mean it. You are a true artist." There was a directness in Tamsen's smile, a crispness to her speech that suggested New England. "Please call me Tamsen. I have a feeling we are going to be friends."

"I'm Medora. And I do hope so." Medora smiled warmly. Earlier she had noticed Tamsen around the camp, and admired the small woman's energy and enthusiasm in whatever she was doing. She had been told that Mrs. Donner once taught school and had brought with her several boxes of books planning on starting a school when she reached California. Medora thought at the time Mrs. Donner was surely a person she'd like to know better. And here she was, making the advancement.

"You know, Medora, seeing your work has given me an idea."

Medora's eyebrows raised in question.

"I've done some writing in the past for the ladies' press." Tamsen's smile removed any suggestion of boasting when she added that she was also an amateur botanist. "So now I've started writing a nature book of prairie life. And seeing your work... I have a very audacious question to ask. I wonder if you'd consider collaborating with me by doing the illustrations?"

"I?" Medora's hand went to her heart. Oh my, to be asked to illustrate a book. "Oh, Mrs. Donner..." Medora smiled, correcting herself. "I mean Tamsen. Are you sure you would want me to?"

Tamsen's eyes were clear and direct. "I'd be very pleased if you would consider."

Thus started a friendship which often meant long walks together out on the prairie gathering specimens to study for the nature book. They found wild tulip, primrose, dwarf lupin, larkspur, creeping hollyhock, and great profusion of yellow buttercups. Tamsen carried a nature book to identify the plants. She examined the leaves, stems, and flowers making extensive notes. Medora sketched them while still in their fresh-bloom state before they pressed the plants between pages of books.

Medora was enthralled with the project. It gave her something to look forward to. And besides it was wonderful to have a friend like Tamsen, who knew and loved literature as she did. They shared marvelous conversations.

However Torrey had not been as fortunate as her mother in finding a new friend. She still desperately missed Effie. Of course there was Lavinia. But who wanted a stuck-up sister for a bosom friend? There was that Virginia Reed who at times acted like she wanted to be friendly--but most of the time she was off riding her pony--the only girl in camp who had a special horse of her own. That was hard to take.

So it was Elspeth she turned to. Elspeth was nearly as old as her mother, and she knew her mother frowned on their friendship. Yet it had been Mama who had first invited the Morgans to join their camp. Right generous of Mama, she reckoned, knowing how her mother felt, disapproving of Elspeth's pipe smoking and the stories she told. To Torrey, Elspeth's stories were right fascinating, scary at times-- intriguing all the same, like her caution about blue hawks.

"A blue hawk flyin' overhead be a mighty bad sign," Elspeth had said.

Torrey had seen lots of hawks, but none of them blue.

"Ye can take it for gospel." As Elspeth said it her eyes bulged more than ever. "It means someone's goin' ter die!"

Torrey gasped and felt prickles of fear.

Her mother was standing near. "Elspeth, that's ridiculous. I won't have you filling my children's head with such nonsense."

"It be a fact, ma'am. My granny saw a blue hawk once. Next day my grandpappy died!"

From then on Torrey kept a wary eye out for blue hawks, hoping she'd never see one. It was best to be cautious.

In spite of the stories, still her mother was right kind to Elspeth. She wasn't so generous with Mr. Morgan when he used his type of language. Mama wasn't even lady-like when she snapped at him and ordered him out unless he could watch his tongue. Torrey smiled to herself. She was sure storing away some bully-right words she'd use in her own mind when Jake made her mad, not that she'd dare say them so anyone could hear.

Besides being captivated by Elspeth's stories, she also found the odd little woman easy to talk to about her own personal feelings, telling her things she could never tell her mother. Nor was Elspeth ever disapproving of things Torrey liked to do. Like the day she waded into that muddy stream, Mama would have scolded her for taking off her shoes and stockings. Reckon it was the wrong thing to do because her legs got covered with door-bugs. After pulling the bugs from her tender skin, the bites started itching like blazes. Elspeth saw the welts and all she said was "What they needs is a dose of my remedy."

She reached into her skirt pocket and pulled out a small deer skin bag and extracted a strange looking root. "Cures most everything," she said as she bit off a piece and started chewing. When it was soft and moist, Elspeth rubbed the root on the ugly red welts. Torrey was amazed. Almost immediately the itching stopped.

Overall, Torrey loved their camping life and traveling, except for helping with meals and the clean-up. And Jake. She stayed out of his way as much as she could. She'd often see him watching her with sort of a smirk like he still aimed to get even for her laughing the time Dulcie dumped him.   And she enjoyed working with her father whenever she could. She was every bit as good as Jake at putting the yokes over the heads of the oxen, fastening the bent hickory poles under their necks that bound the teams together.

Best of all was the grand feeling she got from the prairie. Sometimes her thoughts swelled to bursting; she had to write them down. She was glad Effie had given her the journal. It was now filled with her most private thoughts which included her secret love for her handsome caballero with the very black eyes whose picture was pasted in her journal.

She had once read a romantic story about a Spanish caballero who serenaded a beautiful señorita under her balcony. She pictured herself being serenaded as she peeked coyly from behind a black lace mantilla.

And because her father had promised, when they got to California, to look up the son of that senator they had met in Springfield--the son who owned a *rancho* and had taken to the ways of the Spaniards, it seemed only natural to picture him as *her* caballero--*her Don Stephano*. Each time she wrote in her journal, she'd always turn to the woodcut that had come from her mother's book, *The World of Geography of Today*, written by a Professor Justin Plympton. Not that she had deliberately defaced the book. Its binding was loose and the picture fell out of its own accord. She hoped her mother wouldn't notice it was gone.

After she mixed up flour and water and pasted the picture in her journal, she decided she should know more about those fascinating Spaniards who lived in California. However, she was disappointed that there was little in the book about California except that the Spaniards had taken over the territory to Christianize the Indians, and had built a series of missions. But the missions had fallen into ruin after *secularization*. The dictionary said *secularization* meant "to free from monastic vows or rules, to transfer from ecclesiastical to temporal use, to make worldly." She still wasn't sure what it meant. Maybe Mama could explain.

Mexico had won its freedom from Spain in 1822, which included California. So now the people there were called Mexicans instead of Spaniards. But as Professor Plympton had little to say about the customs of the Californians, Torrey turned to the chapter on Spain.

The professor had summarized the character of the Spanish people: They were temperate, grave, proud, polite, and faithful to their word. Torrey liked that. It was good to know the type of people she'd soon be among. But the professor also wrote that they were superstitious, ignorant, and revengeful. She didn't like those comments, especially when she looked at the woodcut illustration of the handsome caballero astride a beautiful white horse. The professor must be wrong. It was plain to see the Spanish caballero was fearless, dashing, handsome--and romantic!

Torrey picked up her pen, dipped it into a bottle of ink, and in her best penmanship she wrote with a flourish under the picture, the name *Don Stephano*.

The caravan had stopped for the nooning meal. Until now, except when sudden rainstorms struck, the journey had been languid and uneventful until this day. The women started to prepare the victuals and the men, as usual, began tending their animals and checking their equipment for needed repairs. Suddenly a lone horseman charged into their camp waving a newspaper over his head and shouting, "News! Big news for all!"

William looked up, set down the leather strap he was mending as the horseman reined in his pony. The animal glistened with sweat showing it had been ridden hard.

"It's war! We're at war!" the man shouted, and was immediately surrounded by the men of the camp, William among them. "Mexicans have crossed the Rio Grande and attacked our troops! Killed some, took others captive!" He began to unfolded a newspaper and spread the *St. Louis Republican* in front of him so all could see. The headlines were black and startling. WAR DECLARED ON MEXICO.

A chill shot down William's spine spreading to the rest of his innards. War with Mexico? His temples began to pound. What would that mean for California?

There had been talk of war even before any had left the States--trouble with Mexico over the United States' annexation of Texas--trouble with England over the Oregon border. But most figured it was just jaw-flappin' up there in Washington City--politicn', so to speak. With all the preparation it took to get ready for going west, there had been little time to think on anything else, so few had given it much serious thought. Now the news had real impact. They turned to one another, anxiety showed in their faces.

"Could have some disastrous ramifications," said the Reverend Mr. Cronwall. "Especially for us who are headed for California!"

"We could be in for a fight if we continue on," someone said.

"I've been sort of indecisive up to now," said the fellow standing next to William. "Now it's clear in my mind. I'm Oregon bound."

Others felt the same, even some who'd planned all along on California. No way did they want to have to fight the Mexicans instead of starting their farms.

At this point, William had not yet solidified his own thinking, his feelings still in turmoil. He rubbed at the dust on his trousers in an aimless motion. He held himself silent sorting out the thoughts that ran inside his head until he could catch a good one. He finally decided he'd put it to the Lord before making a decision.

Medora, busy preparing the noon day meal, had seen the rider come in, had noticed the commotion among the men, but paid little attention. She was more concerned that Elspeth was again filling her children's minds with nonsense. The odd little woman sat on a camp stool, legs spraddled under her long dark skirt, helping Torrey shell wild peas as best she could even though her right arm was strapped to her chest. Medora figured she had to give Elspeth credit for wanting to be helpful. But she didn't like the way Torrey and Billy, sitting on the ground beside Elspeth, were hanging onto her every word. Torrey's fingers had even stopped the snapping of the peas and Billy sat staring up almost breathless. She'd be thankful when the day came that the Morgans would return to their own campfire.

This time Elspeth had started a yarn about a snake. At the very mention of snakes Medora's innarads knotted. Many years had passed, yet the thought of snakes always brought a flood of agonizing memories. That day she'd let her little golden-haired three-year-old play out in the cotton patch. Then, to hear him cry out that he'd stepped on a snake. And the worst agony of all when he died in her arms.

"Elspeth, please," Medora squeezed out.

Elspeth, absorbed in her story as well as enjoying the attention of her captivated audience had not noticed the effect it had on Medora, so continued. "Thar it whar ready to strike, an' my Pappy with nary a gun."

Billy was wide-eyed and enthralled. "Jimminy whiskers, what did he do?"

"Pappy stood still as the rock he was leant against,'cept his fingers edged toward a loose stone. He threw hit and stunned the snake, then fast as lightnin' strikes, grabbed the snake by hits tail, snapped it like a whip, an' hits head went a'flyin'. Ony a good woodsman like my Pappy whar can do a trick like that."

Billy cracked his arm like a whip. "Like that?" he asked, his expression intense. "I saw a snake just this morning."

Claws of fear gripped Medora. "You saw a snake?"

Elspeth's voice was mater-of-fact. "Bound to be a passel of 'em." She looked at Billy. "But don't you try no tricks like my Pappy did. One thing I kin tell ye though, if'n ye ever do happen ter get bit by a snake, find yerself a good warty toad."

"Enough of this talk," Medora said feeling a rush of panic.

"A toad?" Torrey questioned, as fascinated as her brother.

Elspeth nodded. "Put it smack on the bite. Hif it dies, means it's pulled out the pizen. But hif it lives ye better get another toad right quick and do it over again."

"I said that's enough!" Medora's voice was ragged with alarm. Just then William burst in with his own startling news. "War! We're at war!"

Medora gasped. "What are you saying?"

"We're at war. War's broke out with Mexico!"

Anton, Mike and Eli clustered around full of the same frightening news. Medora's fear of snakes now compounded with another frightening thought. California was a Mexican province. "William, we can't go on," Medora squeezed from a frozen throat. "It's not too late. We must turn back!"

"When we've come this far? 'Course, we're not turning back." By this time William had had his talk with the Lord, although he realized he shouldn't have burst in with the news the way he did and unthinkingly turned a passel of fright onto the women and children. "I reckon I was as alarmed as you when first I heard," he said as though soothing a frightened child. "But actually, Medora, we can view this as a good turn of events."

"Good?"

William's smile now radiated confidence. "Zachery Taylor is a good tough general--good as they come. Mark my word, he'll soon have that skirmish under control. Won't take him long. You'll see. He'll have the Mexicans put in their place. You have to have faith in the quality of our men, Medora."

"But if we are at war..."

"It'll be over. Believe me, Medora. I'tll be over before we ever get there and California will belong to the U.S. of A." William's tone was now firm with his conviction. He looked toward Anton for agreement. The big shaggy head nodded.

Men! Of course they'd agreed. She turned back to the fire. Keep your mind on woman's chores. She began filling the plates and handing them to Lavinia to pass to the men.

All through the meal, as the men sat on storage crates and balanced their tin plates on their knees, the talk went on about the war and the strength of General Taylor and his men, conjecturing on what had actually taken place down there at the Texas border.

Morgan sopped his biscuit around in his gravy, then carried it to his mouth. Thin streams of gravy dribbled down over his soiled leather vest. Medora shuddered and turned away.

"Don't like it a'bit," Eli said. "Can't tell what'll happen now. Bad 'nuff to worry 'bout them damn Mormon bastards out there, ready to waylay us and murder us in our sleeping rolls."

"Mr. Morgan!" Medora said, her anger rising. "I won't have that kind of talk around my children." She had to strike out at someone--feeling so helpless. It wasn't fair that women had so little say in the welfare of their families.

"Now it could be them damn greasers comin' up from the Sante Fe."

Medora seethed. He hadn't even heard her.

Eli wiped the back of his hand across his mouth, then reached into his vest pocket for his bone tooth pick and started probing his yellowed teeth.

"The Mormons haven't bothered us yet," said William. "And certainly, the Mexicans won't come this far north. I reckon old Zack is keeping them tolerable busy down there Mexico way."

The talk continued all through the meal, guesses and speculations from Anton and Jake as they ate their sidepork and peas, as to what they might find if they did continue on to California. Even quiet Mike, Anton's teamster, offered some conjectures. Not everyone was as sure as William, but then, not everyone was as positive as he that the Lord was leading the way. However, in the long run, they all agreed they would not change their plans.

Except for Medora.

William realized she was still struggling with her fear. He wanted to go to her, take her in his arms, assure her it would all work out. But if he did? He felt the usual nagging hurt. She'd just turn away and remind him others could be watching.

War! It sounded so scary! Torrey was eager to be off by herself, think over this new frightening development. She wanted to write her thoughts down in her journal instead of being trapped with the nooning clean-up. Towel in hand, she reached for the skillet Lavinia was washing.

"Can't you wait 'till I toss the water?"

Medora glanced toward the girls. She still hadn't been able to rid her thoughts of the snake Billy had seen, and now war with Mexico. Better keep her mind on the present. She turned toward the girls. "Torrey, please watch what you are doing. If that towel gets against the black, I'll never get it clean."

"Make her scrub it herself," Lavinia countered.

Torrey shrugged. She dried the inside of the skillet and wedged it into a box of straw then spread the wet towel over a crate to dry. "Can I go now, Mama? We're finished." Her mother nodded. Torrey climbed into the wagon.

In spite of the confidence her father displayed, her thoughts were troubled. Papa had said it would be better if California was owned by the United States, but war meant shooting and killing. She thought of her caballero with his strong handsome face, and all the other gallant Spaniards. She had formed a real attachment for these valiant people. To be at war... War was too monstrous a thought.

Torrey reached for her journal wedged in her secret place between the box of winter-packed clothing they might need in the high country and the jars of Mama's special preserves. She plumped up one of the feather comforts and settled herself on the floor of the wagon.

In spite of the many entries, Effie's journal still looked new with its bright gold letters on the cover. The first page still had Effie's offering. Seeing the scrawled penmanship, Torrey felt a longing for her very dear friend. She read:

This is crismas day. I got me this jernal for crismas. I will write in it all the xciting things that happen. It is snowing.

The next page was blank because Torrey figured there should be a separation between hers and Effie's recordings. Her first entry had been made on the day they left Whitherville. That was surely one of the days of strong feelings. She had written about the pain she had in leaving Effie.

I know I will never have a friend as good as Effie. We made a solemn promise to each other. Someday I will go back to Illinois or she will come to California.

She still missed Effie most monstrously.

Torrey flipped a few pages, stopping at random to read a paragraph or two. Momentarily, she forgot about the war. She liked reading some of her entrys before recording the present events. It gave her a certain pleasure. Actually, she guessed it was pride in her writing, not that she'd admit that to anyone else. She figured some of her passages had real beauty. Maybe she'd be a famous writer someday.

She turned more pages and read:

I still don't like Jake, but not as much as I used to not like him. Sometimes I see him looking at me. I can't figure out his look, if he is still mad or if he wants to get friendly. He should go after Lavinia, but snooty Lavinia won't give him the time of day.

Torrey figured it was a good thing she kept the journal hidden. She wouldn't want anyone else to read some of the things she had written.

More pages flipped.

Mama says we have to keep on with our school work. She brought her tin box of books. She gives us lessons in Spanish right after our nooning meal so Papa can learn too. She says it is important so that we will be able to communicate with the natives when we reach California. Lavinia drills Billy and me on some of the other lessons. She thinks she is so smart because she went to the academy in Jackson. But I am teaching Jenny her letters and numbers. She is learning fast and already can pick out some words. She is smart for a four year old.

Torrey turned to the page that had the picture of the Spanish caballero pasted on it. She gazed at the woodcut. Dark snapping eyes, black wavy hair, a sharp cut nose, a proud tilt to his head, and dressed in the colorful Spanish costume--so different from the clothing worn by the men she knew. She sighed. He was so handsome. And below the picture, written in her best penmanship with a flourish, the name, *Don Stephano.*

She turned to a new page in the journal. She dipped her pen into the bottle of ink and wrote:

News has come that we are at war with Mexico. Papa says California will be part of the United States by the time we get there. I wonder how war will effect Don Stephano. I pray no harm will come to him. I pray he will always be the same.

She wanted to add, no matter what happens, I will always love him. But she didn't. Even in a secret journal you had to be careful what you wrote. It could fall into enemy hands.

CHAPTER 7

The big storm struck the day before they reached the Big Blue. Torrey looked up. A strange eerie yellowness colored the sky. "What's happening?" she asked her father as she walked beside him. As she spoke, a little gust of wind worried around them. The oxen had a wild-eyed look as they strained against their yoke.

Then, almost at once, dark clouds rolled in, piled up, one cloud on top of another. Thunderstorms blew in often on the prairie, but this day started out as calm, grew to hot. Not a breath of air stirred. Clouds were light piles of cotton in the blue above. The sun beat down with penetrating heat. The animals hung their heads, and the men slouched in their movements as they walked along side their listless teams. Then, instantly, the atmosphere changed.

"It's going to storm. A real storm this time," her father replied, a worrisome edge to his voice. A gust whipped at them again. "It's coming, girl. It's a'coming!"

Like an echo of the thought, frantic calls came up and down the line. "It's going to storm! Unhitch the oxen!"

The clouds festered to purple and then turned black. There was bustling and scurrying, and excited bellows of dismay from the animals. A bolt of lightening jagged down the sky followed by a deep muttering of thunder rumbling in the distance.

"Quick, Torrey, get out the tent. We'll need the shelter." The wind took the words right out of his mouth. The world became nothing but wind.

Torrey ran to the supply wagon to pull out the tent poles and canvas. Her mother called to Lavinia to get Billy and Jenny into the wagon. Her father and Jake frantically unhitched the oxen so they wouldn't bolt when the storm struck and take the wagons with them.

The whole sky was now dark. The prairie took on a strange purplish hue. Spookey. Mysterious. A sickening feeling of panic surged in Torrey hugging her tight as her skin. She struggled alone with the tent pegs and rope. The wind's menacing claws grappled the canvas as she tried to spread it.

Suddenly, from the dense fold of clouds, the lightening leaped and bounced to the ground. Instantly earth-trembling peals of thunder rolled on and on. Torrey gave a startled cry. The world was cracking apart! Her mother poked her head out from the puckered canvas openig. "Torrey, Torrey, where are you?"

"Mama, I'm all right. I'm helping Papa."

Dancing Girl, tied to the back of the family wagon, rose up on her hind legs and trumpeted in fright as she plunged against the wagon. The rig trembled and wobbled. Screams came from inside.

The wind tore at the canvas covers as the rain struck with a cold, driving violence and a terrifying roar. It beat down the grass and made mudholes where the oxen and horses were stomping. By this time, most of the animals had been freed from their yokes and were pirouetting around, turning to find some direction to escape the stinging rain. Then came the hail.

Icy stones clattered, powerful as rocks slung by tormented gods. Locked in their prison of terror, unable to defend themselves from the pelting hailstones, the animals bellowed in a horrid chorus. Torrey wrestled with the canvas, pulling part of it over her head and her back, but the hail still pounded. She felt dazed.

Dancing Girl screamed again. Her terror cut through the storm. Torrey saw the horse raise once more on her hind legs. This time she reared back so hard the leather strap snapped.

"Dancing Girl!" shrieked Torrey.

The hail mixed with sheets of rain coming down like a curtain dropping on the closing scene of a play. The mare faded to a gray shadow blur behind the scrim of rain, then vanished completely.

"I'll chase the horse down," shouted Jake above the wind. He headed toward the cluster of animals where Dulcie stomped and brayed.

"Oh, Jake! Please! Find Dancing Girl!" Torrey yelled.

He was gone--the young man and the mule, swallowed by the pounding, beating, furious storm.

Torrey was soaked to the skin. The rain streamed from her hair, into her eyes, into her mouth. She even breathed in the rain. William helped her with the tent, then they both crawled in under its protection, whatever protection it offered. Dusty-Dog sneaked in with them with his wet-dog odor. He shook to rid his coat of some of his soaking.

"Dusty!" Torrey yelled. "We don't need that now."

On the outside the pellets pounded the canvas like a thousand hammers, and when the hard round hail stopped, the rain increased in fury. The downpour sagged the tent with some of the water seeping through the canvas. The floor became a muddy quagmire. Torrey shook from cold.

"I'll get some blankets."

William dashed out and returned with an india-rubber mat to place on the ground and blankets to wrap in. Dusty sneaked in under the blanket seeking warmth from Torrey.

Anton stuck his head in between the flap of the tent. His broad felt hat hung limp about his ears. His shoulders glistened with the rain. "Have any exta room in here?"

"We'll make room."

"So busy with the stock, didn't have time to set up a tent."

The stocky German, with his teamster, Mike, right behind him, crawled in. The smell of their saturated blanket coats came with them.

The small tent, designed to accomodate hardly more than two people for sleeping, was crowded. The four sat hunched in a circle, knees drawn to their chests.

"Nothing like a prairie rain for suddenness," commented Anton.

And nothing like thunder to scare the geeminy-crickets out of you, thought Torrey.

"How are the animals doing?" asked William.

"Edgy. But we've herded them together. Line-tethered the horses. Since the hail stopped, now better."

"Sometimes better than us humans," spoke up Mike. "They knows enough to get their asses stuck up to the wind, and heads down. Oh, beg pardon, Miss Torrey."

"Dancing Girl bolted," said William. "Broke her holding straps and took off fast as the lightening. Jake took after her."

"He won't find her in this storm," said Anton.

Torrey's stomach tightened. Lose Dancing-Girl, their only horse! She was one of the family!

The pounding of the rain lessened some, but a thin stream of water still seeped through the canvas roof. The thunder moved on but the low rumble could be heard off in the distance. Thank goodness, it's moving away, thought Torrey. She never wanted to be caught in a storm like that ever again.

"I doubt if we'll move on any further today," William surmised. "Reckon for those who got their tents up, they'll not want to pull them right down."

Anton nodded. "Ja, the trail would be nothing but mud." He took off his soaked felt hat and shook some of the moisture from the mass of unruly hair.

Torrey felt the spray, but she didn't mind. No matter what he did, she always looked upon Anton with deep affection. He was the same as family. He was like a big bear who held his power in check, but you could see it was there by the cord-like muscles that stood out on his neck and the broadness of his shoulders.

She rememberd how frightened she was the first time she saw him that evening they had arrived in Whitherville and he had taken them in. As a six year old, she looked up and saw a big, grinning, jack-o'-lantern face with small, bright eyes and hid behind her father. But Anton gently reached for her and called her his *Liebchen* as he stroked her hair. He told her she reminded him of the little sister he had left in the old country.

Now she saw only the gentleness in his smile when he looked at her with those sharp, blue eyes under the wild, shaggy brows. He still called her his *Liebchen*. She reckoned she'd miss it if he didn't.

As the rain continued its staccato concert on the canvas tent, the men fell to discussing events. They wondered how the war was progressing down Texas way, and wondered what was happening in California regarding the war. Torrey sat quietly, thankful the thunder had abated. In spite of the cold and dampness, it was mighty pleasurable listening to men talk; so much more lively than hearing women brag about their sage stew or fretting over a snotty-nosed kid. Men talked real talk--about their animals, their wagons, their guns. Sometimes they told exciting stories about the Black Hawk War, or coon hunting in the woods--things far more worth hearing.

Anton lit his Meerschaum pipe, carved with the cheerful face of a Burgmeister, Anton said. But when the smoke started clouding the small space of the tent, he knocked out the smoldering tobacco into one of the puddles on the floor of the tent. "Ja, we should do without that," he said.

Thoughtful of others like always, Torrey thought.

The dampness began to penetrate more. Torrey pulled the blanket up tighter to her chin. She was getting some warmth from Dusty curled up beside her leg.

The men went on to the events of the day; the storm, their live stock, whether or not Owl Russell was losing control as their leader. Seemed he'd been imbibing spirits of late. And more pros and cons of fellow travelers.

"One problem," said Anton, "our train is too large--too many animals. We'll have grazing problems ahead."

William nodded. "That fellow headed for Oregon, he's driving over two-hundred head."

"He won't get there with that many," said Anton as he ran stubby fingers through his thick wet hair, shaking it slightly. Again Torrey felt the spray. "Here we've got enough grass. But ahead is alkali soil."

Torrey wondered about alkali soil.

Anton looked thoughtful. "So, a real conglomeration we are. Ja, could be trouble ahead."

There had already been trouble. Anton broke up a fight between two partners just the day before, a partnership that had to continue as one owned the oxen, the other the wagon.

And the hostility that had begun when James Reed had stopped Morgan's runaway mules was increasing between the two. It troubled William because Reed was a man he admired, whom he wanted to know better. Reed had some of those same qualities William had respected in the judge: a canny ingenuity, a blend of shrewdness with forthrightness and honesty, all of the elements needed for financial success. With his own ambitions geared along those lines, friendship with Reed could prove advantageous when they reached the new land. But with the Whitherville contingent following each other in line, Morgan was always around so James Reed kept a reserved distance.

"It strikes me," said William, "that the next set-to could be between Morgan and Reed."

"Ja, it would be good if they had it out between them. Maybe then we'd get rid of at least one."

William bristled. "What's wrong with Reed?"

"A braggart he is. He lets others do his work."

"What's wrong with that? Reed pays his hands well. I look upon Reed as a fine upright gentleman."

Torrey was following their conversation with interest, looking from one to the other. She heard the anger in her father's voice and saw the cloud cross Anton's face. Strange, because Uncle Anton and Papa were the very best of friends, like herself and Effie.

"You'd think Eli would show some gratitude toward Reed for stopping his runaway mules," said William. "That old wagon was almost shaken to bits."

Anton shook his head and now a smile creased his face. "I think maybe it's his treasure. He doesn't want anyone near his wagon."

"Treasure?" Torrey broke in. "Has he got a treasure in his wagon? Like pirate jewels? He used to work the keel boats on the Mississippi. Pirates used to hide their booty along that river. Do you suppose..."

William laughed, and the agitation between the two men faded. "Girl, you do build things up in your mind. Not likely a pirate's treasure. More likely gold from the sale of his farm."

"His brother's farm," Anton corrected.

The tent flap parted. Jake's dripping head poked in. He was grinning.

"You caught Dancing Girl!" Torrey burst out.

"Yep. Got her hobbled now with the rest."

"Good boy," William said. "Come in out of the wet. We'll make room. We haven't got a fire to warm you, but we'll share a blanket."

"I'm awful wet."

"So we all are. Come on."

Jake crawled into the tiny tent on his hands and knees, his wet flannel shirt clinging like skin.

"There's room for you here beside Torrey and me. Torrey, you'll have to share some of your blanket with this shivering lad."

William pushed aside a part of the blanket that covered both him and Torrey and moved aside. Jake squeezed in between them. She could smell his wet hair and his wet clothing. He was clammy cold-soaked beside her. It was mighty crowded with Dusty on one side and now Jake on the other. "It was raining so hard. If it hadn't been for her whinnying--I couldn't even see her. I think she did it to let me know where she was. When I caught her, she was ready to come back, docile as a house cat."

William laughed. "A horse with real horse sense. I appreciate you chasing her down."

Torrey was grateful too--even if it was Jake she must be grateful to. Anyway, her feelings had mellowed somewhat toward Jake. Except--if it weren't for Jake, she'd be the one helping Papa instead of doing women's chores. And then she'd at least have Dulcie to ride.

The rain continued to pepper the tent. The men resumed their talk. Jake sat closer than necessary, Torrey thought. She moved over, practically squashing the dog.

Jake's leg pressed against hers. She pulled herself tight. Then ever so slightly, his leg rubbed against hers, back and fourth. She realized a tingling, like brushing up against nettles. She shuddered away as far as she could, even more onto Dusty. The dog groaned in his sleep but didn't budge an inch.

Torrey thought back to that night of their farewell party when she was dancing with Jake and what he'd said about those ruffles her mother had sewn inside her bodice. Remembering, her anger rose anew. She had slapped him then--and everyone had seen. She didn't want that to happen again, and have to explain. The men were still into their jawing like nothing was going on. Praise the Lord she hadn't screamed out. From the corner of her eye, she sneaked a glance toward Jake. He acted like nothing was taking place, even adding his own bit to the men's talk. Was it just in her own mind?

Oh, he's doing it again! It created such a strange sensation--up the side of her leg and then over to her belly!

Although scarcely any light filtered through the wet canvas, Uncle Anton's gaze dropped to the blanket that covered her legs. His mobile face seemed to tighten, and the deep rubbery furrows between his brows deepened. Torrey felt the redness work up her neck. Could Anton see? She prayed it was too dark in the tent to make it possible. She moved as far away from Jake as she could. Trouble was, there was no distance to move to.

Just when she was afraid she could no longer check an outcry, her father gave

71

a shout. "Say, listen. I believe the rain has stopped. Come, we can get out of this soggy tent."

Saved, thought Torrey. Thank goodness, the fair maiden has been saved!

CHAPTER 8

Anton had noticed a movement under the blanket that covered Torrey and Jake and hoped it wasn't what he suspected, chiding himself on a suspicious mind--or perhaps his own awareness of the nubbins that now strained against Torrey's straight-cut bodice. So fast a woman she was becoming. He thought back to the earlier time when the Dudleys first entered his life. Torrey, with her bright spirit and ready smile had reminded him of the little sister he'd left behind in the old country. Gisela. Twenty years now since he'd seen her--such a long, long time. She now with a family of her own.

Thinking of his sister, a wave of homesickness washed over Anton. Would he ever return to his homeland? As he checked his animals and equipment for damage from the storm, he let memory take him back. Peasant stock he'd come from, as far back as he knew. No royalty could he boast of--like Reed--if it was really so with Reed. But like Reed, he too had come to this country as a youth with empty pockets and now was a man of means. Ja, peasant born--and peasant destined to be if he'd remained in his homeland with little chance of ever rising above his station in life, the reason he'd come to America. And like Reed, here in this new country he had made his own way and had prospered.

He thought back to the small farm in the high country where he'd been born. He'd loved that land. He loved farming, loved tilling the soil. But he had wanted more than a poor peasant's life. His father called him a fool. "You can not change what was meant to be."

But he did--by having the good fortune of coming across a certain book, *Der Wohlberathene Bauer* by Simon Stuüf that gave a scientific method for the practice of farming. Always a reader from the time he'd first started school, he had found the book when browsing in the village bookstore. He saw how the advanced methods for farming could increase the yield of their family plot. He must have the book.

So when he wasn't out tending the goats on the hillside, Anton worked for the village baker washing pans and cleaning the oven. He earned enough money to buy the book. Treasured still, *Der Wohlberathene Bauer* was now tucked into a corner of his wagon. Using its methods had brought him wealth in Illinois. It would do the same when he reached California.

But now, thinking back, he remembered how angry his peasant father had become at the very suggestion of change. His ancestors before him had worked it thus; his son would do the same. Their quarrel was bitter. So when his mother died, Anton saw no reason to remain --except for Gisela. Even now he still felt the hurt of saying goodby. But Bertha, an older sister, would look after the child. She would be loved and well cared for.

But ach, such anger from his father: "You leave, the devil goes with you. No longer do I have a son!" Harsh words from the father he loved. And there were tears from Gisela. His heart was heavy. He was eighteen when he left his homeland, twenty years past. The pull of that distant land was still strong. So far away was his Alpine country--and Gisela. And now the distance growing ever greater as he traveled west. Ja, maybe someday he'd see Gisela again. But not his father, now long gone, buried in the homeland.

For a while his father's parting words had seemed an omen. He wondered if Reed's experience had been as harrowing as his own coming to a new country. He had sailed on a three masted ship at Le Havre going steerage. Thirty-three days in the dark hull of a rat infested ship where they were fed rotted food and received scarcely any water. The smell! The foulness! Vomit, sweat, piss and shit, all together plus the awful smell of death. Now looking back, he could consider he was one of the lucky ones because he did survive.

Arriving in New York was hardly any better, weeks of confusion and panic--he a lost and lonely boy, a foreigner who could not speak the language. He gave his trust and his money to one of his own countrymen and was cheated out of his last few dollars. So he slept under stairwells. He ate what scraps of food he could find. And he longed for his homeland--and Gisela.

At last he obtained work in a cotton factory as a bobbin boy and was paid $1.25 a week. Ach, such riches. At last he'd found the America he'd dreamed of,--land of the free were there was no caste system. He worked hard and advanced to operating machinery and was paid a little higher wage. At night, by candle light, in his rented attic room, he read *Der Wohlberathene Bauer* with the same fervor others read the Bible. Someday he'd return to the soil and put those methods to practice.

During that time he had fallen in love. Twenty years old and in America two years. He could smile now, remembering Maureen with the red hair, more flame than his *Liebchen*. Maureen, a beautiful Irish girl worked in the same cotton factory he did. He envisioned Maureen baking bread in the farm kitchen he'd have someday. Ach, such a fool. Suddenly she married his foreman. Such hurt he suffered. But then, how could he have thought a beautiful girl like Maureen could love an ugly man, such as he. Ja, such foolishness to think.

But the time finally came in '32 to realize his farm. He was twenty-four years of age and had been in this country for a little over six years. He listened to talk of migrating west which meant Missouri and Illinois where land could still be had for $1.25 an acre.

He'd saved enough money to get himself west, and to purchase a few acres in Sangamon County. He plowed and planted vegetables following the instructions in his book, and sent them up river to merchants in Springfield. The productivity of his land amazed his neighbors. They'd shake their heads and say, "What's this talent Zwiegmann has?"

Not talent, Anton knew. Ja, applying the methods in his book that told him how to understand soil and evaluate its potentials. He loved his land. He loved to plow, and he loved the smell of fresh turned soil.

From the earning of his vegetable plots, he invested in more land without ever buying on credit. Thus, when the panic of '37 started and heavy investors were losing their land, he increased his holdings by purchasing property at much less its original cost. His few acres increased to many hundreds. He planted corn, wheat and oats, becoming the most productive farmer in the Sangamon County. Only in America could a poor peasant boy rise to be a land-owner of means. He had a deep love and respect for his adopted country. Yet, here he was, again headed for new frontiers. The restlessness of the humane spirit was something for which he had no answer.

It was fall when the migrating talk became so lively. After harvest, with little else to do, the men gathered in the mercantile. They parked their feet on the fender of the potbellied stove, and their moonrakings mixed with tobacco smoke and was swilled around with the foaming brew William drew from the keg he had set at the end of the counter. The men compared the letters that were printed in the various Illinois papers about the far-off land of perpetual sunshine and told how the Mexicans were eager for settlers and give away huge grants of land for free. It was about that time that he was offered a price for his farm he could hardly refuse. And with his very best friend wanting to go...

In the new country he would once again apply the knowledge he'd learned from his book. He and William would prosper working together. *If Reed didn't come between them.* Naturally, Anton's resentment of Reed increased when he saw William and Reed in deep discussions. That man with his "palace car" and his fine race horse, and the many hired hands who did his labor! He had overheard William and Reed talking of a possible mercantile partnership once they got to California, and his gut had tightened.

True, William's talent was business; he knew little about farming. But in California where ranches could be vast, he and William would combine their skills; he would take care of the growing, William could handle the shipping and business end. Ja, good partners they make. Besides, there was the family, and he with no family of his own. He thought of Torrey. *His Liebchen.*

Anton's shaggy brows pulled together. That time of the storm. Jake--under that blanket--wedged so close to his *Liebchen*. A fresh young man he is. Ja, from now on, my eyes they stake out a watch that is closer. But *noch nicht.* She is still a child. *Or is she?*

CHAPTER 9

The following day the wagon train reached the bluff overlooking the junction of the Kansas and the Big Blue. William looked down at the swift, angry river and heard its sinister sound. The Blue had a reputation as a killer, not much in fall, but with spring rains it could sweep you away. Because of the storm, the Blue ran swift, up twenty feet, and the ford was two hundred yards wide. Terror gripped as he watched the rushing, tumultuous water. *This was the river they now must cross.*

He'd always had a fear of water crossings, even the gentle looking streams. They had already crossed a number, and he knew relief when over them, offering thanks to the Lord when the ground became firm again under the wheels. Never yet had they faced such a full and rushing river as this one!

"No way can we wheel across this time," shouted Owl.

He called the men together and ordered a raft be constructed. But late that afternoon another thunderstorm struck and delayed their work. And that night, James Reed's mother-in-law died. Even though the death was not unexpected, a pall settled over the encampment.

"After all, she was an old lady,"

"Ailing before they even left home. That Reed fellow never should have brought her."

"Just her time to go. We'll all face it some day."

Medora tried to avoid such talk, yet couldn't deny the frightening feeling of foreboding. She was not alone. The pounding of hammers during the construction of the coffin the following morning seemed to echo a thought that hung heavy; how many other such boxes would be put together before their journey's end?

After offering condolence to Margaret Reed, Medora asked if there was anything she could do. Grief lines showed in the other woman's face, and Medora understood her pain. She still felt the hurt she had known--and the guilt for not being there at her own mother's death years ago.

Margaret Reed looked searchingly at Medora. "Yes there is, if you would. "Tamsen says you have a natural artistic talent. I'd like Mama to look as pretty as possible. I've selected Mama's best dress and Tamsen will help me lay her out. If you could do her hair."

"Of course. I'll be glad to." Medora hardly knew Mrs. Reed as the woman suffered severe headaches and spent most of her time in the huge wagon, but hoped she'd be able to arrange the old lady's hair to look most natural.

Margaret Reed had tears in her eyes after Medora finished. "She looks beautiful, Mrs. Dudley. I thank you so much."

"I'm glad I could do it," Medora replied.

A long line of mourners formed to view the corpse in the coffin. As Torrey passed by she thought how peaceful the elderly lady looked. If her eyes were open, she'd be looking right up into the sky--probably greeting her Maker.

The Reverend Mr. Cornwall offered a prayer and everyone sang *Rock of Ages*. They placed a marker cut out of stone. It read:

Mrs. Sarah Keyes
DIED
MAY 29, 1846
Aged 70

After the funeral, the men started work on the raft. James Reed suggested they hollow out a couple of large trees to make pontoons. They'd place logs across them to build a solid platform to wheel the wagons onto. William admired the way Reed took charge as Owl was no where to be seen.

"Ja, the best to get us across," Anton agreed, but William could tell he resented the way Reed had assumed authority. Yet, Anton willingly pitched in to do his share.

The whack of axes mixed with the rap of hammers as the men pitched in. Not so Eli Morgan. He sat on a rock at the top of the bluff and watched the activity.

"Morgan, we need all the hands we can get," Reed shouted up to him.

Eli moved a wad of tobacco from one side of his jaw to the other then shot a brown stream of liquid.

"Well, Morgan?"

"Hell, who made you boss of this job?"

"Someone's got to be. Now get your lazy ass down here and give us a hand if you want your wagon hauled across the river."

"I ain't chancin' my wagon to no shaky raft."

"Got a better way?"

"Hell yes. I'm goin' ter cover my wagon with rawhide, and float it across. Be water-tight then, and won't take no chance on being toppled."

"Suit yourself."

"I'm aimin' to. It'll be a damn sight safer and drier."

Reed turned his back on Morgan and continued directing his work crew.

The sun came out hot and strong. The men worked on through most of the day, their clothes turning dark with sweat. They shouted, cussed, some even joked and laughed. When finished, the raft looked ugly and crude, but strong. Most figured it would get the wagons safely over to the other side of the Big Blue. Cheers went up. It was late afternoon.

"Let's call her Blue River Rover," Torrey suggested, again sticking her nose in where it didn't belong.

"Good idea, little sister," said Owl who finally showed up smelling strongly of liquor. He now bustled around, proud as punch, as though he'd been in on its making. There was little doubt now that the man they'd elected as captain often imbibed more than he should. William had a feeling they'd have a new captain before the trip was over.

The raft was anchored in the water, ready for the first wagon to be rolled on. William walked to the edge of the bank to look down at the river and tasted fear. It plucked at his skin, rising the hairs on his arms. The river had gone down several feet, yet the muddy water still rolled and churned. Eddies swirled on the surface, then sped downstream.

Torrey's arm linked into his. "Geeminy-gee, it does look monstrously scary. The water's so fast."

"We'll make it all right," he said, trying to make his voice sound convincing. Silently he'd been repeating, *Whosoever believeth in Me, behold, he shall not perish.* But his fists, thrust into his pockets, were tight sweaty balls.

Anton strode up with his usual air of confidence. "I've crossed worse," he said.

Bless him, thought William. His friend's sureness lent the support he needed.

"Reed and I talked it over," Anton said. "First, we go on our horses. Ja, to test the current."

Typical of both Reed and Anton, William thought. He wished he had their kind of courage. Still from the top of the bank he watched his two friends, Reed on his grey Thoroughbred and Anton on his sturdy Morgan, cautiously step their steeds in to check on the bottom. At first, Anton's Morgan shrank back, snorting in protest, but soon both horses were in deeper water. The powerful surge of the river pushed against them. The horses started swimming; wide-eyed, necks stretched, heads held high, nostrils opened wide. They made it to the other side and scrambled up the bank. Anton and Reed shouted to the ones waiting on the opposite shore, and then splashed back into the river to return.

"No problem," said the dripping wet Anton to the ones crowding the bank. "We should have no trouble getting the wagons across."

Eli Morgan's face was set with its usual scowl. "Hell, I doubt that. Ye can't trust the Big Blue, from what I've heered. It be a goddamned killer."

William's gut tightened. He could do without suggestion of that nature. He again looked at the water, saw its lethal power, smelled its rank muddiness, watched its rushing strength surging down its course.

"Ready now to go," Anton said. His wagon would go first, loaded mostly with farm equipment and his fruit trees--no loss of lives if worse came to worse--and he a bachelor. He then assigned William to take the rope tied to the back of the raft. "Tie it to your saddle and keep it firm," the German directed. "It's for balance to keep the raft from being swept end-around downstream."

William swallowed. His mouth felt dry.

"Use your mule. She's got the strength. Jake takes your mare. He and Mike, they're up front keeping the oxen in line."

Would he be able to do it? William wondered feeling his legs turn to rubber. He had two wagons and a family. He had to get them across that raging river. And he had to do his share in helping Anton. William closed his eyes and said a prayer.

They double-teamed Anton's best oxen then used two more behind the wagon for needed resistance. Slowly, the wagon started down the steep bluff. At the water's edge the animals turned reluctant. Anton cracked his whip above their heads. Slowly, with steady clumsiness, the bovine responded. The men wrestled with ropes assisting the wagon into place and then firmly secured the rig to the raft. James Reed yelled out orders. Colonel Owl Russell was nowhere to be seen.

Medora, flanked on either side by her two older daughters, watched from the top of the bluff. The wagon looked so unsteady even after being tied to the raft. Would it stay upright when caught in the rapid current in the middle of the river? This first wagon was Anton's. She pressed her hand against her thudding heart. Theirs would be next, and she and her children. As she watched William urge Dulcie into the water and reach for the rope that dangled from the back of the raft, fear traveled up her spine. Why had William been asked to do that task? She knew his fear of water crossings. Why hadn't someone else been asked instead? Would there ever be an end to these nightmares they faced?

As the raft moved from its mooring, the wagon wobbled slightly. It was now into the rushing current. For a moment the oxen panicked when they no longer could feel bottom, but Mike and Jake on either side, calmed the frightened animals and urged them forward. The raft lurched behind. Anton waved his hat in the air and shouted "Hy-yeee."

On the shore, Eli Morgan continued to observe; waiting for his predictions to happen, waiting to yell out, "I told you so." He had already started covering his own wagon with the rawhide, which was taking some time. It would be well into the following day before he'd be able to cross. A few of the other men had sided with him and had removed their wheels and were covering their rigs.

William, still at the water's edge, pulled on the rope to steady the raft. Fear tightened his chest. He dug his heels into Dulcie's shank to spur her into the muddy water. He whispered a prayer. The relentless might of the river washed against his feet, then pressed against his knees. The current was an unyielding power. The chill took his breath away. He knew abject helplessness and terror. *Dear Lord, don't forsake me now!* He could even feel terror in the mule as the rope pulled on the saddle. The river surged against them, vicious, alive, untiring. But the mule fought the river, her strokes powerful, instinctive. William clung with all his might to the saddle. In spite of the yelling around him, he felt a strange isolation. He heard only the roar of the river, felt the danger, felt the enmity of nature.

At last, the oxen scrambled up a muddy slope down stream where the strong current had carried them. They dragged the water-soaked raft and wagon to shore. Cheers arose across the river from the others who eagerly watched this first crossing.

"They've made it! They've made it!"

Medora breathed a sigh of relief and grabbed the hands of her two daughters. "Thank God. Thank God," she muttered.

With the rope slackening, William felt his mule's sharp hooves dig into the muck. Dulcie leaned forward and climbed. They were out of the water!

William took a deep breath and raised his voice. "Praise the good Lord, we *have* made it!" How could he have doubted? Now he felt a certain assurance as he once again plunged back into the watery depths to return to the other side and bring his own wagons over. A start had been made.

Owl Russell finally appeared and started bellowing orders. "The other wagons of the Whitherville unit should go next. The Springfield group will have to wait until tomorrow." He glanced over toward Eli's unloaded wagon. "Mr. Morgan, why are all your belongings out?"

"Tomorrow be my day," Eli replied. "And my stuff will be a goddamned drier than most the others."

Owl turned back to William. "Dudley, better get a move on fast before darkness sets in."

"Right," William agreed, wondering what right Owl had giving orders now. "I'm taking my supply wagon first, then come back for the other."

Billy tugged on his father's arm. "Can I go on this trip?" Excitement made his freckles bold.

"Go on. Climb aboard."

Again, another successful crossing was made and the hard-worked oxen set to graze. Fresh teams would be used for the next crossing. Anton and Jake would remain and set up camp.

"Can I stay and help Uncle Anton?" asked Billy.

William ruffled his young son's bright red hair. "Don't see why not. Mind you are a help and not get in their way."

By now William had a grand feeling of glory. His fear of the river had been controlled--not alleviated completely, but well subdued. He was exhausted, for sure, ached in every muscle from the arduous labor, but still he had a feeling of exuberance. The Lord had shown His love. William was ready to return to bring his other wagon across.

Near sunset the Dudleys' family wagon was jockeyed onto the raft and firmly tied down. Medora, with Jenny and Lavinia, climbed inside where the canvas cover would protect them from the splashing of the animals.

"Torrey, you too," Medora called to her second daughter. "Come get inside."

"I'm going to sit on the board seat," Torrey announced as she climbed aboard.

"You'll get soaked."

"I want to see what's going on."

That girl, thought Medora with a resigned expression. What luck did she ever have in changing Torrey's mind?

The raft was already in deeper water when Torrey heard Dusty-Dog barking from shore. How could they have missed him and left him behind? The dog was prancing and yapping sharp accusations. He darted into the chilling water but backed out just as quickly.

"Come on, Dusty, come on. You can make it," Torrey yelled.

Again the dog tested the water, pulled back, cocked his head and raised his ears at Torrey's encouragement. He finally plunged in. Torrey helped him struggle onto the raft. He shook his big water-soaked body showering Torrey.

"Dusty. I don't need that!"

The dog's entire rump wagged in delight as he planted huge paws against her chest, and his long red tongue bestowed his slobbery affection.

Torrey climbed up onto the board seat. Dusty jumped up beside her and laid his wet head in her lap. What difference did it make? She was already well drenched. She stroked the tan and black head and lovingly pulled his soft floppy ears.

It was great sitting high on the wagon seat. Captain of her ship, Dusty her mate. The water churned and chuckled around the raft. She was on the broad expanse of sea. Wind whipped the sails, gigantic waves were rocking her craft. As the oxen flailed in the current, she was splashed with chilling water. *Ahoy there, sailor. Strike the canvas. We're in for a storm!*

The storm struck!

Torrey felt the wagon bounce and shudder. One of the oxen had bolted and triggered off panic to the others. The raft rocked as swirling rapids caught it.

William, still behind, shouted as he yanked on the balancing rope. Icy spray splashed over the raft as the oxen thrashed. The raft tipped toward the rushing water, tipped toward the churning depths. Inside the canvas cover, Medora screamed. Another lurch and Torrey and Dusty went sailing, pitched from the seat into the wild, flowing water.

The river closed over her. The current pulled. Boiling brown water swept her along. She tumbled head over heals. She couldn't cry out. She couldn't breathe. *This is the end!*

She fought back, but her strength was puny against the strength of the river. She gasped for air and choked down water. The speeding current drove her on. She whammed against a rock. Its jagged roughness tore at her clothes, scraped her skin. Her head broke the water. Sky whirled by. Round and round. A piece of floating driftwood bashed her in the shoulder, but she felt no pain. She grabbed for a branch. It was slippery, slimy. She clutched again and finally encircled it with her arms--hung on for dear life until she was caught in another swirling eddy and felt her life line jerked from her grasp. She tumbled again, over and over. Another object struck her. She flailed the water, reached, grabbed.

"Torrey, quit fighting!"

A voice. From where? She struck out again, blindly.

"Dammit, Torrey. Let go!"

Again something struck.

She was dragged up a bank. She sputtered and coughed. Someone turned her over on her stomach and lifted her in the middle and water spewed out her mouth. She coughed and choked. Turned back again, a mouth pressed to hers. Air was forced into her tortured lungs. When she opened her eyes, Uncle Anton's face was only inches above hers. There were other faces. A circle around her, peering down. There was Billy. There was Mike. There was Jake. Then her father's voice someplace off. "Torrey! Torrey!" Coming closer. "TORREY!"

William was breathless when he pushed aside the others and knelt beside his daughter. Water dripped from his clothing. "Torrey, are you all right? My God, I couldn't get to you. I had to steady the raft to keep it from going over with all the others!"

"She's all right, Will." Anton's voice was reassuring. "She just swallowed some water."

"Thank God for you and Jake."

"Ja, we were close. Jake pulled her in. Medora and the girls?"

"No problem there." William was still breathing hard. "Just shook up. The wagon was well secured to the raft. Torrey was up on the seat--nothing to hang on to. Thank God, you and Jake were here on this side of the river."

William, knelt beside his daughter, took her hand and massaged it with love. "Thank God," he said again. "Thank the good Lord you are safe. How do you feel now, girl?"

Torrey sat up, glanced around with new fright in her eyes. "I'm all right. Where's Dusty?"

"Ach, *Liebchen*," Anton broke in. "You should take lessons from the dog. He swam ashore without trouble."

Torrey looked up at the big German face. Gratitude flooded her. "Thank you, Uncle Anton. I guess you saved my life."

"Nein, Liebchen. Jake reached you first. He saw you go in and yelled to me. Ja, I just helped the boy get you to shore."

Torrey's gaze moved to Jake. His dark curly hair plastered his forehead, and his soggy clothing a testimonial to a recent swim.

"You? It was you who saved me?"

Jake shuffled, looking embarrassed as he jabbed his hands into his pantaloons pockets.

"You risked your life to save me?"

"Twarn't nothin'. I just happened to be there. But by gore, Torrey, you were stubborn as all get out. Tried to drown us both--the reason I had to wham you so hard."

She didn't remember. What happened in the water was only a blur of suffocation and terror. Jake risked his life to save her? A monstrous thought. Jake! *The one she couldn't tolerate.*

Her voice was low. The words had trouble coming out. "Then I reckon I should thank you for saving my life. Reckon I'm beholding to you."

A flash of triumph crossed his face vanishing any previous embarrassment. He drew his hands from his pockets, caught his thumbs in the armholes of his buckskin vest with the fancy beads. His head cocked slightly to a rakish angle and amusement twinkled in dark hazel eyes with the yellow specks adding a spark of roguish intrigue. "Could be you are. Could be I'll hold you to it," he said with a satisfied gleam.

CHAPTER 10

It was Sunday morning. Heads bowed as William led his family in prayer. "We thank thee, oh Lord, for delivering us safely across those torrential waters." His mind added an extra thanks that nothing more serious had happened than Torrey's dunking. Now, on this particular Sabbath Day, he and his family could duly respect the Lord God's commandment to keep it holy; a day for rejuvenating both body and soul. Unfortunately, others must still make the crossing.

The issue had been settled a week past that the caravan would continue to travel on Sunday even though the Reverend Mr. Cornwall had raised his voice in protest with William shouting "Amen" along with a few others.

"Too much time has already been lost," some argued.

"The weather is the one that says we stop or go on."

Owl Russell took a vote. In spite of Reverend Mr. Cornwall shaking a bony finger and looking as though he himself had been smitten by the Lord, it was agreed. They'd push on, Sunday or not, unless unforeseen obstacles prevented them.

So this Sunday morning William was thankful that at least he and his family had reached this farther shore the day before, and he could honor the Sabbath. He included in his prayer a special request that the other travelers would make it over safely in spite of desecrating *this* day.

But thankful as he was for his own day of rest, he felt a touch of guilt as he watched Medora bustle around with necessary chores. She was preparing some broth to take to Mrs. Saunders who was near due and had been feeling poorly. The Saunders was one of the families who had made it over the night before.

The girls were tending other chores with Torrey grumbling. "I hate washing these big black pots. Why can't Lavinia..."

"Lavinia is folding the bedding," Medora snapped.

"But this is the Sabbath!"

"Sabbath it may be. But we still have to eat, and we still have to sleep, and people still get sick and need care. I want no more of your sass, young lady."

That gave William something to ponder. He settled himself with his back against a tree, his legs outstretched, his heels crushing the new buffalo grass releasing a fresh scent of spring. So what about the Sabbath day for the women? Of course, the answer was there in the good book; First Corinthians, eleventh chapter. *Man is not of the woman, but the woman of man... Neither was the man created for the woman,--but the woman for the man.* The Lord had made His intention clear--even for the Sabbath. William rested his head against the trunk feeling at peace.

With hooded eyes, he watched his wife move about the fire dodging the smoke when the breeze shifted. Still a beautiful woman in spite of bearing six children and living through those difficult years in Missouri that had taken two of their children. He had not had her since that night she shared his little tent when she'd given up her bed in the wagon to Elspeth. So little privacy traveling like this. A price one must pay. But the price she was paying, living like this, was even greater.

Guilt edged his feeling of love for his wife. She had not wanted to move on--and yet she was here. Always that sense of commitment--doing what she feels is her duty. *Like that other time.* Then it had been duty to her family to keep them from suffering for her shame, a thought that still stirred up torment inside him even now.

His gaze continued to follow Medora as she strode toward the Saunder's wagon with soup pail in hand, the folds of her dark woolen skirt molding gently to the curves of her hips. He'd like right now to be caressing the smooth white flesh under those folds. He lusted for her still, just as he had lusted for her that time so long ago.

He had been caught by her beauty the very first time he saw her. Like a fresh breath of spring, she and another young lady had come into the Gaylord Emporium where he worked as a clerk. The two flittered among the lavish displays, gay as butterflies sampling nectar, chatting and laughing girl fashion. She, the taller of the two, had eyes so blue and skin so fair. He wanted to look into those pools of blue. A ridiculous thought. Her dress and mannerisms spoke of wealth and culture. He was a lowly clerk behind a counter. It wasn't until later he learned she was the daughter of his employer.

Miss Gaylord came into the store often after that. She'd stop by his counter with a friendly "Hello." She sparkled as bright as sun-kissed dew, and he knew he was falling hopelessly in love. Hopeless indeed, dreaming of someone far beyond his reach. Once he became bold enough to ask her why he had never seen her until just recently. He remembered how her eyes had twinkled with laughter when she replied.

"I was in New Orleans learning Louisiana elegance. I attend Madame Tessier's school. She's a very fine French lady and she took us there so we could learn to be proper young ladies."

He was lost in the brightness of her smile and the sapphire blue of her eyes.

"We dined at tables set with gold and crystal, and were served..." Her eyebrows arched and she wrinkled her nose. *"Bisque d' Ecrevisse a la Cardinal and Escargots Bordelaise.* That's wriggly crayfish and snails, if you please."

He joined in her laughter.

"And we were kept cool by young black slaves fanning us with huge fans of peacock feathers. All that is supposed to prepare us for our introduction to society." She laughed again, and with each musical ripple his heart expanded. Fool that he was.

To behold, but never to possess. He'd heard she was promised to young Chatfield Youngston of the banking family. To see her became torture.

At that time the government had just opened a new county in Missouri for settlement. Land could be purchased for $1.25 an acre. He could leave and put distance between them. He'd also be honoring the promise he had made to his mother. He had saved some money, little enough to be sure, on the meager wage paid a clerk. But it was enough to strike out for Missouri. He purchased an old rickety wagon and a mule named Betsy.

Then, the incredible happened! *Incredible, indeed. He should have known.*

Especially after the shocking news about a duel--and the death of young Chatfield. When he told Miss Gaylord he was leaving, she reached across the counter and grabbed his hands. "Take me with you," she had said.

He could feel his face drain of color. How could his goddess be so cruel? "Please, Miss Gaylord, don't make fun with me."

"I mean it." Her voice dropped to a whisper. Color stained her cheeks. "I know it's not very proper. But Will, haven't you guessed?" There was a tremble in her voice. "I've known how you feel about me. Don't you know that I too..." Of course it was a lie. He should have guessed by the way she stumbled over the words. "Will--I--I--I want to go with you."

His first thought was how impossible it would be. The lovely Miss Gaylord pioneering to a wild and untamed country?

"Please, Will."

He wanted to believe. Oh, days of such innocence. The memory was still bitter even after these many years. Not until later, after they'd arrived in Missouri, had he learned the truth.

They were still using the crowded wagon as a make-shift leanto for sleeping. At that time it still seemed a miracle--this sweet beautiful creature had pledged her love and was now his wife. That night he had satisfied his needs feeling a profound fulfillment, wishing women also could realize the miraculous joy of joining. Of course, that was not a good woman's nature. He felt deep gratitude that she willingly obliged. He lay back, still gently caressing her sweet, smooth flesh. He wished he could express in words the appreciation he felt for her gift. It was then he realized an increasing fullness of her body. Could it be? He felt an overwhelming joy. Yet, she'd told him nothing.

He then felt the movement. Strong. Definite. But they'd been married less than two months and he knew the truth! He seemed to be drowning.

Medora didn't deny it. She confessed she'd had a lover even though she'd been promised to Chatfield. She told about the duel. To escape the charge of murder, her lover had to flee. It was after he was gone that she learned she was carrying his child. And handy indeed was a fellow going to Missouri--a means of escape. She could prevent the heartbreaking disgrace for her family. Fool that he was!

A time of hurt and fury. He loathed her for using him thus. He had every right to abandon her then. But he didn't. He even agreed to keep her secret. To all the world, Lavinia was *his* child. Who would think otherwise?

But he knew. And Medora knew.

In return for his charity, she promised she'd be all that a wife should be. And she was--never denied his male needs.

In time, after the Lord entered his life, the hurt had almost healed, and he'd learned to forgive.

Now as he watched Medora over there at the Saunder's wagon, he counted his blessings. She had been a wonderful helpmate through the years. He could not have asked for more. He'd been the fool then--to believe she could have loved him. And now? Over the years, affection had grown on her part. He was grateful for that. And her pride in his accomplishments. He had seen it reflected in her eyes, in the smile on her dear lips for any of his business accomplishments. But love? He knew it was only her strong feeling of commitment to family--like it was before. *And he was grateful for the crumbs.*

But there was that secret phantasy he had--she lying naked, opening her legs to him, begging him to enter. Of course that never would happen, she the good woman she was.

By nightfall, the rest of the wagons were across the Big Blue. Early, the following morning, the long train was once again snaking across the prairie. But before they could stop for the noon break, a fight broke out when a restless traveler broke out of his place in line and surged ahead. Nerves were becoming taut. Tensions mounted. Most of the emigrants had left their homes long before the wagon train had formed out of Independence. The going had become harder than any had imagined. Disagreements and heated quarrels erupted often.

Sunrise and on the move. Weary animals already protesting. Rest at noon. Look for shade, if there was any--maybe under a wagon. Then on again. At night, exhausted sleep. The next day the same. Sometimes the road was firm, other times it was marshy with mud up to the axles. Creeks to cross. Steep banks to drop down. And the dirt and foulness. The men sometimes bathed in the creeks. Afterwards, more than once, William picked leeches from his tender parts. It was worse for the women--no privacy at all, emptying chamber pots in the morning--or off in groups spreading their skirts to form a screen. No wonder dispositions were becoming frazzled.

One evening, after an especially trying day, Owl jumped to the top of a barrel. "We're too large a group," he shouted. "With so many loose cattle, foraging is going to be more of a problem than ever. I'm suggesting that we separate--the ones going to Oregon and the ones going to California."

A hat went flying and the tosser yelled out, "Yeah, Russell."

Thus came the first separation. The following morning the Oregon contingent pulled out a couple of hours ahead of the ones whose sights were on California taking with them some of the problems such as the fellow with the 200 head of cattle.

William wished the Morgans had been ones to go on with the Oregon group--could save some future problems. He could see a showdown coming between Morgan and Reed with Eli always complaining about Reed's teamsters, about Reed's place in line, about whatever he could think of. Reed, on the other hand, had shown he had a quick temper; Morgan would push him only so far. William wondered if it could cause another split in the party. If it did, he hoped it would be Morgan they'd be rid of.

With all the problems the adults in the caravan were having, Torrey had her own personal cross-to-bear, one by the name of Virginia Reed. Not that the girl was unlikable. It was just that Virginia had a horse and she did not. Papa said it was a sin to covet your neighbor's possessions, but it was not easy to keep from it sometimes. Torrey wrote in her journal:

Virginia Reed does like to show off, always riding around on her pony. She invited me into her Palace Car one day, showing off again. It is like a real parlor inside, with cabinets and drawers and a sheet iron stove. There are special sleeping sections, not just feather quilts laid on the floor. Mrs. Reed was lying down with a wet towel across her forehead. Later, Virginia said she wished I had a horse so we could ride out and explore together. I am not sure I would even want to.

Beside Virginia Reed, there was Jake!

She now was beholding to him for saving her from the river. But she couldn't forget the night of the party back home, and the time in the tent during the storm. She had to admit he was rather handsome though. Other girls in the camp often cast glances his way. Well, they were welcome to him as far as she was concerned. Anyway, she always felt awkward around fellows, sort of tongue-tied except for the pert remarks that were want to slip out.

She was mulling over her problems one evening after supper had been cleared and dishes boxed, when old Mr. Madden got out his fiddle. That meant there'd soon be dancing. Torrey retreated to the shadows of the wagon to sit on a crate where she could watch but not be seen. She loved the dancing but hated the waiting to be asked. If she were pretty like Lavinia... Her sister never lacked for partners.

Torrey tugged at the cord that held her hair tight to the back of her neck and loosened the dark red curls. She shook her head and the mass tumbled free. Mama was always after her to take more pains with her hair. But why should she? It was Lavinia who had inherited her mother's beauty. She herself was more like Papa, and she liked it that way, except his hair was more brown with only a shimmer of red. Thank goodness hers was turning darker the older she got. She remembered the hated "carrot top" teasing of her younger days. And her nose! So short with a silly tilt--not a nice slender Grecian goddess nose like her mother's. Oh, well. Who cared? She didn't want a beau anyway. She'd much rather have a pony.

The tuning screech of the fiddle turned to a lively tune, and the dancers began stirring up dust. Torrey tapped her foot in time with the music. Lavinia was among the dancers, twirling her skirts. Virginia Reed too. While here she was hiding in the shadows, matting the grass with her toes and wondering if she dared go out where she could be seen.

"Why you back here for?"

Torrey jumped. She hadn't heard Jake come up behind her.

"I choose to sit here and watch."

"Cause nobody's asked you?"

"Lot you know. I had plenty of offers."

"Who? Just tell me who."

"No reason I should."

"Well I'm asking you to dance."

"And I'm refusing."

"Trouble with you, Torrey, is you're afraid to be with a fellow. If a man comes within six yards, ya bat 'em off with your smart remarks. Time you start growing up."

Torrey's tip-tilted nose tilted higher, but she could feel the flush stain her throat. "Why don't you vacate my private premises."

"Because I came to ask you to dance."

"If I wanted to dance, I'd be out there now--but not with you."

"So I'll join you in watching." Jake sat down on the crate beside her.

The fiddle twanged a lively tune. The rhythm itched inside her, tantalized her toes. The laughter from the dancers carried along with the music, beckoning, wheedling, seducing. Torrey's head bobbed in jig-time, setting the dark auburn tendrils bouncing. She tried to forget Jake was sitting beside her.

Jake rose and pulled at her hand. "Come on, Torrey. Don't be so stubborn."

The music cajoled and lured. "Well, maybe..."

It was a night to remember. The activity continued later than usual, and Torrey danced every one of the dances and was tolerably pleased that other young men asked her as well, although Jake was by far the best dancer. She gorged on the merriment, bubbled with delight. Her hair, no longer confined by a ribbon, sprayed out, swung around, cascaded about her shoulders. She sparkled with laughter.

Later, when Mr. Madden put away his fiddle, and the campfires were banked for the night, Torrey still overflowed with excitement. She had never before had so many dances. For the first time, she really felt like one of the sought after--almost like Lavinia.

Under the wagon, wrapped in her bedroll, the music still throbbed in her mind. The trembling leaves of a cottonwood seemed to be whispering, "Your own special night." Was it because she'd let her hair flow free--or because she'd made an effort to hold her tongue? Sleep was nonexistent. Billy was rolled up beside her in the deep untroubled sleep of an eight-year-old. Quietly she wriggled free from her blankets and crawled from under the wagon.

The air was cool after the hot day. She hugged her flannel nightgown tight about her, but the chill almost felt good. She darted through the camp. Insects paused their chirring, resuming their symphony as soon as she passed. In the far distance a prairie wolf howled and another answered. She heard the creak of a wagon--the one that belonged to the newlyweds. Some of the men would josh about the night-creaks of that wagon. The bridegroom's face would turn scarlet-red. Whatever went on... Torrey wasn't quite sure.

Now she was alone on the great vastness of the prairie, wrapped in the wonder of night's magic. She stretched her arms skyward as though reaching for stars. She breathed in the flower-scented air. A twig snapped behind her. Her startled cry was cut short as a hand covered her mouth.

"Quiet. It's only me."

Jake!

"What you doing out here alone? That's kind of crazy, you know."

She pulled at his hand. "Doesn't seem like I'm much alone."

"I saw you sneak away. Figured you might catch your death with nothing on but that bed gown." He draped a rough shirt over her shoulders, looped the sleeves in front, his arm brushing across the small nubbins of her breasts. She flinched, but stopped her tongue from a snappy remark. He probably hadn't meant to. The air was nippy, and the shirt felt good covering her shoulders.

He was still in back of her, his arms still pressing against her breasts. Somehow, it had a strange pleasurable feel. She did not pull away.

"It's a nice night," he said.

"Ummmm." For once she was at a loss for one of her pert remarks. It was kind of nice just standing here quiet sharing the night, even if it was with Jake. She'd never had a fellow's arms around her before.

He touched her hair. "I like it loose like this."

Then one hand cupped the tiny mound of her breast. It created a sensation she'd never felt before. She should jerk away, but she liked the tingling feeling. His other arm circled her waist, pulling her tighter against him. She felt an odd hardness against her buttocks. She made an effort to pull away from his grasp, but he turned her around and the hardness now pressed against the place between her thighs. A strange feeling that felt good, like something she wanted to have stay there. But somehow, she knew it was forbidden. She tried to push him away.

His arms were strong. They held her clamped tight like the vice Papa might use for gluing. Was he going to kiss her now? She was glad the night was so dark. *She'd pretend he was Don Stephano.*

His mouth came down against hers. Moist. Greedy. She was smothered in revulsion and jerked away. *Don Stephano wouldn't kiss her like that!*

Jake's arms still held her captive, but she turned her head.

"Sorry. Guess I should take it more careful-like 'till you get used to kissing."

His lips now moved across her cheek with caution, his tongue swiping out, just barely, like a bee seeking honey. She caught her breath in the enjoyment of the new sensual adventure. His lips reached the soft flesh of her earlobe with nibbling pecks, sending dazzling raptures clear to her toes. She was puzzled by these exquisite feelings. She should make him let go, but she was now enjoying this sensuous journey. His voice was husky when he said, "See, you know it feels good. You don't need to fight me. You ain't never been kissed before, have you?"

How could she answer with his mouth covering hers? This time his kiss was more gentle. His fingers worked up the nape of her neck through the heavy dark curls, and traced the shell-contour of her ear then moved to the pulsing beat in her throat. His thumb moved around in a soothing massage. Shock waves pulsed to below the region of her stomach. Why did she have these luscious feelings that made her all quivery inside? A sigh escaped her.

"See how good it is when you let it be."

His mouth again covered hers. She wasn't sure just how to respond.

"Open up," he whispered. "Let your mouth move against mine."

She parted her lips slightly. She liked the feeling so much she wound her arms around his neck to hold his lips to hers longer. The response in him was instantaneous. He opened his mouth wide, his tongue probing like a chisel to force her lips farther apart. He writhed against her, and that hardness that was pressing against her took on a new aggressive life. His hands went down and cupped the rounded cheeks of her bottom, drawing her up harder against that living thing.

That was enough!

She shoved so hard, he stumbled backwards. "For your information," she cried out unmindful of the sleeping camp not too far away, "I don't want to be kissed like that--especially by you!"

Her bare feet hardly touched the grass as she fled back toward the wagons, tearing his shirt from her shoulders and dropping it behind.

Once again in the protection of her blankets, her body trembled as though the night's cold had just caught up. Her heart pounded and her mind whirled as she tensed listening to the movements of the night.

She heard him come back to the camp and crawl into his bedroll over on the other side of their campfire. The night settled silently except for nature's friends chirping in the grass and the deep base croak of a frog down by the creek. But it still wasn't tranquil for Torrey. Sleep evaded her as she thrashed with questions. What had happened to her out there with Jake? She had liked it--and she had hated it--both and together. How could that be? She had wanted him to stop, yet she had wanted him to keep on. Was that an evil in her to want what she hated?

Her thoughts were nagged by her mother's past warnings made in hushed tones and shrouded in embarrassment with the suggestion of sin. *Never let a man touch you. Never let a man have his way!*

Had Jake had his way?

She shivered so violently she was afraid she was going to be sick. What was it men and women did together? Surely, she had stopped Jake in time. And never--NEVER--would she ever let him do it again!

Drowsiness at last overtook her. Finally, in that sweet euphoria that softly closes the door on reality, Jake was no longer there. Yet Torrey again experienced those luscious, delicious sensations as, in her dreams, she was clasped in the arms of Don Stephano. It was *he* who was untapping the wonderful depths of those strange new desires.

It was Don Stephano who was whispering, "I love you, my darling."

CHAPTER 11
California, Sacramento Valley
June 8, 1846

What the devil? thought Steve Magoffison as he puzzled over a message an Indian brought him from Captain Fremont. Fremont back in California? The last time he'd seen Fremont and his old company was when they had stopped here on his rancho on their way to Oregon after Castro had ordered the topographical party out of the province.

The message stated that a large body of armed Spaniards on horseback had been seen on their way to the Sacramento valley, destroying crops, burning houses, and driving off the cattle. Fremont urged every freeman in the valley to immediately meet him at his camp in the Buttes.

There had been other such reports before, Castro's men burning and looting in order to rid California of its American settlers. So far, they had proven to be nothing more than rumors, never any proof of burnings. Steve figured it was just Castro's plan to try and scare the Americans into leaving without actually taking action. But now, coming from Fremont...

Maybe war with Mexico has been declared and Fremont has returned to do battle, although he'd heard no such news. But California was so cut off by mountains and oceans, it often took months for news to reach the province.

More than a month had passed since Steve had set out on his quest to find James Clyman and tell him he was ready to join in the resistance against Castro. He'd caught up with the mountain man at Johnson's place where Clyman was still waiting for Lansford Hastings, the fellow Steve had met at Sutter's Fort, the one with the crazy plan of bringing emigrants to California by his shortcut.

Although Clyman himself was pulling out from the resistance in order to escort the group of disenchanted settlers over the mountains, he gave Steve the names of the others who were ready to get involved. Most were tough mountain men like Clyman himself, who had no property to protect. They just wanted to fight the Mexicans. One was Zeke Merritt, the trapper Steve had met at the fort the same time he'd met that dandy, Hastings. Steve had contacted the men on Clyman's list. All were ready and eager to take action if Castro began to carry out his threats. So far, nothing had happened. Now maybe something had. There was too much at stake to question. Steve decided he'd better saddle up and find out.

The Buttes, not too far from Steve's rancho, were strange up-cropping of land that rose high like great camel humps from the level of the valley floor. Spirit Mountain was what the Maidu Indians called them--a holy place--the roundhouse of the dead.

Steve urged Pepieto, his chestnut gelding, up the dry grassy slopes. He topped a rise and looked down on a forest of canvas tents, enough to house the sixty members of the United States Topographical Engineering Corps, with Fremont's skin tepee off to the side. A pungent smell of burning sagebrush hung over the camp, coming from the various mess fires. Rough looking leather-clad men lounged about, some cleaning rifles. A few were Delaware Indians, their buckskin dress profusely ornamented with beads and porcupine quills. A wave of nostalgia washed over Steve. He missed the old times with the corps; exploring the South Pass together, the Rockies, and then the following year the Cascades and then crossing the Sierra Nevada in the midst of winter. They'd almost perished in the snowdrifts. Times like those created a bond that nothing else could equal.

A small group of horsemen were coming in from the opposite side of the camp, obviously a hunting party returning. Strings of wild fowl swung from some of the saddles. One rider had a deer slung over the rump of his steed. Brent! By God, it was Brent, his long-time friend. Steve spurred Papieto to a lope as he shouted a greeting. Soon ruckus back-slapping and boisterous salutations took over as Steve met with his old comrades.

The flap of Captain Fremont's tepee was pulled aside and a small man with hawk-like features dressed in neat blue pantaloons and a deerskin hunting shirt stepped out. He walked over to Steve, his hand extended. "Mr. Magoffison, good to see you again."

"Thank you, sir. Good to see you again too," said Steve. He had a high regard for the young officer, only a few years older than himself.

From the start of their relationship, it had been one of friendship rather than following the usual protocol of officer and enlistee. But then, Fremont was not one of those by-the-book military men. He had an intensity in his manner that created great friends--or great enemies. Well Steve knew the talent his old commanding officer had for stirring up trouble. Impetuous. Reckless. Obstinate. That sure as hell was the captain--and why his men, all hardened, independent frontiersmen themselves, gave Fremont their boundless loyalty. The Delawares most of all. They'd go to hell for the captain if he'd ask them, which it sometimes seemed he did. A smile played around the corner of Steve's lips as he remembered with affection of past times spent with this feisty bantam leader.

After the initial salutation, the captain retreated to his tepee and Steve turned his attention back to Brent. Hell, it was good to see him--friends since childhood in Washington City and Harvard days and then together with the corps. B r e n t looked just the same, still wearing buckskin. Steve had worn leather gear, too, during those exploring times. Now he dressed in a light loose shirt, a short colorful jacket like the Spaniards wore, and leather *chaparajos* that protected his legs when riding through brush. As for Brent, the buckskin still seemed right. He was a rugged looking man, taller than Steve, although Steve reached six foot. Brent's hair was blond like Steve's, but not nearly as light--more sandy because of its redness. "That red is a mark of your cursedness," Steve used to say. Brent's features were hard and angular, with a nose too bony, a jaw too square, yet with a strong masculine handsomeness that the ladies always found most attractive, as Steve well knew.

"How is it you're back?" Steve wanted to know. "Last I heard you were in Oregon."

"We were. But we got tracked down by the marines." Brent nodded toward a fellow who was talking with some of the other men. To Steve he looked like a dude.

"Name is Archibald Gillespie. He turned up at Sutter's Fort looking for Fremont saying he had an urgent message. He was posing as a man traveling for his health, had come across Mexico. He turned out to be a United States Marine coming from Washington. Our old comrade, Sam Neal, still smiting for Sutter, helped track us down. They found us up on the Klamath. The captain called a right-about face. So here we are back in California."

"Does it mean we're at war? There's been rumors, but we're so cut off from the rest of the world."

Brent shrugged. "Who knows? The captain's not talking. I'd say we were ordered back here for some reason. I cornered Archibald. He said war hadn't happened yet when he was crossing Mexico, but he said they were ready. Maybe so."

By now the settlers and trappers began to trickle in. Steve knew most of the settlers and acknowledged their greetings. One was William Ide, a stockily-built farmer from the northern end of the valley. He'd been a school teacher before he came west, and his manner was astute and precise. The trappers were mostly rangy, foot-loose men with no land of their own to lose, but with strong hatred toward Castro and the Mexican laws. They were eager for action. The roughest and toughest of the lot was Ezekiel Merritt, still wearing his greasy leather togs and foxtail cap he had on when Steve had met him and Hastings at the fort. A fleeting thought--where would Hastings and Clyman be by now? Crossing those salt flats with the trusting people they were escorting? My God!

The day turned hot, and the men hunkered down under whatever shade they could find to wait for others to come.   Some passed around the *aguardiente*, the hot liquor burning a trail down their throats. Some cussed the Californios. "Lazy bastards they be. Just ride their horses, gamble, and fuck their women. They don't work the land like we do. Don't deserve this God-given land."

Steve didn't feel that way. He had many good friends among the Spaniards, finding them a friendly, hospitable people. General Mariano Vallejo of Sonoma, from whom he'd purchased most of his horses, was an especially good friend, one who was openly sympathetic toward the Americans, had even proposed California annex to the United States. He had been the comandante in the northern section before disagreements with Castro caused him to resign. Now his army barracks stood empty as he turned all his attention to ranching. Steve pointed out not all the Californios were like Castro.

The conversation drummed on, turning from politics to farming and the prospects of the future. Finally when the assembly had swelled to a fairly large group apart from Fremont's men, William Ide climbed up on a barrel. "Fellow Americans, may I please have your attention," he called out.

Some "ayes". Some "boos." Someone yelled, "Ide, why don't you keep your ass parked on the ground. We came to hear Captain Fremont, not you."

Another called out, "We want to know if war's been declared."

"Please, gentlemen, hear me out. I have talked privately with Captain Fremont. He asked me to be the spokesman. I said I'd oblige. As for the war, it appears inescapable. But as yet, Captain Fremont has had no actual conformation. Under the circumstances, he wants us to know that it's up to us settlers to determine our course of action." Captain Fremont, sitting on a boulder, nodded agreement.

Steve looked at Brent, his sun-bleached eyebrows rising. "What's our captain up to? He's the one that called us here?"

Brent shrugged.

"But first," continued Mr. Ide, "May I express our gratitude to you, Captain Fremont, for returning to the Sacramento Valley. Your presence here gives us a confidence nothing else could."

Approving shouts came from the men.

Mr. Ide cleared his throat with a couple of loud harumphs to reclaim the focus of the men. "So, fellow Americans--let me say--we have come to this new country planning on making this our home. We were sold the idea that it was a virtual paradise and that land was free. Pshaw! A desolate wilderness instead! But I'm here now, and so are you. And many of us have brought our families. We've gone through untold hardships just to get here."

Irritation pricked Steve. Why didn't the man get on with what he had to say instead of all this school-teacher prattle?

"Most of us have conformed to all the legal conditions," Ide went on. "I, myself, feel I'm entitled to my rights as a citizen. So I say, and I'm sure most of you agree, we will not be forcibly ejected and driven back to the States."

Ayes and yells. A farmer shouted, "Sure, and we won't turn tails and run."

Zeke Merritt yanked his foxtail cap from his head, waved it in the air and shouted, "I's s-s-s-seconds the motion. My damn gun's already cocked, so let's get on."

Captain Fremont climbed upon the boulder he'd been sitting on. He held up his hand to gain attention. "Definitely, you American settlers have suffered great indignities from General Castro. And if the latest reports are true..."

If they were true? Steve again raised an eyebrow as he looked at Brent. Then they were just rumors about Castro on the offensive--or perhaps a ruse of Fremont's to get the settlers to congregate here.

Fremont continued: "Certainly you men would be justified in any measure you might adopt to protect your land and your own safety. The question is, how long can you wait?"

"We're ready now," came a shout.

"Can we expect your support, Captain Fremont?"

"Gentlemen, you must understand my position. As an American Army officer, I am duty bound to remain neutral until orders come from my superiors."

Brent leaned toward Steve, a smile playing at the corners of his lips. "Our captain never let that stop him before."

Fremont's voice trembled with new urgency. "As a representative of the United States government, I can take no overt action. Except..." He paused, to lend added emphasis. "If American citizens are in actual physical danger, then it is my duty to protect them, even on foreign soil."

The captain's sharp gaze traversed the crowd. "I'd suggest a few of you hardy men group together--you men without wives and children, you who have little to lose but everything to gain." His gaze stopped at Zeke Merritt. "Chose a leader."

Zeke grinned under Fremont's scrutiny. He ran a grimy hand through his straggly beard. He shot a brown stream from the side of his mouth.

"If a few of you fearless men take it upon yourselves to confront the Mexicans. And if General Castro retaliates with intentions of bodily harm..."

Mr. Ide broke in. "Sir, are you saying that you and your men could then step in?"

"Protecting American citizens is my duty," Captain Fremont replied his shoulders squaring a little more. "But I can not provoke an action, unless we are at war."

Steve poked Brent in the ribs. "There it is. Our man knows how to flip a coin."

Suddenly, attention was focused on a rider on a sweating horse who was charging up the hill. Steve recognized him as a fellow rancher who had a place on the Sacramento River.

"Got news. Got news," the man yelled, skidding his horse to a stop. "Some Mexicans has just come through my place with a great bunch of horses. Near two hundert, I'd guess. Came from the Vallejo rancho and I'd say are heading for Sutter's Fort."

The man jumped from his horse. "Captain Fremont." He saluted in spite of the fact he was a civilian. "Figured I should report that a Lieutenant Arce is in charge, and boasting that General Castro ordered the horses to use em to drive us Yanks out of California. That's what he said, he did."

Steve felt a surge of excitement. Not just rumors this time. A swelling of energy charged the gathering.

"How many men in the party?" asked Fremont.

"Only a couple of officers and a few vaqueros."

"Sh-sh-shittin' hell, Captain, reckon this is the incident we be lookin' fer," yelled Zeke Merritt, his eyes bulging with expectation. "Let's saddle up, men. Let's go get us some yellow-bellied Spaniards and a string of hosses." Zeke grabbed up his rifle and started toward the corralled horses. Several other buckskin-clad men followed.

"I'm with you," yelled Brent. "Come on, Steve, let's get going."

Steve hesitated. He was willing and ready to make a stand against those damn blue and red uniforms with their bright silver buttons. But stealing a line of horses?

"Hey Steve, what's holding you up?"

Steve watched Merritt who was already swinging up on his horse and yelling orders, evidently taking charge. It was horse-stealing in Steve's book, and he wasn't sure he wanted to be a part of that.

Brent Kendrick was now on his black stallion. He pranced over to where Steve stood. "Come on, fellow."

"I'm going back to my rancho," said Steve.

"What damn talk is that?"

"Kendrick is right, Mr. Magoffison." It was Fremont who'd come up from behind. Steve spun around to face the captain.

"We may not have a declared war as yet, at least as far as we know, but it's war nevertheless," Fremont said. "It's been reported that Castro has six hundred recruits at his Santa Clara headquarters. You can believe they'll be on the march as soon as they get those mounts."

Steve felt torn.

"Strategy is important," said Fremont. There was an unusual glitter in his eyes. Steve knew the captain was chomping at the bit wanting to get into action himself, galling, no doubt, to have to stay back waiting on the side lines.

Steve didn't mull it for long. The captain was right. And Brent was right. Also, that tough mountaineer. An action, such as this, would get something started, yet not cost a lot of American lives. Castro was bound to retaliate if his horses were taken. Then, if Americans were attacked--Fremont would have the right to get in the fight. Now it all made sense.

Steve climbed onto his horse and followed behind the scraggly group who were already heading down through the manzanita and buckeye toward Sutter's Fort.

Near evening they stopped at the fort. Lieutenant Arce and his horses had been there and gone, but it wasn't hard to pick up the trail of a large herd of horses. The men crossed the American River and pushed on toward the Cosumnes River where they camped for the night.

They rose before daylight. Dawn was just breaking when they came upon the camp of Lieutenant Arce. Not even a guard was posted. Peaceful. Sleeping like babies without a care in the world.

Long Bob Semple, a frontiersman who stood six-foot eight in his moccasins, took charge of securing the herd of fine looking *mestenos.* Some whinnied in fright, but hell, with so many, who could tell what was going on? Zeke gave orders with hand signals. He, Brent, Steve, and a Kentuckian noted for his ability to load faster and fire with more accuracy than any other man on the Pacific Coast, moved among the sleeping men, stealthily removing swords that lay beside them. By now, Steve was flared for the adventure. Like old times when he traveled with Fremont.

Suddenly, the early dawn cracked with an ear-splitting yell from Zeke. The Mexicans jumped from their bedrolls and reached for their weapons that were no longer there.

"Hah, you b-b-bastards have to move faster than that," laughed Zeke, his Kentucky long pointed directly toward Lieutenant Arce's middle.

The lieutenant regained his posture. Disgust and contempt crossed his handsome face. He squared his shoulders and glared at Merritt.

"Señor, what honor is this, sneaking up in the dark to catch us unawares? You consider this a victory?"

Zeke howled with laughter. "Looks like a v-v-victory to me. But if you don't think so--want us to return your d-d-damn hosses? Right? Then when you're fuckin' ready, you give us the s-s-signal. Si, señor? We'll move in and take em again--but this time, not so peaceful." Merritt laughed again and the Kentuckian laughed with him as he proudly rubbed his rifle. Lieutenant Arce's head stretched higher above his tight blue collar. His eyes flashed fire.

Zeke motioned for Steve to give the officer back his sword. "All right, you d-d-damned Spaniards. Ye can collect yer riding hosses and be gone. And tell that bastard Castro this is only the start. This time we only took hosses. We're now heading for Sonoma where these hosses comes from and take them fuckin' Vallejos. We'll take their whole damn fort as well with its cannons--any damn thing that might come in handy. Tell that to your fuckin comandante."

The two Mexican officers and their vaqueros wasted little time saddling up and taking off toward Santa Clara. Merritt laughed as he watched them disappear in a cloud of dust. He turned to the men. "Now, it's Sonoma fer us."

Steve looked at Merritt with surprise. "You can't be serious."

"Hell yes. You saw how easy this was. If you catch them lazy yeller-streaked Spaniards unaware, they run like hell if they get the chance."

"But why Sonoma?"

"That's where the Vallejos be."

"General Vallejo? Hell, he hasn't done anything against us settlers." Anger was beginning to throb in Steve's veins. "The general has always been the American's friend."

"The name Vallejo is 'nuff reason fer me. His brother sold me a no-good hoss a while back. As for the general, he's full of sh-sh-shit with his own importance. And there's them empty barracks of hisn. Make us damn good headquarters."

Headquarters! Prickles were rising at the back of Steve's neck. The plan was ridiculous. He certainly wouldn't be party to such a scheme.

William Ide, listening to the conversation, touched Zeke on the arm. "I can see the logic to your plan, Mr. Merritt. It was done in Texas. I'd say the time is ripe for the American's here. Taken just as a political prisoner, no harm need come to General Vallejo. And right you are about those empty barracks. Sonoma will be a good place to set up headquarters for a new California Republic--the Bear Republic we could call it."

Steve turned away in disgust. Mariano Vallejo was his friend. He picked up his saddle and strode over to where his horse was tethered. Brent followed.

"Where you taking off for?" Brent asked.

"For my rancho."

"You're not going to help herd these horses back to the Buttes?"

"I don't like stealing horses. And I'm not going to be a party to what Merritt and Ide are now suggesting. Hell, we're thirty-forty men. It's one thing to take a stand in protecting ones own property. But taking over a whole country?" Steve tossed the saddle over Pepieto's back and tightened the straps. He swung up, throwing his right leg over the saddle. The other men began gathering their gear.

Steve touched his hat. "Adios," he said.

Brent scowled. "Hell, I didn't figure you'd pull out on a job only half done."

Steve wasn't sure about that himself. He just had this gut-reaction. He hadn't felt right about taking the horses. He sure as hell couldn't be party to taking a friend as a hostage. He wondered what would happen in the next few days. What was to be California's future?

CHAPTER 12
The Overland Trail
June 14, 1846

Elspeth's shoulder had healed enough for the Morgans to once again keep their own camp. It was early morning and Elspeth had just stirred up the breakfast fire. At the same time she reached for the iron skillet to fry up some side pork, she glanced up at the sky to check for impending storm clouds. Her face went deathly white and she dropped the skillet. "Eli." Her voice was squeaky tight as though caught in her throat. "Did ye see that?"

"Hell, woman, see what?" Eli was sitting on a packing crate cleaning his rifle.

"The hawk! Eli, that be a blue feathered hawk!"

Eli had seen something flying overhead, but gave it no mind. Hawks were common enough out here on the prairie. No call for his woman to stand there with her mouth hanging open. "Hell, woman. Nothin' but a bird."

The hawk circled, round and round, coming lower and lower, screaming like the devil had its tail. Then it flipped its wings and sped off into a dawn-tinted sky.

"Eli, that be a powerful sign." Elspeth's voice was little more than a whisper. "Could be just the beginning."

"Oh shit, woman! Shet yer damn trap."

"A *blue* hawk, Eli. Means somethin' mighty fearful is goin' t'happin!"

Eli shot a stream of dark tobacco juice from the side of his mouth and gave Elspeth a scathing look. But a short time later, when his wagon broke an axle, he cursed his wife's prediction. Strange how it happened. He was hooking up his wagon when something spooked his mules. They darted crazy and pulled the wagon over a huge jutting rock.

Eli looked at his listing wagon. Hell, he didn't believe in her damn superstitions. Yet... He brushed at the sweat on his brow and felt the presence of doom.

Just those old damn Injun superstitions she was brought up on. Addleheaded, that's what she be. But looking at his leaning wagon--he couldn't shake the damn feeling.

Owl Russell trotted up on his horse. "What's the matter this time, Mr. Morgan?"

"Hell, can't ye see? My damn axle is broke."

"I'm not going to hold up the whole train again while you make your repairs."

Eli looked stricken. There wasn't a tree to be cut within more than a half days journey back. The vast stretches of dry prairie before them gave no suggestion of anything larger than sagebrush.

"Ye can't leave me stranded here alone," Morgan protested.

"I'll ask for volunteers." Owl trotted off.

Volunteers! Hell, he didn't want no volunteers snooping around his damn wagon. He gave the wheel a vicious kick. Goddamned piece of junk. He should have started out with new equipment like Zwiegmann and Dudley. But at that... Hell, his old wagon seemed sound, and putting in the false floor added extra strength to the body. Between the two floors he had hid the money he got from his land sale. But there was also another secret compartment where he'd hid his load of prized ginseng.

"Sang" was what Elspeth and her mountain people called it. That's where it came from. High quality stuff. Its sale would be double what he got in gold certificates from the sale of the farm. By taking it to Californy, he'd sell it to a captain of a ship going to China. Sure as hell, it will mean a lot more profit than selling it to a Cleveland trader, what Elspeth's brother had planned on doing.

Esco, a "sang" hunter in his mountain country of Tennessee, had stopped at their farm to see his sister on his way to Cleveland just before Eli and Elspeth were leaving for the west. With Esco arriving at that time, Eli, often cursing his luck, felt that for once his luck was changing.

Elspeth hadn't seen any of her kin since he took her away from Catalooch Creek, so she was powerful pleased to see Esco--and so was Eli when he learned what his wife's brother had in his pack.

Ginseng. Quality ginseng at that, with roots looking like a little old man with arms and legs sticking out and a prick between its legs. "Man Root," was what the Cherokees called quality ginseng if it had all them parts. Damn proud Esco was that he'd found it. And damn proud was Eli as well.

For centuries the Chinese had been using ginseng for healing and renewing the body, and some claimed, for adding to man's potency. Because it was becoming increasingly scarce, the Chinese were willing to pay a high price for the root, which increased its value so that bloody murders often resulted over the possession of the root. Especially quality ginseng like Esco had.

"But why ye takin' it to Cleveland?" Eli had asked.

"Thar be a trader there. He buys it to send it to Philadelphy fer a ship goin' ter China," Esco replied.

"Ye'll get only half its worth selling it to a trader. Ye'd make a mightier profit if ye went direct to Philadelphia."

"Nope. Cleveland be as fer as I aim. I be right anxious to get back to Catalooch Creek."

"Then let yer sister take it to Californy for ye."

Esco looked puzzled. "Californy? Whar that be?"

"West of the Mississippi a far piece on t'other side of the great Stonies. But once ye get there, yer most to China. Me and Elspeth be headed there now."

It took some doing, but Eli finally convinced Esco. If ye couldn't trust kinfolk, then who could ye trust? He would take the ginseng to Californy for Esco, and later return to Catalooch Creek with Esco's profit. "I'll jest keep a small amount of the money myself fer my trouble, a commission, so to speak."

Eli was glad his brother-in-law hadn't realized the extent of the distance to California, or he might have had some doubts as to whether or not Eli could get back with his fortune. And as Esco put a right good store in kinfolk...

But now, with this goddamned busted wagon, he might not even make it to Californy.

By now Owl Russell was far down the line shouting for the slow ones to get into place. Whips cracked and animals stomped and bellowed as they were jockeyed around. The dust stirred and swirled. Goddamn, they were getting ready to leave! And no one had offered him help! Anger swamped him. What would he do out here alone with a busted wagon?

Eli pulled a fresh plug of tobacco from his pocket and with frustrated force bit off a huge brown hunk. His eyes flashed hate for the whole damn party. Not one sonofabitch had offered. Proof of what he'd always known. No one ye could ever count on--not even that Bible-spoutin' Dudley. No one! Only yerself could ye count on.

A voice from behind caused Eli to spin around. "Colonel Russell says you're needing some help."

It was Rufus Quigley, the tallest and oldest of three brothers. He had come up astride his mule. The two other brothers were right behind.

"That I be," Morgan replied. Morgan had struck up a partial acquaintance with them because they championed mule-power for prairie travel as did he. However, the Quigleys were all single men and traveling light without a wagon. They carried their packs behind their saddles.

Russ, the shortest one, jumped from his mule and peered under the wagon. "Yep, sure 'nuff, you're axle is broke."

"We came to see what we could do to help," said Rufus.

Morgan felt a flood of relief. "What ye want fer draggin' me a tree back from that last stand of cottonwoods? I can't pay much, being a poor man. But I'll offer what I can."

"We ain't asking for pay, Mr. Morgan," said Rufus.

Eli squinted. "Then what be ye aimin'?"

"You're in trouble. We just came to help."

Russ broke in with "Some day *we* might need help. I reckon you'd help us if we needed it." The third brother, who had not yet spoken, smiled and nodded.

Rufus again spoke up. "After Colonel Russell asked for volunteers, we talked it over between us. So here we are, ready to be of service."

Eli still looked at them with suspicion. "Ye ain't askin' fer pay?"

Rufus smiled showing a broad expanse of large sized teeth under a flourishing mustache. "It's only right to be neighborly," he insisted. "Russ here has had experience as a carriage maker. We'll get you fixed up in no time after we once get the timber."

"Beats all," said Morgan, shaking his head. "It's more'n a half a day back to those trees. It could be two days before we catch up with the others again."

Elspeth, who had been boxing up the last of the breakfast dishes as the men were talking, stood up with the load in her arms. The extra exertion started her coughing.

"Here, let me help you with that," Rufus said, relieving Elspeth of her burden. "You sound mighty croupy, Mrs. Morgan." Setting the box down beside the wagon, he turned to Morgan. "I presume your wife will go on with the caravan. Surely, someone will make room."

Eli mulled it over. "Well, maybe the Dudleys," he said.

"Oh no, Eli," Elspeth protested. "The Dudleys be 'bout the nicest folks ye could look fer, but 'tain't right fer me to barge in on em again. I'll be all right here."

Russ frowned. "Rufus is right, Mrs. Morgan. With your cough. It could storm again, and out here with no protection when we're working on the wagon."

Eli wasn't about to let a protesting wife interfere with the Quigleys' concerned suggestion. "Gather up yer needs, woman. I'll ask the Dudleys now before they get movin'."

William, aware that Morgan had a broken axle, had stepped out of sight. Not this time. He'd volunteered enough in Morgan's behalf. Anton followed William.

"There's a limit to helping the bastard," the German said. Anton carried an extra axle but wasn't about to give that to Eli. Only a few other prudent travelers had spares as axletrees were heavy and took up precious room. "He never should have set out in the first place with that makeshift wagon."

"My feelings too," said William. This time he'd decided someone else could assist Morgan, if someone would. Eli had hardly endeared himself to others. But

THE VISIONARIES

suppose no one came forth? William felt only mild guilt thinking now that maybe they'd be shed of Eli.

"If he wasn't so tight fisted he would offer to pay someone to go back and cut him a tree," said Anton. "Some of the single men would jump at the chance for a few more dollars. I'll wager Eli won't suggest it. Ja, tighter than a mule's ass at fly time. You'd think he was dirt poor. You should waste no sympathy on him."

Medora, who had also heard of Eli's problem, approached the two men, her mouth set firm. "This time you're not going to do it," she said.

"Do what?" William asked pretending not to know what she meant.

"You're not going to be the good Samaritan. I know you. Your conscience gets the better of you, and the next thing you're helping him out. This time I'm the one who says no. Your family needs you too, and I don't intend to flounder alone while you stay behind to help the Morgans!"

William affected a concerned expression. "It does seem heartless..."

Medora cut him short. "We did the neighborly thing when we shared our camp after Elspeth's accident. There's others in this caravan who can see to them now."

William swallowed a smile. "I reckon you're right, Medora. My first responsibility is to you and the children." He assumed a troubled expression. "But leaving our neighbor stranded like that, do you think it is right?"

"I do." Medora gave a twitch of her shoulder that said the matter was settled, and turned back to her chores.

Anton looked at William and smiled. "Ja, so now it's the little lady who has given the order."

The first call of the bugle sounded, which meant the wagons were to get into line. Medora went in search of the children. She liked to have them inside when the wagons began to roll. One child had already been injured by falling under a wheel.

Eli Morgan stopped her. "Beg pardon, Mrs. Dudley."

"Yes?"

"Wonder if you'll let my woman travel with ye for a day or two until I get my busted wagon fixed. She's doing a mite poorly."

Medora felt instant resistance. *No, not again!*

"She's getting her duds together. She'll be over directly. Mighty kindly of ye."

Medora raked him with her eyes, her bosom heaved with anger. The effrontery of the man!

Elspeth shuffled up, a bundle in one hand and a pail in the other, her eyes down cast. "Mighty kindly o'ye to let me travel with ye." Her sallow complexion stained to pink with embarrassment. "I feels powerful bad bargin' in on ye again." She kicked at a stone with heavy brogans.

107

Such heavy shoes for a woman to wear! Concentrate on the brogans or else she'd be screaming like a fish wife. Once Elspeth had said she liked those kind of shoes because that's what she'd always wore, when she was lucky enough to have shoes, growing up in her Highland Hill country, and that's what her feet had shaped to.

Elspeth set the pail down on the ground. "I brought over some victuals. Some of my dried sweet 'tater slices that I growed last year; planted by the moon so they made good storin' 'taters. I'll make ye a sweet 'tater pie if ye like."

Medora made herself hold silent though still seething inside. From the thoughts that ran wild inside her head, she wanted to choose the right one. Looking at the pitiful woman in front of her, her anger died and changed to compassion. "Why, thank you, Elspeth. That's thoughtful of you."

"I likes to do my share."

Medora felt ashamed of her earlier thoughts. She put her arm across the bony shoulders. "Elspeth dear, we must do all we can to help each other."

Eli left the two women and walked over to where William was adjusting the yolk for his oxen. Elspeth cast a furtive glance at her departing husband. She then lowered her voice as she reached into her apron pocket and withdrew a small leather bag. "I got somthin' else I want to share with ye. Some of my sang."

"Sang?"

"Shhh." Elspeth lowered her voice to little more than a whisper. "Eli'd be powerful mad if he knew, but hit's all I have that's my own, and ye alays bein so good to me, I want to share what I have."

Elspeth opened the small bag and withdrew a dried root, shielding it from her husband's view by turning her back to the men.

Medora looked at it curiously. "What is it?"

"Hit be my remedy. The best root in the world. Cures anythin' a'tall. Jest now stopped my croupy spell. I chews up a bit an my hackin' alays stops." Her bulging eyes seemed to bulge more than usual. "Hit cures boils, runnin' off, an' anythin' else that ails ye."

"Is that ginseng?" Medora asked.

Elspeth nodded. "That's right, hit be sang. And this be red-rooted sang. Takes ten years t'grow to full time. The white root's more plentiful, but even that's hard to find now."

"Where did you get it?"

"My brother, Esco, gives it to me. Esco's a sang hunter in our Highlands home country. Best sang hunter I know. He knows the right places to look, where the ground be dark and rich, damp like a baby's bottom. And he never chances his luck. Alays passes up the first three plants then digs up the fourth, and never fergits to give his apology fer pullin' hit up. That's the way the Cherokees did, and they'd been sang huntin' long before my pappy come to those hills. So Esco does it jest the way the Injuns did. That's why he gets sech powerful prized quality."

Medora nodded. She'd heard about ginseng, and that it had become a scarce commodity. The root Elspeth had must have real value.

"I's got another one here in the bag. I want ye to have hit."

"Oh, dear no. I couldn't take it."

"Yes, fer ye t'have handy in case anthin' happens to the younguns. This here's the root I've been chewin' off. See--chewed most of t'head and neck parts off already, an' workin' down ter the chest. That's what ye do--chew the part that's like whar hit ails ye. Hit's mighty bitter, though. some likes t'brew hit up like a tea."

Then her popeyes sparkled with mischief. "Even be good fer yer girls. There be some claims hit be a love potion. I'll brew some up fer Miss Torrey." She gave a cackling laugh.

"Brew what for me?" asked Torrey, approaching the two women. Elspeth was so amused, she forgot to keep her voice to the whisper. "Sang. It brews up to a love potion. I'll fix some up fer ye sos to help Mr. Jake with his courtin'."

"Sang!" Torrey's eyes flashed. "Save your sang, whatever it is. Nothing can help Jake with that, as far as I'm concerned."

Eli, starting back to his wagon was close enough to hear Torrey's exclamation. His face mottled with anger. He stormed over to the knot of women and grabbed the root from his wife's hand as well as the small leather bag. "What ye doin' with that?" he demanded.

Elspeth flinched as though expecting a blow, but her voice had resistance. "Eli, that be my sang. Esco gave hit t'me. That hain't from the supply."

"Shet yer mouth, ye addleheaded woman!"

Medora's eyes flashed with anger. "Mr. Morgan, how dare you speak to your wife like that?"

"She be my woman!"

"Right now she's in the protection of our camp, and you're invited to leave!"

William, hearing the commotion came running over. "What's going on?"

"It's all right, William. Nothing I can't handle." Medora glared Eli Morgan down. A bugle sounded again to start the caravan rolling. "Come Elspeth," Medora said putting her arm around the shoulder of the skinny little woman.

"But he's got my sang," Elspeth protested. Morgan had stuffed both the root and the bag into his pocket.

"We'll take care of that later," Medora said, leading the small woman away. All she wanted was to have Eli out of her sight. "Come, I'll help you up in the wagon. It's time to go."

Morgan, back with his own wagon, watched the long line head west, watched until the last wagon had passed him. He was still shaking mad. That stupid woman had exposed the fact that he carried ginseng. He wondered how many had heard. Dudley? *The Quigleys?*

Rufus Quigley's voice brought him back to the problem at hand. "Eli, we better get started. Could be four or five hours back to that stand of timber."

Morgan looked at his listing rig. "I can't leave my wagon unprotected." Yet the only visible signs of life besides themselves was the caravan now being swallowed by distance.

"Reckon not," Rufus agreed. "Never know who might show up and help themselves to your valuables."

"Nothin' much of value," Eli stated. *Did the Quigleys know?* "Only the bare necessities to get me across the country. I'm jest a poor man, ye know. I'd be mighty obliged if a couple of ye Quigleys could go back and cut the tree. I'll stay here with my wagon. Ye can help yerself to my mules and save the strain on your own if ye like."

Rufus nodded. "Russ and I will go."

Eli looked at the man with suspicion. What's up? he wondered. Would they actually go off and let him stay behind with his wagon?

Rufus checked the position of the sun. "We should be back before sundown. Rodney can stay with you so you won't have to wait it out alone. He's not much help right now anyway. Had a bad case of flux. He's still showing some weakness."

"Still wobblier than a newborn colt," Rodney said.

Morgan could hardly believe his luck as he watched Rufus and Russ disappear in the distance on their mules, taking along one of his that would be used to drag back a tree. Rodney rolled under the wagon for a snooze. Reckon seein' has to mean believin'. Eli shook his head and set to rest his earlier fears.

That afternoon another sudden rainstorm came up and bogged the trail, making travel difficult for the wagon train. Some wanted to stop early, but Owl Russell wouldn't hear of it. "I'm not calling a halt this soon in the day. We've lost too much time of late."

It was already the middle of June and they were still 200 miles from Fort Laramie. At least the rain had settled the dust, now so heavy with alkali that made eyes burn. The rain ceased before evening, but the sky hung dark and low. Haste would have to be made for the evening meal before darkness settled in. And it could rain again before they were through.

The men unhitched the teams and drove them to a meadow. It was no longer necessary to corral the bovines since they'd moved into buffalo country. The Indians, with plenty of bison for food, did not need to steal the less desirable cattle. The camp too had enjoyed buffalo meat brought in by James Reed. Although the tasty steaks were relished, some of the men still grumbled, envious that Reed had the freedom to hunt and they did not.

The only fuel available for cooking in this treeless country was the dried manure of the buffalo, but it made a fine, almost smokeless flame if put in a shallow trench with dry grass in the bottom.

Medora handed Torrey a gunny sack and asked her to go out and gather some of the prairie fuel.

"Prairie fuel! Ugh." Torrey scrunched up her nose. "Mama, why can't you call it by what it is--buffalo turds--or more rightly, buffalo..." She didn't say the word, but merriment danced in her eyes anticipating her mother's reaction.

"Torrey, I have a bar of lye soap handy. I declare, I'm going to use it on that mouth of yours. Now go do your chores." Lavinia was mixing up a pan of biscuits without being told. What a blessing to have at least one daughter who gave her few problems.

Elspeth asked what she could do to help, but she was coughing so much, Medora told her to just sit and rest. Elspeth sat down on a box resting her back against a wheel, but her face was tight with worry. Occasionally she'd get up to look down the trail, then up at the sky.

"Elspeth, what *is* the matter?" Her fidgeting was making Medora nervous.

"Hit's 'cause I had a sign this morning. I've been fretin' since."

Torrey snapped to attention. "A sign?"

Elspeth nodded. "I saw a blue hawk flyin'. Means somethnin' fearful will happen. Likely, someone's goin' ter die! I fret about Eli."

Torrey remembered. Elspeth's grandmother had seen a blue hawk and her grandfather had died. Eli? Left behind without much protection. They'd seen signs of Indians. Billy, tossing buffalo chips into the trench, stopped and stared at the scrawny woman, his eyes bright with interest.

Medora flushed with anger. "Elspeth, that's just a ridiculous superstition!"

"It be a fact, ma'am. A blue hawk be a mighty bad sign."

"Geeminy-gee," said Billy. His mouth dropped open.

"Elspeth, I don't want my children hearing such nonsense!"

Elspeth's bulging eyes clouded with tears. "I'm right sorry, Mis' Dudley. I didn't mean t'say somethin' ye wouldn't think proper fer yer younguns to hear. It's jest that I been so anxious. T'was right selfish of me jest to think of m'self."

Medora felt ashamed. She should not have lashed out at the poor woman like that. Those myths were frighteningly real to her. However, she couldn't let her children be influenced by such bizarre fantasies. Thank goodness, Eli should be back with his wagon by tomorrow.

After the evening meal a few falling drops indicated more rain was coming. William hurriedly put up the small tent for himself, Billy and Torrey. Elspeth had already spread her bedroll under the wagon. Medora frowned when she saw it.

"Elspeth, you won't have enough protection under the wagon, and you with that cough." Irritation prickled again. Why, oh why did she feel it her duty...

"Hit jest be that I hain't--(cough)--got my sang-- (cough)--now to stop hit."

"I'll steep some butter with vinegar and honey. That might help."

"I don't like to put ye to bother."

A flash of lightening split the sky. Crashing rolls of thunder followed. Medora's brows drew together. "You certainly can't sleep on the ground under that wagon!"

"Oh Mis' Dudley, I won't put ye out of yer bed again."

"We'll see about that." Yet, she didn't want Elspeth in the wagon either, spraying her cough over Jenny and Lavinia.

Medora picked up a lantern and marched over to the supply wagon. Pulling down the tail gate, she called to her second daughter. "Torrey, come. We have work to do."

Soon boxes and bags were moved. A space was cleared. Bags of flour, beans, and cornmeal would serve as a mattress. And just in time. They'd hardly spread Elspeth's blankets inside the wagon when the down pour began.

At the time Eli had watched Rufus and Russ ride off, it seemed the axle repair was going off better than he'd first expected. But a scant half hour later the two brothers were back with Russ's head bound with a rag.

Russ climbed off his mule and hobbled like he could hardly move his ass around.

"What in hell happened to ye?" Eli asked.

"Got throwed by my mule," Russ replied. "One of those prairie dog holes."

"Wonder the mule didn't break its leg," said Rufus. "Russ got tossed against a boulder. Knocked him clean out. A mighty hard blow. Unfortunately, he's now hardly fit to cut timber."

Rodney, the brother who had stayed behind, came out from under the wagon. "You fellers back already?" He clutched his belly and groaned. "Oh Lordy, the flux is back again." He moaned like he was fit to die.

Rufus looked sorely troubled. "Morgan, it looks like it's now up to you and me to go after that timber. But you needn't worry about your wagon. My two brothers will be here to keep watch."

Keep watch? Eli had a sinking feeling. But what the hell could he do? He had to have the timber. Reluctantly, he left with Rufus. Coming back, dragging a tree, Eli's uneasiness increased as they neared the place where he'd left his wagon.

He turned to the man who was riding a few paces behind him. "Is that smoke up ahead?"

"I don't see any smoke." said Rufus.

"I kin smell the smoke."

Rufus sniffed. "Can't say that I do."

It started to rain, and the only smell then was of the wet earth. It rained so hard that visibility was cut to a scant few feet. Soon night and darkness were upon them with no moon at all. But the image remained with Eli.

The rain had stopped by the time they got back to where the wagon had been left. There was no smoke--nor was there a wagon--only a heap of wet, acrid smelling, smoldering ashes.

And Rufus yelling, "Russ! Rodney!" He was off his mule, running around like crazy. "My God! My brothers! Russ! Rodney!" He kicked something with his boot, stooped and picked up an arrow. "Indians. It must have been Indians!"

"Injuns, hell! Your brothers are gone and so's the stuff in my wagon. I'll kill the son-a-bitches!" Eli made a jump for Rufus. "Ye had it all planned!"

But he stared into the barrel of a gun. "Hold it there," said Rufus, and kicked the arrow toward Eli. "What do you think that is?"

Elli stooped and picked up the arrow. Injuns? A trick, he was sure.

"I'll hunt them down to my dying day," Rufus promised, "and Morgan, you're going to help me."

Help him, hell. Eli still believed it was the brothers who had set fire to his wagon. Hell yes, he'd help hunt them down.

No tracks could be found in the dark in the washed-away soil. They'd have to wait until morning to follow a trail--if there would still be a trail to follow.

Again it started to rain. The two men spread their bedrolls and canvas. Eli staked one of his mules right beside his bedroll, still having his doubts abut Rufus. He tried to sleep but when he'd begin to doze he'd awaken with a start with the sick feeling in his gut. Everything he had was gone--except for his mules and a small amount of gold he had in a pouch strapped around his waist. Thoughts churned through his tortured brain as suspicion grew.

The Quigleys. They'd been goddamned eager to help him. He knew from the start he shouldn't trust them. Did Rodney really have the flux? Was Russ really tossed from his mule? Had they somehow figured he had money hidden in his wagon? Had they heard Elspeth shout out about his ginseng? Their generous offer.

Hell, a fucking scheme, planned beforehand. The hours he and Rufus were gone gave the other two the time needed to tear his wagon apart, find his money and treasure, and set it afire to burn the evidence and make it look like Injuns. They'd probably planted the arrow.

Eli began to shake with hatred. His fury mounted. He reached for his pistol and tossed the blankets and canvas aside. The rain still pelted unceasingly. He released the safety catch on his weapon. *At least one of the Quigleys would have no use for his money!*

Silently, in the darkness of the wet night, Eli moved to the spot where Rufus had spread his canvas. But Rufus was no longer there--nor was his bedroll.

CHAPTER 13

The next morning was bright and clear, a good day for traveling as the rain had settled the dust. Elspeth, insisting on helping with breakfast mixed up a batch of biscuits, wrapped the dough in a wet cloth and covered them with glowing coals. "Nothin' good as ash cakes," she said.

Much too brown and crusty, Medora thought, as she ate one with her coffee. She preferred her Dutch oven for baking, but of course, wouldn't tell that to Elspeth. Instead she thanked the frail little woman for being so helpful. But when they stopped for the nooning meal, and Elspeth was seized with a coughing spell, Medora tactfully suggested Elspeth just sit and rest.

"Hit's 'cause Eli took my sang, reason I be coughin'," Elspeth apologized.

"Don't worry, dear. The girls will help. Torrey, you can start slicing the side pork."

"Ugh. It's so greasy."

Lavinia was already removing the butter churn from the side of the wagon where it hung, the jiggling motion having turned the cream to sweet butter. It was good their milch cow was still giving milk.

A custard sauce would be good over some stewed dried apples, Medora was thinking as she planned the meal. She dug a couple of eggs from the salt barrel. As long as they had no chickens, she was glad the salt did a fair job of preserving.

Elspeth, sitting on a stool by the fire, her coughing subsided, was watching Medora. A spark of amusement flashed in her eyes. "Ye gatherin' eggs from the barrel reminds me of old Henny. Did I's ever tell you 'bout old Henny?"

Oh dear, thought Medora, another one of her preposterous yarns. She hoped Eli would catch up to them this day. Her children had been exposed enough to Elspeth's farfetched tales.

"Ye could al'ays depend on old Henny," Elspeth continued in her soft mountain twang. "Laid a red egg every day o'the world, she did. Times when the hog meat runs out, we would still have fancy eatin's with dried shucky beans cooked with lard, and old Henny's egg--until the day of the weasel."

Torrey's russet brown eyes, all attention, focused on Elspeth. "Why? What happened with the weasel?"

"Torrey please. Keep on with your slicing. I'm ready for the pork."

"Well, hit whar wash day, an' the water in the brass kittle was a'boilin' away when I heered the noise in the hen house, and old Henny squawkin' like her time had come. Hit jest about had. I looks in and sees the weasel. I tries to shoo it out but hit gets hold o'my thumb and wouldn't let go."

"Geeminy-gee," said Billy, eyes like saucers. "What did you do?"

"I wasn't 'bout to let a vermin outsmart me. I sticks my hand in the wash kittle, the weasel still hangin' on. But hit soon drowned and boiled to good pickin's fer the rest of the chickens. But poor Henny. She got so sceered when she'd seen that weasel, she couldn't drop her egg that she was 'bout to lay. It got stuck in her crosswise and couldn't come out. Never again laid an egg."

"Oh, please, Elspeth," said Medora. But actually she herself had been so taken with Elspeth's story, that neither she or the others had noticed Eli riding up on his mule until he was right there at their camp.

Elspeth jumped up in surprise when she saw him. "Eli, thank the Lawd ye be back. Thought maybe I wouldn't see ye again."

"Of course I'm back," but his face was dark as a thunder cloud.

William ran up. "Where's your wagon? Couldn't get the axle fixed?"

"Wagon's gone. Done gone. Burned to the ground."

Elspeth's eyes bulged. "Lord o'mercy. Our wagon's burned?"

"Everything's burned. Every fuckin' thing's gone! Even my other mule! Damn bastard, even stole my other mule."

"Indians?" asked William.

"Hell no. Twain't Injuns. Twas those sonofbitches Quigleys. They robbed me, they did, and sets fire to my wagon, and took off with my other mule. Would have took this one if'n it hadn't been staked by my bedroll."

Now the other men crowded around.

"You saw them?" Anton asked.

"I didn't have to see 'em."

"Sure it was the Quigleys?"

"Hell yes it was the Quigleys."

"If you didn't see them..." said William.

"If I'd a'seen 'em, I'd a killed 'em right then. Those shitasses were gone by the time I found my wagon burned to the ground."

Then Eli told the story; how he was tricked into leaving his wagon, and how he would have killed Rufus if the sonofabitch hadn't disappeared in the night's storm, and how he would have gone after them all if the rain hadn't washed out all signs so he couldn't tell in which direction they'd headed.

"But I'll kill 'em. I'll find 'em, and kill every fuckin' one of 'em." His smokey eyes burned with hate.

Later, William and Medora talked quietly about what had happened, Medora's

116

feelings a potpourri of frustration, sympathy and anger. "You know what that means," she said. "We'll have to let Elspeth continue to use our supply wagon for sleeping. With that cough of hers--we can't turn her out in the weather."

She glanced over to where Elspeth sat huddled on a small barrel, looking much like an old bag of rags, smoking her pipe and rocking back and forth, shaking her head and mumbling to herself: "I knows it. I knows it--when I saw that blue hawk, I knows hit, an' it hain't over yit."

Medora shuddered. Not that she put any stock in what Elspeth was saying. But how could she insulate her children's formative minds against those corrosive myths?

William nodded, feeling no better about it than his wife did--having to put up with Eli. But what else to do?

The caravan traveled on, putting fifteen to twenty miles a day behind them. Long gone was the holiday spirit they had started with. Quarrels erupted often. Reason enough if one slept in drenched blankets, ate cold breakfast when the kindling was too damp to start a fire. And now, some of the animals were sickening and dying from the alkali water. Some of the travelers had been forced to lighten their loads. Along the way--the telltales--a cast off iron cook stove, a carved oak dresser, family treasures; from other caravans that had already passed this way.

With the Morgans now a permanent part of the Dudley group, a sullenness settled over their evening campfire. Elspeth's cough was getting worse. From the luminous brightness of her eyes, Medora suspected consumption. Poor woman. She had enough misery just being married to one like Eli.

Eli continued to bemoan his luck, now with nothing to his name but his mule and his gun, and a sick wife to boot. He spent his days roaming the prairie looking for the Quigleys, but in doing so, came across enough buffalo to keep their camp well supplied with fresh meat.

The dry, dusty drive left even the younger men exhausted by nightfall. Mike was quieter than usual and Jake seldom played his harmonica anymore. Torrey became more impudent than ever toward him. And Anton, although he'd sit back puffing on his Meerschaum, his hands still busy with his whittling, seemed strangely withdrawn as though something was preying on his mind. Medora wondered if it had anything to do with the friendship William had developed with James Reed. She knew Anton resented the man, but some of the other men did too. Personally she liked Mr. Reed. She felt it was a good friendship for William to cultivate, like her friendship with Tamsen. The Reeds and the Donners were intelligent and progressive people.

As for William, in spite of his facade that everything was fine, she could see that weariness now etched his face. She knew he was worried over his oxen. One was bloated from foul water and another one had developed a limp. She had a fierce desire to protect him--like she would the children. Love had not been there in the beginning of her marriage, but over the years a deep caring had come. She owed him so much. That he'd accepted another man's child as his own. Lavinia had never even known a difference. A good man, indeed. It hurt to see this country taking the heart out of him! *If only he hadn't had that obsession to own his own land.*

It was dry sagebrush country they were traveling as they followed the muddy Platte River. In the far distance huge rock formations began to form, like children's blocks piled one on top of another.

"Courthouse Rocks," Anton said. "And Chimney Rock, the great one. Looks like a finger poking the sky."

Crawling slowly onward across the sandy alkali plains, the uncanny visions grew larger, more spectacular, swelling to grandeur. There is beauty here, Medora admitted, and made some sketches. Beauty, that is, if you weren't one of the belabored ants trudging in line, one after another, following the creaking wagons with the everlasting jingle of harnesses, and forever smelling sweat and animal excrement. Oh, and the wind. The never-ending wind. It blew the alkali dust up from the wheels and filled your lungs, mouth, nose, ears, hair, and reddened your eyes. Medora thought of the goggles she'd seen in the stores when they were in Independence. Thirty-seven and a half cents was the price. At the time she wondered why any lady would ever wear anything so unbecoming. But now, she'd gladly pay many times that price to protect her tortured eyes from the glare and the gritty sand. She and most of the other travelers were now suffering from suppurating eyes and granulated lids.

It was afternoon. They were about to start moving again. Medora glanced quickly at the small mirror that hung on the side of the wagon and cringed. How frightful she looked! Her flaxen hair was dull with dust, and her face swollen from mosquito bites. Those intolerable insects--how they swarmed, especially at night.

She rubbed an angry red spot just below her eye, then gingerly picked at the loose, scaling skin on the end of her nose, flicking it off, exposing tender red flesh. Her sunbonnet just wasn't enough protection from the blistering sun and the ever-blowing wind. With forefinger she followed the slender straight bridge down to its tip. *A Grecian goddess nose.* Why on earth would she think of that now? And yet she could hear in her mind that soft French accent. *Ma cheri, you're such a princess.*

A suffocating memory washed over her with a terrible ache. So long ago. So

118

long ago. Rolling green lawns--her grandfather's plantation, the great stately house with its huge white columns. The clop of horses as handsome carriages drew up in front of the spreading terrace. Beautifully dressed people alighting. *He among them.* That teasing smile. Those snapping dark eyes.

Medora shook her head with impatience. Why resurrect such memories?--allow herself to be drenched in the misery of longing for days so long past!

She swept her hand across her forehead to wipe away the sweat, leaving dirt streaks across her fair skin. *Wagon tracks across my brain*! How much longer could she stand it? She ran her tongue over her dry, cracked lips. The day was so hot. And the swirling sand. She could hardly breathe. And always the stomping of animals, the endless turning of wheels.

But the memory was still there in the back of her mind. It was still there as she sat on the cross-seat as the wagon moved on.

Sixteen. She was sixteen at the time. Vulnerable. Ready for love. And he-- the visiting Frenchman with ties to royalty, as he claimed. But it was more than that. Medora closed her eyes. She could still picture his teasing smile, hear that soft rich voice; *Ma cheri, ma princess.* His touch that set her afire. Stolen kisses, fervent promises--the rapture of being in love. But there was Chatfield, and the duel. As always, the thought of Chatfield brought the crush of pain. Men and their honor. A duel meant blood, the smell of fear. It meant death for her dear friend of so many years, and she the one responsible. It meant her lover fleeing. The awful time that followed, and what she did to Will to protect her family. The shame of it. She had seen the longing in his eyes, this clerk in her father's emporium. When she learned he was making ready to leave, and she in such desperate need. She had tried to make it up to up to Will through the years. She'd tried to be a good wife. She'd never denied him his male needs. But now she thought of her own needs, and the walls and fences erected by propriety. It was there in black and white in one of her medical books: "A modest woman submits to her husband to please him, not to gratify her own sexual desires." She'd broken the rules with her lover, so the guilt was there. It helped her stay strong. With Will, when she'd feel the rise of desire, she would push it back as a "modest" woman should. She'd learned from that earlier weakness and had paid dearly. Now, eighteen years later, traveling this dusty trail, she was still paying.

"Medora." A voice startled her from her reminiscence. Her face flamed from her torturous thoughts.

Tamsen Donner was walking beside the wagon. "While we are traveling so slowly, would you care for a stroll?"

"Oh yes. I'd like that." A retrieve from those disquieting thoughts. "Lavinia is watching Jenny, and Torrey and Billy are off..." Medora's arched brows raised. "Who knows where?"

"Bring your sketch pad. We'll look for some specimens. Medora, I'm so pleased you've agreed to illustrate my nature book. What you've done so far--the colors are so vivid. You're truly a gifted artist."

Medora blushed from the praise, and made a modest attempt at denial, but was truly pleased.

As long as the wagons continued their snail-like crawl, it gave the two women time to tramp over the drying grasses and sagebrush. Soon they were absorbed in hunting new specimens for Tamsen's book, and Medora set aside her prickling memories. The two women chatted gaily, enjoying each others company, for the time forgetting the hardships of pioneering--until they came across two small mounds, each with its own crudely built cross.

"More graves," commented Tamsen. "We're seeing more and more as we travel on". The two women moved closer.

"Oh, Tamsen. The size. They must have been just babies." There was a catch in Medora's voice. She knelt to read the simple inscriptions scratched on stones placed at the base of each small knoll.

Richard Ellis, aged two years: June 8, 1846, only two weeks before. Mary Ellis, aged two months--two days later. *Bad water? Spoiled food? An over-turned wagon?*

"The poor, poor mother." Medora brushed at a tear that slid down her cheek. "To lose two of her babies at once." It revived the loss of her own two little boys as though it had happened only yesterday.

"Indeed," agreed Tamsen. "Nothing compares to the pain of losing a child." There was a sob in her voice too.

Medora nodded. "I know. I know." She'd seldom told others of her loss. The pain was too raw--always too near. But now she felt the need to share with this friend. "I had two little boys who died when we were pioneering in Missouri."

Tamsen put her arms around Medora's waist. "Oh my dear." The touch was comforting. "I too," Tamsen said. "I was married to a Mr. Eustis before I married Mr. Donner. It was a cholera epidemic during the Christmastide of 1831. It took my husband and my two children all within three weeks."

"Tamsen, what a dreadful tragedy to bear. Your children and your husband too! Oh, Tamsen. Tamsen." Tears spilled down Medora's face. She felt an overwhelming love for this small woman beside her. The sharing of their sorrows bound them together as nothing else ever could.

A slight gust of wind swirled around their skirts. It sucked up the alkali dust and twirled it into a small funnel between the two graves. Medora felt a twisting of pain akin to the miniature whirlwind, a silent grieving for herself, for Tamsen, and for this unknown woman who had lost these two babies--for all women whose arms were left empty.

For all women who must follow a husband's dream.

And as they stood together, Medora looked down on the brown head that shone with a few threads of silver. They had so much in common--both lovers of literature and learning. They both longed to reach for new horizons, yet accepting the limitations set by a social structure they could not change. They both had husbands who must seek new futures, and to whom they must acquiesce.

Now this other bond, the death of loved ones, the strongest of all. Medora felt a special closeness to Tamsen that she'd never felt for anyone before, a friend she'd always treasure. She offered a silent prayer that their friendship would continue forever.

CHAPTER 14

William carefully dug out the dirt from the deeply cloven regions of his ox's swollen and blistered hoof. He'd already lost an ox to the bloat. Starting out with only one spare yoke of oxen, he couldn't afford to lose another so it meant a constant check to take care of his animals as best he could. He was glad Owl had called a days halt of the caravan for those who needed time for repairs.

Anton, with stiff bristled brush in hand from giving his own animals a needed brushing, stopped for a moment to watch William and see if he needed a hand. He nodded his big shaggy head in approval as William softened the hoof with tallow then fashioned a rough boot from a square of steer skin and tied it over the infected hoof to keep out the dust and sand.

"Ja, for one who's spent his time tending store, still a good farmer you'll make."

James Reed strolled up with warm salutations of camaraderie. William's response was hearty but Anton gave only a cursory nod and went back to brushing his ox.

William frowned inwardly. He wished Anton's attitude toward James wasn't always so abrupt. Reed was a man worth knowing. He was glad his own friendship with James was progressing.

Reed watched the other two continue their labor for a moment then said, "Don't you two ever stop working? You know the old saying--all work and no play,"

Anton grunted. "If we don't, who else?" implying they didn't have all the paid hands that Reed had.

Reed ignored Anton's remark. "Your wagons all in good shape?"

"Tolerable. Nothing that can't wait for repairs until we get to Fort Laramie where we'll have the use of a forge," William said. "Got a little problem with this here bull"

"I was wondering if you could take some time to join me in a hunt."

William's eyes lit up. "Say, I'd like that." They'd been in buffalo country for some time, yet William had not had the chance for the sport himself, and Morgan had kept their camp well supplied with game for his and Elspeth's keep.

"You know old McBride?" Reed asked. William nodded. "He claims to be an old buffalo hunter, so I offered him a challenge. He accepted but then tells me your friend, Morgan, is going along. Now I need a partner to balance it out." Reed grinned. "Don't want to make them look puny by showing them up all by myself."

Arrogant bastard, thought Anton. He'd like to show the braggart a thing or two. However, he didn't think Reed had included him in the invitation. Besides, he had his trees to tend to and he wanted to use this precious stopping time to filter a few barrels of water, make it more fit for drinking.

"How about it?" Reed asked looking at William.

William felt mighty pleased that his friendship with Reed had developed to the point that Reed would ask him to join his hunt. Reed's horse, Glaucus, was the best horse in the entire company, and Reed's daring horsemanship would stack up to any professional hunter's. He'd already brought in more buffalo meat than anyone else, including Morgan.

"I'd like that, indeed. Soon as I finish here, I'm your man."

Reed turned to Anton. "You, Zwiegmann?"

"I have work to do," Anton said, the lines in his face tightening. William, already fantasizing about his trophies, had not even noticed Anton's curt reply. However, he was very much aware of the developing feud between Reed and Morgan, so he was a little surprised when the four hunters all started out together.

They reached a crest of an incline and William caught his breath scarcely believing what he saw as he looked down on a dark wave of flowing, moving creatures. Must be five or six hundred beasts. His pulse throbbed with excitement.

"Time now we part company," said Reed. "You two take the north. Dudley and I will circle around to the south."

McBride, a grizzled old timer, showed a tooth-gaping grin. "Right. But don't get too pissed when we skunk you." James Reed held up his prized Croddock pistol in challenge.

Sitting proudly astride his silver-grey Glaucus, Reed set the pace. William nudged Dancing Girl to follow. They approached the herd downwind. The animals below hadn't noticed them and continued a lethargic graze. Reed made a motion to take it slow.

"Don't aim for the heart," he said softly. "A buffalo bull can run a hundred yards with a bullet in his heart. And if the others see him run, they'll all panic. Aim for the lungs. He'll drop. The others will stand around and watch. They're really stupid creatures."

Steadily the two men followed down the heave of land and closed in on the herd. William cocked his rifle, inserted a cartridge and set the trigger, his heart pounding like an Indian drum. Dancing Girl's ears twitched with apprehension.

The wind changed direction and blew across the herd. An old bull raised his shaggy head and bellowed a warning. The animals began a slow movement away from the approaching men.

"Damn," said Reed. "We'll have to move fast now. They'll stampede when they see us."

He and Glaucus shot ahead, closing in on a gang of ten or twelve bulls. William had to kick Dancing Girl repeatedly to prod her to follow. A thick cloud of dust arose around the buffalos as the now panicked animals took flight. Reed darted into the moving herd, and before William could catch up, he heard the crack of a shot. By the time he again spotted James Reed, the wave had flowed on, Reed with it leaving the fallen game to be butchered later. William passed the young bull lying on the ground with blood spurting from a wound and out its nostrils and mouth.

The plains appeared to be one living, moving mass of bobbing rumps. Horns clattered, the ground rumbled and made thunder in William's head. The dust billowed around, seeped to his lungs, filled his nostrils. Another shot rang out as Reed downed his second calf.

"Next time it's yours," Reed yelled back.

A large bull in crazed frenzy separated from the rest and bounded across the plains. Reed motioned. William drummed the ribs of Dancing Girl with his heels but felt the horse's hesitancy. He nudged harder and finally worked her up to a good fast pace. The air streamed past his face. He pulsed with excitement. Glory! Glory!

Suddenly the old bull turned for battle and came to a sudden stand. His eyes shone hot. Dancing Girl also halted, about a hundred yards distance. Too far for a shot.

"Come on, old girl. Move in. Come on now!" William flipped the reins. Sweat ran down his armpits. His hands were sweaty on his rifle. He dug his heels harder into the horse's ribs. The mare stubbornly refused to move in closer.

"Come on, you dad blamed nag."

She tossed her head in defiance.

"Drad it. Move on!" He was shouting now, but to no avail.

It was now or never. William raised his rifle. He brushed the trigger. An explosion rang in his ears and a puff of smoke curled out from the barrel. The mare reared up--almost threw him.

But the huge buffalo just stood and continued to glare.

William shouted at Dancing Girl. He shouted at the bull. He shouted at himself. But most of all, he wanted to cry with frustration--with shame. He was letting his hunting partner down. He could picture Morgan gloating.

The bull turned and again was off on the run. William kicked Dancing Girl and they were again after the brute. But sadly, the act was repeated. Dancing Girl refused to move in close enough for an effective shot.

James Reed galloped up.

"Go ahead. You might as well get him," shouted William.

James saluted and took off on the chase, William following a distance behind. Disappointed as William was, it was a pleasure to watch Reed and the silver-grey in action. Reed was at full speed. The bull turned around to charge. Glaucus fell back, but then Reed snapped the reins and horse and rider dashed forward, Reed yelling at the top of his lungs. When near enough, he took aim. The ball entered the bull's shoulder and lodged in his lungs. Proudly, the towering animal stood a few seconds in place with blood seeping from his nostrils, then suddenly dropped to the ground.

"Magnificent! Magnificent!" shouted William, pulling up beside Reed. "That was a show to behold."

Before the days hunt was over, James was to shoot another bull and two more calves.

After that first wild rampage, the herd settled down and once again was grazing as though nothing at all had happened to disturb them. This time William dismounted. Dancing Girl was a lost cause--and he had to at least do something toward that challenge. He began to crawl through the tall grass quietly and cautiously toward the unsuspecting cluster of animals. Closer and closer. He edged to within seventy-five yards. Then closer. Silently. Almost afraid to breathe. On his belly, he inched his rifle along beside him. The wild grass scratched his face as he squirmed forward. He heard their snorting as they placidly ate. He smelt the strong buffalo stink. His skin prickled with excitement.

A very young bull raised his head and looked up curiously in Will's direction. *They've heard something!* No time to get any nearer now. It was as though his heart had stopped. *It's got to be now!* William pulled the trigger. The young bull turned to run, but about fifty yards distance, he dropped to the ground, blood foaming from his mouth.

Never had William felt so giddy with triumph. He had stalked and killed a buffalo! The largest thing he'd ever shot before was a coon. This was a monster! A mountain! He raised his arms wide and shouted "Hallelujah!"

The two men went back to their fallen prey and began butchering, cutting off the balls and throwing them away then slitting the jugular to let the blood drain out. William apologized that his horse proved so skittish.

"Some horses just can't stand the smell of buffalo," Reed said. "But you did your share."

They cut off as much of the choice pieces of meat as they could carry, leaving the balance for the wolves. All seven tongues were kept, a delicacy for sure, and proof of their kill. They met the other two hunters who had their share of meat but only five tongues as their trophies.

That evening William strutted proudly through the camp distributing some of their bounty. Soon, dripping grease was bursting to flame as the buffalo meat sizzled over the glowing coals at various campsites. A tantalizing aroma hung heavy in the air. Most agreed there was nothing as tasty as braised buffalo hump and grilled ribs. Later, the children clamored to scoop out the rich marrow pudding with fingers or sticks.

But at the Dudleys' camp two of the men did not participate in the evening's jubilation although they ate their share of buffalo. One was Eli Morgan who glumly complained, "So damned tough, can hardly chew it. Must be from that old bull Reed shot."

The other was Anton who had little to say as he concentrated on his whittling. He was tired hearing William go on about the hunt and his enthusiasm for Reed's remarkable hunting skills. Ja, Reed should be good when he did little else.

Morgan's surliness carried on to the following day. Early the next morning he made ready for another hunt, this time alone.

"Why?" William asked. "We've got enough fresh meat for a day or so. No sense in needless killing."

Eli didn't even reply, just rounded up his mule and was off. He hadn't yet returned when the days halt was called.

After unyoking his working team, William went out to where the loose cattle grazed to check on the ox he'd treated the day before. Good. The swelling was down.

James Reed sauntered up and squatted on his heels. Both men, still in the flush of victory, relived some of the excitement of yesterday's hunt. They were still jawing when William glanced over the prairie and noticed Morgan approaching on his mule. A good sized bundle was strapped behind the big man's saddle. "Looks like Morgan's had his luck today."

Morgan drew up beside them.

"Hunting must have been good," said William nodding toward Eli's poke.

"Good enough. Got me a buffalo skin that's a'ready been cured." He slid off his mule.

James Reed frowned. "Where'd you get that?"

Eli tossed Reed a belligerent look. "From an Injun. A dead Injun, fact is. Reckon he ain't needin' a warm blanket much as I do now."

Alarm spread through William. They were in Sioux country, and the Sioux were known to be hostile. "You killed an Indian?" he asked, dreading the answer.

Morgan tongued his chew to one side. "Didn't have to. He was a'ready dead."

Reed's brow tightened angrily. "Are you saying you took it from one of those scaffolds out there?"

"How'd ye guess?"

A chill shot through William. Reed had told him about coming across the scaffolds when he'd been out on his hunts. The Sioux wrapped their dead in buffalo robes and lay them out on a scaffold to dry for a year or more before burial. William was aghast at what Morgan had done. A heathen custom to be sure, but to the Indians a most sacred rite, and proper respect should be shown.

Reed's face turned purple with rage. He grabbed Eli by his open vest. "You damn fool grave-robber, do you realize what you've done? You've put this whole wagon train in danger!"

Morgan jerked away, giving Reed a shove. "Keep your fuckin' hands to yerself!"

Reed's reflex was automatic. He struck out with clenched fist but only grazed his target. Morgan came back with a forceful jab but Reed, quick and agile, sidestepped the blow and Morgan's fist only cut the air throwing him off balance. His anger heightened to blinding rage. He lunged again at Reed.

The ruckus had not gone unnoticed. Like an army of locusts, men swarmed in from all directions, Anton among them. Several rushed in on the two fighting men, separating Reed and Morgan and pinning their arms behind them.

"What the hell is this all about?" someone demanded.

"The fool robbed an Indian grave," Reed shouted. "Let me go so I can kill the bastard!"

Morgan's smoky eyes sparked with hatred. "Who the hell d'ye think ye be? Ye runnin' this here camp?" he yelled, struggling to free himself from his captors. He managed to break loose and made a dash toward his mule. He grabbed the bullwhip that hung on his saddle. Snapping it back, he cracked the whip forward, catching Reed across the head. William pounced on Morgan, preventing a second blow. Another bystander jumped in to help hold the frenzied Morgan and yank the whip away.

Reed staggered backwards, looking dazed. Blood ran down his forehead. He rubbed at the blood and his eyes blazed with fire. He reached for the long-blade knife sheathed at his belt. He lunged toward Morgan, but Anton grabbed Reed's flailing arm, and jerked it downward. The razor-sharp steel, intended for Morgan, ripped Reed's own trousers and pierced his leg.

Pain and fury masked Reed's face. He turned on Anton. The chunky German wrestled the knife away and tossed it just before a plunging fist caught him in the belly. Anton gasped. Another blow smashed his face just below the eye, and he lost his footing. As he fell, he tackled Reed by the legs and they both went sprawling.

The two men tossed, rolled, and pounded. Blood from Reed's wounds splattered them both. Although Anton was a head shorter, the two were equal in power and strength. Exhaustion finally proved the victor as the men were pulled apart.

Owl Russell run up. "What the hell's going on?"

Eli, cursing and thrashing, tried to break loose from the restraining hands as William filled Owl in with what had started the fracas.

"Let's string him up!" came a cry from someone. "Robbing a grave, the bastard!"

A trial was held right then and there with Owl Russell presiding. The final decision was that Morgan must return the robe. A number of men would go with him and see that he did. After that he'd be banished from the train, left to fend for himself alone on the prairie. He could keep his mule.

Medora was aghast when William told her the decision. "Leaving a man alone on the prairie? That's even more inhumane than hanging."

"It was an atrocious act. For the Indians, that's a sacred shrine," William said. "Actually, he's getting off easy. He'll probably get taken in by another wagon party if one comes along. If not--it's only a day or so to Fort Laramie."

"But what about Elspeth? What happens to her?"

Medora's question came as a surprise. In the demand for justice, William hadn't given a thought to Eli's wife.

"Well naturally--I reckon..." William was stammering.

"You reckon!" Medora's lips tightened, her blue eyes snapped. "Naturally--you reckon! What else? Of course she'll have to continue on with us--or should we turn her out on the prairie as well?"

Medora spun around and walked away, anger roiling inside her. It wasn't that she didn't feel sympathy for the poor woman. But she thought of the weeks ahead. That cough of Elspeth's--lung fever for sure. Could prove a danger to her children. Besides Elspeth's influence on them. Torrey especially, so taken. Problems. Problems. It certainly meant problems. Her anger seethed toward Morgan, toward William, toward all of the men. They thought only in terms of their own sense of justice!

Other repercussions followed. First, Owl Rusell said he'd had enough of the bickering and fighting. Another leader could be chosen. No one objected. Most of the travelers considered Owl Russell was mostly "say" with mighty little "do." And there was his hankering for the jug.

Since the Mormon threat had never materialized, Governor Bogg's name came up again for captain, but so did Anton's.

"A sound sensible man who doesn't take unnecessary chances yet knows how to get things done," someone said about the chunky German.

Reed wanted no part of Zwiegmann as captain. He was not a forgiving man. Because of the German's interference, he was now hobbling around with a wounded leg which kept him from riding his Glaucus.

Anton was outraged and spouted off to William. "If Reed's knife had found its mark, ja, it would have been Reed's neck stretched from a wagon tongue for murder. He should thank me for the favor."

Reed began campaigning for Boggs. Nearly half the members of the caravan, which included the Donners, said they would go along in favor of the ex-governor as captain. However, there were those who wanted no part of Reed or any of his suggestions. They held out for Zweigmann. The arguments became heated. The final outcome was that both men were elected and the wagon train would once again divide. Zwiegmann's party would lead out the next morning, Boggs' party the following day.

"Oh William, it can't be happening," Medora said, tears brimming. Tamsen had become so dear; they had so much in common. And there was the book. Separation would mean the end of doing the illustrations. William too. He must be as upset as she because of his friendship with Mr. Reed. "Do you think Anton would understand if we stayed with the Boggs' party? Oh, Will, I've never wanted anything so much as to keep on with the sketches."

William looked grim. "That's an awful lot to ask of my friendship with Anton. He loathes Reed so. If..."

"But Mr. Reed is your friend too. He's such a progressive man. Association with him could be beneficial for your future."

William nodded. There were many things to consider.

Torrey, too, was upset. She had finally reckoned with her envy over Virginia's pony when she herself did not have a horse and wanting one so badly she could taste it. Although Virginia was a year younger than she, Virginia was a very likeable girl, and they were finally becoming friends. She had lost Effie. She didn't want to lose another friend.

Even Anton didn't like the turn of events. He had not chosen to be captain, but if others had the faith in him... He would do his best to make wise decisions. He looked at William and felt a growing fear. His friend was so keen on Reed. Would he choose to go with Boggs in order to travel with Reed? But Anton was not one to grovel. He would accept what must be. But when he thought of Torrey... *His Liebchen.* Oh, to lose his *Liebchen.*

After supper Anton retreated and squatted in the shadows behind the wagons to smoke his pipe. As yet, William had made no commitment as to the group the Dudleys would travel with.

"Oh, so here you are," William said, spotting Anton. "Why aren't you with us at the campfire?"

"Needed time for thinking." Anton took a deep draft from his pipe then held it in front of him and blew a cloud of smoke.

William dropped down beside Anton and took his own pipe from his pocket. Nothing quite as companionable as a smoke with a friend. In William's mind there had never really been a question of choice--only disappointment. He liked and admired James Reed--a man worth knowing. He felt good that their friendship had ripened. But Anton was his very dear friend of long standing--like a brother. They had started together. They'd continue together. He did feel troubled for Medora's sake. But when decision had to be made...

They sat in silence, drawing on their pipes without saying a word. Finally William tapped his pipe on a rock to empty the ash. "Reckon I'd better go see if anything else needs doing to get ready. By the way, *captain*, what time do we pull out in the morning?"

The lines of Anton's mobile face softened. He removed his pipe and cradled the bowl in his palm, taking pleasure from its warmth. With a finger he traced the carving of the cheerful Burgermeister face. He chuckled. Filled with a rush of relief, he slapped William's knee. "Early. Ja, early. First light come morning we start, and leave our dust for the others."

It was a sad moment for Medora the next morning when she said good-by to Tamsen. She'd miss her friend no end. No more talks on literature. No more prairie walks together. No more excited discoveries of plants for the nature book.

"Why can't men learn to live peacefully together?" she said putting her arms around her friend.

"It won't be forever," said Tamsen. "We'll only be a day behind you, and likely we'll see each other at Fort Laramie if you lay over a day or so. And there will be California."

Medora felt a swelling of love for the tiny woman. "Tamsen, your friendship has meant so much to me, something I'll always treasure. And yes, of course there will be California." Medora smiled. "Ridiculous to get so wrought up. This separation certainly isn't the end of our friendship."

Yet, she had a strange feeling as though this truly was good-by.

CHAPTER 15

"Mrs. Dudley, can ye come?" The voice, no more than a whisper, was tight with anxiety. In the warmth of her bedroll under the wagon Torrey resented the intrusion. Her dream was too pleasant to give up to the sound of voices that had nothing to do with her Don Stephano, and just when her caballero was kissing the back of her hand.

Her mother's response cut in. "Yes, yes. What is it?"

"It's Bertha, Mrs. Dudley. Sorry to disturb ye, but I reckon it's her time."

"I'll be right there, Mr. Saunders."

The wagon jiggled--her mother moving around. The dull thud of receding footsteps meant Mr. Saunders was leaving. Billy, wrapped in a bedroll beside Torrey, groaned in his sleep. She opened her eyes. A faint glow in the east suggested the coming of morning. The wagon trembled as her mother climbed out. Torrey could just barely see her mother pulling a shawl across her shoulders and heading toward the Saunders' wagon. From beyond came the lowing of restless cattle and the sweet call of a whippoorwill. Around her--the scent of damp earth and pleasant smell of crushed buffalo grass.

Torrey squeezed her eyes shut to recapture her dream--her don's flashing black eyes. "Ah, my señorita, I've been waiting so long."

And so had she. My yes, so had she. Now every day of their travel--every day coming closer. Soon she'd meet Don Stephano in person. She was thankful there was now little talk of the war. Everyone had too many problems at hand without concerning themselves with the far distance. Oxen were dying from poison streams. Wagons breaking down. People with the flux. Maybe the war was over by now--Maybe it never was.

The camp began to awaken. Pans rattled. A child cried. Someone swore, and she guessed Mrs. Saunders was having her baby. Scary having a baby, she reckoned, according to the talk of some of the women. Men and children were shooed away like it was something sinful. Then later everyone "ohd" and "ahd" like a miracle had happened.

She'd seen pigs and puppies being born. Revolting with the licking and the cleaning. Of course, humans were different. She really wasn't sure what did take place when a baby was born, and it wasn't proper to ask. If Effie were here, they would guess and speculate together. She did miss Effie so, and now she even

131

missed Virginia. Mama said she was too young to know about certain things--her time would come. Yet she wasn't too young to be constantly reminded to act like a lady. "You're almost fifteen, not a child any longer," Mama was always saying.

Fifteen!

Today she *was* fifteen. This was her birthday!

Torrey felt a tumble of mixed emotions--the thought of new beginnings, new adventures. *Saying good-by to childhood.* A frightening thought. Some girls married at fifteen. Certainly it was not uncommon at sixteen. Then came babies and cooking and sewing and tending things. *Like Mama.*

Mama was sixteen when she married Papa, and seventeen when Lavinia was born. Well, she didn't want anything like that. She thought of Jake and the night that he followed her out on the prairie. In a way, what he did sort of felt good--but not with Jake! There was so much to being a woman that she'd as leaf not have--like that hated monthly business that started a few months past. Papa had said it went with the privilege of being a woman. Privilege, fiddlesticks! Mama hadn't even warned her what to expect. She had thought she was dying when it happened, and no one around 'cept Papa. How well she remembered. It almost ruined what had started out as the most exciting excursion of her life--that trip to Springfield with Papa.

They'd stayed in a real hotel and she had a room all to herself, a room with walls covered with red embossed paper and red velvet drapes at the window. She slept in a bed by herself, not having to share it with Lavinia. Papa's room adjoined hers. They'd dined that night in the hotel's elegant dining room, where they'd met Senator Magoffison. Oh, glory day. Later they'd attended the theater.

Afterwards she was too excited to sleep, her head dizzy from the exquisite evening. She could hear a distant bell ringing--the train bell on top of the old Globe Tavern, Springfield's first hotel Papa had told her. It pealed throughout the night, and Torrey wondered how anyone could sleep at the old Globe and was glad they were staying in this lovely new hotel. Her body still tingled with excitement, but something else--a heavy aching in the lower regions of her belly. Finally she dropped off to sleep.

Far later, when fingers of gray dawn reached between the partly closed draperies, she awoke with a cramping in her stomach. She moved and felt moisture trickling between the crack of her buttocks. Had she wet the bed? She sat up, pushed the heavy coverlet back and pulled up her nightgown. On the inner side of the gown a dark stain spread. Her heart pounded so hard, she thought it would burst through her skin. Dear God in heaven! Was she dying? Papa, come help me!

She was about to knock on the door to the room where her father slept when she was overcome with shame. How could she tell her father? She went back and sat on the edge of the bed, shivering in the semi-darkness. She was terrified. Afraid to tell Papa. Afraid not to.

Papa knocked on the door. "Torrey, time to get up."

She tried to answer, but no sound came out.

"Torrey, are you awake? We've got to get going."

She squeezed out a "Yes, Papa."

An extra pair of wool stockings in the satchel served as padding held in place by her drawers. After dressing she sat on the bed hugging her woolen cloak around her shoulders, but still felt chilled. Her teeth began to chatter.

"Torrey, are you ready?"

Even her toes were shaking.

"Torrey." The door opened. "Torrey, good heavens girl, what's the matter?"

Her face must have showed her shame. She stared at the floor.

"Torrey, what's the matter?"

Tears spilled over. "I can't--I can't tell you, Papa."

Her father pressed his hand against her forehead. "Do you feel sick?"

Torrey nodded. "I reckon. It's awful. I'm too shamed to tell you."

Her father's gaze searched hers and his own face paled. "Torrey, do you know--that is--has your mother explained to you about--well--about things?"

She brushed at the tears. "What do you mean?"

"Has she ever told..."

Even now Torrey remembered how her father had groped for words. "Blast it all. Has she ever told you about becoming a woman?"

She shook her head. Mama never told her anything! She knew something happened to Lavinia ever so often. Her sister became sulky and secretive. Once she'd asked and Lavinia had snapped, "It's none of your business. You'll find out yourself one of these days."

"Has something strange just happened?"

She nodded and again looked at the floor. She still could see the rose pattern woven into the carpet--reckon it was etched onto her brain forever.

"Torrey, listen to me. Don't be frightened. It's God's wonderful pattern for life. He's arranged it so in all forms of life--in plants, in animals, in people--for--for... Oh, blast it all! Now listen. It's nothing you must be frightened of--or ashamed of either. It's God's way of making you change from a child to a woman."

"Papa, I don't want to be a woman!"

He cupped her chin in his hand and tilted her face up. "You are a woman. A lovely woman. Thank the good Lord for the privilege."

Privilege! Rage had battered frenzied wings then as it did now. Being fifteen. Did it mean everything would be different? She didn't want things to change.

But things did change. The Saunders were no longer a family of two. They had a baby boy. Everyone congratulated them and the men slapped Saunders on the back for having the right recipe to produce a son. And when the caravan stopped for the noontime break, a marriage took place. A young man and woman, who'd never laid eyes on each other before the wagon train had formed outside of Independence, were joined in wedlock.

"It looks too much like making a hop, skip and a jump into matrimony without due consideration," Medora remarked to one of the women.

The woman nodded. "Yes. Young people don't always realize what marriage means." She had a baby in her arms, another pulling on her apron, and a swollen belly. I guess she knows, Medora thought.

As wagon master for a much smaller group than the one they had started with, Anton ran a tight schedule to make up for time lost. It was he who had suggested the bonding be performed during the nooning stop. Get the marriage service over in the early part of the day, then there'd be time for celebrating and dancing later during the evening stop.

It was a right beautiful day for a wedding, without the usual plaguing wind stirring up the alkali dust. Hot, to be sure, with the sun bright overhead and only a scrim of clouds streaking the sky. The young couple stood beside the bridegroom's wagon as the Reverend Mr. Cornwall performed the service and pronounced them man and wife.

Torrey sighed, seeing the way the young man looked at his bride. So romantic. Would Don Stephano look at her that way someday?

Everyone laughed when the new husband stooped to kiss his new wife, and finding her sunbonnet a hindrance, fumbled with its ribbons and mistakenly undid the top button of her high-necked dress.

"Must be getting impatient," someone said.

There came good-natured laughter. Even the bridegroom joined in, although his bride blushed to the roots of her dark brown hair.

The atmosphere around the whole wagon train seemed to throb with happy expectancy that day, a wondrous day of blessings and joy. A baby had been born quickly without resistance. A new couple had been joined in holy matrimony. There was the added anticipation for the later festivities. Food donations were planned; vinegar pie, corn dodgers to be topped with sugar drips, dried fruits of various kinds, and plenty of buffalo jerky to munch on. Some of the women started rummaging their trunks for finery they had not worn since their journey began, welcoming the excuse to exhibit some elegance.

"But don't think we've forgotten your birthday with all this other excitement going on," Medora said to Torrey, her sapphire eyes shining with love. "This is an important step in your life. It's the bridge from childhood to womanhood." Her hand reached and lightly caressed the dark auburn hair of her daughter. "My prayers are always for the best in your life. You must know that. I wish we could do more for you now on this very special day."

Medora thought of her own fifteenth birthday; a hundred people had come for her party. There was an orchestra for dancing, and a table laden with delectables: imperial crab, a tureen of turtle soup, platters of mutton flanked with ham, beef and turkey, and cakes and pastries of all kinds. The next day she'd left to attend Madam Tassier's School for Young Ladies. When Lavinia turned fifteen, they'd had a grand party for her, and then she was off for the Female Academy in Jackson. Poor Torrey. If only they could do the same for her. Well, out here on the prairie, she'd at least do what she could.

She sent Torrey to the river to wash some towels, an excuse to get her away. Then quickly Medora rummaged the supply wagon.

"I hope you don't mind if I disrupt your quarters," she said to Elspeth.

"My quarters! Oh Miz Dudley, you know those hain't my quarters. I be ever so grateful ye gives me a bed in yer wagon. Ye be sich an angel."

"They are your quarters for as long as you need them."

Medora found the flour barrel she wanted, then pushing up her sleeves, dug in to extract the dishes that had been buried for safe keeping. By the time Torrey returned, a board had been placed over a couple of barrels and spread with a fine linen cloth and set with the blue willow ware.

Seeing the dishes, Torrey's eyes stung with tears. "Oh, Mama. Your picture dishes!"

The blue and white dishes were Torrey's favorite. At home they'd never used wooden bowls or miss-matched pottery as many of the farm families did. Mama wanted things nice. For company, there was the extra fine china, now left stored with the judge. But for everyday use the table was always set with these blue and white dishes. Torrey loved the picture of the graceful willow tree, the high curved bridge and the lady waiting for her lover inside the teahouse. They'd been in Mama's family for years. They had come all the way from Canton, China Mama had told her. And now Mama had put them out especially for her birthday! Torrey swallowed the rush of tears. *She was fifteen!* She couldn't act like a baby.

"Mama, it is so--so elegant." For once she had such a close feel for her mother. She wanted to say more but the words got stuck in her throat.

Her mother's eyes were misty too. "I wish we could do more. I wanted something special for this very special day."

Her father came up hiding something behind his back, but the slender tip of a riding crop showed above his shoulder. Torrey's heart began to pound. Papa had

135

talked someone into selling him a horse!

He leaned over and kissed her cheek. "Happy Birthday, my dear," and handed her an exquisitely carved silver handled riding stick.

"Oh, Papa, how splendid." Her eyes were bright with expectations. "Does this mean... Oh, Papa, you've got me a horse?"

William hadn't expected his gift to misfire. Of course, he had promised the horse long ago. But he thought she understood that outfitting for the trip had taken most of his savings. The crop he'd found along the trail among a pile of household discards left by some unfortunate traveler. "I wish there was a horse to go with it," he said lamely. But then his face brightened to a smile. "Of course it means a horse--when we get to California. That I promise."

Torrey smothered her disappointment and put her arms around her father. "The crop is grand, Papa. I love it."

Anton also had a gift; this one *was* a horse, a small carved wooden one. "So now I should call you *Miss* Torrey. No longer the little girl who used to sit on my knee," Anton said.

Torrey turned the tiny figure, savoring its carved loveliness. Sleek of line, head arched high, foreleg raised in a stride with a long tail streaking behind, rubbed to a satin smoothness. "Oh, it's beautiful." Her impulse was to throw her arms around Anton, but something in the way he was looking at her suddenly made her feel shy. She touched his arm. "Thank you, Uncle Anton. I will treasure it forever." Then she reached over and lightly kissed his cheek.

It was Anton's turn to look embarrassed. He covered up by stating gruffly that they were wasting too much time with a wedding and now a birthday celebration. "Ja, better we get these wagons under way." He started off, but Torrey grabbed his arm.

"Thank you again, Uncle Anton. I truly will treasure it forever."

She started to climb into the wagon to put her gifts away when Jake stepped up.

"Reckon it's my turn now. Don't have no gift except to wish a happy birthday."

Torrey shrugged. "Not really that important."

One eyebrow raised which always gave him that handsome rakish look. "I'd say it's important. Reckon it now means you're old enough."

"Old enough for what?" She wanted no truck from Jake.

His grin was teasing. "Old enough. Reckon I know you better'n you think. Remember that night after the dancing?" The yellow and green flecks in his hazel eyes sparked with amusement. "Want you to know I'm still at your service."

Oh, how insufferable! "I don't need a thing from you, Jake Stringer!" She climbed over the tail gate into the wagon, her blood boiling. His chuckle followed her inside.

There was an hour left before sundown when Anton called a halt. Eager for the coming festivities, the travelers reined in their teams and scurried about selecting their individual campsites, some argued over whose turn it was to be closer to the river. The drovers headed the cattle toward a meadow. The luxuriant grass that had covered the prairie earlier was all but gone, but the bovine seemed content to nibble on the brown stubs that remained. The men set about with necessary chores while the women hurriedly put a light supper together for their families then turned their attention to preparing for the wedding spread.

Medora, mixing up a party cake she'd bake in her Dutch oven, told Torrey to get a gunnysack and go scrounge for some bison fuel.

Torrey protested. "Mama, on my birthday!"

"Birthday festivities are over. It's time for chores. Take Billy with you."

"Can't Billy go alone this time?"

"Certainly not. I'll not have an eight year-old wandering out beyond the camp by himself. Nor you either."

Torrey scowled, but picked up the limp bag and called to her brother.

They meandered among the cluster of wagons, Dusty-Dog trailing. Friendly greetings were passed with everyone looking forward to the evening's merrymaking. When the two passed by the Hornby wagon they stopped to inquire of Mrs. Hornby how her boy, Tuney, was.

Nine days before Tuney, one of Billy's playmates, had fallen off the tongue of a wagon and a wheel ran over his leg resulting in an ugly compound fracture. As there was no doctor aboard, someone fashioned a crude wooden splint and bound the leg with a bandage. Later, when inquiries were made as to the child's progress, Mrs. Hornby's answer was always, "Tolerable, thank ye."

Mrs. Hornby, a large husky woman, her face tired and drawn, looked up from tending her fire. Her husband sat on a box just staring ahead. He'd had a bad sunstroke several days before which left him nigh useless.

"Afternoon, Mrs. Hornby. Are you coming to the party this evening?" Torrey asked.

"Don't reckon we'll make it," Mrs. Hornby replied.

"How's Tuney doing this day?"

The woman's leather-like skin tightened and pulled at the corners of her mouth. "I'm afeared he's doing poorly, but he don't do much complainin'."

"Can we do anything to help?"

Mrs. Hornby started to shake her head, but then looked at Billy. "Mebbe t'would help to say howdy to him. The tyke gets mighty lonesome. Mebbe he'd like to see his friends."

"Sure," said Billy. "I'll be glad to say howdy to Tuney." He started climbing over the tailgate.

"Jest don't shake the wagon too much."

Torrey hesitated. She hardly knew the boy. But then she thought of the few times she'd been poorly and Mama had kept her in bed. She always welcomed visitors to break the monotony, so she also climbed into the wagon.

The relentless sun beating down on the canvas cover through the day had made it intolerably hot and the stench was awful. Torrey balled her fist against her nostril. How could the poor boy stand it? The child lay on a rumpled blanket on the floor of the wagon, a pail of water beside him. A damp cloth was stretched across his forehead. His face was flushed, a luminous haze glazed his eyes.

"Howdy, Tuney. We came to see you," said Billy. He started to kneel beside his playmate but pulled back because of the overpowering odor and the wild look in Tuney's eyes. The child babbled something that ended in a low, frightening moan. Billy backed out of the wagon, eyes round with fright.

Torrey's impulse was to follow her brother. Instead, she reached over and smoothed the child's stringy hair, so brittle to touch, it almost crackled. "It's all right, Tuney."

The boy said something again. Torrey couldn't understand. Must be a speck out of his head, she decided.

She removed the cloth and sopped it in the bucket, wringing it tight and then replaced it across his forehead. The child's flesh felt as hot as if a fire burned under the skin. His fingers picked at his covers.

Torrey felt prickles at the back of her neck. *Picking at covers--a sure sign of death, Elspeth had said.*

Tuney pushed the covers aside exposing his injured leg. Torrey backed away in horror. The mangled leg had putrefied, the green flesh so swollen it looked like stuffed gut casing ready to burst. And squirming over the oozing flesh was a mass of yellowish maggots!

Torrey pressed her hand to her mouth to hold back the vomit until she could get out of the wagon where she threw up behind the rig. Then, still wiping away the tags of discharge from her mouth, she faced the stricken mother. "How come you let Tuney get like that?"

The woman looked bewildered. "I done what I could."

"The worms! My golly, the worms!" Torrey screamed. "His leg is covered with worms!"

"I figured they be like leeches like old doc back home used to use."

"Those aren't leeches. They are horsefly maggots!"

Others, hearing Torrey shouting and figuring that Dudley girl was sassing a woman twice her age, came running, Anton among them.

"What's going on?" Anton demanded. Torrey told him.

Anton, outraged, demanded of Mrs. Hornby, "Why wasn't I told so we could have done more for your boy?"

Mrs. Hornby's face paled. Grime streaked her face where she brushed at a tear. "I was afeared. Someone told me Tuney's leg would have to come off." She raised frightened eyes to Anton. "What good's a farm boy with oney one leg?"

Anton looked even grimmer after he'd checked the boy himself. "Now--it's gangrene. Too late to be saved"

"Captain, you going to cut it off?" someone asked.

Anton shook his head, pain shadowed his eyes. "I'm not a doctor. The lad's already suffered too much. It's mercy we now have to show him."

Luke, a hired drover, dressed in fringed buckskin, stepped up. "I ain't no doctor either, but reckon I can help. I was surgeon's assistant to ol' Cap Anderson when I was in the army. I'll take a look."

He climbed into the wagon. When he reappeared he stated, "Yep, mortification's set in. The legs got to come off."

Mrs. Hornby gasped. Anton looked angry. "The boy's too far wasted to put him through that extra misery."

Mrs. Hornby clutched the leather sleeve of the drover. "Aye, ye gotta save my boy."

Anton shook his head, sorrow deep in his eyes. "*Gott in Himmel, Mutter*, don't wish more pain for your child."

Luke's mouth set stubborn. "It's her decision, captain. Hell, I've worked on ones worse'n this one and the men were out fightin' Injuns soon after."

Mrs. Hornby looked from Anton to the drover. Tearfully she said, "I have to be trustin'. Do what ye have to for my boy."

Anton's face was hard with disapproval. "I don't like to be a party to such doings. But you're the mother."

A makeshift operating platform was set up. They tied Tuney down and gave him a dose of laudanum to help with the pain. A cloth saturated with camphor was held to his nose. The would-be-surgeon called for a sharp butcher knife, a carpenter's handsaw, and a shoemaker's awl.

Mrs. Hornby's face drained of color when she saw the tools. Medora came over, placed her arm around the woman's waist. "Don't think you should be watching."

"But he's my boy." Mrs. Hornby sobbed.

"I know, dear, but the men will do all they can. Let's go over and wait at my campsite."

Torrey had seen all she wanted to see. Her imagination was already painting graphic pictures having once witnessed the slaughtering of a hog. She climbed into the covered wagon so her eyes could not have a chance to glance toward the scene. Too late she realized that out of sight was not out of hearing distance.

"Lord, we place this lad in your hands. Thy will be done," she heard the Reverend, Mr. Cornwall say.

Luke asked for a knife, and her blood chilled. A moment of silence before a cry of pain. Someone gasped. "Lord a'mighty, look at all that puss."

"Pieson bein' released. Now if you'd kindly hand me that smaller knife. I seen ol' Doc Anderson do it a hundered times. Dudley, if you hold back the skin so's I can start sawing through."

Torrey shuddered. Papa was out there helping!

Then came a pitiful moan that seemed to cut clear through to her innards. Torrey clamped her hands over her ears, the picture vivid in her mind's eye--the small boy stretched on the table. A few days before he was running, laughing, playing. Suppose it was Billy. Why should something like this happen to a child? Questions. Questions. Questions. And no answers. Only intolerable hurting--and anger.

Finally she uncovered her ears, hoping it now was over. But it wasn't.

"Hand me the saw again. This time I'll try above the knee."

Her palms covered her ears again. The throb at her temples felt like a buffalo stampede.

Minutes? Hours?

Cautiously she removed only one hand this time. No voices, but a sound of movement. Was it blessedly over at last? Then:

"Oh, my God. Can't the bleeding be stopped?"

"Hell, I can't see what I'm doing!"

"Stop it!" Her father's voice. Then, "You needn't do more. Thank merciful heaven, this poor child has returned to his Maker."

The wedding festivities were canceled. Instead, a solemn torchlight procession was formed and the members of the wagon train followed behind the wooden box that was carried to the boy's desert grave.

Later that evening, a saddened group settled around the Dudleys' campfire for a few minutes before retiring. Torrey noticed her father had little to say. Papa was such a caring man, it must have been mighty hard for him to be helping with the surgery. She could see her mother's concern the way she hovered over him, refilling his coffee cup before it was empty. When she sat down beside him, she reached for his hand and held it.

A day such as this that had started with joy but had ended with such sorrow certainly was one she should record in her journal. Torrey asked her mother if she could take a lamp inside the wagon.

She took the red-covered journal from its secret hiding place and cushioned herself on the feather comforter. Leaning against a barrel, Torrey closed her eyes, the journal unopened on her lap. She thought of her early morning dream. *Don Stephano.* A hundred years ago. Oh, foolish dreams. There was no Don Stephano. Pretending. Childish make-believe. She felt years older than the girl who had awakened that morning. The things that had happened this day made up the real world. A baby born. A wedding. A small boy died.

She bent back the spine of the journal. It fell open to the page that had the pasted-on picture of the handsome Spanish caballero astride the beautiful white horse. The flicker of the lamp light seemed to catch the sparkle in the man's very dark eyes, and emphasized the lettering done with a flourish that spelled out the name, Don Stephano.

Torrey picked up her pen. Carefully, she unscrewed the top of an ink bottle. Outside voices:

"Reckon it's time to turn in."

Anton's voice: "We'll start earlier. Make up for time lost this day."

Her mother: "Will, Jenny's gone to sleep in your arms. Here, let me take her. Billy, is your bedroll spread?"

And she'd written nothing so far. *Today is my birthday.* Then what? Where were the words that tumbled so freely from her mind. Now only the awful crush of sadness. A little boy dead. But another sadness. Was this saying good-by to her childhood?

Torrey dipped the pen into the inkwell. Below the picture, below the lettering that was done with a flourish, Torrey now wrote in a very plain script *Adios, Don Stephano.* The end of pretending.

A tear rolled down her cheek, dropped and smeared the page. Mama was right. She *had* crossed the bridge.

CHAPTER 16
Fort Laramie,
June 18, 1846

Anton and William topped a rise and looked down on Laramie Creek and, a few yards beyond, the clay walls of Fort Laramie. In the far distance were the grim Black Hills, a reminder of what lay ahead. They had ridden ahead of the wagon train to see about camping near the fort and to make arrangements for needed repairs of their equipment. But they were surprised to see directly behind the fort a forest of tapered lodges alive with scurrying Indians, a couple of hundred or more.

"Josh, what's going on?" William's voice was tight with apprehension. "What are we getting into?" He was thinking of the scaffold that Eli had robbed which more than likely belonged to one of those Indians' ancestors.

Anton shook his head. "Looks like the whole Sioux nation is down there."

And more were still coming, splashing through the creek on horses that dragged travois laden with family possessions. Squaws perched on top of pack saddles with babies strapped in baskets, and the older ones clinging behind. Countless dogs yipped with excitement, some burdened with their own miniature travois, bearing baskets of puppies or other less lively objects.

"Do you think it's a war party?" asked William.

Anton shook his head. "*Nein,* I think not so, not when they bring their whole village. A rendezvous perhaps, to come for trade. Come, we go down." Anton nudged his horse.

William hesitated a moment, but then followed Anton. He wished he had the same confidence that stout-necked German had.

They waded into the creek amidst the Indians. Water swirled around the legs of their mounts. Dogs nipped as half naked Indian children yelled and taunted their horses with sticks. But the smiles on the brown faces were friendly. A big handsome buck, cheeks adorned with vermilion, his ears hung with shell pendants and his neck with beads, looked at them with aloof curiosity, but splashed on by. Anton raised his eyebrows and nodded to William. "See, we have nothing to fear."

William returned a half-hearted smile.

After crossing the creek, they rode up a steep bank to the gateway of the fort, an imposing blockhouse entrance. The Indians, with whoops and hollers rode on, joining their kin behind the fort as William and Anton entered an arched passage.

They passed through a second gate that opened onto a large square courtyard with apartments or storerooms lining the fort's walls. At the far end, marked off by a walled partition, was a corral for the fort's horses and mules.

Indians were everywhere. Some reclined lazily in the sun and others stalked about. Squaws sat in the doorways of the apartments. Children scampered, babies shrieked. Some looked half-breed. There were white men as well, sinewy and weather-beaten, dressed in half Indian costumes. No doubt, French-Canadian traders. One, with a wild red beard, appeared to be haggling over a trade with a big Indian wrapped in a white buffalo robe. They were speaking a language William could not understand--French mixed with Indian, he reckoned. Other white men were checking huge bundles of pelts that were heaped on the ground.

"Ja, see. Here for trading," said Anton.

The two men slid from their mounts and tied them to a hitching rail. William was aware that they were being watched by a stout little man who was leaning against the railing of a stairway that led to a second-floor gallery. The man had a thick black beard and black curling hair that fell below his shoulders. He was dressed in a full-sleeved white homespun shirt and a fringed long leather vest. Throwing away the straw he'd been chewing, the fellow strode over toward William and Anton.

"Good afternoon, gentlemen," he said extending his hand. "I'm James Bordeaux. Mr. Papin, who is in charge of the fort, is not here at present so I'm taking care during his absence. Can I be of service?" His voice was pleasant, heavy with a French accent.

"Ja, thank you. I'm Anton Zwiegmann, wagon master for our party that arrives soon. And this is William Dudley." The men shook hands.

"Can we expect to replenish our supplies?"

"Whatever we have," Bordeaux replied amiably. "It's trading time, as you can see, so our supplies might run low. This is the American Fur Company's main trading post and Chief Smoke and his people have come to trade their furs for guns and powder."

Anton nodded. "Mostly we need the services of a blacksmith's forge to reset our iron tires. Got a lot of shrinkage from that hot desert air. We've been using wooden wedges to take the slack."

The black-haired man nodded. "Mr. Killian is our blacksmith, a very capable craftsman."

Anton looked satisfied. Tongues and axles also would need to be checked and reinforced; packs and canvas covers repaired. The most difficult terrain still lay ahead. Bordeaux assured Anton that the *engages* who worked at the fort would assist as much as they could.

While Anton asked questions, William looked around interested in the activity. Noticing the many doors that appeared to lead to quarters--at least nineteen at the ground level and two more off the gallery above, he wondered if any would be for let. Medora would think it mighty pleasant to be in a room with walls and a ceiling made of wood instead of canvas, a real bed to sleep on instead of a mattress on the wagon floor. *A room alone with Medora.* He thought of her soft body next to his. It had been a mighty long time since he'd cupped those soft warm mounds.

William's attention was brought back to the question at hand when Anton asked where they should park their wagons.

Bordeaux smiled. "Anywhere outside the fort you can find room."

"Are the Indians friendly?" William asked hesitantly.

"*Oui.* The Sioux's war plans at present are directed toward the Snakes, their long-time enemy. As for you emigrants, they are letting you pass across their lands quite unmolested." Amusement played on his lips. "But keep guards posted for your stock. They like to borrow. You should have no problems as long as you show them the normal courtesy they want. They're hospitable themselves, and they'll expect the same from you."

"Ja, so what courtesy do we show?"

"I'd suggest, after you've settled, tell your people to extend an invitation to Chief Smoke to come to your camp for a feast."

"A feast!" William's voice rose in dismay. Feast a whole Indian village? Supplies were dwindling and the trip was not even half over. For himself, his money was short if he had to purchase any more supplies.

"Just show your friendship. Serve coffee and biscuits. In gratitude, they might delight you with some interesting entertainment."

Entertainment? William pictured a demonstration of scalping.

"The squaws will probably paint their faces and put on their dancing dresses. Truly, it is quite an exhibition."

Anton thanked Mr. Bordeaux for the tips and said they'd follow his advice, and now they'd best get back to their party.

William was still thinking of a room alone with Medora. "Are you letting any of your rooms?" he asked Mr. Bordeaux.

"I'm sorry, Mr. Dudley. The apartments are all occupied by our *engages* who work here at the fort, by them and their Indian wives and children."

William face dropped in disappointment. "Of course, I was just thinking of my wife. She's a fine lady, and the trip has been hard. I was thinking how nice for her to have a real roof over her head for a couple of nights."

Bordeaux's eyes narrowed as he stroked his black beard. "Well, maybe so. Perhaps. There's Mr. Papin's apartment. While he is gone, I'm sure he would not object. Would you like to come see?"

William looked at Anton who nodded approval. He'd watch some of the bargaining.

William followed Bordeaux up the stairs to the gallery. The Frenchman opened one of the doors and the two men stepped inside.

It was a large barn-like room with only scant furnishings. A rough wooden bedstead with leather-strip webbing between the frame was pushed against the wall. It had neither mattress nor covers. There were two straight-backed chairs and a chest of drawers. On top of the chest was a tin pail to hold water; a board to cut tobacco upon lay beside it. A brass crucifix hung on the wall, and in the corner suspended from the ceiling hung a scalp with hair a full yard long. A heavy layer of dust lay over all.

Not much to offer Medora. But still--a change from the wagon. "I gather it hasn't been used for some time."

"Not since Mr. Papin left. I'll have Maria give it a sweep. Maria is my wife--Huntkalutawin her real name. She's a daughter of Lone Dog of the Red Lodge band of the Brules. I'll have her spread the bed with buffalo robes."

William's imagination jumped ahead. Dusty robes filled with vermin. He'd have to stop his pleasure to scratch. "Thank you kindly, Mr. Bordeaux. I must not put you to extra trouble. Don't worry about bedding. I'll bring the blankets from my wagon."

"No trouble at all," Mr. Bordeaux insisted.

Well, he reckoned he could remove them later. William motioned toward the scalp adorning the wall. "One thing... My wife is a bit squeamish."

The black-bearded man chuckled. "The trophy? *Oui.* Your misses would probably not appreciate that. I'll have Maria remove it. I'll also have her bring in a tub. Your misses would like a hot bath, no?"

"A real room? Oh, William, that would be heavenly." Medora pictured a four-poster bed, pictures on the wall, lace curtains at the window. "A real roof over our heads. Oh, my gracious!"

But when she learned that it would only be for herself and William--the children would be left with the wagon party outside the fort walls--"With all these Indians around? Oh no, Will, I wouldn't think of it."

"Mr.Bordeaux says the Indians are friendly, and Anton will be here--and Jake and Mike. Elspeth too. Lavinia can take care of Jenny and Torrey can watch Billy. Medora, you need a change. You've been looking peaked of late. The children will be fine."

Medora still hesitated. "Will, I just couldn't."

She saw the disappointment cross his face and felt guilty. She owed her husband some consideration as well as the children. *It would be nice to sleep in a bed under a roof.* "Well, maybe. I guess with Anton here..."

William gave Medora an unexpected hug. She smiled, but glanced around embarrassed to see if others had seen the demonstration.

"I'll go tell Mr. Bordeaux we'll use the room. It'll be a time before it's ready."

Following Mr. Bordeaux's advice, Anton sent Chief Smoke an invitation to come to their camp for refreshments. The women of the caravan started baking stacks of biscuits and opened up precious jars of preserves. Soon thirty or forty painted and decorated Indians came with Chief Smoke and squatted around within the circle of wagons. They consumed the treats with grunts of appreciation and noisily slurped mugs of steaming coffee. Medora told herself that they did appear friendly and apparently posed no threat.

Later, when she and William entered the fort, she was surprised at the hubbub of activity. Hearing snatches of conversation coming from the rough, leather clothed men, mostly spoken in French, stirred pleasant memories. French was such a beautiful language, and it had been a long time since she'd had an opportunity to use it. She wished they didn't talk so fast.

The stocky man with black hair and beard came toward them. His dark eyes reflected his admiration as he looked at Medora. She couldn't help but feel pleased. She tucked an unruly tendril of hair back in neatly under her bonnet.

Mr. Bordeaux extended both hands in welcome. "Ah, at last you have come."

William acknowledged Bordeaux's greeting. "Mr. Bordeaux, my wife Mrs. Dudley."

The frontiersman's slight bow was courteous. "Mrs. Dudley, it is my pleasure."

Medora felt a catch in her heart. *That deep French accent.* An undeniable memory began to stir.

"We are honored to have you grace our humble establishment." His eyes shone with approval. *So very dark.* So very like *his* eyes.

"Indeed, we are grateful to you," said William.

"Mr. Dudley, you didn't tell me your wife was so lovely."

Medora blushed. "How kind of you to say so, Mr. Bordeaux."

"Your apartment is ready. Maria, my wife, has prepared it for you and has taken up a tub. She and the children are carrying up the heated water now so it's ready for your bath."

Medora felt her color rise, having such a personal subject mentioned by a gentleman, but she graciously replied, "How thoughtful you are, Mr. Bordeaux."

"My pleasure, Mrs. Dudley. Later I'd be honored if you and Mr. Dudley would have supper with me."

Again the accent--again the rush of memory, but this time with a disturbing twinge--a memory that should stay buried. A memory that surfaced again with force a few minutes later when a handsome young rider entered the fort herding a stomping band of horses toward the corral. Handsome indeed, dressed in a tight frock of smoked deer-skin. As he turned she caught a full view of his face and sucked in her breath. Her heart did a turn. The same dark wavy hair. A body, lithe and slim that moved with a liquid motion that made horse and rider seem as one. He called out in French for the guard to open the gate. And as though her eyes were a magnet, he looked directly at her, smiled, removed his hat--with the same flourish she remembered, and bowed in her direction. Medora gasped. *Oh no. It couldn't be he!*

But the rider turned back to his herd as he ushered his charges into the corral. The guard clanked the gate shut behind him--and reason returned.

Of course it was not he. This young man must be in his twenties, but as handsome a horseman as Jacques had been to be sure, and with the same vibrant dash. Her memory was of eighteen years past. An illusion, of course. Just a strange illusion.

Mr. Bordeaux brought her back to the present when he said, "Oh, there's my wife now." Medora looked up toward the gallery and saw a plump barefoot Indian woman motioning that the room was ready.

"Don't expect too much," William said as he opened the apartment door. But it was still a shock for Medora when she stepped into the large ugly room, and even more of a shock to see her own coverlet spread across the rough wooden bed.

"How did my quilt get here?"

"I brought the bedding up this afternoon when you were serving Chief Smoke," William explained. He motioned toward a pile of dark buffalo robes heaped in the corner. "Mr. Bordeaux's wife had those robes on the bed. I hope she wasn't offended that I took them off, but I thought you'd be more comfortable with your own things."

William placed the tapestry satchel Medora had packed with things she'd need onto one of the chairs.

"I'll leave you now so you can enjoy the sweet luxury of your bath."

What pleasure to slip down into the watery warmth of the big wooden tub. Oh, how good. Clean water instead of that thick mud from the Platte. She soaped her body with her bar of lavender scented soap she'd taken from the satchel. A warm tub to doze in--let her thoughts drift. She rested her head back against the wooden side, her knees protruding up out of the water in soft creamy peaks. She closed her eyes.

The memory returned. Funny how a suggestion can capture another time like an old melody replays the past. That soft French accent of Mr. Bordeaux's. *So like his.* The young horseman had added to her musing. A mind primed and susceptible. For the moment, down there in the courtyard, it seemed surely he was Jacques Rouleau.

She had truly loved Jacques Rouleau. A school girl infatuation. Still... He was so handsome and so gallant. He had awakened desires in her she had never before known. Even now, with her naked body half submerged in the hypnotic warmth of the bath, she remembered the delicious taste of those kisses and felt that throb of desire his touch had created. She flushed with shame. What kind of woman was she to indulge in a reverie such as this? Especially, in light of what those kisses had led to. She closed her eyes. *The rapture. The ecstasy.* Medora shook her head. Why was she having such thoughts?

She looked at her light, satin flesh shimmering under the movement of the water. The ache of desire was becoming stronger than the shame. *If William were here...*

How many times in the past had she wanted to give in to the sweet pleasure when his hand cupped her breast? But then--always that barrier. Nice women don't indulge in such pleasures. She placed her own hand over the soapy slickness of the pillow of flesh and imagined it was Will's hand that was pressing and kneading ever so gently. Her hand followed down her wet torso, and her fingers twirled in the tangle of pubic hair. Why shouldn't women enjoy the pleasure when it was your husband you were with?

She splashed water over her breasts, rinsing them free of the soap. She studied the creamy-pink of her flesh. She raised her leg, pointed her toe and watched the water trickle down toward her torso. *Proper ladies don't even look at their bodies.* Yet, she was glad her limbs were round and still firm, and that the other parts of her body, which had not been exposed to the drying winds and hot desert sun, were still delicately pink. She touched the dryness of her face and neck. Would Jacques still find her desirable if he saw her now? Again, her mind drifted back to the pleasure of his touch before her guilt turned her own fervor to panic.

With Will... He was always gentle and considerate. He satisfied his needs, then let her be. But suppose this one time she gave in to her own wantonness--the first night in months together in a bed--no one else around. Suppose this one night it was different.

They dined with Mr. Bordeaux in one of the lower apartments; bread, buffalo meat, boiled rice, and tumblers of wine served by Maria on a rough wooden table.

William sipped the wine. "Hmmmm. Very good."

Mr. Bordeaux's pleasure was apparent as he looked at Medora. She was glad she had changed from the practical dark frock she usually wore, to the pale blue muslin that emphasized the blue of her eyes. The lace shawl draped across her shoulders, held in place at the throat by her mother's cameo broach, gave her a feeling of grace. She knew her hair shone like spun gold from the vigorous washing and brushing she'd given it before gathering it to a chignon at the back of her long slender neck, and she was glad she'd thought to rub on some of her lemon-verbena sachet. She was savoring Mr. Bordeaux's admiring glances, and responded with bright gay chatter. Even William was looking at her in a way he had not done for a very long time. It was a lovely evening.

When they finished their supper and had thanked their host, William went out to the camp to check on the children before turning in. Medora climbed the stairs to the gallery alone, still feeling a pleasant glow. Once again she'd been the belle of the ball, even if the swooning swains were only her husband and the chunky little frontiersman. Still, for this one evening, she'd had a chance to once again be a lady of charm. And now she'd sleep in a bed that was off the floor. *And Will would be beside her*. She hummed a little tune as she rubbed on more of the lemon-verbena sachet.

She was already in bed when he returned. "Is everything all right?" she asked when he came in.

"Fine. Except Elspeth had another coughing spell." And Jenny had an upset stomach, but William had decided he wouldn't mention that.

"Oh, poor woman."

"Still no sign of Eli." He had half hoped Morgan would show up here at the fort. Then they could turn Elspeth over to his care. No more than right, she being his wife. "Reckon we'll have to keep Elspeth with us. Can't just leave her here alone."

Oh Will, Medora thought, this one night--let's leave the Morgans and everything that has to do with that wagon train out there beyond the fort.

"Anton is making a check to be sure everyone takes care of needed repairs before we light out again."

Why is he so talkative? Will, can't you see I am here waiting?

She watched him undress. He was still a handsome man with those dark pointed eyebrows and the mustache he kept well clipped. Even wearing his plaid shirt and heavy-duty pantaloons that were beginning to show signs of wear, he had a certain buoyant flair. She remembered how impressive he always looked in his neat broadcloth frock coat and white silk vest he wore when he was managing the judge's businesses.

He was now down to his long underwear. *What would it be like if he removed that too?* She felt her color rise at such a thought--but also, her pulse had quickened.

He climbed into bed beside her.

Now she was conscious of his hard firm figure next to hers. Her own body, well clothed in her long flannel gown, pressed against him. Was it the wine? Was it the scent of the lemon-verbena? Was it those strange sinful thoughts she'd had when she lounged in the tub? The aching desire she'd felt when she'd massaged her soapy breasts began to surface again. Her hand fell across his chest. His underwear was unbuttoned to his navel. She could feel the crinkly hair, and curbed the desire to follow its course down further.

William was aware of her hand on his bare chest, and his desire all but exploded right then. Although he'd been concerned with the camp activities as he undressed, the subject was quite forgotten when he climbed into bed beside Medora. Her hair smelled fresh and clean, soft and silken next to his face. And there was something else--a wild sweet scent of some flower. Already he could feel the swelling in his loins. He'd gone without too long with Medora sleeping in the wagon and he on the ground. He was ready to mount.

"Wait, Will. Please wait." It was only a whisper.

He drew back. The usual hurt and disappointment surged through him. Of course, she didn't want him. She never had. Yet she'd never denied him. It was her obligation, and he'd rightfully taken his privilege. *Her obligation.* It was a bitter taste. But, of course, the way it was with good women.

The tips of her fingers were teasing the tangle of hair. She turned toward him. Her lips were so close. So tempting. He couldn't hold back. he pulled her roughly against him.

But again. "Wait, Will." It was still just a whisper as though the words were difficult to force out, yet her breath was hot on his neck. And it was she who fumbled with the buttons of her gown and released the swollen beauties that gleamed with the velvet richness of polished pearl as the moonlight from a tiny window streamed across them. A wondrous night. It was the first time she'd made the offering. He felt his heart pounding. He kissed the brown puckering, teased the nipples with his tongue. Finally, greedily, and it seemed she more than wanted him to, he took what he could in his mouth, sucking, pulling, surely flushing her with the same urgency that was consuming him.

She clung eagerly to him. He could feel her heart beating against his. It was the first time her lips opened to his. The first time her hands roamed his body. The first time she guided him in, seeming to want him there, wanting more and more of him, matching his tempo, matching his rhythm. Together they came with the final explosion. The first time for her, he was sure, to know the joy of that exquisite rapture.

The sun was streaming through the tiny window when he awoke the next morning. He resented the many things he must do that now demanded he leave the warmth of the bed--leave the sweet, soft sleeping woman beside him. He wanted to take her again, recapture those moments of wonder. Was it because they'd slept apart these many weeks? He had certainly hungered for her. Had she been hungering for him the same way? He still felt the warm glow. That phantasy he'd always had--she lying naked, legs spread, inviting him in. It had almost come true.

CHAPTER 17

Medora awoke slowly, stretched luxuriously, moved her long slender legs and wiggled her toes, enjoying the softness of the bed in comparison to the hard wooden floor of the wagon. Still filled with the delicious memory of the night before, she reached to the other side of the bed. William was no longer there and she felt disappointed. *But last night she'd been so brazen!* Only women of another sort would have enjoyed such pleasure. From what she'd always been taught, she should be hanging her head in shame. Instead, a smile played her lips. She closed her eyes. The remembrance of ecstasy. They had given each other so much joy, and they can again and will. How could something be sinful when it made you feel so lovely?

Afterwards, he'd held her in his arms until sleep had claimed him. Lying together thus, she'd felt a strange new tenderness for the man she'd married eighteen years before. Why had it taken so long to feel this complete sense of belonging? She was glad there'd be another night--away from the camp and the children.

But then her pragmatic sense intruded. She did have family obligations. Much as she'd like to remain here in this bed, dozing and dreaming, she'd best get back to the camp and see how the children were doing.

Medora wended her way through the circle of wagons nodding good-morning to fellow travelers. Most were already busy with chores; the men repairing equipment and jawing among themselves as the women, docile guardian of the hearth, tended housewifery chores made tenfold more difficult out here on the prairie. Women had to share all the hardships of pioneering along with their men, Medora was thinking, yet were accepted only as adjuncts to men, completely dependent on men for their fate. Hardly fair, but the way it was. The courts and the law books said you belonged to your husband, body and soul.

A smile played across her lips. Last night she had broken some of the rules and it had seemed so right. She had shared in the pleasure meant only for the men-- and it gave her a sense of freedom. Maybe it was time to break other rules-- break the bondage. Time women demanded more equal sharing in all roles in life. She'd give it more thought.

Torrey looked up from stirring the breakfast gruel in the big iron pot as her mother approached. Her dark expressive brows drew together in a scowl. "So, at last you're here."

Medora felt a prick of anxiety. "Is something wrong?"

"It's Jenny. She's been puking all night."

Medora sucked in her breath. Guilt mixed with fear as her stomach muscles tightened. What kind of a mother was she to have left her children alone?

The small child, wrapped in a quilt, lay on the floor of the wagon. Lavinia was wiping her forehead with a wet cloth. Relief crossed the older girl's face when she saw her mother.

"Oh Mama, thank goodness you're here. Jenny's been vomiting something frightful all night."

Jenny, seeing her mother, began to cry. "Mama, where you been? My belly's been hurting."

Medora felt a rush of guilt. "Oh my baby, my baby. If I'd known... Why didn't someone send me a message?"

"Torrey wanted to, but I wouldn't let her. Mama, you needed a good night's rest, and I was taking care of Jenny."

Night's rest? Shame was scalding and corrosive. If her daughter only knew...

She took the cloth from Lavinia, dipped it in a pail of water then wiped the child's brow. Jenny began to wretch, horrible twisting dry heaves. Lavinia handed a basin to her mother. Medora raised her youngest child as fear twisted through her. *Dysentery?*

"I tried to do what I thought you'd do," said Lavinia. "I scalded some milk and crumbled in some dried bread and sprinkled in a bit of cayenne pepper."

"You did right. I wouldn't have done differently." *But she should have been here.* "If the vomiting keeps up... Let's steep some white oak bark, or give her a dose of tincture of myrrh. There's some in the medicine tin."

"Elspeth kept saying if she only had her sang."

Medora touched Lavinia's arm. "I'm sorry, my dear, this had to fall on your shoulders. I shouldn't have left you."

Remorse now bore even deeper. Was this punishment for her errant behavior of the night before? For those thoughts of women's rights? A mother's role *was* keeper of the hearth and family. She shouldn't have left her children. There had been a scourge of dysentery among others of the caravan. One family had lost a baby when the small, ravaged body had become too weakened from the sickness. Until now the Dudley family had been spared, but there was no way of knowing where it would strike. She had failed her family. Jenny's illness was definitely her fault.

Later, when William came back from checking the stock, the look in his eyes added to her guilt. When he found her behind the wagon rinsing out some clothes, and out of view of others, he pulled her to him and his hand reached down to caress her buttocks. Medora jerked away. *She wasn't his harlot!* Or was she? She felt unclean.

William looked puzzled. "I'm sorry. I thought..."

"I know what you thought."

"Last night. To me--well, it was so good. I thought it was the same for you."

A hot flush worked up Medora's throat to her face. She could not meet his eyes. Then anger rushed in. Her blue eyes flamed. "Don't you know how sick your youngest daughter was all night? I should have been here."

William nodded, his face showed concern. "Yes I know. But I just looked in on her. Lavinia says she's sleeping now."

"Well, I must get back to my child."

By late afternoon Jenny's cramps had subsided, the vomiting had stopped and the diarrhea tapered off. Medora breathed a sigh of relief and thanked God for answering her prayers. Yet the ugly truth would not go away. She had given into selfish desires by leaving--and then to have enjoyed such lascivious pleasure.

William spent most of his day at the fort's blacksmith's shop resetting spokes and re-fitting the iron tires. Later, when he returned to the camp, he reminded Medora that they still had the room. "Now that Jenny is better..." Anticipation showed in his face.

Medora's eyes turned a frosty blue. How could he suggest such a thing? Her chin jutted. "I will not neglect my children again. Please thank Mr. Bordeaux. It was most generous of him to let us use the apartment, but we'll not be needing it again."

William's face tightened. Last night? A figment of his own desire--his own need? For her, as always--her obligation. "As you say. I'll give Mr. Bordeaux the message." He spun around and headed back toward the fort.

Three days at Fort Laramie found them ready to move on. Anton set the time to pull out for early the following morning. No more time could be wasted. Although this day, the very end of June, was hot enough that rivulets of sweat trickled down his neck and soaked his collar, it was snow that was on Anton's mind. He'd studied the maps in the Fremont Report, and he'd talked to some of the old mountaineers who knew the country. Although they'd been making a gradual ascent for some time, the real rugged mountains were still ahead--the mountains and the vast stretches of waterless deserts. It would be fall by the time they reached the Sierra Nevada, the final barrier to California. Sometimes snows came early. Once the peaks were blanketed with white, there was no getting through the passes he'd been told.

They'd already had some hard going, but now, this next stretch to the South Pass would be worse. Anxiety deepened the creases in Anton's rubber-like face. The weight of his new responsibility was heavy. They'd be gaining more altitude now as they worked up toward the Continental Divide. There'd be danger of Mountain fever--altitude fever some called it, which caused headaches and nausea. No doubt they'd have that to deal with. And poison alkali springs. The cattle would have to be watched closely or they'd lose more of their stock.

Anton spread out a map and was studying it when William came up and looked over his shoulder. Anton pointed with a stubby finger. "From here we head due west to little Sandy Creek then south-westerly to Fort Bridger then make a loop north to Fort Hall."

"Seems roundabout," said William.

"We could try the Greenwood cutoff and by-pass Fort Bridger." Anton stroked his chin in thought. "But that means forty or fifty miles of desert without water. I don't like those chances with our animals."

"But why Fort Hall at all? Going north when we're heading south? If we were going to Oregon--yes. But California? Look where we join Marys River--almost due west from Fort Bridger. That's where we will be headed to get us to the Sierra Mountains."

"Ja, but best we stay to the regular path."

"What about Hastings' shortcut? He claims its the most direct route to California, going south of the Great Salt Lake."

Anton's brows drew together. He pulled on his chin. "I don't know. There's the Wasatch Mountains that way, and more deserts. We should stay with the regular trails that have been proven."

"Josh, what more proof do you need when it's down in black and white in a printed book? I think it's worth considering."

Anton pursed his lips. Caution must be considered when lives depended on his decision. "Ja, we think about it, maybe." He folded his map. "For now--early come morning we start. Time enough to make the shortcut decision after we get to Fort Bridger. I check now the ones who leave with us."

A regrouping was again taking place. Some from other companies had asked to sign up with Anton while those of their own party who were not ready to leave would join later contingents.

Medora thought of the changes. How different from the large wagon train that had left from Independence. Anton told her there would be only nineteen wagons now besides their own three that would be leaving in the morning. She wished their party included the Donners. She hoped they would arrive before their own caravan pulled out. She so longed to see Tamsen again.

Later that afternoon Torrey spotted a snake-like train in the far distance. She came running excitedly crying out. "They're coming, they're coming. I know it's them because of the huge wagon that's higher than all the rest!" Medora was overjoyed.

That evening, with earlier disagreements set aside, the two caravans united in friendship and shared a great campfire. James Reed, his wound healed and again riding his Glaucus, had offered his hand to Anton, his anger forgotten. As for Medora and Tamsen, it was a joyous meeting. Torrey, too, was delighted to see Virginia Reed. She missed having someone to giggle with and share confidences. Not everything though--not like she would have done with Effie. She would never have another friend like Effie. Of course, there was Elspeth who was her friend even though she was older. But Elspeth was sick so much of the time. She now spent most of her time in the wagon. So Torrey was really glad to see Virginia again.

After the evening meal a space was cleared and Mr. Madden brought out his fiddle. Soon couples were stomping and twirling, Torrey, Lavinia, and Virginia among them. Torrey, in spite of intending to keep a fair distance between herself and Jake, danced several dances with him. He was such a sprightly dancer. Often he had her feet flying off the ground entirely, making it a great deal of fun. It was a wonderful evening everyone agreed. Medora and Tamsen sat together watching the dancers and sipping herb tea. The firelight made radiant patterns on their smiling faces.

"It's so good to be with you, my dear friend," said Medora. "I really had a strange dreadful feeling when we parted, that we might not meet again. Such a foolish thought."

"Of course," said Tamsen. "Even though we part again in the morning, we'll get together in California for a certainty. There's our book to finish."

They hugged each other to seal the promise.

James Reed had met an old acquaintance inside the fort, name of James Clyman, and invited him to join their evening gathering. The two had fought together in the Black Hawk war some fourteen years past.

"A frontiersman of the old school," Reed said as he introduced his friend to William and Anton. "Mr. Clyman here used to trap for the Ashley Company and knows this country better than most."

Clyman looked the part of a true mountaineer; tall and rangy, a good six foot, dressed in buckskin and outfitted with the customary rifle with a long knife stuck in his belt. A Roman nose emphasized his sharp, lean face and high forehead. His mouth was a little twisted as if he had lost most of his teeth on one side.

"Lucky to have run into him," continued Reed. "Mr. Clyman is escorting a small party of emigrants who are returning to the States. He's just come from California so can give us some first-hand information."

Everyone was eager to hear what Clyman had to say, with a hundred questions dripping from their tongues. He squatted on the ground in mountain man fashion like he'd never been used to a stool or a chair. Some of the other men squatted around him. Reed produced a bottle of his very fine aged brandy.

"Is the climate and soil all what's claimed?" asked Anton.

"Could say, for the most part. Greatest wild oat fields you ever seed," said Clyman. "While you're pushing through snow in Missouri and Illinois, you could be tramping through full blooming herbage in California--posies so bright as to dazzle yer eyes out, hillsides all covered yaller and purple. January is like a Missouri April."

Anton nodded with approval.

"But later. Don't expect rain. Four to five months of drought. The coast stays green but the Valleys get right scorched."

"And what about the people?" asked William.

"Lazy. Damn lazy. Useless, I'd say. Every man takes his own time to move about his business, like he's pained even to breathe. Half the population is Injuns. Do all the work but kept like slaves. Never get paid a cent for their labors."

William cringed. The thought of slavery always affected him that way. He remembered his own miserable years of indenture.

"Always some kind of a revolution going on. Their damn government changes 'bout every year--each change worser'n the last one. The military and all parts of the government are pukin' weak. Run by imbeciles. Not much respected by anyone. Jose Castro, for instance. He's the present comandante in the north. He's trying his damndest to get rid of all the Yanks. Not that he has a chance. Too many settlers there now."

William's brows went up in surprise. "From all accounts--the letters that were published in our papers was urging Americans to come. Especially the letters written by Captain Sutter."

Clyman laughed. "Sure, from old Cap. He's out recruiting. He needs more Yanks to come. I ain't just pulling your ear. He needs workers at his fort. Got plenty of Injuns for his fields. But he needs men with skills. Got lots of projects going. And he's just laid out a town expecting to sell you Yanks the lots. Is calling his town Sutterville."

William forced himself to silence, but thoughts ran wild inside his head. Land was supposed to be free. The Spaniards were supposed to be a most friendly people. Skepticism crowded his thoughts. This old weathered mountaineer was a man used to the free life of a trapper. Probably, more than likely, would resist any type of civilized ways. He'd have to give second thoughts to anything this old fellow might say.

James Reed broke in. "What's the attitude now toward Americans since the start of the war?"

"War? Hell, what war?"

"War with Mexico."

"You mean it finally got started?" Clyman laughed and slapped his leather covered knee. "'Bout time. I thought Lieutenant Fremont was there to do something 'bout it. I even offered to round up some men to help. Instead, he was high-tailing it out of the country last I heard. Castro said to git, so he was gitting. I got disgusted and left too."

"The word reached us just as we were starting across the plains," Reed explained. "Down in Texas. A troop of Mexicans crossed the Rio Grand and attacked a battalion of our soldiers."

"Well, I'll be damned," said Clyman. "Didn't think them yeller-bellied Mexs had that much gumption. In May you say? I was into the mountains by then. But chances are, they don't even know about it yet in California."

There was more talk of the war. But Clyman figured it wouldn't last long. Americans would sure whop the piss out of the Mexicans. Anyway, it shouldn't make much difference to the Californios. They didn't hold much loyalty to their mother country, Mexico. In fact there was a lot of talk of joining up with England or France. Some were strong for the United States. And now with so many Yanks coming--there was strength in numbers.

William nodded and some of the other travelers looked at each other with satisfaction. There *was* strength in numbers, William figured, and with the number of Americans now headed that way, prospects looked good. Even when he'd first started thinking of California, indications were that the Mexican province would eventually be a part of the U. S. just like it had happened in Texas. And he had harbored in his breast all along that he'd be honored to be just a small contributing factor in the making of that history. Now he was all for getting there sooner than ever.

It was Anton who asked Clyman about the best trail to follow, wondering about the shortcut recommended in the Hastings guide book.

Clyman shook his head. "That's the way we just come. Traveled with Mr. Hastings myself. He dropped off at Fort Bridger, now waiting there to catch the ones going to California. Aims to serve as their pilot."

William's eyes sparkled with interest, greatly impressed. "Say, that's right decent. The one who wrote the guide book will be our guide?"

Clyman's response was hardly reassuring. "He'll be your guide if you take his damn shortcut. But I wouldn't recommend it." Reed's bottle of brandy was still being passed around. Clyman took a double gulp. He passed it back and wiped his mouth with the back of his hand. "We came that way, taking south of the great salt lake. I sure as hell argued against it. But Hastings was set and determined. I finally decided, what the hell. Might as well explore new territory."

"New territory?" someone asked. "But he had it in his guide book that was published last year."

"Reckon Mr. Hastings has got a right good imagination," Clyman chuckled. "Hell, those great salt plains weren't never crossed until Fremont and Kit Carson just done it, and they comes up from the Sante Fe Trail. I can tell you, most desolate country on the whole globe it is, there not being one spear of vegetation and no water. And after the salt flats, we still faced the Wasatch Mountains."

Clyman then expounded on their mountain trek, how they had to fight their way through the brush-choked and boulder-filled canyons.

Anton's brows drew together but he kept his thoughts to himself.

"There were families in your party?" asked Reed.

"Three women and three younguns, riding mules and horses. Of course, no wagons."

Reed looked satisfied. "Well, if women and children can make it..."

"Luck was with us, and like I said--no wagons. We got through. Others might not."

"I'd say if there is a neigher route, 'tis no use to take a roundabout course," Reed said.

William nodded, glad that James Reed saw it the same way he did. The shorter the better, he figured.

But the old frontiersman shook his head as he stroked a grizzly-whiskered chin. "I'd say take the regular wagon track and never leave it. It's barely possible to get through if you follow it, and may be impossible if you don't."

Reed's bottle was now empty; someone else passed around a jug of corn whiskey. Clayman took another swig. So did Owl Russell who appeared mighty soused by now. Although no longer wagon master, he still traveled with the Donners and Reeds.

By now the fire burned low; crimson embers glowed against the blue-velvet night. Above, the stars seemed extra bright in the cradle of the dark desert sky. Long since, the dancers had stopped their twirling and Mr. Madden had tucked his fiddle away most carefully inside his wagon.

Most of the women and children had retired to their feather comforters or patchwork-quilts. If they were going with Anton they'd have to be up before daylight to start the coffee boiling and the side pork frying for a nourishing breakfast before wagons rolled. But a few of the men still lingered and stared at the dying coals, talking and discussing.

Anton got up and stretched. "If you're going with me, you better hit the bedrolls." He walked off toward his wagon.

William took Reed aside. "We'll be leaving before you need be up, but I wanted to ask, what do you think of what your friend had to say--about the shortcut, I mean?"

Reed smiled. "I think his tongue was loose from too much brandy. I remember from the past how that old mountaineer liked to spin yarns when he had a chance for an audience. I'm still putting my stock in Mr. Hasting's book. It's a well written and scientific published manual. The author is an educated man as well as an explorer."

William felt good. "That's the way I see it. I'm glad we agree. And according to Mr. Clyman, Hastings is waiting for us now at Fort Bridger."

"So there should be no problem." Reed's smile displayed supreme confidence. "He'll be backtracking the same way he's just come. When you meet Mr. Hastings at Fort Bridger, tell him to wait, that there is another party coming."

Reed clasped William's hand and shook it in warm comradeship. "Looks like we'll be joining our parties again."

"By George, I'm looking forward to that," said William with a hearty ring to his voice. He was glad Anton and Reed had set aside their differences. "So we'll see you at Fort Bridger in another three or four weeks.

CHAPTER 18

It was a mighty rough pull after they left Fort Laramie traveling the barren land called the South Pass. Push and pull. Chill at night, sweat by day and the wind rising, fierce in the face. Rolling over thirsty sagebrush and dusty sand, coyotes singing at night. Finally they'd reached the very backbone of the continent.

For William it seemed a right awesome experience. The East was truly behind them now. His heart sang with an ardent zeal. He was now in the west, and ready to conquer. But his spirits plummeted when he saw a familiar figure approaching astride a mule.

Eli Morgan rode up, a wry smirk on his boorish sun-browned face, and without even a word of greeting said, "Figured I've jest crossed the Great Divide." His mouth spread to a self-satisfied grin along with an obnoxious chuckle. "So's I pissed to the east, then turned and pissed to the west." He then shook with laughter as though it was one hell of a joke. "Reckon now that makes me master of all the goddamned waters."

Disgust roiled through William. How offensive could one be? Eli himself was hardly a welcoming sight, but strapped to the back of his mule was a bundle of dried buffalo jerky and a hump of fresh meat, and William thought what a welcome addition that could mean for their meager supplies. As the company had changed considerably since Eli had been ousted, few others would know of Eli's episode with the burial robe. And when Eli asked about his wife and said by rights he should be looking after her, William said he'd talk with Anton about Eli rejoining their party.

Although neither William nor Anton wanted Eli back in their party... "Except that we still have his wife," said William.

"But not for long is my guess," said Anton. Elspeth's health had been worsening.

William looked grave. "Perhaps even more reason we should consider. It's a matter of being Christian. A husband should rightly be with his wife at such a time."

They talked it over with Medora as well. "I guess it's no more than right," she said, but not looking forward to having that crude man around their campfire again.

Eli was told he could stay but would be expected to help with the work and to keep their group supplied with fresh game. Eli agreed. Hunting was a skill he was good at--except when it came to tracking down the damn Quigley brothers. From the time he'd been ousted, he'd been searching and found neither head nor tail. But he wasn't giving up. He reckoned they'd joined some other outfit and were well ahead on their way to Californy. He'd never forget them and would track them till doomsday. But he needed a party to travel with. So once again Eli Morgan was traveling with the Dudleys and Anton.

They rolled on over barren upland country, sandy table lands; sagebrush country with grasses scant. William lost another ox when the critter got to a poisoned spring before it could be stopped. Their supply of milk and butter was meager now. With grazing so poor, Bessie, their milk cow, was hardly producing. They had left the buffalo country behind but Eli was still earning his keep by keeping them well supplied with game; prairie hens, antelope, and one day a mountain goat.

The caravan reached the Little Sandy. Some of the party then chose the Greenwood cutoff to Fort Hall instead of staying with the more traveled route by way of Fort Bridger. Anton's group was now down to fifteen wagons.

They crossed the Big Sandy and later the Green River. The trail was dry and dusty and the swirling dust aggravated Elspeth's condition and set her to coughing. She spent most of the time in the supply wagon with a piece of muslin covering her face to guard against the dust. She looks like a bundle of picked over bones, Torrey thought looking in on her, and feeling a helpless pity. Elspeth's cheeks were hollow and sunken, her face pale and waxy except for the bright spots of color high on her cheeks. Her eyes glistened with a strange unusual brightness. Please Lord, hurry us to California, Torrey prayed. The climate there, someone had said, was a sure-fire-cure for the lung sickness which Mama suspected Elspeth had. Nothing must happen to Elspeth.

Mama hadn't liked her using Elspeth's given name. "She's not someone your age, and she is a married woman. It is just not proper," Mama had said, as though being proper was all that mattered, and Torrey steamed. Mama finally gave in about the name because that's what Elspeth wanted.

Elspeth was now her very best friend since she didn't have Effie, or Virginia either. It didn't matter that Elspeth was so much older. Elspeth was one she could talk to, tell her things and not be pooh-poohed as others might do. At first she was drawn to Elspeth for her strange ideas and the stories she'd tell. But then she found that Elspeth listened as well. Torrey began telling her things she'd previously only told her journal--like wanting to become someone famous. Someday she'd write great books--or go on the stage and become a really great actress. Instead of succumbing to the vapors as Mama might do if she thought her daughter was going on the stage, Elspeth was monstrously impressed.

"Laws," she'd said, her eyes almost popping out of her head. "I believes you will. Most certain, the Almighty above has picked ye fer somethin' very special. I knows hit in my bones, and I'll be most proud to say that once I knew ye."

"Oh, Elspeth, that won't ever make a difference. You'll always be my friend." The fact that Elspeth believed in her, *really believed.* Now seeing Elspeth lying in her blankets and hurting so, an awful fear took hold.

The caravan went on, passing Ham's Fork and Black's Fork and the going was better. Finally, nearly three weeks after they left Fort Laramie, they came to Fort Bridger. It was hardly a fort; just two rough log cabins connected by a lashed-pole corral. It had been built three years before by Bridger, an old-time trapper, as a place where emigrants could stop, use the blacksmith shop and replenish supplies at very high prices before going on.

After the desolation they had passed through, it was a pleasant place to stop with plenty of water so the pasturage was good. The stock could graze and recoup their strength. And just as he'd promised, Mr. Lansford Hastings was there waiting.

William was impressed with the man. Hastings had a dash--a dynamic personality, indeed, the kind of a man William took too. He had a persuasive power. His talk flowed smooth as melted butter spread on hot wheat bread. He was younger than William had expected for having so many accomplishments; a lawyer, a writer, an explorer. A sociable fellow as well. It was fascinating to listen to Hastings' tales of his wilderness expeditions. Three times he'd crossed the mountains; the first time to Oregon in 1842. Then he'd gone down to California. A truly superior land, he said with such glowing enthusiasm you could picture the rich growing fields--climate so ideal nobody ever had sickness; soil so fertile it could not be equaled elsewhere--just as he'd said in his book.

And William's vision grew. The land of promise. He pictured his great productive fields--and he, a gentleman farmer. But also, the opportunities a new land offered for productive businesses. No reason why he couldn't do both.

"Only disadvantage at all," Hastings said, "is the present Mexican rule. But that's not for long. Since arriving here, I learned we've gone to war. Now more Americans than ever will be coming. That's why I wrote my guide book to convince more Americans of the advantages of migrating to California, and why I'm here now. If your sights are on Oregon... Well, I've been to both places, and my choice is California. I hope it's yours too."

"Indeed it is," said William. "I'd say you are doing a great service to us all, meeting us here."

Definitely, the man had those qualities William admired. Like Judge Whitherspoon and James Reed. Farsightedness, ambition, a go-getter for certain. But a caring man as well, thinking of the welfare of others. For hadn't he risked the dangers of crossing the mountains for the sole purpose of helping the travelers--of showing them the way over a route that would shorten their journey?

Anton was not as favorably impressed. He'd had doubts before about that cutoff. Now even more so after meeting Hastings. The man had too much tongue. More fitting for a politician than a guide. Yet he could see William had taken to Hastings. Not surprising. So often William was drawn to a person of that nature. Like he'd been to James Reed. Ja, William's nature himself. A visionary, a builder of dreams. But sometimes too eager--too much haste for wise decisions to make. He himself had visions--but always with caution. He wasn't sure they should put their trust in Hastings.

A couple of other companies were also there at Fort Bridger. The grazing was good. It inclined them to linger a few days. The ones with sights set for California mingled and discussed the pros and cons of following Hastings over the shortcut. Many felt Hastings' way was a gamble and still planned to take the longer way up to Fort Hall. But those who would go with Hastings were now carefully inspecting their equipment and making needed repairs. This was the true jumping-off place. Nothin' more ahead 'cept mountains and deserts. No more civilization a'tall till Sutter's Fort in the Sacramento Valley, which was mighty scary to think of.

The women now had time to catch up on the washing. Torrey smiled thinking how funny it looked. They were camping along a stream, and all of the bushes and trees had suddenly blossomed with sheets and shirts, dresses and drawers, spread for drying--like a thousand flags flapping in the breeze.

Four days they spent at Fort Bridger. Billy and Jenny were happy for the chance to play with other children. Torrey was glad to stay put for Elspeth's sake so that her friend could rest quiet and absorb the glorious sunshine and not be constantly exposed to dust. William kept looking for the Reeds and the Donners to arrive. But Anton was anxious to get on. He pressed for taking the regular way, not having much faith in Hastings.

William bristled with irritation. Why was Anton so negative when it came to people he himself admired? Anton hadn't approved of his friendship with James Reed--and here was another man with foresight and boldness. It was as though Anton resented any friendship he might have--too blooming possessive. He owed Anton a lot, and their friendship was important, but still...

"I'm taking the shortcut," William stated deciding it was time to take a stand. After all, he had promised James Reed.

Anton's face molded to inflexible stubbornness. "So soon you forget what that mountain man, Clyman, said. Remember, he traveled the shortcut with Hastings."

"Clyman was running off at the mouth," William argued. "Too much brandy, I think. He admitted they came through in fine shape. And here at the very takeoff for the shortcut, Bridger himself recommends it. You heard him yourself.

Shorter--maybe three hundred and fifty miles shorter. What more proof? The trail's mostly smooth and level, Bridger said. The only Indians to worry about are the chicken-livered Diggers who might try to steel our livestock."

"Ja, maybe in his own interest, so many now taking that Greenwood cutoff to Fort Hall and bypassing Bridger's. Ja, Hastings' route would keep the emigrants coming this way for his fort to prosper."

This time William was determined. In the final test of wills, Anton acquiesced.

The call came. Hastings said those going with him would leave early the following morning. "There's still another party coming," William told him.

Lansford shook his head. "Sorry. It's getting too late in the season to delay any longer. I'll leave directions along the way for the late comers to follow."

Medora also was concerned. "You'd think the Reeds and the Donners would be here by now." She'd constantly been looking down the trail hoping to see that oversized wagon. She was so looking forward to Tamsen's companionship once again, it was difficult to hide her disappointment.

"They may have stayed longer at Fort Laramie than planned," said William. He felt some worry himself but did not want to pass it on to Medora.

The next morning they started out with "geeing" and "hawing," sixty wagons in all, an unwieldy number for mountain trails. Hastings served as pilot and a Mr. Herlan and a Mr. Young took charge of the caravan. Anton was relieved he no longer had the responsibility.

They reached the Bear River Valley where running springs ran clear and hillsides were rich with grass and blue-flax flowers.

How lovely it is here, Medora thought and made some sketches. She checked on Elspeth who still needed to spend most of her time in her bed in the supply wagon. But she does look a little better, Medora decided. The rest at Fort Bridger had done her good.

They camped for the night. The next day they rolled on, pushing over a ridge and then descended into a vast canyon gorge. Medora looked down and grew cold with apprehension. Would they be able to get down that gorge without some wagons crashing? But to Torrey it was exciting--like entering the innards of the earth. They were mocked with echoes which made the cattle uneasy when their lowing was answered from distant peaks. Someone shot of a gun. The sharp report was like the boom of thunder, rolling on and on. Farther on there were fossil sea-shells embedded in the red rock walls. Torrey couldn't believe it.

"How can there be sea-shells way up here?" she asked her father.

William smiled tolerantly. "Read your Bible, young lady, where it tells of rain

165

upon the whole earth for forty days and forty nights."

As they continued down the canyon, fantastic figures cut by the wind and flowing water emerged from granite projections. Torrey's imagination took wing as she stood on a ledge. Strange shapes become towering monsters. Suddenly she felt great claws clamp her shoulders. She screamed. A chuckle came from behind.

"Jake!"

"Scared you, didn't I?"

Torrey swung around, throwing off his hands. Her eyes flashed fire. "You... you... What right do you have sneaking up like that?"

Yellow lights danced in Jake's hazel eyes. "Just come to protect you from falling down the canyon."

"I certainly don't need your protection, Jake Stringer."

"Torrey, why are you always so hot-headed?" His grin was mocking. He lifted a strand of hair that lay curled against her shoulder. "Sure looks purty when you let it hang loose instead of tying it back with a cord."

Torrey pulled the hank of hair free. "It's none of your business what I do with my hair."

"Now Torrey, I've seen you brushing it. Figured you were making it all purty like for me."

Torrey glowered. She gave Jake a shove and stomped away. Unbearable! Her blood churned, Why had Papa ever hired him? So she did brush her hair more and now let it fall loose. But certainly not for Jake's benefit. Not for the eyes of any fellow. Yet deep down, she'd hardly admit it to herself, but she had noticed some of the young men casting glances her way--and sort of liked it. But not from Jake!

He might be a lively partner to dance with, and he added some merriment at their campfire with his jokes and playing his harmonica, but she hated his boldness. It was still in her mind how he'd cornered her in the judge's hallway that night of the farewell party. And that other night on the prairie when he'd kissed her in that repulsive way. Jake was the last person in the world she wanted to have take notice.

For several days the long line of wagons snaked its way down the Weber Canyon with its rocky barriers of ridges and gulches, more hostile country then they'd ever traveled before. They plunged into sharp ravines and edged along narrow ledges. At times the grade was so steep chains were used to lock the wagon wheels to slow the decent. The men stiffened their legs and dug their heels into the dirt as they pulled back on ropes. Some places were so narrow, there was hardly room for the wagons to pass. At one place a chunk of the trail gave way just as the Dudleys' supply wagon was passing over it.

Walking behind the wagon, Medora's heart leaped when she saw the gaping hole. "Elspeth! Elspeth!" She screamed, expecting the wagon to tip over with

Elspeth inside.

William jumped back from up front where he was leading the oxen, and started pushing on the wagon with all his strength to keep it upright. "Anton! Jake! Mike!" he yelled at the top of his voice.

The men rushed to assist, and Torrey as well. "Push hard. Keep it steady!" William's orders were terse, his voice sharp with apprehension. "I'll get Elspeth out."

It was Torrey who could see that the outside rear wheel was now hanging over the cavity. "Oh, Papa, hurry, hurry! I think more of the dirt's breaking loose!"

As the others leaned against the wagon keeping it steady, William climbed inside and lifted Elspeth out.

"I've got her now," Medora said, her heart still racing as she put her arm around the frail little body and led her to a large rock where she could rest until it was safe to get back in the wagon.

"I'm sorry I be such a bother," Elspeth squeezed out between a coughing spell.

"Oh, Elspeth. You're not a bother. Not a bother at all," Medora said, but wishing Elspeth had the strength to walk while they were going down this steep grade.

Anton now took over, telling Jake to get up front and start the oxen. Soon all four wheels were once again on firm ground. William helped Elspeth back in the wagon as Medora fussed over her to make her as comfortable as possible, and wondering if this nightmare would ever end.

Once again the long line of rigs and animals started on and finally reached the bottom of the canyon without further mishap.

Now traveling through the canyon was not as risky, but just as hard. Progress was slow, sometimes making no more than a mile a day. The brush was thick and had to be cleared. Boulders were bridged over with trees and brush. It had been near two weeks since they'd left Fort Bridger. Although there was a narrow Indian trail above, there was no sign that white men and horses had ever been down in this canyon. Suspicion was growing that Hastings had lied.

They reached an impasse where canyon walls rose high, boxing them in. Jungle-thick brush; willows, alders, and twenty-foot high aspen choked together by service berry bushes and thorny wild roses barred their way.

With doubts increasing, Anton cornered Hastings. "I don't believe you ever came this way," he bristled.

Lansford looked indignant. "Mr. Zwiegmann, I admit, with my other party we didn't come down in this canyon but traveled the ridge above. But it was such rough going I decided it would be better to follow the river so I sent a scout down here to check." And with his usual note of bravado Lansford said, "Rest assured,

Zwiegmann, I have everything under control. The Weber River flows out of this canyon. All we have to do is follow it out."

"*Scheiss!* With the canyon walls closing around us?"

Anton stomped away before he'd murder the man. He'd had enough of following Hastings. He would do some scouting on his own, see just how they would get out of the dead-end canyon.

Torrey was glad the jiggling and jouncing had finally come to a halt for Elspeth's sake. She thought how scary it had been when they were coming down the canyon and the trail had given away. It must have been monstrous for Elspeth riding inside. She had this awful tight feeling in her chest when she thought about her friend. Each day she'd look in on Elspeth to see if there was anything she could do for her friend.

On this day, while they men were still clearing for a trail, Torrey looked in at the huddled figure lying on the sacks of meal and flour that served as her mattress. "How are you today?" she asked.

"I be fine."

She sure didn't look fine. "Is there anything I can do for you?"

"I be fine, girl. Jest a might puny today."

The words were hardly out when a violent coughing spasms shook her frame and left Elspeth gasping for breath. When she finally removed the rag she'd held to her mouth, Torrey saw it was stained with blood. Oh, Lord in heaven.

"I better call Mama."

Elspeth shook her head. "No. I be a'right. Nothin' your Mama can do. Ye be an angel to worry 'bout an old woman like me."

"Oh, Elspeth, you're my best friend."

Torrey fought back the tears. She reached for the bony hand and pressed it gently. The skin was dry as sun-burned grass. The lump in Torrey's throat was so big it wouldn't swallow down. Looking at the shell of the woman, Torrey thought of the blue hawk Elspeth had seen that time on the prairie. Mama called it a nonsense superstition. *But was it?* Torrey's fear mounted.

"Reckon we'll be stopped here for a while," Torrey told Elspeth. "The men have a lot of clearing to do. We've come to a fierce tangle of growth."

She thought of some juneberry trees she remembered seeing up on the hillside a piece back where the old Indian trail was.

"Would you like some fresh berries for supper?"

"Could be mighty tasty." Elspeth's voice was thin as a thread. Torrey felt heart-sick, so pitiful it was, almost like the words were too heavy to lift out. Elspeth closed her eyes and Torrey wondered if that meant Elspeth needed to sleep for a while. "I'll be going now." she said and tip-toed away.

CHAPTER 19

The day turned to a scorcher. Not a flicker of breeze. William took off his hat and wiped the sweat from his forehead with his sleeve. Josh, how hot it could be in the middle of the day, yet freezing at night. Different in Illinois. There, when it was hot, it stayed hot, didn't tease you on.

Illinois. If he were still there he'd be dressed in neat broadcloth and joking with his store customers. He'd never ever done this much hard labor, even when clearing his land in Missouri. The tangle of growth seemed impossible to cut through.

He pulled off his glove and inspected yesterday's throbbing blisters. One had burst and looked ugly and red. Hope it wouldn't start to fester. Maybe he'd been wrong, wanting to take Hastings' shortcut. With canyon walls closing down to a narrow gorge, it was now fear they'd never get out unless they'd backtrack to Fort Bridger meaning several weeks of precious time lost. If the snows came early in the Sierra Mountains, no way could they cross over. So feelings were strong.

William put the glove back on and again stooped to slash at the thick brush with his knife. He could hear the swish of Mike's knife ahead and Morgan whacking away behind him. Jake and Anton were off on other missions, Jake shagging down their milk cow who had strayed. Losing old Bessie would mean no more butter and milk, a real loss for the family. And Anton had gone off to scout for a way out of this canyon.

Eli Morgan walked up beside William, his shirt showing large dark circles at his arm pits. "This ain't gettin' us nowhere. I'm calling it quits." He bit off a chew of tobacco and stuffed the plug back in his pocket. "Hangin' is a damn sight bettern' Hastings deserves."

William had heard others of the wagon train express a like view. For himself, he had turned to the Lord, confident that if Hastings or Anton failed, the Lord would see them through.

Eli's jaw worked on his chew, forming a huge bulge in his cheek. He pursed his lips and shot a brown stream from the corner of his mouth then wiped off the residue with his sleeve. "Stupid to keep on clearing when Zwiegmann might find a better way out."

William stood up and rubbed his aching back.

Morgan picked up his rifle that was propped against a tree. "I've seen some antelope signs. I'll see to it we'll at least have some meat in the pot." He headed to where his mule was staked.

Morgan was right, William thought. They were wasting needed energy if Anton finds another way. But suppose Anton doesn't?

He glanced back up at the steep grade they'd come down and thought of his friends, the Reeds and the Donners. James could never make it down in this canyon with that oversized wagon of his. They should be warned to stay up on the ridge and follow the route Hastings' other party had used.

William called to Mike. "I'm going back to camp for a while. Better take a rest too. The sun's too blamed hot for this kind of work."

Medora sloshed a bloody rag in the bucket of water. Elspeth was hemorrhaging badly and she felt so helpless watching the frail little women gasp for breath during her coughing spasms. A lump of sadness lodged in Medora's throat that wouldn't swallow down. Her heart ached knowing the pain Elspeth must be suffering. If only she could do more.

Besides Elspeth, other problems kept mounting. Torrey had gone to milk old Bessie this morning and found her missing. Jake was now out looking for the cow. What if he couldn't find her? The thought was frightening. Their provisions were already distressingly low. She glanced up at the towering walls around them. Another concern the way they narrowed right down to the river. Others were saying there was no way they could get out and accusing Mr. Hastings for bringing them down here. Now Anton was out scouting. She felt an overwhelming tiredness. What more would they face?

After wringing out the rag, Medora swished it around in a pail of clean water. Twisting it once again, she spread it out on a bush to dry alongside several other cloths and towels. Although some activity noise drifted over from other campsites, their own camp seemed unusually quite. The men were still off cutting brush and the children were gone. Lavinia had taken the two younger ones to the creek and Torrey was off picking berries. She shouldn't have let Torrey go off alone. As usual, Torrey had been so insistent. With Elspeth so ill, Torrey wanted to do something special for her friend, and it seemed that a bowl of fresh berries might help. Medora finally gave in telling herself it was safe enough with so many people around. Wagons stretched as far as one could see until they disappeared from view beyond the curves in the canyon. She should have been firmer and said no. Always such a tug of wills between them.

But of late she'd noticed a change in Torrey. The child was not the wild tomboy she was when they had first set out on this trek. Was her attempt at guidance at last taking root? In the past she had tried to impress on Torrey the importance of femininity, a female's only edge in this male dominated world. Now at last, Torrey seemed to be interested in her appearance. Each evening Torrey vigorously brushed her hair--counting one hundred strokes. And she no longer tied it back with a cord but let the curls hang loose around her shoulders--such a wonderful wealth of hair with its rich auburn color. And she complained about the straight cut of her bodices, sometimes borrowing, without permission, Lavinia's shirtwaists which shaped better to her growing breast.

At first Medora had breathed a sigh of relief until she noticed some of the young men of the new additions to their wagon train making excuses to come around to make conversation with Torrey. Torrey was still much too young for courting. Medora had also become aware of Jake's persistent attention that Torrey obviously didn't want. She must talk to William about Jake. He put so much stock in his young hand and apparently hadn't noticed Jake's interest. Or was it that he was not yet accepting that his precious daughter might be reaching *that* certain age.

Speaking of the Devil--As though her thoughts made him materialize, Jake rode up on Dancing Girl--with no sign of the cow. Medora's stomach churned. "You didn't find Bessie?"

"Nope. Scrounged hillsides and gullies. Sorry, Miz Dudley."

In spite of the heat of the day, a patch of cold fear spread down Medora's spine. Their food supply was already woefully low. Without their milk cow there'd be no more milk and butter. "Maybe she'll come back of her own accord when she hears the other cows." she said hopefully.

"I don't know. Cows be such dumb critters."

She said no more but her eyes showed her alarm. She reached for other thoughts--do something with her hands. She turned to the fire, moved the big black pot of beans to another spot on the coals, then remembered Jake had missed their nooning meal. "You must be near starved. Take care of Dancing Girl while I fix you something to eat." Jake nodded then headed for a meadow to unsaddle the horse and let her graze.

William came in mopping his brow with his kerchief. "Too hot to keep working. Decided to wait until Anton comes back." He looked around. "Where's everyone gone?"

"Lavinia went down to the creek with Jenny and Billy. Torrey is off picking berries."

"Alone?" His expression clouded with concern.

"Hardly alone with so many people around," Medora replied not wanting to admit she herself had regretted giving Torrey permission. She came back with, "Will, you're like an old mother hen. Your daughter does well taking care of herself."

"She still shouldn't be wandering off alone."

Medora studied her husband quizzicly. Perhaps he had noticed the recent change in his daughter and the young men casting glances. Did all fathers feel a certain threat when their girl-children reached a certain age?

"You're worrying needless, Will," Medora said, as much to convince herself as to assure her husband. William and his precious daughter, Medora thought with a tug of envy. There had always been such a closeness between those two. Why couldn't she have that same rapport with Torrey?

William sat down on a box, tamped tobacco into his pipe and with a pair of tongs reached for a glowing coal. A sudden spasm of coughing come from the supply wagon. "I better go," Medora said. "Will, I'm so afraid she is nearing the end, poor dear. If only I could do more."

"You're doing all you can. Too bad Eli can't show some concern."

Medora pulled a clean towel from a bush and hurried toward the wagon. William followed his wife's quick movements. A fine charitable lady in spite of all she's been put through, and seldom a complaint. He felt a fierce need to hold her. He thought of that night at Fort Laramie. Would it ever be like that again? For the first time she was his. Really *his*. Even though in the past, she'd never denied him, yet his sexual experience left much to be desired beyond his physical relief. She gave what was expected after marriage vows, but that was all. Nothing more. Only natural, of course, the way it was when you married a lady. And Medora *was* a lady in every way. That made a difference. Men could think, even talk about their body needs, even boast among themselves about their pleasures with certain women--but a proper lady? It was more than he could expect for her to have the same response to the pleasure they could share together. *Or was it that other reason? The ghost between them.* The nagging thought that had always been there. But that one night--that wonderful night... William drew deeply on his pipe then let out the smoke slowly. Perhaps. When the hardships of traveling are over.

Medora came back and put another bloody towel in the bucket. Before she was through sloshing it around, Jack came from the meadow and sat down on a stump across from William.

"No luck with the cow?" Jake shook his head.

Medora filled a bowl of beans from the black iron kettle and spread the last of their butter on a piece of cornbread and handed them to Jake. William watched Jake wolf down the beans. His thoughts had switched to the plight of his friend, James Reed. "Jake, I've got another errand for you."

"William, Jake has been gone most of the day."

"I know. I shouldn't be asking, but I've been thinking of the Reeds and the

Donners. With that rig of his, James can never make it down in this canyon. They need to be warned." He turned back to Jake. "The mare's had a chance for a rest. I want you to saddle her up again."

Jake held his spoon midway to his mouth, his expression showing interest.

"I'll write a message for you to deliver. They may still be days behind us, so tie it to a stick at the top of the trail where they'll find it. Take your sleeping roll. Mrs. Dudley will fix you a packet of food. Traveling alone on horseback shouldn't take long. You should be back by tomorrow."

Jake's eyes sparkled with anticipation. "Yes sir. I'll get back soon as I can."

It was after Jake had waved a farewell, after he'd rounded a bluff and disappeared from view and the loping echoes of Dancing Girl's hooves had faded that William began to doubt his decision. Had he been too impulsive? He should have checked with Hastings first. A message might already have been sent. Jake was much too eager to be off. If Anton found a way out and they were ready to start, how would he manage the two wagons without Jake's help?

But Jake was already gone. William shook his head. No sense to dwell on things too late to change. He looked up at the slice of blue sky directly overhead. On either side were the towering cliffs. Will shuddered, and couldn't shake the feeling of doom. What if Anton couldn't find a way out?

Anton followed the creek to where it flowed into the Weber and paused. Ahead the rock walls appeared to rise straight up from the water. The width between them seemed no more than fifteen to twenty feet. But if they could take the wagons down the river. He nudged his bay with his heels. The horse splashed into the water. This time of year the river wasn't deep, but its bed was rocky and there were places the water flowed in a wild turbulence. Risky for wagons? Ja, considering the boulders in its path, but the wagons could be taken right down through the narrow gateway. His mare stumbled on a slippery rock. Anton leaned forward and stroked her neck. "Steady, *Mein Gretchen*. Steady there, girl."

He continued down the middle of the river for a couple of miles. Finally the canyon opened wider. Ja, a possible way out. He then turned back. He'd also look for an alternative route.

When he reached the meadow where he'd entered the river, he followed alongside the creek heading back toward the wagon camp. He remembered there was an old Indian trail up above the path they'd cleared to come down. If the Indians used it, it had to lead somewhere. He decide to check it out.

Now, on the soft firm ground that bordered the creek, his Gretchen settled to a gentle rhythmic gait. Anton sat back easy in his saddle and let his thoughts wander--as so often of late, to Torrey. Ach, more than he should.

He had been watching the changes taking place. Changes indeed. He had seen a new maturity in Torrey's warm brown eyes, a tempting ripeness in the full curve of her lips. And he couldn't help but notice how her little firm breasts strained against the straight cut of her bodice unless she wore one of Lavinia's. Ja, a child to woman she was becoming. His *Liebchen.*

Of all the four Dudley children, Torrey had always been his favorite, although he loved them all. For eight years he had watched them grow. "Uncle" they'd always called him. He felt privileged. Ja, alone in this country with no family of his own.

Each one so different--Lavinia, the little lady, *eine Schönheit* like her mother in both looks and disposition. Billy, the rambunctious *Junge.* And Jenny? *Das kleine Kind.* She wasn't even born when he'd first met the Dudleys.

But Torrey...

From the start. She'd been his *Liebchen.* A spunky little red-head, so like his little sister, about the same age when he'd last seen his Gisela. Ja, the same fresh eagerness and inquisitiveness that Gisela had. But Torrey's willfulness, which often amused him, was hers alone. Of course, his little sister was a woman now with a family of five.

A rush of homesickness swamped him. He glanced around at the rugged brush filled canyon and thought of the gentle green slopes of his childhood home. Strange how lives change--that he should leave the old country. That the Dudleys should have stopped at his farmhouse for directions that night. Strange how lives become entwined. Suppose he'd never left the old country. Never gone to Illinois. Would he still have been destined to meet the Dudleys--meet his *Liebchen* in some other way? *If he were only twenty years younger.* Ach, where does my mind stray? An ugly man such as I am. *Dummkopf! Nicht das Kind!* He, nearly as old as her father! Such foolishness to think.

With bucket in hand, Torrey waved to a few of the ones she knew as she wandered down through the long line of wagons. Their caravan had changed considerably since they'd left from Independence. She no longer knew too many of their fellow travelers. But now there were a couple of the young fellows who'd been casting glances. She wasn't sure if she liked it or not. At least, now Lavinia wasn't the only one.

She spotted a current bush just off the path but it had already been picked clean. With so many people here, not much chance finding any berries. She'd have to climb the hillside up above the wagons. On the other side of the creek the rocks rose straight and high, but on this side the rise was more gradual. Someone said there was an old Indian trail above.

Torrey started up the bank, her skirt snagging on rocks and bushes. If she could only wear trousers like the men. After reaching the Indian trail the climb was more gradual, and no danger of getting lost as long as she stayed to the path.

She was now well above the noise and confusion of the camp. Right pleasurable indeed. She stopped to listen to the singing of a bird. She watched a spiny horned toad with skin like an armor dart across a rock.

The sun beat hot. Lavinia's long-sleeved shirtwaist was much too warm. Torrey looked around. Why not? There was no one way up here. She unbuttoned the blouse and took it off, tying it around her waist by the long sleeves. That certainly felt better. She was still well covered by her muslin camisole.

Torrey picked up a walking stick and slashed at the shrubbery as she ambled on. A rustling in the thicket made her stop and turn. A furry creature peeked out from under a bush and Torrey thought how adorable. The adorable creature came out from under the thicket displaying a mouthful of very sharp looking teeth. A badger--and badgers could be mean!

The animal charged. Torrey backed away--right into a brier bush. Sharp teeth caught in the folds of her skirt. In panic, Torrey swung her stick striking the badger. The animal scuttled backwards into a shallow ground hole that was not deep enough to protect its protruding head. Torrey raised her stick for another blow but stopped. The poor critter was as scared as she was. However, she wasted no time scrambling out of the briers, picking up the bucket she'd dropped, and getting away as fast as she could before the animal charged again.

A mighty close call she figured when she stopped to catch her breath a fair distance away. For once her bulky skirt had proved useful. Otherwise those sharp teeth would have had her leg. She wondered if she should turn back. No telling what might be around the next turn. Oh, fiddledee. She'd come to pick berries. She wasn't going back empty handed.

A short distance on she came to a spring pleasantly ringed by soft green grass. Just beyond was a juneberry tree loaded with bunches of blue grape-like fruit. Glory be, she'd have her treat to take back to Elspeth.

Torrey pulled down the branches, gathered what she could reach, then climbed one of the sturdier limbs. The berries were fully ripe and extraordinarily sweet. She ate what she wanted and filled the bucket to the brim. She looked at her stained hands and giggled. If Mama could see me now! At least, there was the spring. She'd be able to wash away most of the stain.

Torrey dabbled her hands in the water. It was clear and cold. She took off her shoes and stockings and splashed her bare feet in the spring. The day was monstrously hot. She pulled her camisole over her head and splashed the water up to her face, around her neck and over her bare shoulders. It did feel good.

"You do make a picture," a voice came from behind her. Jake! She grabbed the camisole and covered her breasts.

"Don't let me stop your bath."

A smothering tide of anger washed over her. She turned her back to Jake as she slipped the muslin garment over her head. She reached for the shirtwaist she'd tied around her middle.

"Looking for this?"

Torrey spun around. Jake grinned as he dangled the shirtwaist in front of her.

Torrey grabbed but Jake stepped back out of her reach. His eyes sparkled with malicious enjoyment.

"How'd you get my shirtwaist?"

"Found it caught in some bushes back a spell."

The brambles--when she'd fought off the badger!

"Figured you'd left it as a sign to follow."

"Give it to me," Torrey yelled, and lunged at Jake. Jake was quicker than Torrey, and the garment went behind his back. He laughed and grabbed her out flung arm.

"Damn you, Jake!"

He dropped the garment behind him and pulled the thrashing girl tight against him.

"Let me go!"

"Torrey, quit fighting. You know you've been wanting me."

"Not on your life, Jake Stringer."

"You're just too damn stubborn to admit it."

"Let me go!" She struggled but his vice-like grip held her firm. She felt the harsh roughness of his shirt through the thin texture of her camisole.

A horse whinnied near by and her heart gave a leap. "Some one's coming." She glanced toward the sound and saw Dancing Girl almost hidden in the thickets.

Jake smiled. "Yer really think so?"

"You've got Dancing Girl!"

"I'm on an errand fer your paw."

"Then get on your way and leave me alone!"

"In due time."

Jake rubbed his face against hers. Short stubby whiskers scratched her cheek. She turned her head to avoid his lips. Her heart was thudding.

"Quit fighting me, Torrey." His lips came down hard on hers. Then one of his hands found her breast and squeezed it, sending horrible messages throughout her body. She twisted, worked one hand free and pushed against him.

"God, what a she-devil you are."

Torrey pulled free, turned and ran. Rocks cut her bare feet but she hardly noticed. She stumbled and fell. And Jake was there. He pushed her down straddling her, his knees on either side of her thighs. He grabbed her hands, and pinned them to the ground. She struggled against his hold.

"Why don't you give in just peaceful like? You might find you'd like some lovin'."

"Never! Never with you, Jake Stringer."

He shook his head as though in disbelief, still staring down at her. "I reckon you just like showing off. Why can't you be willing?"

Her heart thudded in her throat, roiled in her chest. She could hardly breathe. He lowered himself upon her. Torrey held her legs tight together, glad the heavy folds of her skirt were between him and her. Oh, God, what next? What's he going to do?

The mocking smile again. "You know, Torrey, you're even purtier when you're mad. I like a girl who's got lots of spunk."

"If you don't let me go, I'll scream."

Jake laughed. "Go ahead and scream. We're too far from the camp for anyone to hear."

His face was just above hers. She twisted and turned against his weight. Oh God, oh God. What now? He held her wrists with one hand and worked the other up under her camisole. He squeezed her breast and pinched the nipple. Pain shot down to her groin. He pressed on her tighter and an ugly hardness down below moved against her. His face was close--a magnified horror. She jerked one hand free and clawed his face. Red streaks oozed blood.

His hand released her breast and he struck her face. "You bitch! You damn little bitch! Don't think you'll get away with this!"

He pressed on her harder. His mouth found hers. Glutinous! Devouring! She thrashed her head from side to side. Grit and stones ground into her scalp. Oh God. Oh God. Please help me! She willed herself to oblivion, not wanting to know more of what might come next.

But suddenly Jake was yanked off her.

"You rotten bastard!" Anton's voice. "I'll kill you. *Gott,* I will!"

Torrey sat up. Where had Anton come from?

But now another horror was happening. The two men were mercilessly pommeling each other with ferocious blows. They fell to the ground and rolled in the mud at the edge of the spring. Anton's thumbs pressed Jake's windpipe. The younger man's eyes rolled back. Jake thrust his knee into Anton's groin. Anton recoiled in a ball of burning pain. Jake broke free.

Up on his feet, he ran to Anton's horse and grabbed the butt end of a rifle that hung from the saddle. He pointed it at Anton.

Torrey screamed. "No, no! Jake, leave him be. I'll do what you want!"

The gun still aimed at Anton, Jake began to work his way back into the thickets were Dancing Girl was tied. Anton ignored the threat of the gun.

"Hold it, Zwiegmann, or you're good as dead."

"You bastard, what you do to this child!" Anton snarled.

"Save yer breath. She's the one who took off her clothes."

Still pointing the riffle, Jake hoisted himself up onto the saddle. "Reckon I'll be on my way. Torrey, tell your paw I'll deliver his message, but changed my mind about California. 'Spect I'll be heading back to Missouri."

Jake then urged Dancing Girl over to where Anton's mare was grazing. Positioning the rifle so it still posed a threat, Jake got hold of the bay's dragging rein.   Torrey, now on her feet started toward Jake screaming,"Our horses! Our horses!"

Anton caught her and pulled her back. Jake saluted with a sneer and headed up the Indian trail.

She tried to break free from Anton's grasp but Anton's hold was tight. "He's stealing our horses!" she screamed.

Jake and the two horses were now lost to sight by the heavy growth that choked the trail. Torrey's bosom heaved with anger. Dark Thoughts ran wild inside her head. Then glancing down, she realized she was still only clothed in her camisole. Shame overpowered her anger. If Jake hadn't seen her half naked...

She slumped to the ground and buried her face in her hands. All her fault--her fault. Their horses gone. Anton almost killed. And the other thing Jake was doing. If she hadn't taken off her clothes. A wave of nausea roiled through her belly. If Anton hadn't come... She'd rather be dead.   She seethed with hate and loathing. How dared he touch her person? The trembling started in her shoulders, spread through the rest of her body. She wanted to hide from herself--from Anton. But no place to go.

Anton retrieved her shirtwaist, draping it over her shoulders. She slipped her arms in the sleeves and pulled it tight around her. Anton sat down beside her, gathered her to him.

The comfort of his arms quieted her trembling, but unleashed the tears. He drew her head to his chest, running his hand through the tangle of hair. He rocked with her until the tears subsided. Then: "*Meine Liebling,* my poor *kleine Liebling.*"

Suddenly she was aware of Anton's arms. He had seen her so scantily clothed. Fire burned her cheeks. She crossed her arms in front of her as though to cover

179

herself more. She stared at the ground unable to face Anton. "There was no one around. I needed to cool off--the reason I took off my shirt." A futile explanation.

"It's all right, *Liebchen*. I understand. It's not your fault." Anton rose. "Come, we start back for camp before darkness sets in. Where are your shoes?"

"At the edge of the spring." Then her voice choked, became only a whisper. "Anton, I'm so shamed."

"*Liebchen*, it's all right. It's over. We forget it, ja?"

She looked up, her eyes pleading. "Please, Anton. Don't let anyone else ever know what happened."

"If Jake comes back..." Anton's face was threatening. "I'll kill him. Ja, I will."

But then he looked at her, and the love was deep in his eyes--in his heart. He nodded that he did understand. "Ja, I promise," he said. "No one will know."

CHAPTER 20

It was now late in the day. Torrey had not yet returned from picking berries. Medora, aware of the worry shadows in William's eyes, tried not to show her own rising panic. Lavinia and the two younger children had long since come back from the creek. She knew she should not have let Torrey go off alone. William, glancing down the long line of wagons, finally said he was going out and find her.

Medora nodded, but just then caught a glimpse of Torrey working her way toward them through the heavy brush and trees. "Wait, Will. There she is now coming with Anton." Her breath escaped in a sigh of relief.

"'Bout time," William said and started off on a run to meet them.

Medora, curbing her impulse to follow, watched as William joined them, then waited anxiously for the three to get back to the campsite. As they drew closer, Medora could see both Torrey and Anton looked scuffed and bedraggled. A new tide of alarm swept through her. Hurrying to meet them she gasped out, "What happened? Torrey, are you all right?"

Torrey's eyes were cast down. "I'm all right, Mama."

She's not all right, Medora thought, her fear tightening. "Torrey, I can see something's happened." Medora persisted.

"I said I'm all right."

Medora studied her daughter. The fear crept to her chest and lodged there. She saw no apparent abrasions but Torrey's hair was mussed and tangled and she had a strange stricken expression, guarded and withdrawn. Medora reached out, but Torrey pulled back. Medora felt a stab in her heart. My dear, I'm your mother, don't shut me out. Always that wall between them.

Medora turned to Anton. A bruise showed red and ugly on his face and his shirt was torn. "Anton, you tell me what happened."

Anton scowled. "Robbed. That's what. Robbed by that young man of yours."

"A misunderstanding, I'm sure," William intervened, a look of denial darkening his expression. "Anton says Jake stole his horse, and Dancing Girl too. You know Jake. It's just a prank. Jake's not a horse thief. He's joshing you, Anton. I'm sure that's all it is."

"No prank. He stole our horses." Anton's voice bristled with anger. He then told Medora the story--his version, about how he'd come across Torrey picking berries when Jake rode up. When he noticed Jake's bedroll tied to the saddle of

William's horse he became suspicious and demanded an explanation. Jake became hostile. "We both lose our tempers. First a fight with the fists until he gets hold of my rifle. He then takes off with both, your horse and mine, my rifle as well."

"Jake was on an errand for me," William said defensively. "I told Jake to take Dancing Girl. He'll be back. Of course he'll be back," William insisted.

Anton's eyes narrowed to slits. "Make up your mind, William. You've lost your Dancing Girl and I've lost my Gretchen."

William still wasn't convinced. Later, when he had Medora alone, he had an explanation. "Anton is often too blunt. Jake probably resented Anton's questioning, and that led to the fight. Give the lad time. He'll cool off by the time he does my errand, and he'll be back with both the horses."

Medora wasn't so sure. She still had this dreadful feeling that Anton wasn't telling all. At supper Torrey only picked at her food, and climbed into her bedroll early. If only she could reach her, Medora thought over and over.

That evening a message was sent out by Hastings announcing a meeting would be held concerning options for routes that could be taken to get out of the canyon. Children were put to bed early, tucked in with extra quilts to guard against the night's cold. Someone built a fire near the bend of the creek. Most of the men turned out, and the women too now figuring it was high time they be included in the decision making. The men hadn't done too well so far. It was now their children's lives they must think on.

William spread a blanket for Medora and sat down beside her. Lavinia tucked in the two younger children then joined a family named Clark with whom she'd become aquainted. At least Lavinia posed no problem, Medora was thinking, making friends easily yet always conducting herself with lady-like decorum.

For William, the shadow-shapes that danced on the canyon wall added to his closed-in feeling and gut tightening when Anton had told of the routes he had explored that day and said it was possible to take the wagons down the river between these canyon walls. He thought of the Big Blue and other river crossings, even shallow streams. Somehow, he'd never lost his fear of water crossings. He was relieved when Anton offered an ulternative--the old Indian trail up to the ridge.

He looked at Medora and could see her strained troubled expression. Still worried about Torrey. He reached for her hand. "Torrey will be all right. Naturally she's upset, but Jake will be back with Dancing Girl."

Medora did not reply. He is still attributing Torrey's baffling behavior to the loss of the horse she was thinking, but she knew there was more than that. But right now Will's worry was how to get them out of this canyon. She'd seen his face blanch white when Anton suggested taking the wagons down the river and noticed the relief when Anton told of the Indian trail. She wouldn't burden him more with her own suspicions about Torrey. As for him believing in Jake... So typical of Will. He saw only the good in people. He couldn't believe Jake was anything other than his trustworthy hand. Like believing in Mr. Hastings. He had been impressed with the man at the start of their journey, but Hastings had endangered all of their lives lying about his shortcut. Now, she wondered if Will still had faith in Hastings just as he did in Jake?

By the time most of the travelers had gathered, all anxious to learn if there really was a way out of the canyon, Hastings climbed upon a barrel and started waving his arms. "Friends, fellow travelers." As usual, his voice burst with undaunted cheer. "Our good friend, Anton Zwiegmann, has been out scouting. He's here to present us with a couple of options for leaving this canyon."

Anton changed places with Hastings. From the barrel he looked down on the cluster of people, a shadowy mass except for the ones within the firelight's glow. Anton raised his voice to carry out. "We got two ways to go. Either one will get us out of this canyon. Ahead, the canyon gets like a funnel. The Weber cuts through the mountain, but walls go straight up. No banks to speak of. I took my horse down the river to see. The flow is fast, but not too deep. Ja, we can make it with the wagons by going down the middle of the river itself."

"Hell, Zwiegmann, we ain't no ducks," shouted a voice from the shadow.

Anton ignored the interruption. "About five miles we go, then the Weber empties on to the great Salt Lake Valley. We have to watch for boulders, but Ja, we can do it."

As Anton told about the river, William grasp on Medora's hand tightened. She eased her hand away to massage her cramped fingers. William gave her an apologetical look. He hadn't realized he was squeezing so hard. But as Anton talked, William pictured the foamy turbulence of the river, its rush over the rocky bed. He knew what its force would be. Five miles down a rushing river? No way. No way. They'd go the other route for sure.

From Zed Clark, the family Lavinia had joined, came a question: "Zwiegmann, you said there's another way?"

A woman's voice cut in: "I'd say let's go back to Missouri."

"Ja, there's another way," Anton went on. "A mile back is an Indian trail. It goes up to the ridge. Mr. Hastings says from there you can see the Salt Lake Valley."

"That Injun trail? Zwiegmann, you must be loco," shouted a red-shirted man. "I've been up on that Injun trail. It's way too steep and too narrow for wagons."

"We make it wider, but it takes a couple of days. We double team our wagons.

For steepest places, we use a windlass, help pull them up. Even then it's not easy. There'll still be ridges and gullies. Mr. Hastings came that way with his other party going east. Talk it over among you. We can go either way." Anton stepped down from the barrel.

A hub-bub of discussion followed. The talk buzzed strong, a blend of speculations, fear, desperation, and anger toward Hastings for taking them down in this canyon when it hadn't been tried before. Finally red-shirt jumped up on the barrel. "Hell, there's too many of us with no one thinking the same. Me--I'm taking the river. Them who wants to join me, can. The others can go climb the hill."

A far majority decided on the water course. Mr. Hastings would escort them. The next morning wagons were hitched and loose cattle rounded up. They started out following the creek toward the river. Twelve wagons stayed behind, Anton and the Dudleys among them and the Clark family as well.

Anton's choice would have been the river, but he knew of William's fear. Crossing so many water ways during their trek, he'd always been aware of his friend's tension. Yet William always splashed on which proved his courage. Ja, tackling what he feared. But now they had a choice. Not good, one way or the other. But still a choice. He wouldn't put his friend's courage to test this time when there was the alternate way.

Once again the men, now only from twelve wagons, gathered up their shovels, picks and bowies and began hacking away to make the Indian trail wide enough for wagons to use. They cut away shrubs and trees, sent huge rocks tumbling down the mountain side. Short handed for sure. Fortunately, the Clark family had five strong grown sons if you counted the freckle-faced youngest of the clan who was only fourteen, but a good strong husky lad.

William noticed with approval the way the Clark boys pitched in with nary a grumble among them. Wished he could say the same for Eli. Morgan was good at swinging a pick because of his size and his strength, but all the while he peppered the space with his usual complaints and profanity.

On the second day, Eli called it quits. "I've had enough of this shit. Time we had some fresh meat in the stew pot." He picked up his rifle and took off.

The others stuck with it, combining strength and determination. The men chipped away at the banks. A young Clark's ax slipped, but fortunately only slashed his boot. Another man stumbled and fell against a tangle of thorns. Tempers flared. Yet the narrow Indian trail widened enough for wagons to make it up the steep incline.

Late on the second day a member of the other party who'd taken the river came back. "We all made it through. No mishaps a'tall," he told them. "I'd suggest you'd do likewise. Mr. Hastings says he'll wait a day for you to join us at the big black rock."

William still had doubts about tackling the river. And by this time the Indian trail had been widened nearly to the top of the ridge and seemed safe enough for the wagons to make it up the steep incline.

On the third morning they were ready for the climb. Anton took charge. "Be sure everything inside the wagons is secured and tied down. We use at least six yoke of oxen per wagon. We'll change off and give the teams a rest between pulls. Near the top we'll have to use the windlass."

Double teaming, William thought. He'd lost two of his best work animals and was now down to only three pair of oxen for each wagon and a couple of rangy beef cows which weren't much good for heavy pulls. "You know I've only got six good working critters," he told Anton. "If we're only going to get one trip from a team."

"We'll use some of mine," Anton replied. He had fared better with his stock. He still had six pair of strong oxen and only one wagon to pull. He also had eight beeves that could be put to the yoke if need be, and two non-producing milk cows. For riding stock, Anton still had two other horses besides the one Jake had stolen. "We'll use three pair of yours and three pair of mine with Freddy for the wheeler," Anton suggested. "We'll switch and rest the ones we have to use a second time."

The wagons waiting their turn were to stay at the present campsite near the creek. "What about us women and the children?" Medora asked.

"You stay here until we have all the wagons at the top," Anton replied. "After the wagons all up, then you will climb to the top. A steep climb, ja, but you can make it."

"What about Elspeth? She's much too ill to leave her bed."

Anton looked grave, but nodded his shaggy head. "Ja, she stays in the wagon with plenty of blankets for padding."

"Elspeth has made it over some other rough places," William reminded Medora hoping to ease her concern. "We'll take care. She'll be all right."

Clark offered to take his wagon up first. "With my strong boys, I've got enough muscle to get my rig over the stumps. It will be a good test for the others."

An hour after the Clark wagon started up the steep incline, the youngest Clark, whose name was True Trevor, came back down saying all had gone well. "The windlass worked tolerable good. Got the wagon up over the final hump without nary a snag." His freckled face beamed. "Pa says the rest o'you will do right smart. He told me to stay down and help you with yours."

"Much obliged for the help," said William.

The morning had turned hot. Anton had already removed his coat and was down to his shirt sleeves. "A scorcher today. And it's early yet. Better your supply wagon goes next before it bakes like an oven for poor Mrs. Morgan." Eli had not

185

yet returned from yesterday's hunt, so Mike started helping William with the yoking and hitching.

"You're short handed, so I'm going up with the wagon and help," Torrey told her father.

"No, you stay here with the rest of the women until we get all the wagons to the top."

Torrey's face set with that determined look. "True Trevor said there were some real hard places going up. He said at times it took all of them pushing together just to keep their wagon steady."

"Not the kind of work for women-folk," her father insisted.

"'Spect I'll be going regardless."

William shook his head. Not much sense trying to argue with that strong-willed daughter of his. And he could use another pair of hands.

Medora cushioned blankets around Elspeth. She placed a corked bottle of water within her reach. The frail woman lay quiet, eyes closed. For a moment, Medora had a touch of fright seeing Elspeth so still. Then Elspeth's eyelids fluttered.

"They're ready to start up the trail now, Elspeth dear. Is there anything more I can do for you?"

The heavy eyelids opened. Elspeth shook her head, rolling it against the pillow. She said nothing, fearful of starting up the coughing again. Medora reached in gently squeezing the other woman's hand. "It will be a steep climb. At least you're well cushioned with the extra blankets. Are you comfortable enough?"

Elspeth nodded.

Will cracked his whip. The wagon lunged. Medora stepped back as the wagon creaked and began to roll toward the Indian trail. Anton had gone ahead, checking the trail. She watched Torrey trudging behind the wagon and knew it would be useless to change the girl's mind, and just as well in case Elspeth needed some help. She looked up at the sky. It would be near noon by the time they got back for the next wagon. They'd be hungry. She and Lavinia would prepare something simple and have the wagon packed and ready to go.

The bawling oxen and jolting wagon worked on up the erratic grade, back and forth, following the switchback path. At times the vehicle scraped against the side of the cliff, hit stumps and trembled. Occasionally Torrey looked inside the wagon to be sure Elspeth was riding well. The trail got steeper. The oxen had difficulty keeping their footing. One time the wagon shuddered and stalled against a large rock. All hands pushed to get it over. The wagon rolled on. An overhanging branch ripped a tear in the canvas top. Anton swore in German, but William held his tongue, not being a swearing man.

Torrey felt the sweat running down her back and soaking her camisole. It seemed like they'd been climbing forever. Finally they neared the top. Above Mr. Clark and a couple of his sons peered over a ledge.

"Hold it," hollered Anton. "Time to attach the lines so the windlass can help with the pull." He shouted to the men above to toss down the ropes and he and William attached them to the wagon.

Torrey looked in the wagon. "You all right, Elspeth?" The woman nodded. Lordy, but her eyes looked heavy. Torrey felt a clutch at her heart. "This is the steepest part. You want Papa to lift you out and carry you up?" Elspeth shook her head. No, she didn't want to be moved.

The oxen were getting restless. Torrey moved up to the front to calm the jittery critters. She talked softly and patted Freddy's big sweaty head. "Almost there now, boy. Just a little bit more."

Her father came up beside her. "I'll take over the animals now. You go back and ask Anton what he wants you to do."

Anton was making a second check of the ropes to see that all were secure. "Ja, you and the boy there, stay at the back of the wagon. Steady it best you can. Mike and I will be one on either side." He looked up above and yelled. "Ready down here. You can start cranking in."

William cracked his whip, but the oxen were reluctant to start up again. Mike, who usually was so quiet, had a booming voice when he did let go, which he now did hoping to start the weary beasts moving. Instead, it seemed to confuse them. The team started forward, but wavered back and forth in a snake-like motion. Torrey, at the back, pressed with all her might trying to hold her end of the wagon steady.

"Push, True Trevor, push!" she yelled.

"Watcha think I'm doing?"

The wagon made a sudden lurch ahead then started shifting. "*Beim Teufel noch 'N' Mal!* It's leaning," shouted Anton, throwing his weight against his side of the wagon. "Mike, pull on your side!"

"I'm pulling."

Torrey grabbed a corner, straining her weight against it, pushing as hard as she could away from the edge of the road. She could feel the wagon leaning. She strained against it even harder.

Anton yelled, "Watch it, Torrey! It's going! Get out of the way!"

Anton jumped to the back, shoved Torrey out of the way as the wagon leaned. Torrey screamed. A rope snapped, and the next one too from the strain. With heart pounding and eyes not wanting to believe what she was seeing as the wagon turned on its side, rolled over and began a plunge down the mountainside, yanking the

187

twelve yoked oxen with it.

"Elspeth! Elspeth!" Torrey screamed, crawling to the edge of the road to follow with her eyes the terrifying decent of the wagon.

It was rolling, tossing and turning. Wood splintered and flew in all directions. Animals bellowed in panic and pain. Down, down. Torrey watched in horror. *She should have pushed harder!* The wagon turned over and over, crashing trees in its path. Dirt roiled up and around it. The contents went flying.

The three men were now scrambling down the steep side of the mountain. Torrey followed, slipping and sliding down the steep bank. Her skirt caught on a protruding wedge and jerked her back. She tore it free. It gave way so suddenly that she lost her footing and began rolling. She grabbed a straggly branch and stopped her fall, then slid the rest of the way down to where the crashed wagon had landed; a jangled jumble of bellowing animals, splintered wood, twisted metal, and a snow-storm of flour.

"Elspeth! Elspeth!" Then Torrey saw her.

Elspeth had been tossed from the wagon about halfway down and caught from a further plunge by a heavy thicket. She lay in a crumpled heap at a grotesque angle, her face pressed to the earth. William reached Elspeth first. He gently turned her over and looked into the bulging unseeing eyes then drew down the puffy eyelids.

Torrey pushed her father aside and closed her arms around the lifeless form. She brushed at the ground-in dirt on Elspeth's face, pulled a twig from the blood-matted hair. Every ounce of her being cried a denial. "It's all right, Elspeth. It's all right," she said over and over again.

Then her father's voice coming from somewhere. "Torrey, you've said your good-bye. Come girl, you must let her go." His hand rested on her shoulder.

"Let me be," was Torrey's response.

"Torrey, there's nothing more you can do now."

"I need to be with Elspeth!"

William looked at his daughter with sorrow in his heart. Grief had to have its own time. Perhaps she needed more time to say good-bye to her friend. He turned and walked away.

He started looking at the wreckage with a feeling of helpless despair. Anton and Mike were already tramping around looking for whatever could be recovered. Bags of rice, beans, and flour had all torn open, their contents strewn over a large area of ground. William picked up one of the bags that still had rice trapped in its folds. He reached in, trailed his fingers through the grain. Maybe five or ten pounds left from a hundred pound bag. They'd be needing every bit of foodstuff that could be salvaged. He stooped and picked up a greasy slab of bacon, already rancid from the long exposure to the many warm days of travel. It was covered with ground in dirt, but it was still worth keeping. Under a wagon wheel he recognized the small satchel that contained Medora's prized medicines and remedies. He tugged and pulled before it finally worked loose, for all the good it did. Every bottle, every jar, every twist of herbs had been smashed and mixed to a gooey slushy mess. He hated having to tell Medora that there was nothing left to be saved.

Slowly he tramped over the dried grasses and looked through the thickets for whatever could be found. He picked up a piece of broken blue and white pottery. Medora's willow ware. He gathered up several more broken pieces. Only dishes, but they meant so much to Medora. Foolishly he tried to fit some of the broken pieces together, then let the fragments slip from his fingers back to the soil. How would he tell her? A larger piece held in a tangle of shrubbery caught his eye. He pulled it free and was surprised that it was still whole. The only one. A sauce dish, Medora would call it. He traced the edge with his finger. There was one very small chip. *This one little dish--all that is left.* He put it in the bag burying it in the few pounds of rice.

He continued to wander the hillside. Total destruction. Some of the oxen were already dead. The ones still alive were bellowing in pain. Twelve of their best work animals. Anton had already sent Mike up to get his rifle. The animals would have to be put out of their misery. Freddy too. William took the big tan bloody head in his hands. Large dark eyes begged for relief.

Guilt weighted William's shoulders. Half of the oxen were Anton's, and he alone was to blame. Anton had never wanted to take Hasting's shortcut. As for getting out of this canyon, he knew Anton had favored the river. If it hadn't been for his own unreasonable fear... Why hadn't he left the decision up to his wise and dependable friend? Why hadn't he put more faith in the Lord?

There was at least two more months of travel ahead of them over deserts and mountains. How would they survive with most of their food supplies scattered? Anton had some in his wagon, but not nearly enough. Anton's rig was filled mostly with heavy farm equipment and his potted trees--what they needed to start their farms--if they ever got there.

William glanced over at his daughter, still holding the dead woman in her arms, looking as though in a trance. *Elspeth's death.* That too could be placed on his shoulders. If they hadn't attempted to climb this mountain--if they hadn't come down in this canyon...

Torrey did not know how long she sat with Elspeth in her arms. Panic surrounded her, but strangely off in the distance. Men's voices; her father's and

Anton's--and others.

"Lord, what a mess." "Doesn't look like there's much to save." She could hear the crazed bawling of injured oxen. And gun shots, one after another. Why were they shooting the poor critters? Death and dying. Everything was death and dying. Her friend was dead in her arms. She should have pushed harder against the wagon. Elspeth... Elspeth...

A hand pressed her shoulder. "Come girl." Her father's voice. "We've taken care of all we can now. We've got to get back down the mountain."

Torrey looked up with fear in her heart. "No. I have to stay with Elspeth."

"She'll be taken care of later."

"But Elspeth is my friend."

"I know. I know."

She felt so strange. The awful pain in her chest was dissolving to a void of nothingness. Why was she here? Why was she holding a bundle of torn rags that her father was trying to take away. She clutched the bundle tighter.

"Torrey, you must let her be. We have to get back."

She released her hold. Her father pulled her to her feet, his arm comfortingly around her waist. She wasn't sure where she was. Everything seemed unreal. She saw Anton stretch a blanket over the torn bundle of rags. Strange thing for Anton to do.

Medora was getting restless. She wished the men and Torrey would return. It was taking them longer than it had taken the Clarks to get their wagon up to the top of the ridge.

Everything was ready to go when the men did get back. She and Lavinia had secured all loose objects in the wagon as Anton had instructed. The coals from the morning fire had been smothered with dirt, and pans and dishes stored away. They'd have just a quick meal--cold beans and cornbread. The men only need hook the teams and take off.

Why didn't they come? If she'd wander toward the Indian trail maybe she could see. But the children were playing down by the stream and she hated to leave. Lavinia was visiting the pleasant Mrs. Clark. Seemed she'd become mighty friendly with the family. Because of their five handsome sons? Medora wondered. She'd best do something useful instead of fretting.

Medora removed her sewing basket from the wagon. One of William's shirts needed mending. Soon her needle was making quick stitches. It was then she heard a commotion in the far off distance and felt a rush of fear. A crack of a tree? Animals bellowing? Medora dropped her mending and started to run.

Just then Jenny screamed, "Mama, Mama!"

Medora spun around. Jenny was running toward her holding out her hand. "My finger. Mama, my finger."

My God, what now? She could still hear the distant cry of oxen. Was her whole world exploding at once?

"A bee. I saw the bee."

Medora took the small hand. Indeed, she could see the stinger. Carefully she pulled it out. "There, my darling. Now it will feel better."

Jenny was still crying. "No, it still hurts. Mama, it still hurts."

Gun shots in the distance! *Oh God, what now?* Another shot and another!

"Mama!"

"Yes, my darling." Her stomach was a churning mass of anxiety, torn two ways.

"Mama, It's still hurting."

"I know, my dear." She wanted to run and find out what was happening. Instead, she took Jenny's arm and led her over to the stream. "I'll fix you a mud poultice. You'll see. It will take the sting away." If it didn't work, she had a salve in her medicine satchel that would help--as soon as she could get it.

Medora dabbed cooling mud on Jenny's finger. The child's sobs subsided as she watched her mother with interest. It was then Medora looked up and saw William and Torrey coming. Thank goodness, at last. But when she saw their bedraggled appearance... Quickly she rinsed her hand in the stream and rushed to meet them. "What happened. What's wrong?"

"Now calm yourself, Medora." William had hoped to ease it to her gently. But how? "We had an accident. The wagon went over a drop."

"Oh, dear heaven." Medora's face blanched and her eyes widened. "Was it badly damaged?"

"Smashed to smithereens, I'm afraid."

"And Elspeth?" She was afraid to ask. "What about Elspeth?"

"God rest her soul, she's now with her Maker."

"Oh, poor woman." Medora closed her eyes for the moment and said a silent prayer. Perhaps a blessing. Elspeth had suffered so much these last few days. Perhaps it was the Lord's way of putting her out of her misery sooner.

Torrey looked at her mother. *Just poor woman?*

"At least, she's now at peace," her mother said.

Doesn't she care? Mama, Elspeth is dead!

"Was anything saved?" her mother asked.

Didn't you hear? Elspeth is dead!

"Not much. The oxen had to be put out of their misery. It was about a seventy-five foot drop. They were all too badly injured."

"All the oxen? Oh dear heaven, what will we do? Even Freddy?"

"Even Freddy."

"Our provisions?"

"Not much left. We scraped up what we could. Anton and the other men are bringing down what we salvaged--and Elspeth."

Elspeth is dead! It was like an echo in Torrey's mind. The rest of what had happened was still just a blur--the scramble down the mountain. She remembered her father's strong hand leading the way. But now hearing her father tell her mother about the oxen--and Elspeth. The horrifying realty rushed back with overwhelming pain. Her friend up there on the hillside, and Mama only saying *poor woman.* She doesn't care that Elspeth is dead. She only cares about the other losses!

Her father reached into the bag he was carrying and pulled out the sauce dish. "Twas a miracle that this was saved."

Her mother took it, turned it in her hand as though she'd never seen it before. She traced the blue pattern with the tip of her finger, ran her finger around the edge and stopped at a nick, rubbing it over and over again. Then she clutched the sauce dish to her heart. Tears shimmered down her face.

Torrey felt a rush of fury. *Her broken dishes! She's crying for her broken dishes. She didn't cry for Elspeth!*

"This is all that's left?" Her voice was only a whisper.

"That's all I found still whole. I'm sorry, Medora. I'll get you the finest set we can find when we get to California."

Torrey saw the liquid misery glistening in her mother's eyes while her own eyes smarted with anger.

"I used those dishes when I was a child," her mother said, and then still holding the dish to her heart, turned and walked toward the wagon. A stepping box had been placed under the tailgate. Medora stepped on the box, and raising her skirt just slightly in her usual ladylike manner, she climbed into the wagon. Torrey watched in disbelief. *That dish means more to her than Elspeth!*

CHAPTER 21

They brought the Clarks' wagon back down before they laid Elspeth to rest that evening. No one else wanted to risk going up the hazardous trail after the plunge of the Dudleys' wagon, especially since the other group had made it safely down the river. The men had gone back and gathered up some of the boards from the smashed wagon and fashioned a coffin. Eli had not yet returned from his hunting expedition, but no more time could be wasted waiting for his return.

Medora, with the help of a couple of the other women, laid Elspeth out. They washed the dirt and blood from the dead woman and Medora brushed the snarls from her hair.

"Skin and bones," one of the ladies remarked. "Not much of her a'tall."

"She's been suffering so dreadfully these last few weeks," said Medora. "The blessing is that her pain is now over."

Hearing her mother's words infuriated Torrey. She bristled with anger and it mixed with her grieving. These last few days had been more than she could bear. Starting with Jake, the hurting was relentless: a devouring, bottomless chasm of shame and pain.

They placed Elspeth in the box and Medora rested the dead woman's head on one of her own embroidered pillows with the crocheted lace edge. She arranged a spray of lupine on the corpse's chest and crossed the claw-like fingers over them.

"She looks almost purty now," one of the women said.

William gave the service, starting with "I am the resurrection and the life, saith the Lord; he that believeth in me, though he were dead, yet shall he live..." and concluding with, "Grace be to you, and peace, from God our Father, and from the Lord Jesus Christ."

"Amen," came from the others, and they nailed the box closed.

As it was about to be lowered into the shallow grave, Eli Morgan road into the camp, a dressed antelope slung over the rump of his mule. "Got me a badger too," he said as he trotted his horse up to the group. "Badger be mighty fine eatin', rich like bear." He stopped when he noticed the box. "Who ye got in there?"

William stepped up. "I'm sorry Eli. It's Elspeth, God rest her soul." He explained what had happened.

Eli's eyes narrowed to accusing slits. "I was again' comin' down this canyon from the start, but you wouldn't listen to Zwiegmann and me. Dudley, it were yer notion to take this shortcut, and it were yer wagon that killed my woman. I hold ye to blame."

William paled, for he had already been castigating himself. If they'd stayed with the proven route to Fort Hall. If it wasn't for his fear of the river...

Medora's eyes flashed with anger. She had to squeeze her hands tight to keep from lashing out at this despicable man. "How dare you imply such a thing? What ever did you do to help your wife through her suffering?"

Anton, also incensed, grabbed Morgan's arm and swung him around. "No one's to blame. *Mein Gott,* man, it was an accident. It could have happened to anyone."

Later, Medora, sensing William's torment, took his hands. "William, you can't hold yourself responsible for all that's happened. There's been scarcely a family that hasn't had some misfortune. As for that Eli Morgan..." Her fine features flared with indignation. "He pretended he was grieved. But you know he wasn't. He never even asked for the cover of the box to be removed. He didn't even care to say a proper farewell!" But then her voice softened. "Poor Elspeth. Poor dear soul." A tear slid down her cheek. "Rest in peace, dear Elspeth."

The next morning, feeling the pressure of valuable time lost, the small party broke camp right after breakfast amid the usual bawling cattle, barking dogs, and shouting men. William looked around for Eli, needing his help.

"Saw him leave early on his mule heading for the river," someone said.

A mixed blessing, William thought, not wanting Eli's accusing eyes upon him. But, without either Eli or Jake, he definitely was shorthanded. Torrey, aware of her father's need insisted on helping him yoke the team. She wanted hard work--exhaust her body so her mind wouldn't dwell on past happenings.

The eleven wagons followed alongside the creek to where it flowed into the Weber. Tramped brush and cropped grass indicated where the larger party had started down the river four days before. Again Anton took charge and would be the first to put his wagon in the river. The Clark wagon would go next. William chose to be near the end of the line. He wished he wasn't going in at all.

Anton started giving instructions. "Hoist your flour and all your spoilables up as high as you can get. The currant's right strong but you've got to Keep those wheels on the bottom. If your loads not heavy enough, weigh your wagon down with rocks or it might float away. Ja, for even more drag, you can chain your rear wheels. You'll only need one yoke of oxen." As for the loose cattle, Mike and one of the Clark boys would herd them along after the eleven wagons were well under way.

As the men started their preparations, Medora welcomed the free time. She had rushed through morning chores to get under way. Now, while waiting, she hoped there would be enough time to tend some of the other necessities. Here the river water was fresh and clear. No telling how much good water they'd have when they got to the great salty lake. Maybe there'd be enough time to launder their hair. Luckily, she still had a bar of good soap--left in the family wagon after its last use, which brought to mind what they had lost, and now what they faced.

Most of their provisions were gone--scattered and left on a hillside. How would they survive? And the other things. Elspeth. She missed the odd little woman. And Torrey's grieving--and not able to help. She felt so helpless. The thoughts were so crushing--like looking through a long dark tunnel with no end in sight. But dwelling on things she could do nothing about was not getting things she could do done. Medora straightened her shoulders and called to Lavinia.

She found a nice spot along the creek slightly up from where the men were preparing the wagons for the river. She filled a basin with the clear water and she and Lavinia took turns washing each other's hair. She hoped Torrey would have enough time after helping her father. Then, while Lavinia sat in the sun brushing her long honey-colored hair, Medora lathered her hands with soap and started in on Jenny amid whimpering of "You're getting soap in my eyes," and "Mama, you're pulling too hard."

"Oops, oops. Sorry, my dear. I do declare, a rat has made a nest in your hair."

Jenny giggled. "Oh, Mama, that's not so."

"Sure enough. One's been here."

Torrey stepped up, her skirt streaked with mud and dirt smudged her face.

"Lands sake, you do look a sight."

"What else, when I'm helping Papa?" Perverseness colored Torrey's tone.

Medora could see the misery in her daughter's eyes, knew how she was hurting because of Elspeth's death. "I know your father must be grateful to have your help with both Jake and Mr. Morgan gone, but if you are finished..."

Torrey appeared not to hear. Why was it so difficult to reach the girl? She wanted so much to help ease her pain--comfort her child. She ached because she was a mother who had failed to protect her child from life's cruelties. If she could only break the barrier between them. "I just thought while we're waiting our turn-- Perhaps you'd like me to launder your hair like I did Jenny's. The water is so soft and nice here. It would make you feel fresher."

Torrey's face set hard as a piece of carved marble. "Whatever freshening I need, I can do it myself."

"As you say." Medora felt bruised by her child's rejection. Torrey ladled water from a bucket into the basin and started to wash the grime from her hands and her face. Medora, watching, felt an overwhelming desire to put her arms around Torrey and draw her close, but checked the impulse.

"There's still a smudge on your face." Medora reached for a cloth that hung from a bush. "Here, let me get it for you."

Torrey glared. She splashed more water on her face and scrubbed so hard her cheeks flamed red. Medora stepped back. What is it? What have I done? Why are you so angry with me? She felt as though Torrey was blaming her for Elspeth's death.

As Torrey finished her cleansing, Medora handed her a towel. Torrey took it without a word and rubbed her face with such vigor Medora wondered if she'd have any skin left.

"I hope that now meets with your approval," Torrey said, throwing back the towel. She turned and started back down toward the wagons. Medora watched with an ache in her heart.

William had parked their wagon, while waiting his turn, slightly apart from the others. Torrey was thankful for that. She wanted no useless conversation, especially with her mother. She was glad her father was off jawing with some of the other men. She needed time alone. The pain was too hurting, and all Mama cared about was how her daughter looked. She didn't care how she looked. Elspeth was dead, and Mama didn't care. She still saw her mother clutching that dish to her breast and tears filling her eyes. It seemed like an iron band was squeezing her innards. Elspeth had looked so still in the box. Pain against pain. Torrey crawled into the wagon.

She brushed at the tears that ran down her face. Her nose, too, was running a stream. She reached for the hem of her skirt to wipe her nose and noticed the dirt on the skirt. Yes, Mama, I do look a sight. So what if I do? I don't want to be like other girls, fussing to make men look at me. *Jake had looked!* Her temples pounded. Her stomach pumped anger. Emotions mixed and tangled. Elspeth. Mama. And Jake.

Her gaze was drawn to her mother's sewing basket over in the corner. The bright handles of her mother's scissors protruded like a hand waiting to be grasped. The mud on her skirt. All right, Mama, I'll take care. Torrey slashed quickly, cutting away the offending streaks. There, Mama, dirt's all gone. Will that please you now?

Torrey sat back, appalled at what she had done. What ever had come over her? Now what to do? Take the skirt off and hide it? Pin the slashed pieces together? Papa would be calling her any minute to help launch the wagon.

She rummaged through the trunk that stored their clothing. She'd slip on another skirt and hide the damaged one. A pair of her father's old pantaloons was on top of the folded garments. She took out the trousers and held them up. Papa hardly ever wore this pair. She'd have to help Papa the rest of the way to California, doing the work of a man. Why be hampered by a bulky skirt that catches on bushes and gets in the way?

Torrey quickly pulled on the trousers and then looked for something to tie around her middle to hold them on. She found a stretch of rope. She flexed her legs. It felt odd to have them encased in such sturdy material, but she liked the feel. No more secret nods from Mama that her skirt wasn't properly down. And she'd tie her hair back like she used to--keep it out of her way. There'd be no more female falderols that might give men ideas.

Like Jake! She ran her fingers through her hair. *Jake always liked it hanging loose.* When she'd quit tying it back, had she given Jake an invitation to do what he did? Was she after all to blame? A shudder ran through her with sickening force. Jake grinning--the feel of his hands. Her mind swam with confusion. Was she going to puke? She pulled herself as tight as the knot in her belly. The scissors were still there beside her. Well she'd make sure no other man would ever want to look at her again.

Torrey grabbed a heavy hank of hair. Bright auburn tresses soon littered the wagon floor. That would fix Mama as well with her notions of what's proper and what's not. Elspeth, with her heavy brogans and her clay pipe, was never a fine enough lady for Mama. Well, Mama, wait till you see your daughter now. For the first time since Elspeth's death, Torrey's grief was nullified by a certain amount of satisfaction. Mama was in for a monstrous surprise!

William walked to the edge of the river. He listened to its voice, heard the chortling of its strength. He watched the foamy turbulence as it rushed over the rocks. The lunge of fear returned--the same he'd known when he'd faced the Big Blue three months back. But that watery hurdle had been crossed successfully, except for Torrey's dunking. They'd crossed many others after the Big Blue. No reason to think this would be any more hazardous. Except--five miles? A mighty stretch to travel down stream with wagons. He was glad his wagon was to be near the last to enter--gave him more time to work up his courage.

Anton went in first, wanting to test the rocky bottom. One of the Clark boys had offered to assist. In his usual no-nonsense manner, Anton prodded his unwilling animals into the icy waters but allowed them to gingerly pick their own way. Watching, William's heart jumped every time the wagon shuddered and leaned. But young Clark was there to push. The wagon would straighten and then go on. The water rose quickly to the wagon bed. It didn't look too bad--if the water didn't get much deeper. But with those several miles ahead...

The third wagon was now in. No trouble at all. Then the fourth with the fifth and the sixth next in line and the seventh getting ready. His time would be coming up sooner than he wished, William reckoned, so he guessed it was time to call Torrey. At first he had told Torrey he wouldn't need her assistance as Perrigrine, the oldest of the Clark sons, had offered to help. William suspected Perrigrine's offer was partly so he could watch Lavinia as she followed the narrow ledge just above the water line along with the other women and children. The ledge made a good footpath and less risky than tramping down the middle of a river with its fast flowing current. He wanted Torrey up there as well, but her thimble of a nose had gone up as usual. She would help with the wagon.

As William walked up to tell his women folk it was time to get started, he found Medora waiting with Lavinia and the two younger ones, ready and set to go. Dusty Dog wagged his tail in greeting. "We're next, soon as the Granger's wagon goes in." He glanced around. "Where's Torrey?"

"She's already down at the wagon. Didn't you see her?"

"I was watching the others get launched."

Medora's eyes were shadowed with concern. "She's taking Elspeth's death so hard. I wish she'd accept some comforting. It breaks my heart."

A muscle twitched in William's face. "If she hadn't been there to see it happen. A frightening and sickening sight." He sighed. "That's why I gave in to letting her help me now--take her mind from her pain. She's so determined. I'd rather she go with you and the children." He shook his head. "Well, guess it's time for us." They started toward the wagon.

"Torrey, our turn next," William called out as they approached the rig.

"Coming, Papa," came a muffled reply. Torrey climbed out of the wagon.

Lavinia and Medora gasped. William's eyes got bigger, not believing what he saw.

"Geeminy whiskers!" burst from Billy.

Medora choked out: "Victoria, what have you done?" Abject horror reflected in her eyes. Triumph in Torrey's.

"How could you?" Lavinia said in utter shock.

Billy started to laugh. "You sure do look funny." And Jenny followed suit with her giggle, her hand covering her mouth to stifle the outburst. Then she pointed. "You got on Papa's trousers."

Indeed she had, rolled up at the cuff and held in place at the waist with a twist of rope. William still stood open-mouthed too astonished to comment.

"What's the meaning of this?" Medora demanded.

"Papa's shorthanded. He needs my help. I won't be hindered by a bulky skirt and hair getting in my way!"

"So short! Did you have to cut your hair so short?" Medora still could hardly believe her eyes. "It will be months before you'll look proper again!" Short it was, cropped to within an inch of her scalp. How could she? *How could she?*

Torrey's eyes flashed. "Proper! I don't care a tinker's damn 'bout being proper. You think being proper is all that matters. Well, Mama, it's not. Only caring about people is important. But you wouldn't know about that!"

"Torrey!" William's voice burst out in shocked outrage. "Don't talk to your mother like that!" He was as stunned as Medora at Torrey's outburst as well as the sight of his daughter's short cropped hair. Her beautiful hair. The one child of his who'd been so generously blessed with such a crown of glory--that rich copper main that fell past her shoulders in those thick luxurious waves. Now, hardly more than a stubble! And attacking her mother so cruelly! "Apologize to your..." But Torrey was gone, a flash of a dark blue shirt and baggy trousers disappeared among the trees. For a moment William made as if to follow, recognizing the turbulent misery in Torrey's eyes. His child was desperately hurting, and his immediate impulse was to protect her, set up a bulwark against her pain. But he stopped short and turned back to Medora. Color had drained from her face. Hurt was there as well, in the dark pools of those usually clear blue eyes.

"Does she really think I didn't care about Elspeth?"

"She's a child. She's mighty grieved, perhaps more than any of us realized. And such a shock what she went through." He thought of Torrey up on the hillside, holding the dead woman in her arms.

"But why cut off her hair? It doesn't make sense."

"Who ever can figure out Torrey?" Lavinia cut in.

"I'll go find her," said Billy, darting off toward the growth that had swallowed his sister. Dusty Dog, excited with the sudden activity, barked at his heels.

"Hold it, son. Come on back," William called out. Billy returned with dragging footsteps. "Let her be for now. I reckon it's grieving that needs some aloneness."

Then came the call: "Dudley, you're next. Granger's rig is already in." William looked perplexed.

Medora's heart felt so heavy. She wanted to go to her daughter, hold her, tell her she did understand. But she knew it was her father Torrey wanted. "Will, go find her. It's you Torrey needs." William nodded and motioned for the next wagon to take his turn.

He found Torrey huddled against a rock in a cluster of trees, her face swollen from crying. He gathered his child to him and held her without speaking. Finally he said, "I'm sorry I shouted at you the way I did. But you're wrong about your mother. Your mother did care. She nursed Elspeth the same as she'd have done for any one of you children. You know that."

"Elspeth was never good enough for her."

"Your mother had a different up-bringing from Elspeth. She was just afeard you would learn bad habits."

"Elspeth was my friend."

"I know she was. Elspeth was friend to us all. We'll all miss Elspeth--even your mother." He kissed the top of her forehead. He knew in time the hard edges of grief would soften--but it would take time.

"Come now, we'll have to be going or be left behind." He ran his fingers through the short stubble of hair and smiled. "You'll have to wear a hat now or you'll sunburn during the day and catch your death at night."

Torrey gave him a watery smile and touched her head to his shoulder. "Papa, I do love you so."

The Dudleys' wagon was now the last to enter the river. There had been no casualties so far, yet William offered a silent prayer as he grabbed the rein of his oxen to lead them into the water. *Lord, don't desert us now.*

He glanced toward the cliff that rose almost straight up from the river except for that narrow ledge that served as a footpath. His family, except for Torrey, was there following behind some of the others. Lavinia strode ahead, then Medora with a firm grasp on Jenny's hand. Lagging behind was Billy, the dog at his heels as usual. The boy stopped, picked up a stone and skimmed it into the water. Torrey should be there too instead of behind the wagon along with the young Clark whose gaze definitely followed Lavinia.

William splashed in, pulling on the reins of the oxen. Torrey came up beside him, an old soft felt hat of his covering her head. It was still a shock to see no hair about her shoulders.

"Want me to lead the critters?" she asked.

"No. You stay back with Perrigrine. The animals are apt to get skittish."

But she had already taken hold of the strap and was leading them out farther. The oxen bawled as they slipped on the stones of the streambed. The water churned around the high wheels of the wagon, almost up to Torrey's slim waist.

"Torrey, it's getting too deep!"

"I'm all right, Papa."

The wagon scraped a high rock and tipped. William pushed his weight against it and Perrigrine jumped fast to lend his support. The wagon righted as the oxen moved on further into the river. William splashed up beside Torrey. "That's enough, girl. This river's too dangerous. I want you up on the bank with your mother."

Torrey scowled. "I'm as strong as Perrigrine." She pulled the ox whip from her father's hand. "Reckon I'll be needing this to keep the critters in line."

"Torrey, I insist!" Just then a rock turned under William's foot and he fell backwards. By the time he'd scrambled back on his feet, Torrey was several strides beyond him. He shook his head as he watched her go on. Never could change that girl's mind once she's set to.

For five hazardous watery miles the eleven wagons rolled on down the center of the Weber River. Some places the flow was gentle. More often it foamed and crashed as it rushed over rocks, its deafening roar mixing with panicked cries of the animals. The larger boulders threatened. The wagons leaned far on one side and then on the other. Time and time again, both William and Perrigrine lent all the strength they could muster to keep the Dudleys' wagon upright. Some of the wagons mired in the mud. The men had to team together, turn the wheels by the spokes to get them out of the mire. Other times the wagons were held back to keep them from rushing too fast upon a lower-lying rock and being dashed to pieces. Once Torrey slipped and William lunged to reach her.

At last they were through the canyon. A grassy plain opened before them. Exuberant "hurrahs" burst forth from the small company. They had gotten through the narrow gorge without harm to anyone or any of their critters. The Wasatch Mountains and its rugged canyons were behind them. William bowed his head. *Thank thee, oh Lord, and forgive a sinner for having had doubts.*

It was the sixth day of August. Ahead lay the Great Salt Lake that they'd skirt to its far southern end where they'd rest a day or so. There they'd stock up by cutting grass for their animals and filling their water barrels to last a day and two nights in preparation for the forty mile stretch of waterless salt flats. "No problem at all," Hastings had assured them earlier, "If you take those precautions."

Traveling now should be easier. No more rugged mountains and canyons to conquer until they reached the Sierra Nevada, and that last hurdle would be crossed early in September, long before they'd be threatened by snows. William felt a return of his usual euphoria. The Lord *was* leading the way. He raised his arms and shouted, "Now onward to California!"

Others shouted too.

Except for Torrey.

The grief for her friend was a raw open wound. Someday she hoped it would not hurt so much. But she'd never forget the other. Jake's attack. It had been a violation of her private self. No. She would never forget. Men! She didn't want anything to do with men again--now or ever!

CHAPTER 22

The eleven wagons forded a river and then picked up the tracks of the earlier party. Traveling straight across the open county, they were making good time. Spirits were high. A virtual paradise compared to what they had been through. The greatest challenge now ahead would be the dry run over the salt flats. Hastings had said a day and a night to cross it which didn't sound too ominous. By late afternoon they could see the black rock landmark where they hoped Hastings and the Harlan and Young party would be waiting. As they approached they saw two horses and a mule, but no wagons. Three men sat around a campfire.

William's spirits plummeted when he recognized one of the men as Eli Morgan. He hoped he'd seen the last of the man when Eli took off before they started down the river. His guilt over Elspeth's death was torture enough without Eli's accusing eyes scraping the wound.

The wagons pulled up and formed an uneven semicircle. Two of the men rose and came over, but not Eli. One was a runt of a man, the other a giant, at least six foot six without his boots. The short one--William thought he looked familiar.

"Name's McCutchen," the big man said offering his hand to William who was the first one to step over. He nodded toward the fire. "Reckon you already know Mr. Morgan. And this is my partner here, Charlie Stanton."

William grinned. "Thought I recognized you, Mr. Stanton," William said shaking the little man's hand. "We started out together from Independence. You stayed with the Reeds and the Donners when our party separated."

"Still with them," Stanton replied. "George Donner is now captain of our party."

"George Donner?" William looked surprised. "Governor Boggs was captain last time we met at Fort Laramie."

"He was. But our train split at Little Sandy, part going up to Fort Hall. Donner was elected captain for the ones who'd take Hastings' shortcut."

The big fellow grinned. He had a broad open face and William liked him instantly. "And me and my wife and baby joined up with his party at Fort Bridger."

Medora, hearing the name of the Donners, jumped down from the wagon eager for news of their friends. "Oh, please tell how is everyone? How is my dear friend, Mrs. Donner?"

"Tolerable," Stanton replied. "Everyone in good health considerin' the terrain we've been traveling."

Then McCutchin broke in to explain that after leaving Fort Bridger their wagon train had started down the Weber River Canyon following the tracks of the other party until they found a note written by Hastings advising them against any further decent. Hastings suggested that a couple of horsemen search him out and he'd give directions of a better way to reach the valley of the Great Salt Lake. So it was McCutchen, Stanton and James Reed who set out to catch up with Hastings and finally had done so the day before.

"James Reed?" William said in surprise. "Where's Reed now?"

"Gone back to our party. Our horses were right done in by the time we got through the canyons. Reed traded his horse with someone in that other party and took off right away to let our families know we're not lost."

"His grey thoroughbred?" William asked in surprise.

The little man broke in. "Hardly his thoroughbred. Don't reckon he'd ever trade that fine horse. It was one of his mares he was riding."

"Hastings went with him a short spell back to point the way," the big man continured. "Me and Stanton are headin' back come morning."

William then asked if they had met up with a young fellow with dark curly hair, name of Jake Stringer. McCutchen shook his head. William swallowed hard, still finding it difficult to believe Jake was a common horse thief.

Later, Medora wrote a note to Tamsen for the men to deliver when they returned to their party. In it she told Tamsen she hoped they still might catch up and again be traveling together. If not, she would look forward to meeting them when they reached California.

Early the next morning the two men took off heading back toward the Wasatch to rejoin their own party and the eleven wagons swept westward following the tracks of the pervious party. Although Anton was against Eli rejoining their group, William argued it wouldn't be Christian to turn a man out alone in the desert where there'd be little chance of finding game. No one in Hastings group had been willing to take him in. So once again Morgan was riding with the Dudleys. Medora worried about one more mouth to feed when their provisions were so low. After the crash of their supply wagon, only a meager amount of provisions had been salvaged. They had bought a few supplies from some of the other travelers, whatever could be spared, and had hoped to purchase more supplies when they rejoined the Hastings' larger group. Now that hope had been dashed. Medora prayed they still might catch up. In the meantime, she had started a daily rationing of their food supply.

Following in line, the eleven wagons cut across spurs of hills and shallow valleys. By evening they came to a place that was pot-marked by numerous springs that varied in size from six inches to nine feet across. Torrey was fascinated as she knelt to fill the pans and buckets with the sparkling clear water. "Look, Billy," she said pulling her brother down beside her. "No matter how much I dip out, it fills right up to the top again, yet it never runs over." Dusty Dog looked too, lapping up and enjoying the fresh cold water.

Medora was relieved to see Torrey finally showing an interest in something. The girl had become so withdrawn, boxing up her feelings, making herself unapproachable. Medora felt heartsick not to be able to do anything to help ease her child's pain. She'd even asked Lavinia's help. "She needs to open up to someone. You two so close in age."

"I know, Mama. I wish I could." Lavinia's expression showed her own concern. "But you know Torrey. She won't let anyone help."

The following day after a long hard drive over barren hills and arid sagebrush plains they came to a lovely green meadow with more springs, a good place to camp for the night. Anton was the first to see the message tacked to a board.

"From Hastings," he said. The men crowded around, but Anton was already swearing under his breath. "Tells us one thing--now says something else."

"I'll be damned," said one of the men looking over Anton's shoulder. The message read: *2 days--2 nights--hard driving across desert before reach water.*

"Why didn't he say so in the first place?" said another. "Hell, thirty-five or forty miles on level plains shouldn't take no two nights and two days."

"Lying bastard," mumbled Eli. "The shit-ass came this way before. He knew all a'time how long it should take."

Anton felt the anger but wasting time complaining didn't serve any purpose. He assessed the present landscape. "At least, there's plenty of good grass we can cut to take with us. All right, men, let's get busy. Better fill all your empty kegs with water." Anton's eyes narrowed to slits. "Our lives depend on our animals. We'll need all we can carry." And Medora, with Lavinia's help, began preparing enough food to last them a couple of days knowing there'd be no chance of finding fuel.

The next day they crossed a sagebrush desert, climbed another pass a thousand feet above the valley. As they topped the pass, Anton squinted against the shimmering glare of the setting sun. Ahead another sagebrush desert. Beyond that stretched the white salt flats. In the very far distance was the shadowy outline of a mountain, their nearest hope for water. Forty miles Hastings had said? *Gott im Himmel.* Must be eighty miles or more! The water supply for their stock was already mighty low. He cursed Hastings in his anguished thoughts.

To avoid the mid-day blistering sun, they traveled most of the night by the light of a three-quarter moon, bumping over sagebrush and rocks. By this time, their small party had become a formless disorganized group stringing out across the barren hills and desert, every family for itself. Medora noticed Lavinia's disappoint when the Clarks' wagon disappeared from view. Was something going on she hadn't noticed between her oldest daughter and one of the young men? All nice and well mannered, she had to admit, and with such imaginative names from a very pragmatic down-to-earth family--Perrigrine, Dulancy, Nahum, Plutarch and True Trevor. Perrigrine and Dulancy were the eldest and possibly marriageable age. But still... destined to be just farmers. Medora sighed. Can't blame a mother for wanting the best for her daughters.

Finally at the base of the mountain the Dudley group, now alone, made camp only long enough to rest the critters and, with caution, dole out a bit of the water from the kegs. The children whimpered in their sleep from the piercing cold, but morning brought a scorching sun. It wasn't fair Medora's tortured mind kept saying seeing the plight of her children. If women had a say, none of them would be here now. Surely there would come a day when women would make their voices heard.

They rolled on over powder fine dust that boiled around them and burned the eyes. Up another steep ridge. The wagons scraped against volcanic rock. And then, worst of all, came the sand dunes and sucking sand. The oxen flagged and wagon wheels sunk to their hubs. Strain showed in the faces of the travelers as bodies drooped from pushing through the ash-like sand. The two days and two nights had already been spent. The water kegs were near empty and the cut grass almost gone.

On the third day they finally reached the flats where not even sage could grow. The sparkling white crust seemed to stretch on forever. At least the hard surface made traveling easier--for a while, that is. But the mid-August sun beat down mercilessly and the glare seemed more than a body could stand.

Suddenly Mike shouted, "Water! Look ahead. By God, there's a lake!" He started to push the loose oxen harder. But there was no lake. William thought he saw a line of men marching in single file. He stopped. The marching men stopped. He moved on and they moved too. The sun is making me loco, he was thinking. Others were seeing things too.

"Don't let the images fool you. It's the heat. Makes like a mirror. Known to happen in the desert," Anton said.

The blinding glare--the burning sky--twisting dust devils with stinging salt blasts. Poke the oxen to keep them going. Roll on, Roll on. Lag in the legs, but keep pushing on. Eyes red and stinging, lips cracked and puffed. They passed collapsed animals left behind by the earlier party, and abandoned wagons. One they recognized belonged to a family named Granger who'd come down the river with them. Water was all but gone. Medora gave the younger ones lumps of loaf sugar moistened with peppermint oil to suck on.

"Forty miles?" Eli grumbled. "Hell, we've at least gone sixty. I'll kill that damn Hastings once we catch up--if we get out of this hell-hole alive."

They came to the sink which meant they were about halfway across the salt flats. Anton's wagon, heavily leaden with his farm equipment, broke through the thin crust first and sank several inches into a salt water slush. Then William's wagon sunk too, heavier now with the salvaged supplies.

The oxen bellowed. A couple of the beeves looked near ready to collapse. "Get them unhooked," Anton yelled. "Their feet are sore already. That salt slush is stinging them more. Morgan, give us a hand."

Torrey, pitched in to help--anything to help deaden the pain of Elspeth's death. The shame of Jake's attack. The anger she felt toward her mother. The animals were freed of the yokes, and Mike took over the herding.

"How much water do you have left?" Anton asked William.

"None for the critters. Hardly even enough to get the family through the rest of the day." William's face mirrored his fear.

"We've got to get our animals to water. Our own lives depend on them." Anton pulled on his chin as he looked off toward the far distant mountain, no more than a shadowy outline in the blur of the heat. "That must be Pilot Peak ahead where Hastings said was a spring."

"Lying bastard," grumbled Eli. "Never make it. Critters already done in."

"Ja, the oxen can make it if they're not pulling wagons. Mike and I go ahead on our horses with what kegs we can carry. William, you and Morgan push on with the cattle and we'll meet you part way with enough water to get the cattle to the spring. Then soon as they've revived, we'll go back for the wagons and the family."

William looked surprised. "Leave Medora and the children alone?"

"It's our only chance," said Anton.

Eli's lips hardened to a scrunched up ball. "Hell, I ain't no bull-whacker like Mike. Better I go with you for the water."

Anton's jaw set firm. He knew Eli couldn't be trusted. Likely, after they reached the spring he'd just keep going and never go back to rescue the others. "Long as you eat our victuals, you're one of the hands, and you take orders from me."

Eli glared.

While Mike saddled their horses, Anton checked the drooping oxen. "Keep a close watch," he told William. "No telling what thirst-crazed animals might do. Some could go completely crazy."

William tightened with apprehension. If that should happen, what would he do? He didn't have the knack with animals like Anton. He turned a worried face toward Medora. "It could be late tomorrow before we get back."

Medora's own fear had mounted thinking of being left here alone, just she and the children. She tried to hide her feelings. "I guess there's no other choice," she said as bravely as she could. Little choice, indeed. If she'd had a choice they never would have left Illinois.

Torrey broke in saying she'd go with her father. "I can walk along with a bull-whip to keep the critters moving on."

William shook his head. It was out of the question. Walking would only work up more of a thirst and Dulcie was their only mount. "No, Torrey. You stay and help your mother. Morgan and I will make out." He began to unload some of the supplies from the wagon. "But I can use your help with this. We'll make enough room here inside the wagon so you can all stay under cover from that blasted sun. Keep both ends open to catch the breeze."

If there was a breeze, Medora thought.

William turned to Medora. "During the night, let Dusty Dog be in the wagon with you. He'll help keep you warm."

"We'll make out," Medora assured him, needing the assurance as much for herself. Two days now since they'd seen any of the other families. Were they the last ones in this forsaken land?

She stood in the sliver of shade beside the wagon as she watched William, Eli, and the animals became shadowy objects in the distance. Alone. She and the children alone on these blinding salt flats. Silence closed in. Now not even any animals to break the silence. The children as well as Dusty Dog had climbed into the wagon to escape the blistering sun.

"Mama, come in out of the sun. You could get a stroke," came Lavinia's voice from inside the wagon. "I'm getting Billy and Jenny bedded down for a nap."

"I'll be in presently."

It was so quiet. So silent.

Anton had said thirty of forty miles before they'd reach the spring. She'd heard him caution William that thirst-crazed animals could go crazy, and Will with so little experience with stock. Would he and Eli be able to keep them in line? What if something happened to William? Fear rolled through her, tightened her chest, made her almost feel nauseous. If something happened to William and she alone with the children on these salt flats. She rubbed her hand across her forehead, her brain feeling fuzzy from the heat. Her legs became rubber. She sank down to the hard white crust that appeared to be whirling. Above, the blazing sun was spinning in space. She must collect her thoughts. Think other things. She closed her eyes. Think cool running water. Think lilacs blooming by her doorstep. Think pleasant thoughts of her childhood--green rolling hills in Virginia. Her loving family. Her grandfather's plantation. Picture herself as a young girl dancing in the great chandeliered ballroom. And Jacques? What was it like the first time they met? She squeezed her eyes tight, trying to bring up Jacques' image. Think. Think. But the only image that appeared was William's--Will looking at her with troubled eyes. Gentle, positive, forgiving William. Right now she wanted him beside her, feel his arms holding her close. Protecting her. She wanted to press her head against his chest, feel the prickles of his few chest hairs. *She wanted to feel him inside her.* William. William. If something should happen...

"Mama. Mama, I need some water." Jenny's voice from inside the wagon. "Mama, I'm thirsty.

Blood pounded in her ears.

"Mama."

"Yes dear, I'm coming." Medora pushed herself up, climbed into the wagon. She reached for the bottle she'd hidden in a corner under a blanket. She'd use her thimble as the measure. Surely, someone would come back soon.

The gentle tint of early dawn colored the slopes of the mountain as Anton and Mike approached its base. They had traveled nearly thirty miles from where they left the wagons, riding most of the night, stopping only for a couple of hours to rest their mounts and get a few winks of sleep. Now, just beyond the edge of the sand was a thicket of willows--and there the spring. Cool, fresh, wonderful water.

Some of the ones they'd been traveling with were already there. The Clarks were there with their five sons, and Perrigrine asking about Lavinia. Others had been there and gone, the ones who had managed to make it to the spring with their oxen still pulling their wagons. Others, like Anton and Mike, had come with empty jugs and kegs to take water back to the exhausted animals they'd left behind.

"How far back did you leave your wagons?" Zeb Clark asked.

"About thirty miles. But Dudley and Morgan are pushing the cattle without the wagons."

Clark nodded. "Yeah. That's what some others have done. We were lucky. Got here all intact, and now about ready to take off again over that desert. But there's Grover here, and a fellow named Smith. They had to leave their wagons behind. Maybe you can all start back together."

Anton, in consideration of their horses, gave himself and Mike a couple of hours to rest. They filled their empty jugs and fastened them to their saddles. Anton hoped they wouldn't have to go back too far before they'd meet up with William and Morgan herding the cattle. Granger and Smith were ready to return as well. The four set off together.

William found the traveling at night harder than he expected, and certainly Morgan wasn't the most agreeable partner to work with. The thirsty cattle, consisting of William's three yoke and Anton's three, plus the extra beeves, were reluctant to go on. A cold wind came up and cut through their clothing. The salt blew like dust, and the cattle, facing the wind, bulked at its sting. Dulcie didn't like it either. She switched her long dark ears and ducked her head. William pulled his bandanna from his own face and covered the mule's eyes to keep her going. At least his family would have some protection inside the wagon.

They passed more abandoned wagons. In the moonlight, looming up from the white glittering crust, they looked like ghostly tombs. By morning the wind had died down and the scorching sun took its place. The need for water increased. The cattle, their tongues hanging out, became frenzied. A volcanic outcropping ahead had the look of green--a sure sign of water. William's spirits heightened. He and Morgan hurried the cattle on. But it proved to be nothing more than greasewood.

By mid-morning William's shirt was as wet from sweat as though he'd gone swimming. He wished that he had. The sweat ran down his face and stung his cracked swollen lips. He swiped his tongue across them just to collect the moisture. He still had a swallow or two in his canteen, but he'd hold off as long as he could. His head throbbed from the merciless sun's rays. He imagined himself splashing in the spring once they got there.

The cattle were stringing out more now, the weaker ones barely stumbling along. Some were bumping into each other as though they couldn't even see. Extreme thirst could cause near blindness, Anton had once told him, and they might try to head back to where they last had water. Suddenly, a young steer, eyes rolled back with hardly more than the white showing, turned and with a burst of new energy started running in the opposite direction from which they were headed.

"Hey, get that critter back in line," William yelled to Morgan who was riding to the rear.

"Get him yerself," Morgan yelled back. He made no attempt to head the steer off.

William's anger rose as he kicked his mule and made a wide swath around the wayward animal.

Morgan watched William with lethargic interest. What in hell was he doing here, cooking in this goddamned sun, playing herd to Dudley's and Zwiegmann's stock? The reason, of course, he had tried to join up with someone in Hastings' party, but not a damn one had offered to take him in lest he could pay for his keep, and with his money all gone... And there'd be no game in the desert to shoot. At least that shit-ass Dudley couldn't say no, still beholding for causing the death of his woman. But hell--playing nursemaid to a bunch of damn cows! He wasn't askin' fer that.

He wasn't askin' fer the way his damn luck had turned sour when he'd thought, for once, it was goin' right when he'd started west with the gold from his brother's farm and that choice supply of prized ginseng. If his goddamned woman hadn't opened her mouth about the ginseng. She'd al'ays been bad luck for him, from the time he first took her behind that rock. Good riddance at last.

Morgan's mood turned blacker the more he thought of all that had happened. The more the sun beat down. His tongue got so thick it filled his mouth. Maybe he'd even die of thirst on this goddamned desert. He lifted his canteen to his mouth. Dry as a bone. He gave it a furious toss.

Without any help from Eli, Willian finally got the crazed steer back in line. Others started causing problems, stumbling and lagging behind. Dulcie was so tired William had trouble making her work. One ox lay down and wouldn't get up. William dismounted, pulled on his tail and got the bovine back on his feet. Another broke loose, started running in circles and frothing at the mouth. He headed toward Morgan.

When Morgan saw the ox coming his way, he dug his heels into the flanks of his mule to get him to move in a hurry. The mule did, but not fast enough. The ox lowered his head and a curved horn caught the mule on the rump, tearing the flesh. The mule's hind legs struck out as Eli grabbed his revolver to shoot the ox. A shot rang out just as Morgan was tossed from the saddle. His gun went flying. But the bullet had caught the ox in the shank and it dropped to the ground. Morgan made a quick grab for his whip before his mule took off. He cracked the whip across the fallen animal's big tan face. A pitiful cry rang out. Morgan slashed again and again. Blood spurted from the animals eye, from its snout, and Morgan kept slashing.

William dashed up. "Stop it! Stop it! You're killing the critter!" He tried to grab the whip away from Morgan, but Eli's hold was firm. Eli's big fist struck out and sent William spinning. Morgan returned to his frenzied slashing, across the animal's face, across his neck, across his rump. Blood flowed from both the animal's eyes and the gashes up and down his spine.

William got up and lunged at Morgan. He threw himself onto the much larger man. His fist connected with Eli's nose. He felt the crunch of bones before Eli caught him in the middle with his huge fists and knocked the air from his lungs. William felt another blow strike his jaw. His head snapped back. He hit the hard white crust of salt and sand and felt the heavy kick of a boot. Lights flashed, then merciful darkness.

With the plains so level and open, visibility was possible for miles. Anton saw the small herd of animals coming toward them when they were still at a distance. He was sure the two men riding mules were William and Morgan. He thanked his *Gott im Himmel* that they were making it all right. But the animals appeared to be lagging. Naturally they would be. Then he saw more trouble developing.

"Looks like William is shagging down a stray," Anton said turning to Mike. "Come, we make it faster. They need the water."

Anton put his horse to a lope. Mike and the other two men followed. They weren't far away when the shot rang out and they could see the rest of the ruckus. Morgan's mule ran past them, a bloody wound across its rump. Granger turned his horse to chase the mule down as the other three spurred their animals to a faster gallop toward the scene of destruction that was taking place. Anton's temples pounded. His eyes shot fire. He saw the brutal attack on a helpless beast that then turned on his friend. His gun was out of its holster and cocked before he skidded his horse to a stop. His shot cracked the desert air.

But Mike had been as fast as Anton. It was a matter of reflex, rather than thought. He pulled his horse up besides Anton's and kicked Anton's mount in the rump. The horse jumped in surprise, and Anton's shot went astray. The gun flew from his grip. Blind with rage, Anton jumped from his saddle and plowed into Morgan, pulling him off from William.

The man Smith had also jumped from his horse and retrieved Anton's gun. Pointing it skyward, he pulled the trigger. Anton and Morgan jumped apart, wondering which one had been shot. Smith lowered the gun so that it was now aimed at them. Noticing Morgan's revolver not far away, Smith told Mike to pick it up. His voice calm, as though it was an every day discussion of weather, Smith said. "I know it's been a mighty hot day. We've all felt the strain. And there are times men do unreasonable things if he's been out in the sun too long. But whatever the problem, I'm sure we can handle it in a more civilized manner." He again looked at Mike and nodded toward William. "Better see to your friend."

William opened his eyes when something touched his face--wet and wonderful. He looked up at Mike. Then Mike held a jug to William's lips. He gulped in huge blessed drafts of precious water. "Not too much right off," Mike said. "Reckon this desert makes people go a little crazy," which was quite a bit of talk coming from Mike.

Sometime later, five men squatted on the salt crust to have a quick smoke before parting. Eli was not among them. By this time, the animals had all been watered and the injured ox put out of his misery, but valued time had been taken from the urgent tasks still ahead. The five men were all anxious to get back to where they'd left their families.

211

Anton had examined William's abrasions and found no broken bones, which was a wonder considering the force of Eli's punishment. He had placed his own saddle to William's back for a prop to make him more comfortable for that smoke.

"I'm all right," William protested. "You don't have to fuss." One eye was swollen shut and the flesh around it turning color. His lip was cut and swollen and the bruised ribs that had received the brunt of Eli's kick, made it painful to breathe.

Granger looked at Anton with admiration. "For someone to buck a feller as big as that Morgan, I say you showed a powerful lot of guts."

"I should have killed the *Schwein*," said Anton. "I would have if my teamster here hadn't kicked my horse."

"You were lucky he did," said Smith. "If you'd have killed Mr. Morgan, you'd have been charged with murder. The course we just now executed was far more legal." Smith had read some law before he'd headed west. And it was Smith who had suggested they hold a trial right here and now.

A jury of four men was selected--the possibility of bias being overruled. Smith had acted as judge.

The jury found Eli guilty of unwarranted cruelty against both animal and human. The judge passed the sentence. For the second time since their journey began, Morgan was to be banished from all present company without benefit of food, and not allowed to join present company for the rest of the travels to California. His canteen had been retrieved and filled. Granger had brought back Eli's mule, and as its injury proved only minor, Eli was told to mount and be on his way.

The men finished their smoke. Anton arose. "We've still got to get our cattle onto that spring. The amount of water we brought back for them can't sustain them for long."

The other men got up as well, dusted the loose salt dust from their clothes.

"And we'd better get our kegs of water back to our families and teams," said Smith.

William arose also, but painfully. "Lets waste no more time," he said with determination. His family had been left alone too long with so little water.

"Want to wait here?" Anton asked looking solicitously toward his friend. "We rig our shirts up for a shelter."

"Absolutely not," William responded with determination. "Let you take the cattle back to that spring without me? By George, for days I've been thinking of splashing in a spring. Now, let's get on our way."

CHAPTER 23
High Desert Country
September, 1846

Medora welcomed with great relief the news that Eli Morgan had been banished from their party. Even now, a month after the ferocious beating, anger still churned in her bosom at what that man had done to her husband. She thanked The Almighty that Anton and the other three men had arrived when they did, or her children might now be fatherless and she a widow. After their rescue from the salt flats, by the time they too had reached the spring, they learned that Eli had managed to join another group. By now he must be far ahead of them.

Now both of the Morgans were gone from their lives, Medora thought, relieved that they were rid of Eli, yet she still felt a clutch in her heart when she thought of Elspeth. In a way, she'd learned to love the plucky little woman and even missed her. The children too, for they all had adored her. Torrey still showed her grief. It saddened Medora that she could do nothing to help her daughter. Torrey still shunned any comfort she offered.

Now, trudging along behind the wagons, she watched William up ahead with a nudge of concern. She noticed the weary droop of his shoulders as he prodded the worn-out oxen on--with his usual optimistic banter--come on fellows, got to keep going, not much farther. William and his unconquerable spirit. At least he had help from Torrey--Torrey with her short-cropped hair and still wearing her father's trousers that she herself had cut down and restitched for her daughter. Such an independent nature was that girl. She was one who'd never be subservient to a man--perhaps the way it should be.

At the spring they had rested a few days. What a treat for the children to splash in the wonderful clear water. It gave William a chance to partially recover from his beating and the animals to revive their strength. They regrouped with several other families and once again started out. All would have liked to stay longer but ahead was the towering Sierra Mountains to cross before snow covered their peaks.

For a while the country got better--although still treeless desert. Occasionally they came to well-watered meadows and sometimes saw antelope herds which supplied them with much needed food. As they traveled on they often saw small clusters of naked Indians watching them from a distance. To Medora's relief, they never came close. She certainly would not want her two young daughters exposed to their unclothed manhood.

Finally, reaching the Mary's River (on Fremont's map called the Humboldt) meant they had rejoined the main California trail. Now the country worsened. The soil was rocky and grass very poor. The river was no more than brackish half-stagnant pools of water. "Ugh, it's full of wigglers," Jenny cried. "At least it's wet," her brother replied. "Undiluted horse piss," Anton called it. But they drank it because there was no other. What passed as meadows had already been trampled and cropped by the parties ahead. Once again it became necessary for each family to strike out on its own.

The Dudleys and Anton where once again traveling alone when they found a note attached to a stick dated nearly two weeks before and signed by Governor Boggs They knew the Boggs Party had chosen the regular route going up to Fort Hall rather than chancing Hastings' shortcut. "Ja, and now are probably a hundred miles ahead," said Anton with a shake of his head.

The note warned them to keep a guard. Here the Indians were more hostile and liked to steal stock. Diggers, they were called. Miserable people, indeed, having to exist on roots and insects in that wasted desert country--except for the cattle they'd steal.

That night William said he'd stand guard, but in his exhausted state he dozed. It was then the Indians sneaked into their camp, killed a couple of their critters with arrows and made off with several others. Medora and the children huddled together in fright, but cattle was all the Indians wanted. Now they were down to the five yoke for the two wagons plus a few of Anton's scrawny beeves.

"At least, I still have my two horses for Mike and me, and you have your mule," Anton said to William.

Poor old Dulcie, thought Medora a couple of days later as she watched William shag down some of the loose cows to get them in line. Doing double-duty now. Pack mule sometimes. Sometimes used for scouting. Sometimes hitched up with the oxen when a bovine gave out. She didn't like that much, and showed it by twitching her ears and kicking up the dust. A lady with a mind of her own.

Medora and the children walked most of the time to save the poor worn beasts. When Jenny gave out, she and Lavinia took turns carrying the small child. What a blessing was Lavinia, always helping with seldom a complaint. It wasn't fair, Medora thought. This lovely daughter of hers should be back in Illinois being courted by eligible young men instead of tramping through this ash like soil that covered them in clouds of white dust making them look like stalking corpses.

Torrey too was working so hard helping her father. A necessity now because Mike was gone. For weeks they'd been on short rations with their food stock dwindling down to nothing. William had seen Medora stint on her own portions to give more to the children. She'd become so thin. The only game they saw was once in a while a scrawny lizard. That's when he decided something must be done and said to Anton, "Others have sent ahead for supplies to Captain Sutter's fort in Sacramento."

Anton nodded. "Ja, the same thing I've been thinking. We send Mike. He takes my other horse."

But for one who often put more trust in humane nature then was prudent, now William had some doubts. Mike was a single man with no family to come back for. "Do you think..."

"He'll come back," Anton said with assurance. "He's not like that thieving Jake. Ja, Mike we can trust."

So they fixed Mike up with a canteen of water and as much food as they could spare. Anton had an extra pistol. "Maybe you find game when you get out of this hell-hole desert." And they waved him off.

The country continued to worsen as they crossed the long waterless stretch across the Mary's sink. The plains were now utterly destitute of vegetation with the exception of an occasional strip of sage on the swells. Humans and animals were becoming mad with thirst. Suddenly the oxen lifted their heads and started to stampede. Anton began yelling. "Head them off. Don't let them get to those pools!" He had scouted ahead and knew the stock had smelt water.

They had come to what appeared to have been, at one time, the center of volcanic activity and now was pockmarked with several pools that had steam rising above them. It took all of them, including Medora, Lavinia, and Billy to stop the crazed stock from stampeding toward the tantalizing scent of water which was much too hot for them to drink. But no one had thought about Dusty. The dog, also crazed by thirst, made a mad wild plunge into a bubbling boiling pool.

Billy saw the dog. "Dusty! Dusty!" he screamed, and started after his pet. William reached his son just in time to pull him back for the dog had already been scalded to death.

Billy stood stiff but trembling, trying to be the brave man he was supposed to be. Medora reached for him, tears streaming down her own cheeks, and cradled him to her bosom. "It's all right to cry," she whispered to her brave little son. "We all loved Dusty. It's all right to cry when we lose ones we love."

The sobs started, gasping and painful. Medora rocked her child gently back and forth as she sat with him on a hard grey rock. She pushed aside the soft red hair that clung with sweat across his forehead, kissed the top of his head and felt his need. Finally the heartbreaking sobs became only a whimper but Medora continued to hold her child. They clung together, neither one wanting to let go. She thought of Torrey's grief at the time of Elspeth's death. If only she could have given Torrey the same comforting.

It was a heart broken group that grouped together that evening. Medora dolled out their scant amount of sustenance handing each a biscuit and one piece of boiled bacon that she'd scraped off as much of the slimy yellow coating as she dared from the rancid slab. She poured each of them a cup of coffee made from the boiling water scooped out of one of the cauldrons. How much longer, she wondered.

By early October they had finally reached the Truckee River, now crossing and recrossing its twisted course as they climbed ever higher up the slopes of the Sierra Nevada into blessed pine covered forests. Bullwhip in hand, William urged his remaining two yoke of oxen on followed by Anton's rig. Anton rode ahead scouting the way. Torrey, behind on Dulcie, was driving over the rocky terrain the few loose cattle they had left. She circled around, poked a stray with the end of her stick, and yelled, pushing them right along. Good as a man, William thought. Heavy chore for such slim shoulders. Though the course was steep and rocky, it was a welcome relief after the two devastating months of desert travel they had finally put behind them.

William cracked the whip above his wheeler's head to push the critters on. Poor worn beasts--so thin that sagging pockets showed behind their hipbones. He had only two yoke of oxen left, Anton only three pair, after the Digger's attack. They were now approaching the Sierra summit. Once over that final barrier, they would be there--California at last.

The Truckee River made a bend. It had been going south, but now suddenly turned west. Up ahead, Anton stopped his gelding and craned his neck to look up. William did too and caught his breath. Above the tall pine trees, jagged granite spires pierced the sky. A startling view, awe-inspiring in its grandeur, wild and rugged. He walked up beside Anton. "Some sight."

"Ja. Like the Alps in my own country."

Spectacular beauty indeed, but they had to get their wagons up and over that granite wall. It was as though nature was conspiring against them. "How will we do it?" William asked.

"There must be a pass. We'll double team."

"Double team! Josh, man, we've only got five yoke of oxen between us, plus those scrawny cows of yours. Good thing we didn't eat them."

"Why we didn't."

"Maybe some other will arrive," William said hopefully.

Anton shook his shaggy head. "I think now we are the last. We'll find a way.

We unload the wagons. Carry up on our backs if we have to." Anton flipped the reins of his horse. "I now look for a meadow with good grass. We'll rest our animals, maybe a day or two." He nudged his gelding and started ahead.

William turned, hearing Dulcie's snort behind him as Torrey rode up. "Are we going much farther today?" she asked.

Even after two months he still wasn't used to seeing his daughter's hair so short, although it was now a cap of short curls. But still--that wealth of copper that used to hang past her shoulders... And wearing his trousers. At least they fit better after Medora had cut them down. His little girl. She looked like a boy. But William masked his feelings.

"What's the matter, girl, playing out?" She'd never admit to playing out, but joshing kept things light. Why was she driving herself so? She was determined to do more than her share, and men's chores at that. He blamed himself. The Lord gave man freedom of choice. Unfortunately, the toll for making the wrong choice could be incredibly high; like taking Hastings' shortcut.

"One of the cows has gone lame," Torrey said.

William's spirits plunged further. They couldn't worry about losing more stock now, not with that granite wall ahead. "A little rest should help. Anton is looking for grazing now. It's the crossing and recrossing the river. The water softens their feet, then walking over the rocks. Wears their hooves right down to nubbins." She shouldn't have to worry her pretty head about the critters. "They'll be all right with a little rest time," William assured her.

Anton reappeared from the heavy forest coverage. "Up ahead. Not far. A nice sunny meadow."

"There's your answer, girl."

It was a beautiful meadow, lush and green and surprisingly open considering the heavy growth of tall pines that surrounded it. Near by, through the trees, the shimmering blue of a lake could be seen.

"Like a sparkling blue diamond." Torrey said.

"Truckee Lake, according to the maps."

To the east end of the lake, only partly visible amongst the trees, Torrey noticed a log structure. "Look. A house!"

"A house! Where's a house?" came from Medora as she climbed from the wagon then lifted Jenny down. Lavinia and Billy had been walking behind and now drew nigh.

A log house it was, partly hidden by the trees, weathered and somewhat dilapidated--the first man-made structure they'd seen since they'd left Fort Bridger.

"Could someone be living in it?" Torrey asked.

"What do you make of it?" William asked turning to Anton. "Think trappers hole up in it during the winter?"

"Trappers wouldn't stay here in winter. There'd be no game. Snow thirty-forty feet deep they say." He looked thoughtful. "It's probably the cabin the Stevens party set up in forty-four."

"Of course. That must be it."

"Who were the Stevens?" asked Torrey.

"The first wagon party to make it over these mountains," William replied. "The first ones who proved it could be done."

"Then why would they build a cabin if they made it over the mountains?" Lavinia asked.

"Snow," Anton answered. "Got trapped by snow." He looked skyward and studied the little puffs of white scuttling across the blue. "Hope those clouds don't mean snow for us."

William looked up and studied the fish scale formation. "Rain maybe. Those kinds of clouds pass quickly. It was November when the Stevens' party got caught with snow."

Most emigrants knew about the Stevens, the party who'd made the first successful crossing with wagons two years before, a caravan that included women and children. Certainly it had been a contributing factor for the present migration. But the Stevens party had arrived too late in the fall. The snow prevented them from getting over the summit with their wagons. Using snowshoes, the party went on, except for one young man who stayed behind to guard the equipment until the snows cleared.

"I reckon that's the reason the cabin was built," said William after relating the story to the children.

"Someone stayed here alone?" Torrey asked in surprise.

"Until he was rescued the following spring when they came back for the wagons."

"Geeminy-gee," exclaimed Billy, his face bright with interest. "He sure must have been brave."

"Reckon so," said his father, tousling the boys hair. "As brave as you'd probably be under the same circumstances."

"Can I 'splore the cabin?" The child didn't wait for an answer before he started off across the meadow.

"Hold it, son." Billy paused and turned with a look of disappointment.

"Oh Papa, let him go." Torrey's eyes suddenly shone with the spark William hadn't seen for some time. "I'll go with him. Please Papa, I'll come right back to help with the unhitching."

How could he refuse? It warmed his heart to once again see enthusiasm shining in her eyes. "But show some caution," was his reminder, although he was sure earlier parties would already have routed out anything of danger.

Torrey and Billy ran off. *A child once again,* William thought watching his daughter. The way it should be. Except--a hurting feeling of loss as he watched. No exuberant, prancing, barking dog followed behind them. Poor Dusty Dog. Never again to be chasing after Billy. Never again would he himself feel that soft muzzle work its way into his curled palm. William ached with the memory--and the bitter truth of what he'd put his family through to follow his dream.

After turning the oxen loose on the meadow to graze, they set up camp beside a clear running stream. Anton figured a couple of days here for the animals to gain some strength before tackling the summit. The next day he and William left to scout out the best way to get over the forbidding height.

Medora looked forward to the couple of days of rest for themselves as well as the animals. The children wanted to hunt berries so she gave her permission providing they not stray far and all four stay together. Now, with everyone gone, Medora took the time to do some chores. She first shook out the white dust that had collected in their packed clothing. Then she checked their meager supply of food. Her disheartening estimate was one scant meal from the remaining rice, a couple of days, possibly three, for biscuits if she made them no larger than walnuts, and a little of the rancid bacon. The frightening reality was that there was still two or three more weeks of mountain travel after they got over the summit. How would they survive without food? Her stomach muscles tightened. If only Mike would get back.

She went through all of the boxes on a chance of finding a hidden jar of preserves or relish but found nothing except the little sauce dish William had rescued from the crash that she had carefully packed among the towels. *This one last piece of her blue willow ware.* Memories flooded her with an ache that throbbed her whole being--memories of so long ago--the one last thread of her heritage, of her past. She picked it up and ran her finger around its edge and felt the tiny nick. A lump rose in her throat. Like life and its flaws.

Her eyes misted and the blue willow tree and curved bridge shimmered through her tears. She pictured her family's linen covered table set with the willow ware and a bouquet of blue larkspurs in the center. A time of dignity and genteel living, the kind of life she had wanted her children to know. Medora brushed at a tear that slipped down her cheek. She had wanted only the best for her children. But Torrey's protest nudged her thoughts. *Why is all that proper stuff so important? Maybe for you and Lavinia. But I'm me, Mama. I'm not like you. I'm not like*

Lavinia.

A spot of moisture had collected in the dish. She wiped it away. Had she tried too hard to impose her old way of life on her two daughters? All these years, had she tried too hard to cling to her past? A life now gone forever. Lavinia had accepted it but Torrey had a mind of her own.

Medora shook her head as thoughts churned. What her family had been through these last few months, still going through. Survival is really what matters. Not fancy dishes or linen table cloths. Survival and a chance for their future, whatever that future may be. Was propriety all that important? Carefully Medora placed the sauce dish back in its cushioning. Past to the past where it belongs. As it should be.

A shot in the distance startled her from her reflections and her heart somersaulted. The men? Had something happened? She calmed her thoughts with a smile. She was jumping to unlikely conclusions without any reason. More likely a shot meant a squirrel for the stew pot, food they were desperately in need of. Then came another sound, the crashing of twigs in the distance. A bear? Where were the children! But their laughter soon filtered through the heavy thicket of trees and Medora breathed a sigh of relief.

The distant sound became more definitive--the roll of wagon wheels coming up the trail. They weren't the last ones after all. Maybe the Donners. Hope against hope.

A wagon came into view followed by two other wagons a short distance behind. Not the Donners. Disappointment at first, but then Medora recognized the Clarks' wagon, the family with the five well mannered sons. After the crash of their wagon, then the trek down the river and the beginning crossing of the desert, they had become quite friendly with the Clarks before each party found the need to strike out on its own. Anton said he'd met them again at the spring but the Clarks had left by the time they got back to the spring with the cattle. Naturally, they assumed the Clarks would be far ahead by now. But who could tell. Different routes had been taken in crossing the deserts.

The children emerged from the forest. When Billy recognized the Clarks' wagon, he started running and shouting, "The Clarks have come!" To him, fourteen year-old True Trevor had become his hero.

Medora also rushed to greet the newcomers. "Oh, it's so good to see you again."

Mrs. Clark grasped Medora in a motherly embrace, and in her warm hearty voice said, "I've thought of you so often, wondering how your family was making out after losing your other wagon and most of your supplies." She was a robust woman with a round, motherly face and salt and pepper hair pulled tight in a bun.

Medora had always liked the plain but friendly couple. It was good to be with them.

Mrs. Clark's eyes fell on Billy and Jenny. "Sakes alive, you two younguns--I declare you've grown a tad taller."

Not really taller, Medora thought. It's their thinness. Makes them look taller.

By this time, the other two wagons the Clarks had met along the trail, pulled up along side the Clarks' wagon and introductions were made. The Thornbergs, a man and his wife had three small children which delighted Jenny and Billy who spirited them off right away to show them the cabin. The other family was young Sam English, his elderly father, and his wife, Electa, with their baby born just three days before. Electa was still reclining in the wagon with her new-born infant.

"I'm seeing to it she stays there," Mrs. Clark told Medora. "Sweet little thing she be--not a day older than your Torrey, I swear. I helped the baby come into this world. I told Mrs. English she's to stay put and I'd tend to what needs be done. These younguns want to get up too soon. Don't know the peck of trouble they're in fer if they do. Ten days, I tell her. That's when things slip back in its proper place. So she's got to stay put until then before taking over her chores."

Medora smiled to herself. She didn't put much stock in the ten-day theory, but many women believed it. And if it meant ten days of rest, well, why not? Probably the only rest she'd have for years to come. She then asked if any might have met up with a family named Donner, but no one had. Now that they were already into October, Mrs. Clark was sure that they were the last ones on the trail. "We lost time repairing our wagon and then time spent with our little mother. Reckon your friends have already settled themselves in California."

"Yes, you probably are right," Medora agreed.

Not long after the three families had settled in, William and Anton road into camp with a killed deer stretched across Dulcie's back, explanation for the shot Medora had heard. Her spirits soared. First the Clarks had come, and now food! A deer meant eating for the next several days and if they stayed put for a couple of days she'd be able to cut and dry some strips for jerky. Good luck was smiling. Maybe even Mike might show up with more supplies.

William and Anton had heard the hubbub of talk and excitement as they approached the camp and knew more families had arrived. "Today we're really in luck." Anton remarked. "First the deer--now some help to get us over the top."

During their scouting expedition, they had found overgrown ruts that indicated earlier wagons had skirted the north side of the lake to its western end and then tackled the rugged crags above. It appeared more recent parties had taken a route south of the lake. Although it was six or seven hundred feet higher, the approach was easier, and perhaps would be best.

That evening the four families had a real celebration. Intoxicating aroma rose from the Large chunks of deer meat suspended over coals tantalizing tastebuds long before the meat was ready to be served. Each family contributed to the feast. Mrs. Clark mixed up wheat flour biscuits and boiled rice that would be seasoned with drippings from the roast. There were the sweet fresh raspberries the children had gathered. Mrs. Thornberg contributed plum preserves and stewed dried apples. While they waited for everything to be ready, Perrigrine entertained by playing his harmonica. A gay party indeed. The English's wagon was backed up toward the fire so Electa English could participate in the festivities and still follow Mrs. Clark's firm dictates.

As darkness set in it turned right cold but the men had gathered plenty of wood, a luxury indeed after weeks of nothing but desert sagebrush to burn. A great fire blazed that they gathered around.

Old Mr. English said the fire was fine to warm ye on the outside. "But I got somthin' better for the inside." He went to his wagon and brought out a partly filled bottle of brandy and passed it around to the men folk. "I've been savin' it for a special occasion like this now that we're jest a hop-skip-and-a-jump to Californy."

The evening wore on. The women compared notes on their children and shared prized recipes that they'd try once they reached civilization. The men talked about their teams and their experiences; how many animals they'd lost, and about encounters with the Diggers, and how they'd tackle the next problem ahead.

"I'd say ten yoke per wagon up the steepest climb, one wagon up at a time, and rotate the teams," said Anton.

"I'll share my manpower," Mr. Clark said, proudly indicating his five sons.

William nodded. "Mighty generous of you. Reckon we'll need all of your lads to get the wagons up that grade."

Torrey broke in. "I'll help too."

"We'll see about that," William said.

She'll get her way, thought Medora. The way she twists her father around her little finger. She couldn't help the envy she often felt for the camaraderie shared between father and daughter. Why couldn't it be the same for her and Torrey? At least a little understanding. Instead, the gulf between them now even seemed to have widened. Why was Torrey so difficult?

Medora glanced toward Lavinia sitting beside Perrigrine and looking right fetching with a blue ribbon in her hair that matched the color of her eyes. Lavinia had an instinct for what was most becoming. She hoped her daughter's charm and natural sweetness would not be wasted on some unworthy oaf in California. Perrigrine? A possibility? A farmer type like Anton, but apparently well educated. He seemed quite taken with Lavinia.

Her gaze shifted to Torrey with her short cropped hair still wearing her father's trousers. Why hadn't she at least put on a skirt for this celebration? Dulancy, the most handsome of the five brothers, sat down beside Torrey but she rudely got up and moved away. Medora sighed. Any other young lady would surely enjoy the attention of a young man as handsome as Dulancy.

What was it with Torrey? Medora wondered. There was a time, after her fifteenth birthday when she appeared to be showing some of the natural female interest in the opposite sex. But then came the change. If only she could reach the child, Medora thought with a wrench of her heart. If there was only some way.

The next morning a light snow covered the ground. Even though it melted as soon as the sun came up, the men's voices took on a new urgency.

"The animals are so worn. I'd hoped we could lay over another day," said William.

"I hoped so too," said Anton. "But now..." He looked skyward. The ridges increased on his forehead. "I don't know."

"Early October? Too damned early for snow," said Mr. Clark.

"Ja, but not safe to take chances."

It was disappointing to leave the lovely meadow so soon, but the travelers once again got underway. Going around the south part of the lake the trail proved no great strain on their teams until they were within three hundred feet of the summit. At that point, there was a relatively level area which made a good place to halt and prepare for the last steep climb, a thirty-five degree slope. "For that short distance, we carry the loads up on our backs," said Anton.

"Hell, we ain't no pack mules," complained Mr. Thornberg.

"We're pack mules today," said Anton, and started unloading the farm equipment from his wagon.

Mrs. Clark came over to Anton, her shoulders set firm, her hands on her hips and her lips a determined line. "Not Mrs. English. She's not to leave her bed."

Anton nodded. "The little mother, ja. She stays in the wagon. Even with the *Kind*, she can't weigh a hundred pounds."

Electa stuck her head out from the puckered canvas opening. "Oh no, I ain't. Me and my baby ain't chancing staying in the wagon going up that steep rock." She started to climb over the tail gait but Mrs. Clark rushed over.

"Child, you get right back in there. This is only your fifth day!"

"We'll use extra precautions," Anton promised.

Electa's fear still showed, but she ducked back in, no match for Mrs. Clark's determination. William looked doubtful. He had not forgotten his own crashed wagon--and Elspeth.

The unloading got under way. Everyone pitched in, including the children. Light weight bedding and clothing was left but heavier boxes removed to be carried up later on the shoulders of the men. Dulcie would cart up the heaviest pieces.

Five pair of oxen were driven up to the plateau where the summit leveled off. The men at the top cut two forked tree trunks, pounded them into the ground and placed a log between the crotches to be used as a roller. Below, five yoke of oxen were hooked up to the first wagon going up and a long chain stretched between it and the teams at the top that would help pull with the roller keeping the chain from dragging. Thus the first wagon was hauled up successfully, climaxing with joyous shouts and hurrahs. The oxen were unhitched and brought back down. The English's rig was next.

Electa had watched the first wagon go up. That was enough for her--Mrs. Clark or not. When the men came to hitch the wagon, Electa was out and had parked herself and her baby on a blanket under a tree. "Thank ye kindly, but I'll climb up that rock myself with my baby," she said, and wouldn't budge from the blanket. Medora offered to carry the baby. Electa shook her head. She didn't want her baby out of her arms. Medora understood, remembering how it was when she'd had her babies.

While waiting their turn, Medora strolled through the forest, enjoying the peace and beauty. Patches of wild flowers were so colorful. She waded through ferns, and climbed moss-covered rocks. Why hadn't she brought her sketch pad along? She took in deep draughts of the fresh incense of the forest. She loved the tranquility.

When she returned to where their equipment had been unloaded, she made a quick check for her children. Billy and Jenny were playing hop-scotch with the Thornberg children and Lavinia was knitting and chatting with Mrs. Thornberg. Mrs. Clark was asleep under a tree, and the little Mrs. English--bless her heart--was stretched out on a blanket, preparing to nurse her baby. The young mother would not chance the ride up in the wagon. Good, Medora thought, remembering Elspeth. She spread a blanket. A good time to relax and watch the action.

For the poor weary beasts it was a slow belabored climb up the steep incline. The men used sticks to prod them on. Two of the men were at the back of the wagon pushing to keep the vehicle from tipping as it jiggled over the rocks. And, yes, there was Torrey pushing right along side them.

Medora sighed. It seemed an obsession for the girl to do men's chores. Torrey could be so pretty if she tried. How would she ever attract a proper gentleman when she acts like a man herself? Not that she wanted marriage as yet for either of her daughters. It was just that preparation had to start early, like Lavinia's innocent flirtation with Perrigrine last night. Certainly, marriage wasn't a guarantee for happiness. But a spinster's life? Dear Lord, she wouldn't want any of her daughters to have such a fate.

224

Medora leaned her head against a tree and closed her eyes, but couldn't rid herself of her concern for Torrey. Of course, as short handed as the men had become, her father had needed her help. Still, there was last night's rejection of the young Clark boy. And there was the rejection she herself felt. The ever present question--why? It had started with Elspeth's death. She understood Torrey's grief, but that was two months ago. Time should have started to heal. Had she done something wrong? And cutting off her hair? To get back at me? It didn't make sense.

A mother's duty is to help her child. How could she when she didn't know the cause of the pain? If she could only break through Torrey's tough shell.

Torrey's journal. Dared she?

She had found the journal tucked behind a packing box when she'd helped remove their belongings from the wagon. For safe keeping she'd put it in the tin box with the other books.

Of course she couldn't. *She wouldn't.*

But the thought nibbled away, eroding her feeling of honor. Just a child's writing, Medora told herself. But still, it is a personal diary. Everyone has a right to one's privacy.

But it's a mother's responsibility to council her child. Hesitatingly, Medora opened the tin box and took out the red-covered journal. She wouldn't read much-- just quick glances, just enough to see if she could find a clue to Torrey's troubled behavior.

The journal fell open to a page with a picture pasted on it, a handsome Spanish caballero astride a white horse. She remembered the picture. Removed from her geography book! Below the picture Torrey had written the name Don Stephano. At the bottom of the page, somewhat smeared, was *Adios, don Stephano.*

Medora shook her head. A childish notion of some sort. But she'd have to reprimand Torrey for damaging a book.

She turned to the front of the journal. The day of leaving. Medora was impressed with the details and colorful writing--Torrey's lack of restraint concerning her emotional parting with Effie. A twinge of conscience. She *was* snooping. Might she come across something Torrey would not want her to read?

Still, she *was* the mother.

She turned a few more pages. Most journals recounted little more than date, weather, and place. But Torrey's was vivid with colorful description, somewhat ungrammatical and with a few misspelled words, but her impressions were vibrant. Medora was amazed. Torrey certainly had a flair for the written word.

A further entry brought a smile. Jake had pulled Torrey from the river. *I suppose I'm beholding to him since he saved my life. I still don't like him. I wish*

225

he'd just disappear.

And then another. Medora caught her breath. *Mama wants to make me what I am not. I will not be like Lavinia, even though that is what Mama wants.*

Medora closed the book with a snap. Is that what she thinks? I'm trying to make her like Lavinia? She felt the blood rush to her face. She mustn't read more. It was as though Torrey was looking over her shoulder.

Then hesitatingly, Medora again opened the journal.

There was quite a bit about Elspeth. Again Medora smiled as she read: *Elspeth says if you swallow a thimbleful of salt before you go to bed and dream of a man who gives you a drink of water, he will prove to be your true love. I tried it, and I dreamed I was dying of thirst on the desert plains. A handsome man with very light hair saved my life with a cupful of water. I wonder who the light-headed man can be.*

So Torrey does have some romantic inclinations. The date of the entry was July 15. Before they'd reached Fort Bridger.

She turned more pages. July 25. That was after they'd left Fort Bridger. The account was an exciting tale of going down into the Weber canyon along the narrow and dangerous trail. She does have a gift. Reading the journal was like reliving the hardships--a treatise to be preserved as a memorial to endurance. But still no clue for Torrey's unreasonable behavior. Medora turned more pages.

August 2. August 3. August 5. And a couple of more dates. Medora's brow drew together. Strange, all those entries on the same page. No vivid descriptions, just short cryptic entries.

August 2. We can not get through the canyon. We lost Dancing Girl. Lost Dancing girl? Nothing about Jake stealing the horse.

August 3. Most of the party is going down the river. Papa doesn't want to, so we will go to the top of the mountain.

August 5. We lost a wagon.

And that was all! Not a word about Elspeth's death. Was the hurt too deep to put down on paper? Her own eyes filled with tears. Oh, Torrey, my dear child. She herself should have been more understanding. But Torrey wouldn't let her get close.

Medora brushed at the tears and glanced at a few more pages. The same brief entries.

August 6. We took the wagons down the river to the Salt Lake Valley.

She turned back some of the pages. August 2 was when the short entries had started. *We lost Dancing Girl.* Three days before Elspeth's death.

A sickening thought now seized Medora. That was when Torrey started acting so strangely. What was the story Anton and Torrey had told? Torrey was picking berries up on the Indian trail when Anton came along, and then came Jake. Anton and Jake were involved in a scuffle and then Jake took off with the horses.

Was that the whole of the story? *Jake!* Medora felt an awful trembling. Torrey would never even mention his name. *What had actually happened?*

Suddenly, shouts from above. The men were coming back down with the oxen. The Dudleys' wagon was the next one to go.

With shaking fingers, Medora opened the tin box and hurriedly replaced the journal.

But the sickening thought had now taken possession. Oh, dear God. What really happened to my child on that Indian trail? What had actually happened with Jake?

CHAPTER 24

Once they were over the summit, William figured the going would be easy the rest of the way. Now, more than a week later, he knew how mistaken he had been. In many ways the terrain proved even worse--not the sucking sand of the desert, but often so rocky it stone-bruised the hooves of their animals, and where the forests grew thick, there was no grass for grazing. A couple of places they'd used ropes to let the wagons down the steep granite cliffs. Again they were traveling alone, the Dudleys and Anton, as each family, eager to get down to the valley, saw no reason to wait for one another.

A couple of mornings they'd awaked to a light covering of snow. Now walking beside his oxen, William looked up at some gathering clouds and wondered what was in store. Thus, he did not see the large jutting rock in the pathway until he heard the splintering of wood. He turned and saw the wagon sag. A broken axle! That was all they needed!

Anton poked his head under the wagon. "Looks like you did it up right this time."

"I reckon," William said as he kicked the listing wheel. "At least we've plenty of trees to choose from."

Anton grunted and went back to his own wagon to get an ax.

They cut down a slender but strong looking pine. As William started shaping the tree trunk to size, the hatchet slipped and gashed his leg. Blood spurted and pain shot through his body.

Medora rushed over. "Oh, dear God. Torrey, quick, bring a towel."

Anton yanked a kerchief from his neck and fashioned a tourniquet while Medora ordered the children to scrounge every bush they could find that had spider webs strung on their branches. "The webs will help stop the bleeding. Now! Hurry! hurry!"

After tending William's injury, she bandaged it with old torn sheeting. The drawn look on her face showed her frightened concern.

"It's all right," William assured her. "Now let me get on. I've work to do."

A couple of days later the wound began to fester. William kept it to himself at first, trying not to limp and being careful not to wince when his rough trouser leg rubbed against his injury. Medora had enough to worry about--once again being nearly out of food. Mrs. Clark, bless her, had insisted on leaving them a little flour and some dried beans and rice before they separated even though their own supplies were getting low. He knew that morning Medora had used the last of the flour for biscuits and had put the last of the beans to soak.

"If only Mike would get back," Medora said wistfully.

"Ja, he should be here by now. Unless..." The German's pliable face creased with deep furrows. "Unless he had problems." Mike had been gone over two weeks. Not that Anton had doubts of his teamster's trustworthiness. Mike wasn't like that rascal Jake. But it could be a risky trip traveling alone.

"When Mike comes, can you make us some rising bread?" asked little Jenny.

Medora hugged her small child. "Indeed I will."

Anton winked. "And maybe Mike brings sweet preserves to spread on it."

At the time Medora and Anton were wondering about Mike, a half days journey away Mike was making his way up the mountain. Riding one mule and leading another one heavily loaded with supplies. Captain Sutter had been right generous providing him with a goodly supply of provisions. He just hoped to God he wasn't getting back too late, considering how short of food his party had been when he left them on the desert.

Mike had taken longer than he'd figured to make the trip to the fort, probably longer than his boss had figured. He hoped Anton wasn't thinking he'd pull a stunt like that damn Jake Stringer, but he reckoned Anton knew him better than that. You just couldn't count on everything going right.

The second night after Mike had left the Dudleys' camp, still in desert country, he had pulled under a heavy stand of brush that he hoped offered enough coverage from the eyes of marauders. He hobbled the horse Anton had given him to ride and for added security looped the rein to his boot while he caught a few winks of sleep. He was awake before sun up for an early start. The rein was still looped to his boot but there was no pull when he moved his leg. He scrambled up. The horse was gone. How had those damn Injuns cut the rein without him knowing? He reckoned he was lucky to still have his scalp, but he hated losing Anton's horse.

On foot and half starved, Mike eventually reached Sutter's Fort in the Sacramento Valley. He'd taken little food with him and had found next to nothing on the way. A few chipmunks, a squirrel or two. He'd dug a few wild onions. He hoped to God his friends were making out better than he. The Dudley younguns had such hungry looks when he'd last seen 'em. Christ, it was bad enough to be hungry yerself. But that pleading look on the faces of those little tykes...

A crash of twigs behind him made Mike swing around in his saddle, his heart pounding. He reached for the revolver Anton had given him to use. Not likely

Injuns here--but could be a grizzly. Somewhat below, through the network of trees, Mike glimpsed a man on a horse with a bright colored blanket over his shoulders and a large brimmed hat on his head. Some of Sutter's tame Injuns dressed that way.

"Hi-ye," came a yell. Mike halted the mules. The man riding up on a handsome chestnut was not an Indian. Nor even a Spaniard in spite of the serape he wore. Very light hair straggled out from under the broad brimmed hat.

"Howdy," Mike said. "Thought you might be an Injun at first."

The man grinned. "Not an Indian. A Yankee vaquero, you might say. Got a rancho down in the valley." He pulled up beside Mike and extended his hand. "Steve Magoffison."

"Mike Sullivan."

"Glad to make your acquaintance, Mr. Sullivan. You taking supplies up to some stranded travelers?"

"Yep." Mike responded in his usual laconic way.

"I'll ride along with you if you don't mind. How far back are your people?"

"Left them in the desert. Reckon they're someplace in these here mountains by now."

"Get the supplies from Sutter?"

"Yep."

"Good man, Captain Sutter. He never turns down anyone in need."

They rode on in silence for awhile, then Magoffison said, "I'm on an assignment for Captain Fremont, looking for recruits for a California Battalion. Of course, you know the United States is at war with Mexico."

"Heard tell." Mike thought back to the day the horse rider had brought them the news when they'd first started out on the prairie and the excitement it had stirred. Yet he had still been surprised to see the American flag flying over Sutter's Fort as he approached. He soon learned from a disgruntled Captain Sutter it had been flying there since early summer. On the 7th day of July Commodore Sloat, with his Pacific squadron, had sailed into Monterey Bay and took possession of the seaport pueblo and all the other coastal settlements. A few days later Colonel Fremont secured Sutter's Fort in the name of the United States and renamed it Fort Sacramento. However, Mike felt mighty proud to know California now belonged to his country. It would make settling here a lot better than putting up with them Mexican foreigners. But as long as California had already been captured, why were new recruits needed? He looked quizzikly at the blanket-draped man. "Thought we already took all of California," he stated.

"We did. But there's been an uprising down in the southern part of the province," Steve explained. "Colonel Fremont has been commissioned to recruit four or five hundred men to put down the rebellion. He asked me to ride out to meet up with some of the incoming emigrants and sign them up for the battalion. How about you? It means rations and twenty-five dollars a month."

Mike looked thoughtful, then nodded. "Be right proud. Not for the money. But to serve my country. Soon as I get this grub up to my people." He looked at the dark clouds scudding across the sky. "Reckon I better get a move on. Don't want my people to be caught in snow without no food."

The day had been pleasantly warm, but as evening approached a chill filled the air. Medora wondered if there'd be snow again this night. They'd stopped to make camp, and the fire Anton had set was starting to blaze. She looked over at William. He sat huddled in front of it looking chilled. His face was drawn and peaked as he stroked his injured leg.

"Are you all right, William?" Medora asked.

"I'm all right," he replied.

Medora frowned and placed her hand on his forehead. "William, you're burning with fever!"

"It's just been a hard day," he said.

"It's more than that. Let me look at your leg."

"I'm all right. Quit fussing."

Torrey was watching. Her innards tightened. She didn't like the worry tone in her mother's voice.

In spite of William's protest, Medora insisted on seeing his injury. When she'd first bandaged his leg she had slit both his trousers and his underwear to be restitched later when his leg no longer needed to be bandaged. Now she carefully unwound the bandages that covered his left thigh.

Medora gasped. "Oh dear heaven! It's now septic." The yellow puss oozing from the injury and the red line starting up his leg was a sure indication of blood poisoning. She felt her own blood chill. "Why didn't you tell me?"

"What's to tell? We've got to get down these mountains."

Medora called to Torrey. "Quick. Get some water heating." She turned back to William. "A hot compress will draw out some of the poison." If she only had some of her remedies for a poultice such as her beech tree leaves and bark of basswood root. Or even some old moldy bread or a little of the rancid bacon--if only they had some left.

The fire was not yet coals when Torrey hung the kettle on a trivet over the flame. She willed the water to hurry and heat. She felt so scared, it was hard to breathe. She thought of that little boy who had died out on the prairie from his injured leg. *Dear God, don't let anything happen to Papa.*

Anton brought in an armful of split wood and dropped it beside the fire. He looked at William's injury and shook his head. "Ach, not so goot. Ja, mortification has set in."

"I'm all right," William insisted. "Quit stewing, you two."

He wasn't all right, Torrey knew. Oh, dear Lord. She stuck a finger into the kettle to see if the water was hot. It had hardly started to warm.

Medora reached for the food box. There was panic in her eyes. "There's only one piece of dried deer meat left. I'll use it for broth. That will help build his strength."

"Ja, goot," The alarm was in Anton's expression as well.

"Will you two quit fussing over me!"

Torrey added more wood to the blaze. The fire flamed surrounding the kettle. She again tested the water. A little warmer, but not hot enough. Her mother had started for the wagon. She had to know about Papa.

Her mother was frantically searching through some of the boxes. When she saw her daughter she brushed at the tears that streamed down her cheeks. Torrey's own belly roiled with terror. Mama crying? She was always so strong.

"Mama..." Fear dried her mouth. The words come out in pieces. "What--you--looking for?"

"Oh dear God, I'm hoping--maybe some of my medicine got put in one of these boxes." Her mother's voice was as tight as her own, and she realized her mother was just as scared. *She loves Papa as much as I do.*

"Mama, you gotta tell me about Papa," she whispered. "Is Papa going to die?"

"No, he's not going to die! Don't suggest such a thing." But the tears were coming afresh, streaming down her cheeks so fast brushing them away was futile.

"Mama." Torrey reached for her mother, now her own tears flowing.

Medora's arms tightened about her daughter. *Finally--finally*--went through Medora's troubled thoughts. She relished the feel of her child in her arms. It had been so long. They clung together, each desperately needing the strength of the other--sharing their caring--and their fear.

At last Medora pushed her daughter away, her voice bristled with resoluteness as she stated, "No. Your father is not going to die. We won't let it happen."

Torrey breathed a little easier. Fate itself would not dare defy her mother when her hackles were up.

Medora edged to the back of the wagon. "No medicine here. That water must be hot by now. A hot poultice will do wonders." But once again her arms encircled her daughter, holding her again in a supportive embrace. "Torrey, it's been so long. I do love you, you know."

Torrey, pressed her head against the soft warm breast and wished she could stay there forever. "I know, Mama. I know. And I love you too." The words came out choked. She wondered why she'd kept her mother at such a distance for so long. Medora too wished this moment could continue. Why had it taken something like this to break down the walls? But she had to get back to her husband.

She had Torrey and Lavinia tear a flannel petticoat into wide strips and dipped the rags into the boiling water. Gingerly she pulled out the steaming cloth and when her hands could finally tolerate the heat, she wrung it out. She fashioned a poultice and carefully placed it around William's swollen leg.

Watching her mother, the tight knot was again forming in Torrey's innards. She knew Lavinia had put the piece of jerky into a pan of water for the broth, but such a small piece. Papa would need more than that to fight the poison. Maybe if she could find some wild onions to add a little more nourishment. If she were lucky, she might even find a bush with a few late berries.

In spite of her show of strength with Torrey, Medora's anxiety also had increased as she looked at the small piece of jerky floating in the pan of bubbling water. Such a tiny piece of meat. It wouldn't make much of a broth. If only Anton could shoot a squirrel to add to the stew pot. So concerned was she for Will, Medora did not notice Torrey leave the camp.

Although Billy was aware his mother was fretting over his father's bad leg, it wasn't enough to put a damper on the amount of energy a boy could store up in his body, especially when there was a huge boulder near the camp that needed to be climbed. Now, up on the top he became a scout looking for Indians. Far below among the trees he saw a movement. He curled his fingers to his eyes and made a spyglass. Sure enough. There was something down there. The figures came out into a clearing. Through the spyglass he could see two men on horses and one horse trailing--or maybe a mule. He felt prickles of excitement. "Someone's coming! Someone's coming!" he shouted.

Anton scrambled up the granite boulder beside the child. Billy was still looking through his spyglass. "I think... Maybe it's Mike. Sure looks like Mike."

Anton looked too, but without the need of a spyglass. Ja, two men and a pack mule. Billy was right. It was Mike! Anton slid back down the side of the huge rock then started on a run down through the trees to meet the oncoming travelers.

Supplies! A time for jubilation. Food! Flour, beans, dried meat, coffee, corn, fresh apples--and bacon!

Billy and Jenny danced around. "Hooray, Hooray! Mike is back! Mike is back!"

To Medora the bacon meant she could make a real poultice for William's injured leg to draw out the poison. That would be far more effective than just the hot water poultice. And the food meant nourishment for her family.

William, ignoring his weakness, mustered enough strength to rise and greet the two men. He embraced the teamster. "Mike, you are a sight for sore eyes." Then he turned toward the tall stranger.

"A friend I met on the way," Mike explained. "Meet Mr. Magoffison."

William offered his hand. "Magoffison you say?" his expression quizzical.

The stranger nodded. "But just call me Steve."

"Your father... Is he a senator? Senator Magoffison?"

The tall man's very blue eyes snapped with interest. "Yes, yes. You know my father?"

"By George," William said. His excitement made him forget the pain in his leg. "Senator Magoffison's son." He shook his head, hardly believing it. "I saw the senator shortly before we left Illinois. In Springfield. He told me about his son. I promised I'd look you up soon as we settled in California. But here--up here in the mountains?"

Steve looked as surprised as William. "This is an unexpected pleasure," he said beaming. "My father wrote that a friend was on his way." He shook William's hand with enthusiasm. "I can't tell you how pleased I am to meet you." Then he plied William with questions, eager for any news William might have about his father.

Soon the men grouped around the campfire, all itching for the exchange of information as Medora and Lavinia happily went through the bags of provisions and began the preparation of a sumptuous meal.

Torrey had gone farther from camp than she intended with little results for her effort--a few straggly wild onions. At least they would add some flavor to the watery broth her mother was fixing for her father.

Although her thoughts were mostly filled with worry for her father, she was also thinking of the few minutes she'd spent in the wagon with her mother. It had been such a long time since she'd even been nice to her mother. Now she wondered why. First she'd been so mixed up over Elspeth's death, hurting so and thinking her mother didn't care when she knew that really wasn't so. Mama had done all she could for Elspeth. Torrey ran her fingers through her short curls as though she could pull out the answer. Reckon my head wasn't working right, still mixed up over what had happened with Jake, and Mama always pushing... Fix your hair. You're old enough now to act like a lady. And when she did--brushing her hair and letting it hang loose, talking to the other fellows, giving Jake those ideas. Shame and anger still burned. Anton had been good to keep her secret. She wouldn't want Mama, and especially Papa, to ever learn what actually happened.

Darkness closed in quickly in the mountains, not that Torrey was afraid of getting lost. In the distance she could hear shouts from Billy and other camp noises. Good as a compass, but she'd better get back before her family started to worry. She stumbled over rocks and fallen limbs, and was relieved when she got close enough to see the firelight's flicker through the trees.

She smelt a tantalizing aroma! Bacon frying? Coffee boiling? Her empty stomach contracted with hunger pains. Was her mind playing tricks? She groped her way in the darkness as fast as she could but stopped short when she heard a horse whinny almost beside her. There was just barely enough light to make out its bulk. Its face had a white blaze that shone in the darkness. Her hand reached out and stroked a silken mane and sleek shiny sides. Must be sixteen hands high. A beauty, she could tell by the feel. Not Anton's gelding or the one he'd given Mike to ride. The horse tossed its head proudly. Oh, to have such a horse. Then, a short pace away, came the braying of a mule. Maybe Mike was back!

Torrey turned and was about to dart into camp with shouts of joy when she stopped short of the perimeter of the firelight's glow. Her mother was bending over the fire, a large spoon in her hand stirring something. Mike was there, talking to Anton. And a stranger too, talking with her father. The stranger's light hair was longer than hers. Torrey's hand went up to control her unruly short curls. She looked a sight! Not that it really mattered. But still ...

The firelight played on his face. A nice face indeed. Torrey liked the straight cut of his nose and the firmness of his jaw. When he smiled, deep creases lined the sides of his cheeks. His hair, though mussed--he must have removed a hat--hung in a tangle of waves, long past his ear lobes. The firelight turned it to gold. She had a strange ridiculous feeling like she wanted to touch it.

Her mother looked around, a frown on her face. "Goodness, I'd hardly realized it's turned so dark. Where's Torrey?"

Anton looked up and his brows drew together. "Sometime ago. She said she'd go dig some wild onions. Ja, I better go look."

Torrey knew she should make herself known, but at the moment she was still interested in the stranger. In spite of her father looking mighty puny, he was leaning toward the man listening intently to what he was saying. In spite of his pinched look of pain, he was smiling and he called the man Steve, like he'd known him a time. Billy stepped up and touched the stranger's arm and addressed him as Mr. Magoffison.

Magoffison! Stephen Magoffison? It couldn't be. Not her *Don Stephano!*

Torrey's heart began beating in a crazy erratic way. Her mind's eye flashed to the picture in her journal--the handsome caballero with the flashing dark eyes and very dark hair dressed in elegant Spanish clothing. The man had on some Indian blanket pulled over his shoulders. This man's hair was so light, and certainly his eyes weren't black like her caballero.

"Tell me more about your ranch, or is it a rancho?" her father was asking.

The man smiled. "Rancho--in California."

"The senator said you were breeding a special type of Mexican horse."

The blond head nodded. "Palominos. Yes, a truly handsome animal. Trim of line and light in color. Almost golden with a white tail and mane."

"Then not the horse you were riding."

"No. Pepito is my trail horse, the kind that runs wild in great bands in California, a remarkably strong, sturdy breed."

Hearing the conversation was proof enough. There could be no doubt. The stranger had to be the same Stephen Magoffison her father was to look up.

Torrey's emotions were in turmoil. How could he be so different from the dark handsome hero she had dreamed she would meet? It was as though she'd been cheated. Anger began to simmer. This man was no different from some of the other young men who'd traveled with them in their wagon party--men like Jake! Men she wanted nothing to do with--ever!

Yet he had a nice smile.

She moved her foot. A twig cracked. Her mother turned and peered into the darkness. "Torrey, is that you?"

"Yes, Mama."

"Thank goodness you're back. We were about to start searching for you."

Hesitantly, Torrey stumbled forward. She tugged at the old shirt to pull it down over the worn trousers. Her father looked up. "Oh, here's the other member of our family. Torrey, come meet Mr. Magoffison."

Steve got up and offered his hand. "Howdy, young fellow. It's nice to meet more of the Dudley clan."

Torrey felt the redness creep up to her face. She was glad there was this much darkness. Billy held his hand in front of his mouth and started to snicker. "She's a girl, Mr. Magoffison."

It was now Steve's turn to look embarrassed, but he covered it with a smile. "I do beg your pardon,--*Miss* Dudley."

CHAPTER 25

After the supper mess had been cleared they grouped around the fire for talk--after they'd stuffed themselves like hogs. The food was so good; fresh cured pork, slabs of hard cheese, and hot biscuits with gravy. They'd finished off with more biscuits slopped with butter and honey. And then afterwards, when talk time came, they sipped fresh brewed coffee and munched crisp apples from Captain Sutter's orchard. Only William, feeling puny with fever, didn't stay up to talk. Medora fixed a bed inside the wagon.

Torrey chose to sit slightly back out of range from the flickering firelight's glow. She felt somewhat embarrassed in her unladylike clothing. She ran her fingers through her short-cropped hair. Why was it taking so long to grow out? Lavinia had changed her frock and had combs in her hair. Torrey noticed how her sister leaned forward when Steve was talking. She didn't know why that irritated her so. He was a man like a dozen others they knew.

Steve--he'd insisted they call him by his given name--was telling about California. Torrey sat at attention, not wanting to miss a word. She wanted to know all she could about the caballeros--even if there wasn't a real *Don Stephano*. She still felt disappointed that the real Steve had turned out so differently from what had been in her mind. His hair so light. His eyes... The firelight caught a spark but she couldn't be sure of the color. Probably blue. Certainly not the deep velvet black of her hero. And the flickering light showed a stubble of whiskers on his square cut jaw. Her caballero might sport a handsome mustachio, but surely he'd never need a shave. To have fashioned her dreams around someone such as he! It was like discovering her lover was dead! The sad ugly truth. *He had never existed.*

Anton, too, was interested in learning more about the Californians. "What are they like--the Spaniards? Or are they called Mexicans?"

"Spanish. Mexicans. Either one. Mexico is their government, but they like to claim their Spanish blood. They think of themselves as Californios." Steve's expression showed the fondness he felt for the people he'd been mingling with the last two years.

"Are they friendly toward us foreigners?"

"For the most part. They are a hospitable people. I have some very good friends among the Californios."

"Even now--since the war?" Medora asked.

"Not much has changed, at least here in the northern part. Most of the natives go about their lives the same as always, although there are some who never liked the Americans--if they've had bad experiences in the past--been robbed of their cattle or cheated in other ways. And there was General Castro who, indeed, was making it difficult for the Americans. He was the comandante here in the north, and was determined to rid California of its Yankee settlers. A political ploy. Castro figured if he could get rid of the Americans, the Mexican government would appoint him as governor over Pio Pico."

"Where is this general now?"

"Mexico, I presume. He high-tailed it as soon as the United States took over."

"Was there much resistance at that time?" Anton asked.

Steve smiled, and the lines deepened in his cheeks. Torrey had a funny quirky feeling. Those creases flashed so quickly. She liked it when he smiled.

"None. Commodore Sloat sailed into Monterey and raised the American flag. That was it."

"Hard to believe," said Anton.

Again the creases deepened in Steve's cheeks and once more Torrey had the strange fluttery feeling. In the firelight his hair shimmered like gold. She wondered how it would feel if her fingers made trails through those glimmering strands. She only half listened to what he was saying. Political talk could be boring.

"Anyway, the Californios, for the most part, don't have a strong feeling of loyalty for their mother country," Steve continued. "Some, like General Vallejo, had already been pushing for annexation to the United States. After the take over, it was pretty much business as usual. Most of the natives continued on with their lives the same as always--except for an uprising in the southern part."

There was more talk about the political situation and Steve told how, even before the arrival of Commodore Sloat, a few of the American settlers rode into Sonoma and took possesion of General Vallejo's headquarters. "Someone made a flag and drew a picture of a bear on it, raised it and declared California the Bear Flag Republic." Steve's eyes twinkled. "Only, the picture on the flag looked more like a pig than it did a bear. However, it was only three weeks later when the United States officially took possesion of California."

What Steve didn't tell was his own involvement in the horse-stealing incident, which he wasn't proud of. He was glad he had refused to go on to Sonoma, especially when his friend, General Vallejo, had been made a prisoner. Since then, the general had been set free, which was no more than right.

Unlike her young daughter, Medora was interested in the political talk. There had been so little written about California in her geography books and she wanted to know more about the people they'd soon be associating with. "Tell us more about the Spanish communities."

"The pueblos? Well, most of the Mexican settlements are along the coast on the other side of the Coast Range. Of course you know California was all Indian country until the Franciscan monks came up from Mexico to build their missions and Christianize the heathens. Then soldiers came to keep the Indians in line and make them do the padres bidding so presidios were built. After that came the settlers and the pueblos. However, inland it was still Indian country until Captain Sutter established his fort. Now a few American have started farms."

"But what about the great Mexican ranchos?" asked Medora.

Torrey now came to attention. "And you have a rancho? I remember the senator telling and that you're raising horses?"

Steve smiled and again the creases appeared making Torrey feel like jelly inside. "Palominos. A very special breed. I also run some cattle. But my place is in the Sacramento Valley and nothing compared to the great Mexican ranchos near the coast. When secularization took place after Mexico won its independence from Spain, the vast mission lands were devided up and given as land grants to the chief military officers."

"Ja, so what about the Americans? Where are they settling?" asked Anton.

"Most are settling inland away from Mexican influence."

"Why?" Medora asked. "Are the Mexican--you call them Californios--are they unfriendly to the Americans?"

"On the contrary, even now with the war going on. They're a very hospitable people, but their lifestyle is so different. The Americans who have migrated here are industrious, hard working farmers. They think the Californios are lazy, don't take advantage of this wonderful land they have. They see the Indians treated like slaves and made to do all the work,."

Anton nodded. He could understand the reasoning.

"Another thing that's hard for red-blooded Yankees to understand is the strong caste system," Steve continued. "The big land owners, especially those with some Spanish blood, call themselves 'gente de razon' meaning people of reasoning. Beneath them then are the artisans and the *pobladores* of the pueblos. At the bottom are the Indian peons."

Anton's mouth tightened. He knew about the caste system from his own homeland, the reason he had left the old country. And Medora was thinking that would be something William would not tolerate well because of his own servitude during his apprentice years.

"But don't get me wrong. There are many fine people among the Californios," Steve continued. "It's just that their way of living is different from ours. Great horsemen they are. In fact, children are placed in the saddle almost as soon as they can walk. So their life revolves around rodeos, horse races, bear hunts, and week long fandangos, something else most Americans can't understand."

Torrey, across the fire from Steve was now wide-eyed with wonder as she followed every word Steve said. She pictured herself riding horses all day and dancing all night. A wonderful way to live. She thought of her earlier dreams of her caballero. Her gaze lingered on Steve with his Mexican sarape draped over his shoulders. What if his hair was light as sun bleached straw and his eyes blue as the sky? He had a rancho and raised horses. He was as much a caballero as her dark haired, black eyed one had been. More so. Because Steve was real, and sitting across the fire from her now. Her Don Stephano? She closed her eyes and thought how it would be to dance all night in his arms at a real Mexican fandango.

Steve leaned over and poked the fire with a twig. Sparks flared up and a flame blazed hot. He glanced back at his audience and continued with his commentary. "Another thing our frugal Americans find hard to understand is the little care the Californios give their horses. Everything grows so well, produces so well... A rancher might have as many as fifteen thousand head of cattle, maybe eight thousand horses all just left to roam wild." The creases in his cheeks deepened as he chuckled. "Even children. It's not uncommon for some families to have twenty--twenty five children."

Such abundance was hard to believe, thought Medora, while Torrey was thinking that that was where she'd draw the line with so many kids. She wasn't sure she'd want any at all.

"With so many horses, they don't bother to give them much care," Steve continued. "They ride them hard, then just turn them out to pasture and pick a fresh one."

Ja, thought Anton. He too would heartily disapprove. No matter how many animals you have, you give them as much care as you can. On this long trip, how deeply he'd regretted what his poor animals had suffered. The more he heard, the more he understood why the American settlers were distancing themselves from the Californios. The Central Valley sounded good to him.

Lavinia was also listening to Steve's story of the Californios with rapt attention which Medora couldn't help but notice. Suitor material? She couldn't help but speculate Lavinia being of marriagable age. This young man she'd highly approve--obviously intelligent and showed good breeding. Torrey, farther back in the shadows, seemed interested as well, an interest Torey hadn't displayed since–*since Jake?* In spite of her guilt for having read her daughter's journal, the thought of Jake was still in Medora's mind, and the question: What had actually happened?

An unwanted thought pummeled her thoughts thinking of what had happened to her so long ago. *But not Torrey and Jake!* The thought made her nauseous. *That time she herself, in the name of love, had shamefully given in to her body's desires* . But Torrey had no use for Jake. Yet, something had happened. Torrey's obvious rejection of anything male--except for her father and Anton.

If only she could council her child--tell her she must not judge all men by Jake. The thought of those few minutes of sharing in the wagon returned, holding Torrey as she had years ago--treasured moments she'd hoped now meant a better understanding between them. She wanted to tell her child there are many good men. Like her father. Like Anton. Spinsterhood was still the threat--an unhappy fate for any woman. But Steve had apparently sparked an interest in both her daughters.

Medora glanced toward the wagon. She should check on her husband. With Mike's arrival with the provisions, there was now more promise of Will's recovery. Things were bound to be better from now on.

Early the next morning they were ready to continue the trek down the mountain. A cold rain had pelted them during the night, but the morning broke bright and clear. Clouds drifted eastward leaving only feathery streaks across the sky.

Steve looked up above the tree tops to the peaks beyond. "There must have been a real storm up there last night," he said. "I'll wager there's plenty of snow now on top. No point in my going up any farther. No other wagon parties will get through now. It's a good thing you folks got down to this lower elevation." He remembered the time he'd crossed the Sierra with Fremont, how their horses had floundered and they had to tamp the snow down with mauls to get the horses through. With wagons, it would be impossible.

Medora looked worried. "What if there are still others?"

Steve shook his head. "They'll never make it now."

Medora felt chilled. What if Tamsen and her family were still behind them? No, she mustn't have such thoughts. The travelers had taken different routes over those four hundred miles of desert, and both the Donners and the Reeds had far more oxen than they had, and thus could make better time. More than likely, they were ahead of them now.

"Have you come across a family by the name of Donner?" she asked Steve.

"I don't recognize the name, but then, so many emigrants have come in to Sutter's Fort this season, even before Colonel Fremont started recruiting for his battalion."

Of course he wouldn't know. She must put the thought of her friends aside. More than likely they were already down in the valley, maybe even settled in a house by now.

Torrey watched the men hitch the wagons and offered to help. Mike smiled kindly. "Won't be necessary, Miss Torrey, not with three of us now."

So she stood around with nothing to do. She'd thought earlier of putting on a skirt, but sure as she did Billy would ask how come. What could she say--even to herself? After all, nothing had changed. Steve was a man--the same as Jake. But she had brushed her hair a second time to subdue the short unruly curls. Little good it did, so she covered her head with a scarf.

A moan came from the wagon. Torrey looked in on her father. Alarm spread through her. He looked so frightfully ill. "Papa, is there something I can do?"

"Nothing, girl. You're Mama's doing all that needs be done."

"Steve says we'll be down in the foothills in a few more days. There's a man named Bill Johnson who has a ranch down there. Maybe he'll have the medecine Mama needs, or maybe some good moldy bread. Mama says that would be the best thing to bring your fever down."

"Don't fret so, girl. I'll be fine."

From up in front Anton called our, "Let's move out." A whip cracked and the stomping oxen began to move on. But before the two wagons had gone a hundred yards there was a creak and a groan of cracking wood. Anton's wagon tilted as a wheel crashed and splintered.

"*Donnerwetter!*" he shouted. "That's all we need now!"

Torrey viewed the wreckage. Now more time to fret away while the men did the repairs. She stood by and watched them split pieces of pine and whittle them to spokes. She followed Steve's easy grace of movement, his obvious strength. He towered over the stocky German. He must be at least six foot tall. *And that very light hair.* Such a contrast to his sun-browned face. She'd never favored light hair on men. It was better on women--like her mother. Even Lavinia, although neither had hair as light as Steve's. Again she thought of the picture in her journal. Dark hair and dark eyes--that's what she liked--if she wanted a man. But after Jake-- never! Yet, she couldn't keep her gaze from following Steve.

Time dragged. The men didn't need her help. Mama was fussing with Papa. Lavinia had her embroidery out, making pillow cases for her hope chest. Ugh! She, herself, would as lief be doing something more meaningful--like walking up stream.

"Not too far from camp," Medora called as Torrey started out. "It's too easy to lose your way in the woods."

"Mama, I've never been lost yet."

"I know you haven't dear. It's just a reminder to be cautious."

"I'll follow the creek. That way I can't get lost."

The sun was out but a cold breeze came down from the white peaks above and chilled the air. Torrey pulled the heavy cotton shirt tighter to her body and wished she'd worn her father's old wool plaid. They were still in heavy pine country, although now there were other trees; oaks and some with shiny red bark and dark glossy leaves which Torrey thought most beautiful. There was a heavy growth of shrubs as well. Manzanita, Steve had said. The Indians ate its berries. And a spicy smelling plant that grew close to the ground. Her boot crushed the leaves and released a pleasant pungent scent. Bear clover. Steve told her that too. Bears like to roll in it.

Why did her thoughts keep going back to Steve? *Her make-believe caballero?* Indeed! What a childish fantasy that had been. Now that she was older--*and wiser...* She'd realized that months ago--she had written "*adios*" under the picture. What difference did it make that he looked so different? He was just another man. And she wanted nothing to do with any man--ever! Better to keep her mind to the beauty around her. Were they in California now? Steve had said the Sacramento Valley was a great level plain. *Steve again.*

She stopped at a little pool that eddied off the main flow of the stream. She trailed her hand in the icy water. It teemed with tiny silver fish. Sometimes, when the sun hit just right, Steve's hair shone with that same silver glow. She tried to grab the darting slivers, but they slipped through her fingers like mercury. She wandered on. It was so peaceful. She could stay here forever, but their trip was almost over. Two more days, Steve had said. There she was, thinking of him again--his smile, the way the lines in his cheeks deepened--like this morning. He had smiled at her and she had turned to jelly. In the daylight she saw the color of his eyes. Blue. So very blue. Like the sky above. More blue even than Mama's. She reckoned she liked blue eyes on a man after all.

A huge boulder loomed in her path. The only way she could keep following the creek was to cross to the other side. Torrey jumped from one rock to another, until one started to roll. Her foot slipped. She hit the water with a splash. She cried out in shock. It was freezing cold! It made her body ache. As quickly as she could, Torrey scampered up on the opposite bank, soaked to the skin. Her scarf had slipped off her head and floated down stream. It could keep on floating. She wasn't about to get back into that icy water.

There had been only a light breeze when she started out. Now a chilling wind swept down from the snow-covered peaks. Icy fingers penetrated her wet clothing. Her muscles tightened. Her teeth began to chatter.

Torrey looked for shelter. Across a short stretch of meadow was an outcropping of granite with a shelf protruding where she could stretch out on and dry.

At last, protected from the wind, the sun's rays felt warm, but her clothing, layered as it was, remained wet and clammy. Knowing she should get back to the camp, she stepped away from the shelter of the rock, but the wind became ferocious and cut through her wet clothing. In her wet garments, she'd be an icicle by the time she got back to the wagons.

Quickly she pulled off the soggy twill trousers and heavy cotton shirt, wrung them out and spread them across a manzanita bush. Then, a sickening memory. Once before she'd removed some of her clothing when she thought she was alone in the woods--and look what happened! But now--what choice? With the wind blowing and the sun still warm, her clothes would get partially dry in short order. She huddled in the shelter of the rock. Her camisole and drawers still clung to her body, wet and uncomfortable. The wind mocked as it whistled through the trees. It was a long way back to the wagon, and it would be only a matter of minutes for her lightweight undergarments to dry. No one around, with the men still busy repairing the wheel.

The wheel was mounted on the wagon. Anton stepped back to admire their handywork. "Looks pretty damn goot. It should get us the rest of the way down the mountain."

Steve agreed. Not a true wheelwright's job, but sturdy enough. They need only hitch up the animals and be on their way.

"But Torrey isn't here," said Medora.

"Torrey? Where's she gone?"

"For a walk up stream. I didn't think she'd be gone this long."

Steve frowned. "She went off alone?"

Medora didn't like Steve's look of concern. "She often takes off alone. But she's aware of directions. She won't get lost."

"That's not the problem," said Steve.

Medora caught her breath. "Indians?"

"Probably not. I was thinking of bears. I've seen some signs."

Medora's face lost its color.

Steve regretted what he'd said. "Don't worry, Mrs. Dudley. I'm sure everything is all right, but I'll go look for her anyway." He picked up his Hawkins rifle that leaned against a tree.

"I should go too?" asked Anton.

"That won't be necessary. You and Mike get the wagons ready to roll."

Steve found it easy to follow her trail, mountain explorer as he'd been in the past. He came to where she'd crossed the creek and did likewise. He moved across the meadow then saw some signs he didn't like--tramped grass, fresh bear droppings, and broken branches of choke cherry. Old Bruin had recently been feasting, and still could be near.

He rounded an upthrust of boulders and pulled back in surprise. Torrey, naked, was stretched out on a ledge. Obviously, she hadn't heard him. Shocked, his immediate reaction was to leave quickly before she discovered he had seen her. Instead he stood mesmerized.

Lying on her stomach, her head resting on her arm, she was turned just enough so that one firm breast was exposed. To think he'd thought her a young boy at first. No question of that now. He felt a flush of embarrassment for his intrusion, yet was enjoying the loveliness before him. His pulse quickened. Such long lovely lines, the satin brightness of her flesh--the rounded curve of her hips. He knew he should slip quietly back through the brush then make enough noise to alert her that someone was coming.

For Torrey, the sun had felt good on her flesh. Maybe she dozed. She was barely conscious of the trill of a bird. But then she had the feeling someone was there. Torrey opened her eyes. She saw the boots first. Wet. They'd crossed the stream. She raised her gaze without making a move. Panic made her rigid. *Steve!*

Thoughts of Jake flashed through her mind.

"Excuse me, Miss Torrey." Red mounted his neck as he turned away. "I didn't mean... I didn't know..."

Torrey couldn't move. Her heart pounded wildly. If she could only reach her clothing draped over the bushes.

"We're ready to start," Steve said.

"Just go away."

"You shouldn't be out here alone. This is bear country, you know." Steve smiled to himself. In more ways than one.

"Just leave. Go away." Oh, dear God--thinking of Jake. "Don't come any closer."

"Get your clothes. I'll not look."

He started to move away so that Torrey could reach her garments, but suddenly stopped short. Not more than thirty yards away stood a grizzly--seven foot tall at least, watching him with small beady eyes.

He heard Torrey gasp.

"Stay quiet for a minute. Don't move," Steve said softly. He moved with caution and gathered Torrey's clothing, then edged backwards toward the rocks, watching the bear for any hostile movements. From the corner of his eye he could see the naked contours of a white leg. Carefully he dropped the bundle of clothes within her reach.

"Just gather them up and get ready to run. See that madrone tree over there, the one with the shiny leaves? Wait until I move in the opposite direction, then dash for that tree. Shinny up it as high as you can get."

"What about you?" Torrey whispered.

"Never mind about me. I've got my rifle."

The bear dropped down on all fours, sniffing and swaying his brute head from side to side, but he still kept his eyes on them, appearing more curious than anything else. He lumbered slowly forward. Steve moved away from Torrey, then said, his voice strained with tension, "Now get! Move fast!"

He heard a movement behind him, and caught a flash of a naked body making a dash for the tree. The quick movement surprised the bear. The beast was again on his hind legs as though to better study his prey. God, what a creature. Must weigh a thousand pounds. Its shaggy hide was marred with bald spots and scars from old battles. Steve could see the power in the massive forepaws, with claws a full three inches long.

"Hi-yee!" Steve yelled, distracting the bears attention from Torrey. Old Bruin looked at Steve and snarled. Steve positioned his rifle and pulled back the hammer. It was the first time he'd ever come face to face with a grizzly and yarns told by others flashed through his mind. "You got to hit 'em dead center or you're a goner."

The grizzly moved closer. Steve felt his heart pound against his chest. One shot, he kept thinking. One shot. There'd be no time to reload. The animal came on. They were now trading stares. Steve could smell its strong wild stench. The animal growled low, sort of a mumble.

Steve worked forward, but the toe of his boot caught in a root, throwing him off balance. His shot blasted out, embedding high in the bear's shoulder. He heard Torrey scream. The bear, only slightly injured but now thoroughly enraged, focused his attention in the direction of the scream. He lunged for the tree. His tremendous weight hit with such force, it set the branches to trembling as though buffeted by hurricane winds. High among the branches Steve saw a bare leg--a bare arm clutching a limb.

Thank God she's climbed out of his reach. She had dropped the bundle of clothing.

The grizzly raged with fury. He scattered the clothing. He shook the tree again and again with his massive strength. *My God, don't let her slip!* Steve reloaded his gun: pouring in the powder and ramming the ball home so quickly it seemed only one movement. He crept closer. The grizzly snarled and turned toward Steve. The second ball found its mark. It penetrated the animals mouth and embedded in his brain. With a thundering crash the grizzly was down. He gave one more frenzied roar and then lay still.

Steve dropped to the ground gripped by a fierce weakness. Rivulets of sweat poured from his arm pits. He buried his head in his arms.

How long did he sit huddled? He heard a twig crack. Finally a touch on his shoulder.

"You can look up now, Steve. I'm dressed."

He raised a haggard face. "Are you all right, Miss Torrey? My God, that was close."

"I'm all right," but her voice was shaky. "I'm beholden to you, Steve. I reckon I have you to thank for my life."

She dropped down on the grass beside him. She started trembling as shock set in. His arm went around her waist. She looked up, fear still mirrored in her eyes-- still trembling. He stroked her hair. The action unleashed her tears. He held her face against his.

A strange awed feeling consumed him. He liked the feel of her in his arms. He thought of that lovely naked body on the rock, and drew her closer. *But she's only a child.*

Torrey pulled away, stared up into his eyes with unvoiced questions. He had not noticed before their rich russet coloring. And hidden yearnings? Surely, he was looking into the eyes of a woman with untapped passions waiting to be unleashed.

He reached for her hand and pressed her palm to his lips. Nor did she withdraw it. He caressed the softenss of her face. He lifted her chin and brought her lips to his. Her response was hesitant at first, then yielding. He was aware of his own escalating desire.

What was he thinking? Crazy! A reaction from what they'd been through. Crazy, but he couldn't let her go.

Torrey's trembling had lessoned, feeling the gentle strength of Steve's arms. And the kiss. She liked being in his arms, pressed to be even closer. Nothing at all like with Jake. Steve had even turned away when he had caught her naked. She reckoned not all men were like Jake.

Finally Steve broke away. He stood up, reached for her hands and pulled her to her feet. "Forgive me, Miss Torrey. I had no right. It was the reaction from what happened."

"It's all right, Steve. I was so scared."

Torrey looked at Steve, puzzled herself by her own reaction. The kiss seemed so right, as it was now when he once again drew her close. Steve took her face in his hands and looked deep into her eyes, and she was awash with turbulent feelings. He picked at a little manzanita twig that had caught in her hair. His fingers moved through the tight mass of curls. His eyes probed hers with unvoiced questions.

"You are so lovely--so young." His voice was ragged and husky. Steve pushed her away but held her gently by her shoulders. He started to pull her close again; hesitated. Then took her hand. "Come now. Time to get back to the others."

CHAPTER 26

The poultice was not working! Medora's chest pinched with alarm as she knelt beside her husband on the wagon floor. She'd been terrified when she'd changed his bandage a short time before and his wound looked so much worse, yellow and streaked, festering with puss. His eyes, luminous and round, glowed with fever. She was flooded with fear. Had she been too late with the poultice? Never before had she felt so apprehensive.

She placed a wet cloth across his burning forehead. "Does that feel better?" she asked, her throat so constricted with fear it was a wonder any sound came out. William's response was an indiscernible mumble. She leaned over him again. "William, William, do you hear me?" Again only the muttered response.

Anton stuck his head in the wagon. Seeing William's glazed eyes, he shook his head. "Ach, not so goot, but Steve says there's a doctor at Sutter's Fort."

"Sutter's Fort! That's at least a week or more off! Oh, Anton, what else can I do?"

Anton nodded. "I think so, you're doing all you can. I'm sorry, but we've got to get going, that is, as soon as Steve and Torrey show up. The ride will be bumpy so make him as comfortable as you can."

"Torrey and Steve?" Another attack of panic. "They haven't returned?" William's sudden soaring fever had scattered all else from her thoughts. Now a new chill went up her arms and down her back. What was it Steve had said? Bears? Oh, God, he'd seen some signs!

William groaned and she snapped her attention back to him. "Yes, dear, what is it?"

"Barrel--barrel of pickles--put in the corner."

Oh dear God, he's now completely out of his head, back tending his store. *If only he were.*

"Yes dear, we'll take care of the pickles." Best to play along as she did with Jenny's make-believes. She felt she was drowning in a sea of alarm. She again dipped the cloth in the bucket of water and wiped his burning forehead. She ran her fingers through his damp hair. "Oh, William. Don't you dare give up. I need you so. Don't you dare. Do you hear me? Don't you dare!"

He thrashed about on the horsehair mattress. His arm flung wild and knocked over the pail of water. Medora grabbed a towel and started sopping. When she finished mopping up the mess, she started backing out of the wagon, empty pail in hand. "I'll be right back," she told an unresponsive William.

Just as she stepped down from the wagon, Torrey and Steve emerged from the forest. Thank God. She breathed a sigh of relief but her held-over concern still sharpened her voice as she demanded to know why Torrey had been gone so long.

"It's all right, Mama. I'm sorry. We are back now, but we did have a scare." Torrey looked up at Steve with glowing eyes. "I'd have been a goner if it weren't for Steve. He saved my life."

Medora gasped. "Why? What happened?"

By this time, the others also had gathered around with a chorus of questions. Torrey, enjoying the sudden shock she'd stirred and liking the attention said, "We met with a bear, big as a giant and ugly as sin."

Billy's eyes went round. "A bear?" And Jenny's echo.

Medora felt her legs go weak. "Oh, dear God in heaven." How much more could she take? She suddenly felt faint.

Lavinia's arm went protectively around her mother's shoulders. "It's all right, Mama. Torrey's here now." She glared at her sister. "She looks a mess but she's safe." Then directing her remarks to Torrey: "Do you have to be so dramatic considering what Mother has been going through?"

Steve broke in with an explanation. "I'd just come across Torrey when Old Bruin showed up."

"Steve had me shinney up a tree," Torrey spoke up not sure how much Steve would tell. She wasn't about to let the family know Steve had caught her naked. "Then he shot the bear dead. If he hadn't come along..." Torrey again cast an adoring look toward Steve.

There were more questions, and more answers by both Steve and Torrey, neither one giving a total explanation. Then glancing down, Medora realized she was still gripping an empty pail. "Oh, dear, your father. I've got to get back."

Torrey's face blanched white. "Papa? Is he worse?" She started toward the wagon.

Anton grabbed her shoulder to stop her. He took the pail from Medora and handed it to Torrey. "Your Mama is taking care. Here, she needs more water in this bucket." He then turned to the others. "Time's wasting. We better get a move on." And before long, they once again were under way.

The rest of the day, as they jiggled over the very rough road, Medora sat on the floor beside William's mattress trying to keep him as comfortable as she could. When he shook with chills she tucked the blankets tighter around him and sponged him for the fever. When they stopped to camp for the night she let the two girls prepare the meal leaving William's side only to stretch her cramped legs. When

Torrey brought in a cup of tea, she braced William against her chest so he could sip the liquid. If only it could have been brewed from her willow bark, the best tonic for bringing down fever. But it, like her other remedies, had been lost with the crash of the wagon.

She remained beside her husband all through the night. Often William talked crazy, sometimes calling out names she'd never heard before. More often he called out her name--or Torrey's. Sometimes he mentioned things she'd almost forgotten. But most of the time he just lay tossing and moaning and shaking with chills even though his head dripped with sweat. She kept sponging his skin, wiping one section at a time, especially where heat was generally the greatest, such as his armpits and his groin area, but careful to keep the rest of his body covered because of the chills.

Time passed slowly, and sitting beside him all through the night her thoughts mixed with thoughts of the past. Once she dozed--and dreamed. Jacques. That first magical time with Jacques. Jacques was a poet in the way of his touch. She awoke with a start and felt a rush of guilt. But the dream still nested in her thoughts. Such a long time ago--a love that had changed her life and brought her to shame. A poet's touch stirring her own weakness, creating desires only a fallen woman should know. She relived the heartbreaking memories of the past: Chatfield's death, banishment of her lover, tricking William, separation from her beloved family because of her own wanton desires. The shame of it--still a bitter cup.

Sitting beside William throughout the night, memories of Jacques faded as thoughts of her life with William took its place. Those difficult first years in Missouri. William accepting Lavinia as his own. Lavinia had never known the difference. Sleeping beside him these many years, how often she had felt the rise of desires even though his touch was not the poet's stroke of Jacques. Still haunted by the taint of her first experience and awareness of her own weakness, she had learned to turn her face to the wall. But Will was an understanding man, never demanding more than she felt right to give. A good man. But a stubborn man--the reason they were here. And resentment seeped in to dim her fear of losing him, resentment as she relived some of the hardships they'd just been through, crossing the plains, starving on the desert, now fighting for his life, and who knows what still lay ahead. She had left a home she loved to follow his dream. *Thy desire shall be to thy husband, and he shall rule over thee.* It was written in the Bible. And a flash of a Tennyson's quote--*For man is master of his fate.* But what of woman? A woman must follow in the wake of both man and fate, and it didn't seem fair. She'd followed William because she had no choice. *And now she might be losing him because of it.*

William groaned and thrashed about. A leap of fear vanquished her traitorous thoughts. She resoaked the cloth and once again wiped his feverish brow. *But now if she should lose him...* The thought sent a chill racing through her body. She leaned closer so that her face was just above his. "Will, do you hear me? Will, you're not going to die! Do you hear? I'm not going to let you! I'm not! I'm not!"

She dipped the cloth and again wiped his blistering brow. A tear rolled down her cheek. *Will, I need you. We all need you.* When she carefully removed a section of the cover to sponge him around the groin and could see his private part coiled limply in its bed of pubic hair, she thought how vulnerable it looked. She wanted to stroke it, bring it to life, and then blushed with shame. *To have such a thought at a time like this!*

But her mind slipped back to that night at Fort Laramie. At the joy she'd given him. That night for the first she'd felt complete. She had joined with her husband, willing and wanting. A union such as that could not be wrong. The admonitions she'd read in the proper books, restrictions of society drummed in by propriety, the hard rules a woman should follow: *A modest woman submits to her husband to please him not for her own sexual gratification.* And her mother's voice; *duty--always duty, more important than her own body's urgings.* Barriers of freedom that had been erected. Why shouldn't loving and touching be a natural relationship for both men and women? Who had made the restrictions?

She replaced the covers, tucking them carefully around him. *Time she shattered the myths--break down the barriers of the day. If he recovers.* Oh, God, please give me that chance.

The early morning sun was making inroads through the dense covering of branches announcing the start of another day. It seeped through the white canvas covering of the wagon. Lying on the floor beside William's mattress, Medora had just dozed off. A soft touch on her face startled her to attention.

"Medora?"

She jerked herself up. "William?" In the shaded light she could just barely make out her husband's face and saw his eyes were open.

"Medora, have you been sleeping here all night?"

"Oh, William." Tears of relief clouded her eyes. She reached over and pressed her hand to his forehead. His fever had broken!

"You gave us such a scare. But now--Oh, William, I know now you are going to be all right." She leaned over and kissed him on the forehead. "William, you do know I love you."

His eyes reflected his love and his fingers stroked her cheek. "Even after what I've put you through?"

Her answer was a soft gentle kiss on his lips.

Now with enough food to keep them going, everyone had thought the rest of the trip surely would be easier going down the west side of the mountain. Everyone except Steve. He knew the terrain was as difficult, if not more so, than any they had already traveled. Even on the lower slopes the road was intolerably bad, steep and rocky, almost impassable at times. The forest was so dense, little grass could grow. The rocky terrain made their fatigued oxen foot sore and they had become frighteningly thin for lack of grazing. Often everyone had to pitch in to prod the poor creatures on or help push the wagons up an incline. Going down the steep grades, the men had to lock all four wheels to keep the wagons from running away, and often a windlass and ropes were used to lower the wagons down a cliff.

One ox so hungry and fagged with the hard pull laid down in the middle of the road and refused to get up. Anton screwed its tail but the exhausted beast just put his head down on a pine needle bed and closed his eyes.

"Kindness to him will be to put him out of his misery," said Anton as he reached for his pistol and shot the ox in the head. Ironically, that night they camped at a spot where a previous party had buried a man. A tossed torn mattress lay near by. Anton turned it over and saw it was stuffed with corn husks. "Too bad old Felix couldn't last another day," he said sadly. At least the rest of their stock now had some fodder.

The weather turned warmer as they descended the mountain. William was improving and walking some of the way with the aid of a crutch Anton had made, yet not strong enough to help with the work.

After a hard day of pushing the animals over the difficult terrain, they all enjoyed sitting around a fire after supper was cleared. This one evening Anton had gathered enough wood and built a large glowing fire looking forward to a smoke and a talk with Steve. Now getting closer to the great Central Valley where he'd likely settle, he thought it would be a good time to sound out one who had already established himself there.

William still needed his rest, so Medora fixed his bed in the wagon and tucked him in before she joined the others around the fire. She told the two younger ones they could sit for a spell and share an apple if they were quiet while the grownups talked. Torrey would get their bedrolls ready while Lavinia put on a pot of coffee.

Before Torrey started her chore, she glanced toward Steve already settled by the fire with the other two men. She was satisfied there was enough space for her beside him as soon as she finished her chore. She spread the children's bedrolls under a tree, stretching a canvas covering over the two lower limbs in case of rain. But by the time she finished, Lavinia had already served the coffee and had taken her place beside Steve. Torrey glared at her sister. *Lavinia and her scheming tricks.* Her sister was so intent in smiling up at Steve she didn't even notice. Torrey tightened with anger. She wanted to scream at Lavinia to leave her love alone. But not wanting to give her sister the satisfaction of thinking she cared, she was able to restrain the scream letting it out silently a bit at a time. She squeezed down beside Anton on the other side of the fire where she could keep a watch on Lavinia and Steve.

As Medora joined the others she glimpsed Torrey's scowling expression and realized it was directed toward her sister sitting beside Steve. A bit of sibling jealousy over Steve? At least she was now displaying a normal interest in the male species. Whatever had happened between Torrey and Jake still troubled her. She probably would never know. She still felt ashamed for having read Torrey's journal, but relieved that Torrey evidently had put Jake behind her as it should be. But Steve? Of course, it was only normal for a young girl on the brink of womanhood to have some interest in the opposite sex. He was a handsome young man, indeed. But much too old for Torrey, only fifteen and certainly too young for courting. Steve surely must be in his mid twenties at least. Medora again glanced over at her older daughter. But Lavinia? Her thoughts began spinning like leaves caught in a breeze.

When William had first talked about California, one of her concerns was for Lavinia approaching marriageable age. In that far-off remote country populated only by mountain men and adventures or people of a culture so different from their own, what was her daughter's chances of meeting eligible young men? Now, looking at Steve, she decided California did have some eligible bachelors. A Harvard graduate and son of a senator and such a likeable young man. Lavinia, now eighteen, was of courting age. Indeed yes, she could approve of Steve as a suitor for Lavinia. But Steve seemed to be dividing his attention equally between the two girls, showing no favorite but charming to both.

For a few seconds Medora thoughts floated on a sea of uncertainty. Of course, Torrey was out of the question. But Lavinia? She shouldn't be meddling, but yes, there were things a mother could do: *A way to a man's heart*...? She'd drop hints of her daughter's cooking skills, arrange time for tête-a-têtes. Medora smiled to herself. She'd like to welcome Steve into the family.

While Medora's mind churned on, Anton lit up his Meerschaum pipe. Now with a steaming cup of coffee in hand and as wisps of smoke curled above his head, he looked over at Steve. This was time for that talk. "You say your ranch is in the great Central Valley?"

Steve nodded. "Up on the Feather, about fifty miles north of Sutter's Fort. Wild but beautiful country."

"Most what we know about California comes from the letters printed in our Illinois papers praising California's superior weather and soil. Especially letters written by Captain Sutter," Anton continued. "He writes about the great Central Valley of California."

Anton's remarks suddenly put Medora's matchmaking plans on hold. Yes, she well remembered those glowing letters, the reason they were here around a fire in the mountains and William fighting for his life.

Steve smiled. "Yes, convincing, indeed. One of the emigrants I met showed me the clippings he carried with him."

"You mean there's little truth to the letters?" Anton asked.

"Oh, there's truth all right. The valley is all Captain Sutter claims. But he sends those letters to the eastern papers to get more Yanks to come. He needs skilled workers for his many enterprises."

"Ja?" Anton looked surprised. "His interest is other than agriculture?"

"Captain Sutter has many interests. Agriculture is certainly one. He has huge fields under cultivation; at least twelve hundred acres sowed in wheat, a hundred in barley and great herds of horses and cattle. But his tamed Indians work his fields and his Indian vaqueros work the herds. He also employs American hunters and trappers to traipse the mountains and bring him pelts. But inside his fort--wait till you see his many other enterprises; blacksmithing, barrel making, flour milling, a distillery for his wild-grape brandy. He even makes and blocks hats. And down by the river he has a tannery for different kinds of leather goods. Only now, most of his workers have left to join the battalion."

Anton nodded. "Sounds a very enterprising man."

"He also plans to build a sawmill, a gristmill, and has started a town he calls Suttervill. So he needs the people to populate his town, another reason he sends his letters extolling the virtues of our great Central Valley."

For Medora, Steve's words were painting a picture different from what she had previously imagined. Sutter was building a town. It wasn't all just wild Indian country. A burst of hope swelled in her bosom. "You mean a town with houses and stores?"

The creases in Steve's cheek deepened. "Well, not just yet. Those are Sutter's plans."

Medora's hopes plummeted.

"Except for inside his Fort. A few settlers have started some farms, but it's still mostly Indian country. It's only been seven years since Captain Sutter first came, the first white man in these parts. The governor then granted him the land in hopes he'd tame the inland Indians."

Medora's innards were tightening again.

"Has he--tamed the Indians?" Anton asked.

"He's had a couple of uprisings. But Sutter has a way with the Indians. He supplies them with food and pays his Indian workers with chips they can use for purchasing goods. But as a reminder, he also has cannons mounted on the four turrets of his fort. That helps keep the Indians in line."

Anton looked thoughtful. "I'm a farmer, not here to work as an artisan for Captain Sutter in his fort. I ask advice. Would you say the valley is the place we should settle?"

Steve beamed. "You won't go wrong. It's wonderful virgin country. Still wild, but, as I said, a few settlers have started some farms, but still few and far between. We need more settlers. The Maidu Indians are a friendly, gentle people, not like the Miwoks on the other side of the Cosumnes River, twenty or more miles south of the fort. Sutter's had some trouble with them."

The fear was back for Medora. It *was* wild Indian country, and by Anton's intense interest it seemed apparent it was the country he would choose! If Anton did, William would too.

Steve added more fuel to the fire. Still enthused with his subject, he went on to tell how it was when he first crossed the snow covered mountains with Fremont three years before and looked down on a valley so rich with vegetation and the abundance of wild life he knew he'd never find a more fertile land.

As Steve enthused, Medora's innards tightened. Unsettled land--Indian country! What she and her children had to look forward to.

Anton took another deep draw on his pipe. To him, the Central Valley sounded good. If Captain Sutter could tame the Indians, so could he. The more they talked, the eager he was to reach the valley and look over the land where he'd have his farm. Of course, the farm would come after they returned from putting down the rebellion in the south for it was no more than right, he figured, that he help protect the land he would soon be claiming. It wouldn't take long, Steve had said, as the majority of Californios welcomed peace. Then they'd all be back.

It was time to turn in for an early start in the morning. Anton tapped the bowl of his pipe on a rock to empty the ashes. But one more question to ask Steve. "What about land grants now? We came thinking we'd have free land."

"That will be a question. When Commodore Sloat raised the American flag in Monterey, he told the natives their Mexican land grants would still be honored. But some are so vast, like the Vallejo brothers' in the Napa Valley. Some Yanks have already claimed squatter's rights there. Don't know what will be the outcome. I met another party heading there just as I was starting up the mountains. Boggs. Yes Boggs was the name. I was told he had been a governor in Missouri."

Anton's eyes twinkled. "Boggs, ja. We started out together from Independence. He took his party up the long way while we chose the shortcut. Look where it got us--the last ones to get over the mountains, because we were fools enough to follow a hoodwinker named Hastings."

"Hastings? He and his party pulled into the fort just as I was leaving. He and several of the single men of his party signed up for the battalion." Steve's thoughts went back to the time he first met Hastings at Sutter's Fort. He remembered how troubled he'd been then wondering if some poor emigrants might put their trust in his wild shortcut scheme. Here were some who had. They were lucky they had made it.

As the men talked, Medora thought it was good to learn of the safe arrival in California of the different ones they had traveled with. Like tying up loose ends. She asked if he had met a family by the name of Clark.

Steve looked thoughtful. "Clark? Yes I did. Nice family. Had five sons. Some were all fired up to join the battalion.

It was then Lavinia's expression sharpened with interest. "Did Perrigrine sign up?"

"Sure did. A real nice fellow. I think he was the oldest. Real anxious to get going although his pa wanted him to stay to help get a farm started."

"Might they still be at Sutter's Fort?" Lavinia asked a hopeful gleam in her eyes.

Steve shook his head. "Took off before I left. The older couple and the two youngest boys might still be there. The three older fellows are probably in San Juan Batista by now. That's where captain Fremont is organizing his battalion."

Lavinia looked disappointed. "They were all so helpful to us, I was in hopes we'd see them again when we reached the valley."

Medora was thinking the same. The Clark family had helped in so many ways, and she especially liked buxom Mrs. Clark. She was glad to learn of their safe arrival in California. If only there was news of the Donners.

An acute deep-souled feeling swept through her. She almost felt the presence of Tamsen sitting beside her. Her very dear friend. The many things they shared. The discussion of loved books they had read, walks together on the prairie as they collected specimens for Tamsen's nature book, doing the sketches for that book. The day they looked down on those two little graves and learned for the first time they'd each lost babies of their own. The sharing of grief drew them closer than ever. There was the promise when they parted, if they didn't meet again on the trail, they would surely meet in California. She thought of that first snow storm they'd experienced soon after they had topped the summit. She had wondered at that time if the Donners might still be behind them. So once again, she couldn't help asking Steve. "You are sure you didn't meet a family named Donner?"

Steve shook his head. "Can't say I did."

"Or maybe Mr. James Reed and his family?" The Reeds and the Donners were such close friends, they'd still be traveling together. It could be Steve might have met one and not the other.

"So many families arrived this fall. I'm sure your friends were among some of them," Steve said with a reassuring note.

Medora clasped her hands together and said a silent prayer. She must believe Steve was right, and she would meet her friend once again when they were all settled in California.

CHAPTER 27

Torrey knew she was in love. Her dark haired, dark eyed caballero had been exchanged for a blue-eyed blond giant of a man with creases in his cheeks that deepened when he smiled. She could close her eyes and relive the time he had held her in his arms and their lips had met. She still felt the rapture of that moment. Nothing like Jake. Jake had been put out of her mind forever. Now her one problem was Lavinia.

Lavinia, all gussied up in her printed shirtwaist with matching ribbons in her honey colored hair. Lavinia, batting those sapphire blue eyes as she gazed up at Steve like he was the last male creature on this blessed earth. Lavinia and her tricks. The way she monopolized any free time Steve had. And Mama helping.

Yes, Mama was part of the problem--*Mama plotting!* Torrey was sure of that-- Mama saying, since her own time was so taken nursing their father back to health, that Torrey must help her sister more with the cooking and family chores so that Lavinia could have some free time--*free time to walk off with Steve.*

It definitely seemed like a conspiracy between Mama and her sister--with all Mama's prattle to Steve. Mama's honeyed words about Lavinia's achievements. Lavinia had such a love for household duties, and a special knack with fine cooking, with the proper ingredients of course. Nor had Mama failed to mention that Lavinia had attended a female academy of culture before they had started west, and how accomplished Lavinia was on the piano, how the family enjoyed gathering around for a sing-along while Lavinia played. "The piano is now stored with our friend, Judge Witherspoon," she'd heard her mother tell Steve, and that would surely be one of the first things they'd have shipped around The Horn as soon as they were well settled in California. She'd even invited Steve to join them so he could hear Lavinia play--like her sister would be performing on a concert stage. The only good thing was that Steve said he'd be delighted to come which meant she'd at least get to see Steve again--when the war problem was settled.

The more Torrey thought of her mother's apparent plot to get Steve and Lavinia together, the more resentment crept in. Why hadn't Mama included some good points about her other daughter--how well she could ride and handle horses, how she had helped her father with the beeves when he had no other? The hackles rose at the back of Torrey's neck like thorny prickles. But of course, those weren't the all-important lady-like accomplishments that Mama put so much store in. But

Steve's rancho was in wild untamed country. Surely, what he would need most of all was help with his horses and cattle, not fancy cooking or listening to someone play the piano.

Resentment swelled to anger. Torrey thought back to the many times her mother had tried to make her into something she wasn't--make her like Lavinia, the daughter she was most proud of. Lavinia with her lady-like manners who thrived on domestic chores--and could play the piano!

Torrey's brows drew together as she turned over in her mind some of Mama's preaching. A nudging, deep in her head. Was femininity really a woman's most powerful advantage? *Could Mama be right?* If she wanted to attract a man--*attract Steve*, was it important that she act more like a lady? Torrey looked down and rubbed at a grease stain on the made-over trousers. She thought of the evening she first met Steve and he had mistaken her for a boy. She didn't like to admit Mama might be right--but if she had to compete with her sister... So in spite of Billy's smart aleck remarks, Torrey was again wearing a skirt. She'd prove to Steve how mistaken he'd been at that first meeting. She'd make him remember the kisses--like she did--that time after killing the bear.

Torrey's fingers ran through her short-cropped hair. If it would only grow out faster. She was now brushing it a hundred strokes every day and pulled on the short curls to stretch them longer, yet her hair hardly covered her ears.

Lavinia and Steve. A pricking thorn. And Mama helping. Torrey's lips set to a determined line.

It was a surprise to Medora, albeit a relief, to see Torrey had abandoned the trousers and was again wearing a skirt. Did this really mean a change in Torrey? She was also relieved that now with three able-bodied men to handle the wagons and push the oxen Torrey's assistance was no longer so crucial. She'd felt guilty that so much of the family chores and the care of the children had fallen to Lavinia. Now Torrey could be of more help. If only Torrey was more inclined. And more willing.

She desperately wanted to guard the closer relationship that had developed between herself and Torrey since the day in the wagon when they thought William might die. But now once again Torrey was showing resentment and she didn't know why. She'd have to tread lightly, watch her own tongue. But sometimes it was hard. Medora glanced over at Torrey who was sitting on a wooden crate slashing at the potatoes she was peeling for their nooning meal. Medora gasped. The girl was wearing her very best skirt, one she herself had spent many hours putting in tiny tucks at the waistline and a ruffle at the bottom.

Medora couldn't check her outburst. "Torrey, why are you wearing your very best skirt?"

Torrey looked up, her eyes clouding with resentment. "You're always after me to dress more like a lady. I do, and you fuss at me anyway." Torrey slammed the paring knife into the bowl.

"You have older skirts to wear while we're still in these rugged mountains."

Torrey screwed up her face and glared. Medora knew she was skating on thin ice yet felt so helpless. "I'll get you an apron."

"Ugh. I hate wearing those cover-all things. I've got a towel under this bowl." Torrey picked up the knife and went back to her slicing.

Medora watched silently for a moment trying to check her own anger. Torrey was cutting the potatoes much too thick for frying. The men were at the creek now washing up and would be here for their dinner any moment now. She hated to say more, but... "My dear, you'll have to slice the potatoes much thinner if you expect them to be cooked by the time Lavinia is ready to dish up the pork."

Again Torrey slammed down the knife. "Then maybe Lavinia should slice the potatoes."

"Torrey, please don't be so difficult." Medora turned feeling heart-sick that the wall was up again between them, yet as she started toward the wagon to help William down, she couldn't resist one more reminder. "Watch that grease in the skillet when you put in the potatoes. It's sizzling hot."

Torrey's lips tightened to a thin line. As though I haven't fried potatoes a thousand times she grumbled to herself, but then glanced toward the creek. Her heart did a turn and her vexation toward her mother vanished. Steve was coming up drying his hands on his kerchief.

Torrey cast him a smile--for all he noticed. Lavinia had just picked up the box of dishes. Steve stopped and relieved her of the box. Lavinia smiled up at Steve and said something, but they were a bit too distant for Torrey to hear. She raked them with her eyes, her lips tightening to a thin line of aggravation. The knife slipped. She felt a stab of pain and a streak of red tipped her finger. Damn women's chores. She glanced back over at Lavinia and Steve. Now they were both laughing at something Steve said. Torrey seethed with anger.

The lard in the frying pan smelled hot. She'd better get the potatoes in before her mother had another suggestion. Torrey dumped in the sliced potatoes. The grease splattered and burnt her hand. Damn again to women's chores. Driving oxen was a lot less hazardous.

The noon meal over, the two girls washed the dishes as Medora helped William back into the wagon. The men hooked up the animals and once again they were underway. The road, cluttered with rocks and brush, made traveling slow and uneven.

Torrey could see the oxen were lagging and figured they could use some pushing. In spite of her skirt with the ruffle on the bottom which would surely cause her mother more displeasure if it caught on the brush, Torrey grabbed an ox prod and stepped up beside Steve. Lavinia had him before their nooning meal. It was her turn now. "Need some help with these critters?" she asked.

Steve smiled down at her and she felt crinkly feelings race around inside her. "Guess we can always use some help," he said. "But better watch with that fancy dress."

Torrey beamed him a smile bright as the sunny day. At least he had noticed she was wearing a skirt.

The terrain became increasingly rough and uneven, the oxen edgy, to Torrey's chagrin, leaving little chance for conversation between her and Steve. A huge rock blocked the trail. Anton called back to Steve. "Need your help here if you can break away from that pretty girl you're walking with."

That left Torrey alone to drive the oxen as the three men dug and pushed and finally removed the huge rock from the trail. Eventually the trail became so choked with manzanita and chokecherry, they had to stop altogether to clear enough of a path for the wagons to get through. A reminder of clearing the trail in the Wasatch canyon.

William poked his head out from under the wagon cover and said he'd had enough of the stale air inside. "If we are staying here for a spell, I might as well get out."

"Might as well," agreed Anton. "We'll have to do a lot of cutting through these thickets." He shook his head in disgust.

"I'll help Papa," Torrey said starting for the wagon.

"Ja, help your Papa," Anton agreed. "He needs a rest from this bumpy road, and the critters as well. We might be here an hour or so cutting the brush."

Torrey looked back at her mother walking with Jenny about fifty yards behind. "I'll take care of Papa," she called back. Torrey helped her father down, handed him his crutch and let him lean on her shoulder and they started for the creek. Her mother had assumed such a protective watch over her father, like no one else could do anything for him, and Torrey had missed the companionship they'd always shared. As long as Anton didn't need her, she could have a little time with her father--if Mama didn't horn in.

Actually, Medora had watched Torrey help William from the wagon and was glad to see the two together. She knew how much Torrey loved her father, knew how frightened Torrey had been. She watched the girl assist her father to the edge of the stream, clear a spot and spread a canvas for them to sit on. She said a prayer of thanks that he had been able to make the short distance to the creek.

Torrey tumbled down beside her father, rolled over on her stomach, cupped her chin in her hand as she gazed up at him. Not a very lady-like position, Medora thought, but smiled to herself thinking how Torrey seemed to vacillate--a lady one moment (when she was around Steve), a tomboy the next.

Lavinia came up and said as long as they had time to waste, she'd take Billy and Jenny on a little walk up stream.

Medora smiled at her daughter. "That would be nice, dear. The children never get tired exploring. But not too far," and realized, for the first time since William's illness, she had a little time for herself. She removed one of her books from the tin box and settled down on a blanket. From the distance came the hack of scythes and axes and occasional voices spiced with swearing as the three men cut away the heavy growth. William and Torrey were within view but too far to hear their conversation. By the changes in Torrey's expression, Medora figured the girl was bringing her father up to date with happenings during the time he was fighting for his life and hardly aware of what had gone on. Medora felt a poignant touch of envy. Those two. They had always had such a close relationship, a relationship she'd often envied. Why hadn't she been able to have that same rapport with her daughter?

She thought of that troubled time after Elspeth's death when Torrey had become almost hostile. The hurt was still a weight on her heart. But the recent time in the wagon when they'd clung together in their fear of losing him. Medora closed her eyes reliving those few moments of holding Torrey close, and Torrey saying. "Mama, I love you too." It had seemed the wounds between them had healed. And they had--until now. Now again... A lump of pain attacked her chest. What was she doing wrong?

She knew Torrey resented her stressing the importance of proper deportment and a woman's role in the society they must live with if their lives were to be fulfilled. But it was a mother's duty to teach her children these roles. How else was a child to learn? It was written often enough--and preached often enough; a woman's role in life was as the docile guardian of the hearth, dependent on men for their fate. Not really fair, but the way it was. Women were acceptable only as adjuncts to men in their roles as daughters, wives, and mothers. She thought of the quote in one of her prized literary books. "Stay within your proper confines and you will be worshipped. Step outside and you will cease to exist." The courts and the law books said you belonged to your husband, body and soul. The man owned the money, the house, his wife and the children. Hardly fair, but the way it was. Lavinia had taken the instructions to heart. But Torrey?

Medora swallowed to push down the feeling of uncertainty that was rising and clogging her throat. But children are not all the same. Torrey was such a strong independent person, so different from Lavinia. No chance of Torrey ever becoming the underling of a man. And how she had always rebelled when compared to her older sister. *Is that still the trouble?*

Medora sighed. She wanted a good life for her children--wanted for them what she had known herself in her earlier years; a lovely time of civilized culture and social graces. A sweeping ache of nostalgia surged through her as she thought of that long ago time. A time when a genteel nature and fine manners were woman's's most important asset. Certainly no place for a bold, forward woman who refused to remain within the sacred sphere. *Like Torrey?*

Even traveling the plains. And Medora thought of the many pioneer women who had shared the heavy labor with their menfolks, who certainly had displayed their remarkable stamina under the most trying conditions. Yet even most of them had retained their purely feminine roles and duties, regarding themselves not as partners but as long-suffering conscripts. Not fair, my daughter, but that's the way it is. The way it will always be--unless...

Torrey was still looking up at her father and now chuckling. Medora wished she could hear what the two were saying. But this is their time together. She owed that to both of them.

Torrey still on her stomach, still in animated conversation, raised one leg wriggling her foot behind her. Her skirt slipped down exposing a black stocking-clad leg and the bottom edge of her drawers. Medora gasped in shock. Suppose one of the men came up and saw her in that very unlady-like position? She checked the impulse to cry out and tell her daughter to put her leg down where it belonged and see that it was properly covered with her skirt. Then the humor of it worked to a smile. Torrey, you are incorrigible. No doubt, she has forgotten she's no longer wearing those cut-down trousers. Maybe those trousers are what she should go back to wearing, at least until they reach civilization.

Medora glanced down at the book that still lay unopened on her lap, a book of Emerson's essays. She should take advantage of this time as planned. She fanned a few pages. A paragraph caught her eye that suddenly seemed so pertinent to her present thoughts as she read, "A healthy discontent is the first step of progress. Times are changing. Women should have more rights of choice." From the profound writings of Emerson? True. How very true. She did agree, but it would take a woman with boldness and a very strong will to start righting the wrongs, Medora thought as she again glanced over toward Torrey and William. The kind of woman who can face a new country with courage and hope for the future; one who knows her own value. And rather than surrender to submission, she would become a builder along with her man. *Like Torrey?*

Now both black-stockinged legs were scissoring the air, the girl quite unmindful that her skirt was hiking farther up her bloomers. A smile crossed Medora's lips. Her eyelids lowered in speculative thought. Yes, her daughter was that kind of a woman, one who knew what she wanted and had the courage to pursue it. And strangely, Medora suddenly felt an inexpressible feeling of satisfaction.

Lavinia and the two younger ones followed the creek a short ways up stream. The day had turned warm and sunny, a contrast to the days of snow and rain they'd encountered coming down the mountain. New shoots of grass were sprouting and greening the bank. Lavinia thought how pretty it looked. But time now to turn back. "By now the men may have cleared enough of the path, and we better be there," she told the children.

Billy and Jenny were splashing in the water trying to catch wriggling tadpoles to deposit in a jar Billy had carried. "I've got one," Billy cried out, depositing his squirming trophy into the bottle.

"Well, so you have." Lavinia smiled at her brother. "Hurry and get some water in the jar so it can swim around."

"I got one too," Jenny screamed, but the tiny polliwog squirmed out of her hands and back into the creek. "He's gone. He's gone," she cried.

"All right, one more try," Lavinia said. "Then we have to get back to the others." She knelt beside the small child, and when Jenny captured another one of the creatures, Lavinia wrapped her hand around Jenny's to prevent the tadpole from escaping. "Quick, Billy, bring the jar."

By the time they got back to the wagons, the men had cleared quite a distance ahead but were still whacking away. Torrey and her father were still at the edge of the creek and her mother had cushioned herself on an old blanket and was reading until the children interrupted by excitedly showing off their tadpoles. Then they ran down to show their prizes to their father and Torrey.

Her mother resumed her reading, and as the children now were kneeling at the edge of the creek in search of more tadpoles with Torrey's help, Lavinia decided it was now her free time to do what she loved doing. She rummaged in the wagon and took out a small satchel that contained her fancy work of a pillow case she was embroidering. She settled down against a tree and selected the colors of thread she would need. She stretched the cloth over a small wooden hoop and started working on an intricate design of roses she was doing in cross-stitch. So absorb was she in her work, she didn't hear the footsteps that had come up from behind.

"Well, I guess your mother isn't the only artist in the family."

Lavinia looked up at Steve in surprise, a touch of red creeping up her cheeks. She smiled. "Oh, not really. I have a pattern I'm following. Mama does it all from the heart with her sketch pencils and brushes."

"And yours isn't from the heart?"

Lavinia chuckled playfully. "Well, yes, of course. It is something I love doing when I have time. But Mama's is her own creativity." Lavinia loosened the material from the hoop and spread it across her lap, smoothing out the wrinkles. "See, I'm just following a design I stencilled on the pillow cases. I'm embroidering them for my hopechest."

"Hopechest?" Steve's eyebrows raised in question.

The color in Lavinia's's cheeks heightened. "Oh, that's just something we girls call a box or a chest that we use to store linen or things--well, in anticipation of marriage." She dropped her gaze, her cheeks flaming.

Steve's eyes danced in merriment. "I'd say it will be a mighty lucky man who'll be laying his head on that fancy pillow."

Lavinia looked up at Steve. "Oh, now you are teasing."

"Would *I* tease with something like that? No. I say a very lucky man indeed." He scrutinized the young lady before him, Lavinia with her honey colored hair pulled gently to the back and tied with a ribbon that matched the blue of her eyes, eyes blue as rare jewels. He thought how true his words really were. He studied the lovely young lady before him, the delicate contours of her face, a nose straight as a Roman princess', so like her mother's, and sweet rosy lips just right for kissing. In the few days he had been traveling with the Dudley party, he couldn't help but observe some of Lavinia's sterling qualities; a sweet caring nature, patient with the younger children, and a great help for her mother. A lucky man indeed who would claim this young lady. "So is there all ready a lucky man?"

Lavinia blushed even more.

"I see there is. Someone you've left heartbroken back home? Poor fellow. I can't believe he'd let such a jewel get away."

Lavinia pulled a tuft of grass and threw it at Steve. "You're still teasing." She stared at him for a moment as though juggling a thought around in her mind, then said. "Well, in a way, you are almost right--but not anyone back home." She paused as though debating whether she should tell him more. "No one knows. I haven't told anyone." She paused, studying the man before her. "Actually, it's my family. I don't want them to know. Mama might try to discourage me." Her expression sobered, her gaze searching the man before her.

Steve plopped down beside her. "Be assured, your secret will be safe with me."

Lavinia continued to study the man who was now sitting beside her. "I feel like it's bursting inside me. I want to share it with someone." She still searched his face. "You already know him."

Steve looked surprised. Surely it couldn't be Mike who hardly ever said a word. And Anton was almost as old as her father. There was no one else they had met since he'd joined their party. Suddenly a sinking feeling ran down his gut. *She couldn't mean me.*

"Remember when Mama asked you if you had met a family named Clark?"

Steve looked puzzled. "Yes I remember. The family that had five..." Steve's face broke into a smile. He suddenly felt relieved. "One of the Clark boys?"

Lavinia dropped her gaze, and pulled another tuft of grass in her embarrassment. Then admitted. "Yes. It's Perrigrine, the oldest. I know it seems crazy. We first met when we were in the Wasatch Mountains, only then I didn't think much of it--just a very nice fellow, always so polite and respectful. The whole family was nice, and they all helped my family when our supply wagon crashed. Then we separated as we were crossing the desert, but were all so happy to see the Clark family again when they joined us at the lake just before we crossed the summit." The color in Lavinia's cheeks heightened again. "It was during that time when our families were together again that Perrigrine told me he loved me--said he had loved me ever since we first met. I guess it was then I realized I loved him too. We made a promise; he'd find me wherever we are when we get to California. But we decided not to tell our families. They would say we hadn't known each other long enough. Maybe we haven't. But I have this feeling for him--and he has for me."

Steve reached for Lavinia's hand. "I'm very happy for you. I remember your young man. Perrigrine struck me as a very fine fellow."

Lavinia's eyes shone as she looked up at Steve. "Oh he is. He plans to help his father start his farm, but then he wants to have one of his own. And then..." Lavinia giggled in embarrassment. "You must think I'm awfully forward telling you this. I had to tell someone, and I look on you as my friend. But please. Please don't tell my parents."

Steve felt his own feeling of exuberance--happy for Lavinia's joy and thinking what a very lucky man young Perrigrine Clark was to have claimed this lovely woman's heart. But also a sense of relief that it hadn't been him. He wanted Lavinia as his friend but without romantic entanglements. For he already knew who had claimed his heart. But as young as Torrey was, he knew that had to be far in the future.

CHAPTER 28

The pine growth of the higher altitude had given way to groves of oak and brush which meant they should be out of the mountains and down to the valley by nightfall. Unfortunately, a heavy rain during the night had washed out a part of the trail they were following. In its place was a slide of thick heavy mud. Anton frowned as he assessed the problem. With the dense growth all around, there was no other way to go. "We'll have to use ropes again to let the wagons down," he said shaking his shaggy head in disgust. "Another delay. Two or three hours to get back on solid ground, so let's at it men."

Steve and Mike began to unhook the oxen as Anton barked the orders. They'd lower his wagon first. Mike would be on the tongue to keep the long wagon from jack-knifing. Steve volunteered to ride the front seat to direct the descent and apply the wagon breaks when needed--a dangerous job if the rope should brake.

Medora watched for a while, her throat tightening with anxiety as Mike strained on the tongue to steady the wagon while Anton pulled on a rope to keep the wagon from tipping. She closed her eyes and issued a silent prayer. Now so close to the end of their journey, nothing must happen to hinder them from reaching their goal.

Torrey, standing beside her mother, was also watching, her eyes focused on Steve sitting in his precarious position. Once again she was wearing her trousers. Not one to be hindered for long by female dictates, and thinking Steve didn't seem to notice anyway, she'd decided a skirt was too impractical.

Of course Medora had noticed and wondered why Torrey had switched back to her old worn trousers, but she wasn't about to comment and risk a petulant reply. Better leave well enough alone since Torrey's defiance toward her had again resurfaced.

The first wagon reached a lower slope and appeared past the most hazardous part of the slide. Torrey breathed easier, and Medora did too. The men appeared to have everything well in control. However, it would still be some time before both wagons would be back on sound ground.

"No point in just standing here watching when there are other things to do," Medora remarked to her daughter. She was thinking of a scenic spot they had passed a short ways back and at that time had thought how much she'd like to sketch the scene to add to her collection of documenting their travels. "I know your father would like to be out of that wagon, and as long as we will be here a while..."

"Guess you're right," Torrey said. "Not much gained by just standing here. Besides, I noticed a bruise on Dulcie's hind leg. Reckon I better tend her."

Medora watched her daughter head for where the mule was pastured and felt a heaviness in her heart. She had savored the closeness she and Torrey had shared during the time William's life was in question. Now she was still asking herself what had gone wrong and wondering if it had something to do with Lavinia and Steve? Surely Torrey couldn't blame her for that. She shook her head. No figuring out Torrey.

Medora poked her head in the wagon and asked William if he'd like to get out and sit where he could watch the action. He would, but she sensed his inner turmoil. He wanted to be sharing the labor with the other men and it was causing him undeserved self-reproof. Although he was improving daily, he was far from strong enough for physical activity. Medora wished she could do something to ease his guilt.

She helped him out of the wagon and arranged a comfortable spot where he could watch the other men tackle the slide with the wagons. She hesitated for a moment then finally said, "Would you mind if I leave you for a short while?" She told him she had seen a beautiful view she'd like to sketch of the towering snow capped peaks in the distance.

He nodded. "Of course you should go."

Medora removed her pencils and sketch pad from the wagon then checked to see that everyone else was accounted for. Lavinia was reading to the children and Torrey was already rubbing lard on Dulcie's leg.

"You are all right?" she asked feeling some guilt in leaving him.

"Of course I'm all right." There was a sharp edge to his voice. "You don't have to treat me like an invalid forever. Reckon you need a little free time to yourself." Then his voice softened and his eyes spoke his love. "Medora..."

She turned back to face him. "Yes Will?"

"Guess there's no words to say what I really feel--what you did for me--what I've put you through."

Moisture filled her eyes. "Oh, Will. Don't you know its enough to still have you. I was so frightened for a while." She wanted to put her arms around him, but there were so many around to see. Instead she let her eyes speak her thoughts and said only, "Oh Will..." Then she turned before she got maudlin. "I won't be gone too long."

William watched his wife as she walked away, tall and straight, her dark skirt brushing lightly against her legs. A lady still in every way in spite of all she's been through. The hem of her skirt caught on a bush and she bent to free it. Such nice rounded hips. Josh, how he'd like to fondle those lovely rounds. He felt the rise of his growing lust. Gad, it had been so long. He pictured her lying on a mattress, naked, legs open, waiting for him--wanting him, arms reaching up to pull him to her. *Not that she ever had. A wish. A shameful wish.* Medora was a lady, not a harlot. It was enough that she never denied him his physical needs as a good wife should. He should count his blessings. Yet, deep down, he knew he wanted more--*like that night at Fort Laramie.* Why had that one night been so different? He thought of that other man, the faceless one who had fathered Lavinia. *What had her response been with him?*

Gently Torrey rubbed lard on Dulcie's bruised leg then tied a piece of torn petticoat around the injured part to keep out the dirt. "There, Dulcie. That should make it feel better." She rose and lovingly rubbed the animal's broad snout and stroked the mules long ears. "You're a real good friend, Dulcie. You've sure done your share on this trip. Won't be long now, and we'll be down in the valley. Then I'm going to feed you all the carrots you can hold."

The mule snorted as though it understood every word Torrey said. Torrey was about to put the cover back on the lard can when she rubbed her hand across her face. "Feels almost as rough as yours," she told the mule. I wonder..." If the lard was good for softening the scabs around Dulcie's bruised and chaffed leg, well... She rubbed her cheek and touched the bridge of her nose with its sprinkle of freckles and thought of Lavinia's peaches and cream complexion her sister so carefully protected from sun and weather by always wearing her sunbonnet. Was that why Steve was so attracted to her? Torrey fingered out a gob of lard and rubbed it across her nose and massaged it well into her cheeks.

Oh, drat. Why should she care? Yet, thistles of anger pricked her insides as it often did of late. Anger toward Steve and anger toward her sister. Steve was now spending far more of his free time with Lavinia then he ever spent with her. And anger toward her mother because Mama was purposely making it so, always insisting Lavinia take more time from chores. Like Mama wanted Steve to have a chance for courting. Well, Lavinia could have him! The anger was bitter as gall in her belly.

But she'd already had a talk with herself, worked something out between her heart and her head. Steve was now a part of her past, added to the incredible past few months--violation and death, thinking of Jake and Elspeth. And almost losing her father. Then love. Now heartbreak. She'd grown up a lot in these past few months, and done a lot of thinking of late. Ahead was her future. So what would she make of her future?

Definitely, she'd live her life her own way, not be ruled by what her mother deemed as proper. She'd be a woman with vision. An independent woman who did not have to rely on a man.

Only at night... So no one could hear, her face would be buried in her pillow-- and the sobs would come. She still loved Steve. Reckon she'd love him all the rest of her days.

The lard on her face felt good making her skin feel smoother. Maybe it would help the freckles disappear. If only her hair would hurry and grow longer. Maybe, just maybe...

Medora settled herself on a grassy spot and felt lifted by the beauty that stretched before her. Across the canyon in the far off distance were the higher snow capped peaks. Near by a stream of water cascaded over rocks in a miniature waterfall. A breath-taking scene, indeed, as had been many others she'd seen as they traveled over these rugged Sierra Nevada Mountains. Later she would be able to look over her sketches and recall the beauty--and forget the hardships they had endured.

Hardships indeed, thinking of these last few months. The worst was when she thought she might be joining the ranks of the many others who had lost loved ones on this journey. So many graves they had passed; dysentery from poisoned streams, drownings when crossing the rivers. She thought of the little boy who had been run over by the wagon and the two little graves she and Tamson had found on the prairie.

Medora leaned back against a tree and closed her eyes, thankful the journey was almost over. Her thoughts strayed back to the many families they had traveled with, all starting west for a better life, never dreaming the hardships in store. Up before dawn to start the fires, packing and unpacking, airing out wet bedding, all women's chores. And the many women with their swollen bellies. Her heart went out to them. How had they endured the constant bone-shaking jiggling of the wagons or walking the hundreds of miles? And those who gave birth while traveling. One woman in their party had died in child birth and left four young ones. But pregnancy was part of family life. It was men who made the decision to go West and the women were expected to be strong enough to serve the common needs of the day--strong enough to meet the uncommon demands as well. Women had to accept what their men decided. So unfair. So unfair, thought Medora. Yet, here we are. Medora's thoughts continued to wonder. Someday that will change. Someday? Why someday? They were entering a new land now--a new life. It was time for a strong woman to come forth and say it's time women take more control of their own lives. A strong woman like Torrey? Medora smiled. Yes, maybe Torrey.

But why was she thinking such thoughts now with their journey almost ended? Another day or two and they should be down in the valley. She should count her blessings. William was recovering and her family was still all together.

Medora sat up, reached for her sketch pad but then noticed a pair of shiny-backed beetles headed toward her. She picked up a stick to brush them aside but paused her assault when the lead beetle stopped. The one following caught up and climbed on the first beetle's back. A mating position? Medora smiled to herself thinking of watching such an intimate act. But the most natural act in the world for all forms of life. How could it be wrong? It was only her own culture that shrouded such a God intended act in a cloak of impropriety as though it were sinful. And as she watched, she felt an arousal in her own private parts. It had been such a long time since she had lain with William, even long before his injury, with so little privacy. She thought of her vow made that night in the wagon when Wiliam's fever was raging. It was time to shatter old myths, break down the barriers of the day--*if he recovered*. She wished William were here with her now.

The beetles completed what they were doing and went on their way. So absorbed was Medora in the insects' action as well as her own body's responsive need, she hadn't heard the shuffle of leaves behind her.

"So here you are," William said.

"William!" Medora jumped up in surprise, her face aflame. Could he read her thoughts? "How could you make it this far?" she demanded trying to hide her confusion.

William grinned. "I'm no longer the invalid you're trying to make me. I wanted to share the view with you."

"Oh, William. Here, let me help you." She took his crutch and assisted him to the soft grassy cushion and sat down beside him.

"Yes, it's really a spectacular view," he said as he gazed out beyond the canyon to the snowy peaks beyond. His arm encircled Medora's waist and pulled her to him. He touched her cheek with his lips and then nestled in the softness of her neck. "It's been such a long time," he whispered.

His hand cupped her breast, and she liked the feel. Yet she said, "William, we can't. Your leg is not yet healed."

"Maybe that's the healing I need." His fingers were undoing the buttons of her bodice.

"We might hurt your leg."

"Drat the leg."

"Someone might come."

271

"The others are all busy." The round jewels he wanted were now free of the clothing and spilling into his hands.

Medora gasped and felt her nipples harden. She wanted him to squeeze and knead, wanted to forget all caution. She turned her face and his lips found hers and his tongue explored. She knew it was dangerous, yet her arms went around his neck and pulled him close. Forget all those old admonitions. She wanted to give. But her leg touched his and she felt him flinch. "Oh, Will, I'm sorry. We can't. It's too soon."

"There are other ways." His hand pulled up her skirt and worked to the top of her drawers where he tugged on the drawstring and slipped the undergarment down. Medora raised her buttock so he could slip them down farther. His fingers stroked the silken skin of her thighs, then sought the soft mound of hair and the tiny crevices and creases of her desire, already wet and wanting. "Oh, oh," she moaned. "Oh, Will."

Her pleasure was so exquisite, she wanted to do the same for him. She reached for the buttons of his fly, released his hardened member, cupped it, stroked it, squeezed it, felt it grow fuller, drinking in its pungent smell. Her mouth found his mouth and opened to him. There seemed nothing but shapes and shadows as she cleaved to him. But she wanted more and more of him. She'd have to watch to be careful as she straddled him. Again she moaned another, "Oh, Will."

Her hair spilled down over him, warm and fragrant from the afternoon sun. Through it he glimpsed her eyes, translucently blue and lovely. He nestled his head between her hot swollen breasts. Her yielding. Her giving. Her wanting. The dream he never thought could be was materializing in her sweetness. She was enfolding him in her arms, drowning herself in him. Caressing. Fondling. Guiding. He felt her smooth belly press against his and he clutched the back of her knees then moved to the moist crevices and those warm throbbing parts. He could contain his passions no longer and drove into her, and heard her cry out. Then again the muttered, "Oh, Will... Oh, Will!" She belonged to him as she never had before.

Finally he lay spent, and Medora beside him. He closed his eyes, savoring the sweetness beside him. He could hear the soft gurgle of water over rocks from the nearby stream. He could smell the spice of the crushed grasses, and the soft dampness of the earth beneath it. He could smell the sweetness of the woman beside him.

She brought his hand to her lips. "Oh, William, William. I do truly love you." She studied his face and saw moisture forming in his eyes.

"I've been praying these many years to hear those words."

"Oh William... When I thought I was losing you..." Then she smiled. "Husband, I think we have a lot of catching up to do. But now, guess we should get back to the others before they start wondering what we are up to," and she laughed in the glory of the final acceptance of her newfound freedom.

The second wagon had been safely lowered over the spill and the party was ready to go on. Torrey saw Mike driving the oxen toward the wagons and yelled that she would follow with Dulcie to be sure the mule wouldn't lose her bandage. Just then Dulcie brushed against a tree and disturbed a nest of yellow jackets. The wasps swarmed angrily and Dulcie took off like a lighting flash in a summer storm throwing the pack strapped to her back and scattering its contents. With their target gone, the yellow jackets now attracted by the lard on Torrey's face began to swarm around her. Torrey screamed as she swatted at the stinging insects.

Steve, just about to put a yoke over the lead oxen's head heard Torrey's scream. He dropped the yoke and ran toward the yelling girl. He grabbed Torrey up in his arms and rushed toward the nearby stream. Plunging in, he pushed Torrey's head under the rushing water. Torrey struggled, came up rasping for breath. The wasps were still buzzing. Steve pushed her head down once again.

Torrey fought to be free of Steve's grasp, rose coughing and choking and sputtering, "Let me go, let me go." Water cascaded down her face from her water-soaked curls. "Leave me be," she screamed between gasps for air.

Steve pulled off his kerchief that was tied around his neck and started scrubbing Torrey's face. His voice raised trying to calm her. "It's that damn grease you've got on. Yellow jackets are meat eaters, don't you know?" The wasps were now swarming around both of their heads. Steve ducked under the water pulling Torrey with him as he worked out into the deeper water. Torrey fought to break free but Steve held firm. Finally he raised his head and brought Torrey up with him. The wasps had dispersed to find other booty, but Torrey was still fighting. Steve held her at arms length. As his arms were longer than hers, her fists only flailed the air. Her anger had now blown to rage. "Let me go. Damn you. Let me go!"

"Hold it there. Just hold it," Steve yelled back. Then a smile began to twist his mouth, deepening the creases in his cheeks. "My, such language coming from a young lady."

"It'll be worse than that if you don't let me go."

Steve began to chuckle. "I don't blame those wasps for attacking. I could eat you myself, make an entire meal of you, leave nothing but maybe a straggly red curl or two."

He pulled her against him and started kissing the red welts that were already rising on her forehead. His lips moved down her nose till he found her mouth. He groaned. "I've been wanting to do this again ever since the first time."

Torrey's resistance began to crumble. What was he saying? What was he doing? A thousand daydreams coming true?

Steve had worked them back to the shallow part and they were now just sitting in the water. He held her at arm's length so he could study her face, and dipped water up to sooth the reddened welts. He then deposited another kiss on the big red welt on the end of her reddened nose as the stream flowed around them.

Torrey's heart was hammering like a sledge hammer going amuck. What did this mean? What about Lavinia?

"Seems like I'm always saving you from some critter or another. Do I have to marry you to keep you out of trouble?"

Surprised, Torrey pulled back so she could look up into his face. "You mean what you're saying?" she asked. Her thoughts were reeling. Her head felt weightless and her heartbeat raced.

"I mean it," he said and his eyes were soft with a liquid glow. "Only remind me to ask you that again--say in a couple of years from now.

A couple of years? You bet your tooten she'd remember.

Just then she heard Uncle Anton yelling, "Hey Steve--time we got rolling."

"I'm a'coming," Steve yelled back.

He reached for Torrey's hand and together they splashed up the shallow stream bank. And Torrey's heart was singing.

Their march commenced early the next day, with weather mild and most pleasant. They were determined, if at all possible, to force their way out of the mountains before nightfall to reach Johnson's place, the first settlement in the valley of the Sacramento. They had already travelled a number of rising and descending hills, had covered three or four miles. The two younger children were making a game of running ahead of the slow moving teams.

Anton and Mike were driving the weary beast while Steve walked beside the wagons to push against them if one leaned too far on the uneven ground. Lavinia and Torrey were a few paces behind him, walking together for a change. A stretch farther back were Medora and William. Still unable to contribute much to the work, William insisted he had to walk some of the time in order to recover his strength and he had the aid of his crutch and Medora's assistance.

As they hobbled along, Medora's attention was focused on the three young people ahead. Lavinia, as usual, looked sweet and lady-like in a dark walking skirt and freshly washed shirtwaist. But Torrey? Medora was puzzled about Torrey. The girl had a buoyancy in her stride like she had conquered the world. Occasionally she gave a hop-skip-and jump or would swing to catch a limb as though charged with more energy than her slight frame could contain. Back to her tomboy ways, Medora reasoned, and just as well. She had been wrong to think she could ever change her, and now wouldn't want to. Torrey would choose her own path in life. Whatever that might be, it would be right for Torrey.

As for the child's romantic infatuation toward Steve, it apparently had run its course since she was again wearing her grimed trousers and an old flannel shirt, no longer trying to impress Steve. Often the case for a young lady Torrey's age. No doubt, she would experience many more flirtations before Mr. Right came along.

But what puzzled her the most was that morning, before they'd started out, Torrey had put her arms around her and kissed her on the cheek and said, "Mama, I do truly love you." So whatever had caused Torrey's perverseness toward her was now gone. Something else to be thankful for.

As for Steve and Lavinia. She'd often seen the two in deep conversation and felt sure something was developing between them. The time would come, she was sure, he'd ask William's permission to court Lavinia. She knew both she and William would happily welcome Steve into their family as a son-in-law. Only now, and Medora smiled to herself, what a diplomat Steve is, showing no favoritism to either girl, treating both in a safe brotherly fashion.

The wagons were now ascending another hill. Far up ahead raced Jenny and Billy. When they reached the crest they started jumping and shouting and turned to face the others who were still treading up the hill. "We can see it! We can see it! The valley's down there. We've reached California!"

Medora's heart began to race and she cried out, "Oh, William, we must be there!"

Anton and Mike started running up the hill leaving the oxen to trudge along by themselves. Steve grabbed a hand of each of the girls to follow. Anton was the first to reach the top where the children were still dancing. He turned and shouted, "They're right. It's the great Central Valley below." He pulled off his hat, tossed it and gave three huzzah. Soon it seemed all the hills and valleys were ringing with the shouts of joy and hallelujahs, "California! California. We're here!"

Anton shook hands with Mike and Steve, then hugged the two girls. Such joy shared by all. They had crossed the plains, the deserts and the mountains of Western America and finally were here. They had reached their goal.

As the children continued to dance around, the three men and the two girls looked down at the valley below, each now lost in his or her own vision of the future.

Anton stood in deep thought as he looked down on the vast flat plain, now brown and dry after a summer's draught. It's only brake was a broad line of timber through the center indicating the course of a river. But what he saw was a land of abundance. Choice agriculture land, and agriculture was the guardian of the nation. Brown and barren now, but he pictured great fields of winter wheat. You planted in the fall and reaped the harvests in the spring. He also saw great orchards in bloom irrigated by water brought from the river by digging canals. Of course, all in good time. After the trouble in the south had been settled.

For Mike there was little speculation. He would go with Steve to join Fremont and the California Battalion. Later, he'd wonder around and see more of California.

And Steve? His deep blue eyes sparkled with eagerness. "You can't see it from here, but my rancho is down there, just a little more north, more in foothill country. Wonderful country." He could hardly wait to see it again, see how his Palominos were doing, how his Indian vaquero had been getting along overseeing things while he was gone. He turned toward Anton and Mike to tell them he would be leaving them as soon as they reached the valley. "Only for a quick check of my rancho," he explained. "I'll meet you at Sutter's Fort in a day or two and we'll go on together to join the battalion." Settling that uprising in the south wouldn't take long. Then, when peace was assured for all of California, he'd return to his rancho and get on with raising his horses. He cast a furtive glance toward Torrey. Another couple of years? Would she still be waiting?

Torrey, standing beside him, had her own vision of the future. To her, the summer-dried grass was not brown at all. Below she saw miles and miles of golden prairie, rich pasture land for raising the golden Mexican Palominos with their flowing white tails and manes that Steve had told her about. Beautiful horses Steve had said.

She pictured herself riding a Palomino, riding beside Steve--always beside him--forever and ever. Again she thinks of him as her caballero lover. What matters that his eyes are blue and his hair is yellow. The warm glow in his eyes, as they sat in the stream, had told her all she needed to know.

Now, wanting to share this wonderful view with her father, Torrey glanced down the hill to see if he and her mother were coming. They were, but hobbling along slowly. She figured Papa could use another arm so started down the hill to meet them.

Lavinia, although still standing beside Steve, was thinking of Perrigrine as she gazed off in the far distance at a hazy outline of another range of mountains. Steve had said Perrigrine and his brothers had left to join the battalion that was forming on the other side of the coast range. Was he over there now on the other side of those mountains? So far away.

She was glad Torrey had gone to help her father as she wanted a few minutes alone with Steve. Anton and Mike had moved over to look at the valley from another view.

"I had hoped for a moment to speak alone with you as long as you'll be leaving us when we reach the valley," she said.

"Just for a day or so," Steve replied.

"What I wanted to say was how much your friendship has meant to me." She hesitated a moment with embarrassment. "I've had beaus in the past--nothing serious, of course, but I've never before had a man as a friend. It's been so nice, our talks together. It's meant a lot to me." She hesitated a moment, then looked up at Steve. "And thanks for keeping my secret."

Steve smiled down at her and squeezed her hand. "I'd never think of betraying a confidence."

Lavinia looked around furtively to see if anyone was paying attention to them. "One thing more." She could feel the color rush to her face. "If you see Perrigrine..." She glanced down in embarrassment. "Would you tell Perrigrine that I'll be waiting?"

"It surely will be my pleasure."

Having witnessed the excitement up on top, Medora wished she could run ahead as she and William treaded slowly up the hill. She was as eager as the others to look down on the fabled land the others were cheering about. In her mind she pictured the beautiful green rolling hills of her beloved Virginia and figured the great Sacramento Valley must be much the same. But when they finally arrived at the crest and looked down on the flat dry plain, her disappointment was like a rock in her stomach. It rose to her chest and spread like dead ashes. When her heart quieted it lay like stone. This is what they'd risked their lives for?

She glanced over at William to see if his disappointment was the same as hers, but his eyes were misted in awe. "So much land," he said in a reverent tone. "Medora, did you ever think there would be this much unpopulated land to choose from? And from all reports, such fertile land. We should bow our heads and give thanks to our Lord."

He and Torrey bowed their heads and Medora followed suit as he led them in prayer. After the amens, the three stood silent for a moment looking at the valley below, each one lost in his and her own vision.

Anton strode up. "Ja, what you think?"

"A lot of land down there," William said. "Enough to have our choice."

"Right for wheat," Anton said.

William nodded. But he was not seeing wheat fields like Anton. He was seeing a land of multi-opportunities. A new country to be settled. A chance to be putting his own mark on history. He had come for land, and he'd have his land fulfilling the promise made to his mother. With Anton's help, he'd farm some land. But he was also thinking of Medora's arguments when she was resisting their going west. She had said "You're a businessman, not a farmer. A good businessman at that. You've proven that with the Judge's affairs." And there were the talks he and James Reed had shared; not on farming but on business. With so much land and so many opportunities, why couldn't he have both? People would be coming and settling in the valley. They'd need merchandise and supplies. There was no doubt in William's mind. The Lord had led, and he had followed. Below was a land to conquer. Again he offered a prayer. He had reached *his* "Promised Land."

Medora felt a tug on her skirt and looked down at Jenny. "Mama, I got to go weewee," the small child said. Almost glad for the distraction, Medora took the child's hand and led her to some brush out of sight of the others, but her thoughts were still on the barren sun-burned plain with the only trees to be seen were those that banked a river. It was a sad longing in her heart that pulled at her silently and painfully as she again compared the brown plains with the beautiful green hills of Virginia. Ridiculous, she knew. She had heard of California's rainless summer. So what else could she expect this time of year with the rains just starting? But she'd also heard of California's abundance. so a shock, indeed, to look down on such a vast barren plain.

"All through," Jenny said as she pulled up her panties and looked up at her mother with wide questioning eyes. "Is that really California down there?"

"Yes dear, it's California. But California is a very big place. Even these mountains are a part of California. What we were looking at down there is the great Sacramento Valley which will probably be our new home."

Jenny clapped her hands, her face wreathed in smiles. "Will we live in a real house again?"

"Someday. Yes, someday we will," Medora said.

Jenny's face was still vivid with expectations. "I'll have a real bed again?"

"You'll have a real bed. Someday, I promise." She stooped and pulled her child close. "Yes, someday you will have a bed again."

The child's arms encircled her neck. "Mama, I love you."

Medora's eyes filled with tears. "And I love you too." She kissed the nest of soft brown hair and suddenly was flooded with an overwhelming feeling of gratitude. She should count her blessings. In spite of all the hardships they've faced, what they still must face, her family has come through it together. And that was what counted. Her greatest blessing.

She rose and took Jenny's hand. "I think we should get back to the others."

Medora stood beside her husband and felt William's arm go around her waist as he drew her close. She was no longer mindful that others might see. She thought

278

of yesterday's stolen moments by the stream and felt a rush of joy. She had finally shaken all the old shackles. She had become her husband's true partner and knew it was right.

William adjusted his position. "Oh Will, you've been standing too long on your injured leg, and all that walking up this hill." She'd best get him back to the wagon.

"A lot of land down there," William said not even aware of his fatigue. His gaze was keen with his boundless vision. "It's hard to think it's so big. Medora, you'll see. We made the right decision by coming here"

Medora smiled. William, the perpetual optimist. He's already dreaming and planning, ready to conquer this new world. She looked at him with a loving and proud gleam in her own eyes. "Yes, husband. I'm sure we did." But seeing the stress lines around his eyes, she added with a shadow of concern, "Will, you can't keep taxing your strength. Let me help you back to the wagon."

His arm draped her shoulder for the support he needed as her arm encircled his waist. "Just a minute longer," he said.

The two stood silently looking down at the brown valley below, William building his dreams and Medora thinking how it was pioneering in Missouri, living in a dirt-floored cabin, cooking over an open hearth. Now she'd be doing it again.

But aware of the nearness of her husband, she thought of the many years they'd shared together, the children they shared--and now her new found expression of love. She was suddenly overwhelmed with a feeling of tenderness for this man beside her. So what if she once again must live in a make-do shelter. She'll make of that shelter a home. Her home will be her dominion, a place to shelter her family. For isn't that her purpose in life? The way it should be. What she really wanted most of all.

Medora sucked in a big draught of the crisp exhilarating air, filling her lungs and clearing her mind. Determination now was a dynamic force to get on with the journey. They were wasting time just standing.

She reached for William's hand. "Husband," she said, "we'd better get started down that hill if we're going to reach the valley before dark." She nodded to Anton. "As soon as I get William settled in the wagon."

Soon saddles were squeaking, cattle lowed and Dulcie brayed in protest. Dust rose around the turning wheels of the wagons. Once again they were on their way. Medora glanced back only once at the mountains they were leaving. Ahead was the valley, a new country to be settled--a new life for her and her family. With her husband's head cushioned on her lap, Medora leaned over and pushed a stray hair back as she planted a kiss on his forehead. She smiled as she looked into his eyes. "This is it, husband, the last leg of our journey."

Whatever that new country held for her families future, Medora knew she was now ready. She started to hum a tune as their wagons continued their roll down the mountain.

* * * * *

HISTORICAL NOTE

The Mexican uprising in Southern California was soon resolved and Captain Fremont received a final surrender January 1847 and was temporarily appointed Governor of California. The newly arrived emigrants as well as the California Mexicans were able to get on with their lives as planned. But it was not until the United States won the Mexican War and the Treaty of Guadalupe Hidalgo was signed February 1848 that California actually became a part of the United States.

As for the Donner Party, they were trapped in the Sierra Mountains by the early snows. Forty-two perished, forty-seven survived. When the first rescue party from Sutter's Fort arrived in February 1847, George was too ill to travel and Tamsen refused to leave him but insisted their five children be taken out. George soon died but whatever happened to Tamsen remains a mystery as her body was never found. James Reed and all of his family survived, and he went on to become a successful businessman in San Jose. You can visit The Donner Memorial State Park located on the east edge of beautiful Donner Lake with a turnoff on Interstate 80.

* * * * *